Of Breath and Blood

A Novel of Suspense featuring Detectives Daniels and Remalla

J. T. Bishop

Eudoran Press, LLC

Dallas, Texas

J. T. Bishop/Eudoran Press LLC
6009 Parker Rd. Suite 149 #205
Plano, TX 75093
www.jtbishopauthor.com

Publisher's Note: This is a work of fiction. Names, characters, places, and incidents are a product of the author's imagination. Locales and public names are sometimes used for atmospheric purposes. Any resemblance to actual people, living or dead, or to busi-nesses, companies, events, institutions, or locales is completely coincidental.

Book Layout © 2014 BookDesignTemplates.com
Author photo by Nick Bishop
Edited by G. Enstam, P. Creeden, C. McGuire and C. Marquis
Cover by Judy Bishop
Cover Photo by photocosma

Of Breath and Blood/ J. T. Bishop. -- 1st ed.
Paperback ISBN 978-1-7325531-7-0
Hardback ISBN 978-1-7325531-8-7

To Dad…
I love and miss you.

Other Books by J. T. Bishop

"I'm telling you, it was an accident. She fell and hit her head. Must have slipped on the stairs."

Detective Aaron Remalla shook his head. Going into a third hour of questioning, he gritted his teeth while his head pounded. "That's not what the evidence shows, Marcus." He leaned forward in his seat. "You know more than you're saying. Your girlfriend's head was caved in, and you had specks of blood on your shirt. Neighbors have heard you argue in the past and they've seen bruises on your girlfriend's face. It doesn't add up." He splayed out his hands. "Just tell us the truth, and this will go a lot easier on you."

Marcus groaned and held his head. "I'm telling you. This is all a big misunderstanding. I didn't kill her. I didn't touch her."

"I don't believe you, Marcus." Remalla pointed. "We've been canvasing the neighborhood and searching the area as well as your apartment. You better hope they don't find something that implicates you."

"There's nothing to find. I swear," yelled Marcus. "Why won't you believe me?"

Rem sighed with impatience. "Your record, for one thing. You have a history of domestic abuse. You want me to go over it again? This isn't the first time you've roughed someone up, only this time you escalated to murder." He leaned closer. "Just tell me. She got in your face, and you lost it. That temper of yours exploded and you decided to show her who was in charge, only it got out of hand." He squinted. "Nobody likes men who beat up women. Now your crimes have caught up to you and it's time to pay the piper."

"You've got it all wrong. I didn't touch her."

Tired, Remalla checked the clock on the wall. "It's been a long day, Marcus, and I'd like to go home. But if you want to draw this out, then we can. I got no problem sitting in here and hanging out with you all night if we have to."

"Why can't I leave? I didn't do anything."

"Maybe after you tell us what really happened, then we can talk, but right now, something isn't adding up, and I think you know what it is."

Marcus dropped his head. "It was an accident."

The door to the interrogation room opened and Remalla's partner, Detective Gordon Daniels stepped inside the room. His normally pressed pants and jacket looked rumpled, but his blond hair remained perfectly gelled back. Rem wondered how he managed to keep it that way after grinding days like today.

"Bad news, Marcus," said Daniels. "Looks like they found the murder weapon. Your golf club. Hidden in a trunk in your storage shed. You really should learn how to hide things better."

Marcus' eyes widened.

Remalla whistled. "Oh, dear, Marcus. That's not good."

"That's not mine," said Marcus.

Daniels tipped his head. "Well, you better hope that the traces of blood on it aren't your girlfriend's, and we don't find your fingerprints, cause if we do, you're going to have to explain a few things."

Marcus' face crumpled, and he held his head.

"Care to tell us now?" asked Remalla. "Before the evidence tells us instead?"

Daniels put his hands on his hips and waited. "Any day now."

Marcus moaned, and Rem thought he heard a sob. "I didn't mean to do it. I swear it was just an accident."

Rem raised a brow at Daniels. "You hit her with the club?"

Marcus hugged himself. "She just made me so damn mad. I didn't mean to swing it so hard. She just needed to learn her place, and then she fell down the damn stairs." He moaned again and started to cry.

Rem almost moaned, too. "Okay. Now we're getting somewhere." He slid a notepad and pencil over to Marcus. "I need you to write it down. Tell us exactly what happened. From the beginning."

**

Daniels sat at his desk and stared at his computer monitor. It had been a long damn day, and he couldn't wait to get home, hop in a shower and get some sleep. He eyed his partner who sat at his own desk across from him, looking just as weary. His long, dark, shoulder-length hair was tied back with a band, but sections had come loose and hung in his face. His eyes were red with fatigue, and he leaned back and rubbed them.

"Tired?" asked Daniels.

"Does the Grinch hate Christmas?" asked Rem.

"I hear you."

Rem sat up. He wore a Bruce Lee T-shirt which sported a coffee stain after one of the many cups Rem had drunk that day had spilled and he hadn't bothered to clean it. "You think Lozano will let us finish these reports in the morning? Marcus isn't going anywhere."

Daniels eyed his captain's office. The window shade was open, and Lozano was meeting with Titus and Georgios, two other detectives in the Robbery/Homicide division, and they appeared to be having a lively discussion. Daniels shook his head. His and Rem's history with Titus and Georgios had always been rocky. While respectful of each other as colleagues, they hadn't always gotten along. "Cap's currently occupied," said Daniels. "Maybe we can sneak out and deal with his wrath tomorrow if he wants the reports tonight."

Rem turned to look. "What the hell are they talking about in there?"

Georgios' voice raised, although Daniels couldn't make out what he was saying. "They caught those liquor store robberies down on the south side last week. From what I hear, they haven't made much progress."

Rem frowned. "Didn't the cashier get shot at the last robbery?"

Daniels nodded. "He did. Died this morning. Their robberies just became a murder investigation. No wonder they're frustrated."

The voices from the office rose, and Titus, his face red, stood, pointing at Georgios. Georgios stood, too, yelling at Titus.

"What the hell is going on in there?" asked Rem.

Lozano stood also, yelling at both men, and Georgios faced the captain, and yelled something at him.

"It's not good, whatever it is," said Daniels.

The arguing continued, and Rem and Daniels watched as Georgios walked up to Titus and shoved him.

"Whoa," said Rem.

Lozano yelled again, but Georgios turned, yanked the door open, and stormed out of the office. "You piece of shit," he screamed. "I thought you were my partner."

Titus was right behind him. "You're losing it. I can't work with you like this."

Georgios whirled on him. "You can't work with me? I've been dragging your ass around for months, and now you're blaming me for this mess?"

Lozano followed them out. "Both of you get back in here. We're not done." His voice boomed through the squad room. Rem and Daniels were the only two left at that moment. Rem slunk in his seat, and Daniels picked up a pen and pretended to look busy.

Georgios exploded. "You can take your office, my stupid-as-shit partner, and your crappy captain skills, and go fuck yourself with all of it. I've had enough."

"Georgios!" yelled Lozano. "You step out that door, and your career is over."

Titus took a step forward. "Come on, man. Something's wrong. This isn't like you. Maybe you should talk to someone."

Georgios' dark skin went darker, and he pointed at Titus. "I don't need your, or anyone else's help. This has been a shitshow from the beginning, and the only reason it's held together this long, has been because of me." The creases in his forehead deepened. "And now you're both going to stab me in the back." He sneered. "This is the thanks I get? After all the long hours and hard work, and sweat and blood I've put in?"

"Nobody is blaming you for anything," yelled Lozano. His rumpled jacket looked just as wrinkled as Daniels' and he jabbed out a hand. "But you flying off the handle doesn't help anything. Now get back in my office."

"No," said Georgios. "I'm done. I'm pissed and I hate you both."

Titus tried again. "What's gotten into you? Whatever it is, we can figure it out. None of this is worth your job, or our partnership."

"I don't want to figure it out," screamed Georgios. "I'm not the issue here. You are. You both are. In fact…" He reached inside his jacket, pulled his weapon and pointed it at Titus. "Maybe it's time I listened and did something about it."

Rem and Daniels jumped from their seats and Lozano and Titus went still.

"I could take care of you right now," said Georgios, his hand with the gun shaking. "Then maybe I can get a good night's sleep." He blinked several times, and a trickle of sweat ran down his cheek.

Titus raised his hands. "Take it easy."

Rem eyed Daniels and Daniels, who was only steps away from Georgios, put his hand near his own gun on his waistband.

Rem took a step away from his desk, his hands in view. "Hey, Georgios," he said, his voice calm. "What are you doing?"

Lozano quieted his voice. "Put the gun down, Georgios."

Georgios looked between the men in the squad room. Sweat poured off of him and he seemed confused. "You don't understand." He waved the gun.

Daniels took a step closer.

"What don't we understand?" asked Titus, his eyes rounded.

"I can't...I can't..." Georgios shook his head. "I can't think."

"Just take it easy," said Rem. "It's nothing that can't be fixed."

Georgios swiveled toward Rem, the gun following. "You shut up. You don't know what's going on." He aimed his weapon. "You and Daniels think you know everything. Like you're shit on toast. Well, I'm sick of it."

Daniels stepped a little closer, his gaze on Rem, who tried to keep Georgios talking.

"Shit on toast doesn't sound too appetizing," said Rem. "Personally, I'm more of a jelly or peanut butter guy myself." He took another step from his desk, his hands still out. "Why don't we go get something to eat? We're all tired. It's been a long day. I think we just need to chill out." He tipped his head. "What do you say?"

"Put the gun down, partner," said Titus. "You don't want to do this. Let me help you."

Georgios whirled back toward Titus. "I'll do whatever I damn well please." He briefly squeezed his eyes shut and then opened them. "If I could just think in peace."

"Listen to your partner," said Lozano. "Put the gun away and we'll talk."

Georgios acted like he hadn't heard Lozano. "I should have done this a week ago, when these damn voices started." The gun wobbled in his grip, and Georgios' voice trembled. "If I had, then you would all understand." He eyed Titus. "You want all the recognition, partner? Well, you got it. I can't take it anymore." He raised the weapon and put it toward his head.

"No," yelled Titus.

"Georgios, stop," yelled Lozano, stepping forward.

"Don't." Rem ran forward and Daniels tackled Georgios, grabbing at the weapon, and pushing it away just as it discharged. A loud boom rocked the room, and Daniels shoved Georgios down to the ground. Titus jumped on top of Georgios along with Daniels, and Georgios struggled and fought beneath them. Rem grabbed for the gun still in Georgios' hand and held it down, trying to pull it from Georgios' grip.

Georgios grunted and cursed, but Daniels and Titus grabbed at his arms, pulling them back. Rem dislodged the gun and held it, while Titus pulled out his cuffs and managed to secure them on Georgios' wrists while Daniels did his best to control him.

Rem handed the gun to Lozano and helped Daniels hold Georgios down. He fought and screamed until the handcuffs clicked on and then went quiet, as if all his anger had dissolved, and went slack against the floor.

Daniels, breathing hard, stood along with Rem as Titus sat beside his partner. "You two okay?" Daniels asked Rem and Lozano, his heart thumping. He swept his no longer perfectly gelled hair back with his fingers.

"Fine," said Rem, looking pale.

Lozano watched his men, and tucked Georgios' gun in his waistband.

"What the hell happened here?" asked Rem.

Georgios whimpered, put his forehead on the floor, and began to sob.

"I wish I knew," said Lozano, his face grim. "I wish I knew."

CHAPTER TWO

Marjorie Daniels rinsed the glass in the sink, put it in the dishwasher, and flipped it on. Eyeing the clock, she wondered when Gordon would get home when she heard the back door open and close. After a few seconds, her husband walked into the kitchen, his face drawn and weary.

"There you are," she said. She wiped her hands on a dishcloth and tightened the sash on her robe. "I was about to text you again."

"Sorry, babe." He dropped his badge and keys on the front table. "It's been a hell of a day."

She walked over and gave him a hug. "You look exhausted."

He wrapped his arms around her. "I am."

Pulling away, she squeezed his waist. "You hungry? Did you have dinner?"

"Not really, no." He stepped back and pulled his gun from his holster. "Honestly, I think I'm too tired to eat." He opened the front closet and the gun safe, secured his weapon and locked the case.

"You should eat though," she said. "I know you're beat, but why don't you run upstairs and take a quick shower while I heat something up for you. I have some chicken and rice in the fridge. It won't take but a second."

He closed the closet door and swiveled toward her. "You should head up to bed. You must be tired, too. I can heat my own food."

"I don't mind. Besides, I'd like to talk to my husband at least for a few minutes before we go to sleep." She rubbed his arm. "Go on. Get cleaned up. You'll feel better and then you can eat."

Walking up to her, he took her hand. "I got pretty lucky when I met you." He kissed her forehead. "How's J.P.? He asleep?"

"You're darn right, you got lucky. And yes. He's asleep. He had a play date with his cousin, Lucy. He's pretty tuckered out, like his dad."

Gordon nodded. "Okay. I'll go give him a kiss, take a shower, and I'll be back in a few." He squeezed her fingers. "It's good to come home to you, you know that?"

"It's good to come home to you, too." She patted his butt. "Now get going."

He smiled, gave her a quick kiss, and headed up the stairs.

Marjorie went back into the kitchen and pulled out the chicken and rice. She added some to a plate and returned the rest to the fridge. Hearing the shower start up, she put the plate in the microwave, set it on low and flipped it on. The microwave hummed, and she found a glass and filled it with water and ice and set it on the counter.

Sitting at the table, she waited for the food to warm and for Gordon to return, smiling and reflecting on how happy she was. Her son, J.P., had just turned one; she'd been married almost six months; she had a sexy, handsome detective husband who loved her and whose partner had accepted her with ease and whom she'd come to love; they lived in a happy home and were blessed with good friends and family. Life couldn't be much better, although Gordon's job did occasionally put a damper on things. She'd spent more than one sleepless night worrying about him, plus he'd had a few injuries and hospital stays she'd had to deal with, but he loved his career and she'd come to accept it. It was who he was and she couldn't ask him to be any less.

The microwave dinged, and she sat up, smelling the chicken. She grabbed a napkin and silverware and brought his water over, too. Not long after, Gordon came down the stairs wearing his robe, his hair wet and combed, but his eyes less fatigued. "Smells good," he said, sitting in his seat. "Thanks."

"You're welcome." She sat beside him. "How was your day? You and Rem catch any bad guys?"

He took a sip of his water. "Arrested a guy who killed his girlfriend. Finally got him to confess."

Marjorie frowned. "God. That's awful."

"At least he'll be spending the rest of his life in jail. Or at least most of it." He ate some chicken and rice and sighed. "This is delicious."

"Feeling better?"

"Much." He ate a few more bites. "And then Georgios lost it."

"Georgios? Detective Georgios?" she asked. "What happened?"

Gordon shook his head. "Pulled his weapon on Titus and Lozano. Was shouting at them and blaming them for whatever was going on with their case. Rem tried to talk him down, but then he aimed the weapon at himself."

She straightened. "What? You're kidding."

"I tackled him, and he fired randomly. Thank God he didn't hit anyone. I got him down and Titus cuffed him, and Rem got the gun away from him." He sighed and shook his head. "It was terrifying."

She took his hand. "I can't believe that. He tried to shoot himself?" Her heart thumped at the thought of her husband almost getting killed. "Are you all right?"

He stretched his neck. "I'm okay, just stressed. My neck's in knots."

Marjorie stood, went behind him and began to knead his shoulder muscles. "You are in knots. You're as tight as Rem's high school prom suit he tried to wear to that policeman's charity event."

He chuckled. "I thought those buttons were going to give way at any second."

She smiled at the memory. "He must have been a scrawny kid." She used her elbow to dig into a knot on his neck.

He moaned. "God. That feels good."

"Finish your food."

"I think I'm done." He groaned again when she dug into another knot.

She thought about the incident with Georgios. "Why do you think he lost it? Was he that stressed? Or was it something else?"

He sucked in a breath when she bore down on a particularly tight spot. "I don't know, babe. They've been dealing with a stressful case. He said something about not sleeping well."

"You and Rem have dealt with stressful cases and lack of sleep, but you've never lost it like that. Rem's been through hell and back, and he's never gone that far."

Daniels nodded. "I know. I've never seen anything like it. You would think we would have seen the signs. But it just came out of nowhere. Titus said he'd been acting odd the last couple of weeks, and they'd been bumping heads, but he didn't expect this."

"Poor man. I hope he gets some help." She rubbed her fingers up his neck and into his hairline.

He groaned again and leaned back. "Lozano put him on paid suspension, and now he's at the Green Oaks Psychiatric Hospital on suicide watch. His poor wife is a mess. I just saw her for a few minutes at the station, but she looked terrified."

"That poor woman. I can imagine how she must feel." She ran her hands into his hair and massaged his scalp. "Better?"

He sighed deeply. "You have no idea."

She hugged him from behind. "You sure you're okay?"

He scooted back in his seat and pulled her around, and she straddled him on the dining chair. He brought his hands to her waist and pulled her in. "I'm okay." His eyes held hers and she saw that familiar gaze.

"Why, Detective Daniels, I do believe you are getting frisky." Her body heat rose as his hands found their way under her robe and he ran them up her thighs. She arched against him. "I thought you were tired."

He sat up and kissed her neck. "When it comes to you, my love, I'm never too tired." He trailed his lips up her neck and nibbled her chin. "What do you say we go upstairs and get more comfortable?"

She found the tie on his robe and opened it. "I don't know. I'm pretty comfortable right here." Seeing his muscular chest, she ran her hand down from his shoulders to his abs. "You want anything else massaged?"

He sucked in a breath and groaned, then raised his mouth to hers, and she slanted her lips over his and kissed him hard.

Their hands exploring, they discarded their robes, and Marjorie took her time, successfully taking her husband's mind off his troubles.

CHAPTER THREE

Remalla sat at his desk, feeling as if he'd just left it. After the incident with Georgios, he'd gone home, finished a leftover pizza from his fridge, taken a hot shower, and hit the hay. Lozano had told him and Daniels to take an extra hour in the morning after their long day and Georgios' near fatal shooting.

Rem shook his head at the memory, still hearing the gunshot. Looking over, he saw the hole in the drywall, and said a silent thank you that no one had been hurt. He couldn't help but think of the fear he'd seen in Georgios' eyes, and his shaking and sweating. If Rem was honest, it almost as if he was on something. Titus had sworn that was not the case, but they'd taken Georgios' blood for a drug test, so they'd know the truth soon enough.

The coffee machine beeped, and he stood with his mug. He poured a full cup, added sugar and cream, and sat. Despite the extra hour Lozano had given him and Daniels, Rem had arrived at the station early. He'd had a restless night, still seeing Georgios waving that gun and hearing the boom of the weapon firing in his dreams. He found it difficult to get out of his mind.

Scratching his head, he took hold of a folder and opened it. They still had to finish the paperwork on Marcus, so he picked up a pencil and made some notes, recalling the interrogation from the previous day. While sipping his hot coffee, though, his thoughts wandered back to

Georgios. He recalled the yelling, the gun shaking in Georgios' hand, and the boom came again.

"Good morning."

Rem startled and almost spilled his coffee.

"Sorry," said Daniels, pulling out his chair and sitting.

Rem dabbed at the drops of coffee that had escaped his mug and dripped on the folder. "Haven't been here ten minutes and I've already made a mess."

"That's hardly a record," said Daniels. "I believe the time to beat is two minutes."

Rem smirked.

"You're here early. I figured you'd squeeze out an extra thirty minutes of Lozano's one-hour gift." Daniels rolled his chair in and opened a green juice he'd been carrying.

"Yeah, well, I didn't sleep too well. Figured I might as well get an early start. Maybe finish some of this paperwork."

Daniels drank from his juice. "Still thinking about what happened?"

Rem raised a brow. "Yeah. Aren't you?"

"Kind of hard not to."

Rem closed the folder and held his coffee. "I keep wondering about what pushed him over the edge. I mean, I know we didn't always get along with the two of them, but nothing seemed out of the ordinary as far as I could tell."

"We have been a little pre-occupied with our own case. It's not like we've been bored. Something like that, you probably wouldn't notice unless you'd spent a lot of time with them."

Rem sat back. "I wonder how Titus is doing."

"It can't be easy, seeing your partner fall apart and almost shoot himself," said Daniels.

Rem hesitated, thinking back on his own struggles. "You ever worry about me doing that?" He fiddled with a pad of paper on his desk and felt Daniels' stare.

"Is that why you couldn't sleep?" asked Daniels. "You think that could have been you?"

"God knows there's been a few times where I felt I was close to it."

"There's a difference between thinking about it and actually doing it, you know?" Daniels leaned back in his chair. "And no. I never worried about you doing that."

"You didn't? Why not?"

"Because I know you. No matter how bad it may have gotten, you'd come to me first. You're a talker, Rem, and as long as you keep up the chatter, I know you're planning on hanging around. It's when you stop talking, that I worry."

Rem tapped at his desk with his finger. "My mom always did tell me I didn't know when to shut up."

"Your momma was right."

The squad door opened, and Lozano walked in. His yellow shirt complemented his brown skin, but his face still reflected his fatigue. Rem suspected Lozano's night had been worse than his.

"Mornin', Cap," said Rem.

"Good morning." Lozano stopped at their desks.

"Morning, Cap. How are you?" asked Daniels.

"I've had better sleep on my worst stake outs," said Lozano. He loosened his tie.

"I hear ya," said Rem, rubbing his eyes.

"I need to see you two in my office," said Lozano. "After last night, we need to discuss what happens next." He walked away.

Daniels sighed and stood. "I'll bet you a steak dinner, we just inherited Titus and Georgios' case."

Rem joined him as they headed toward Lozano's office. "You owe me a steak dinner anyway, after you set me up with Donna."

Daniels' eyes widened. "I thought you liked Donna. Said she was cute."

"Cute didn't cut it when she told me she works as a mortician and is a fruitarian. You left that part conveniently out."

"So, she likes fruit and is good with make-up. You'll save on restaurant bills and she's probably dying to talk to someone when she goes out. Seems like a win-win. What's the problem?"

"I ate two bananas and an apple on our date, and she showed me pictures she'd secretly taken of dead people she's worked on. I left starving and had a nightmare of a walking corpse with too much blush and lipstick."

Daniels' face fell. "Oh."

"Yeah, oh," said Rem, walking into Lozano's office. "That steak better be thick and juicy." He sat in a chair across from Lozano's desk, and Daniels sat in the one beside it.

"What steak?" asked Lozano, sitting at his desk.

"The one Daniels is going to buy me for my pain and suffering," said Rem.

"I don't think Daniels makes that kind of money," replied Lozano.

"Tell me about it," said Rem.

"How about this?" said Daniels. "I'll take you to that hot dog stand you like. You can get the biggest dog you want. Unlimited toppings. Cheese, ketchup, mustard, chili, buttered popcorn, whatever you want."

"Buttered popcorn?" asked Lozano.

"Don't knock it till you've tried it," said Rem. He eyed Daniels. "Make it two and you're on."

"Two it is, and I'll buy you an apple, in honor of Donna." He raised the side of his lip.

"You can keep the apple. Give it to the Cap instead," said Rem. "He's watching his waistline."

Lozano grunted. "If my wife makes me eat one more no-carb meal, I'm going to scream." He patted his belly. "A man needs some pasta every now and then."

"Just say the word, and I'll hook you up, Cap," said Rem. "I know a guy who makes a mean spaghetti and meatball."

Daniels grimaced. "You're not talking about Joey, are you?"

"Yeah, I'm talking about Joey."

"Don't go for it, Cap," said Daniels. "Last time he took me there, there was a hair in my salad."

Rem raised a hand. "The man has three dogs and two cats. What'd you expect?"

"They're not supposed to be in his kitchen," argued Daniels.

Lozano huffed. "I think I'll pass, but I appreciate the thought."

Rem shrugged. "You change your mind, you know where to find me."

"Anyway," said Lozano, with a sigh. "We need to talk about the case Titus and Georgios were working on. The liquor store robberies and now a homicide. Since you two are finishing up your current case, I want you on it."

"I figured," said Daniels. "How are Titus and Georgios, by the way? Have you heard anything?"

Lozano nodded. "Talked to Titus this morning. He's taking a few days. Going to be there for Georgios' wife and he'll be checking on Georgios. Georgios will be at Green Oaks for at least seventy-two hours. I'll be talking to the chief about him today."

"You think he still has a career left, if he recovers?" asked Rem.

"The man fired his weapon in the squad room, and almost killed himself or potentially one of us. I'll do my best to back him up, but the odds aren't good," said Lozano. "It's still early though. There's a lot to figure out before we get to whether or not he gets his job back." He paused. "He may not even want it back, based on what I saw yesterday."

"Yeah," said Rem, tapping on the arm of his chair.

"Getting back to the case," said Lozano. "Based on the updates I got before all hell broke loose, and what Titus has filled me in on, I put everything I have in here." He handed Daniels a folder. "Titus is going to send you more via email, so keep an eye out."

"Got it," said Daniels, opening the folder.

"What exactly are we dealing with here?" asked Rem.

Daniels' cell phone buzzed. He pulled it from his pocket, smiled, shook his head and turned it off. He returned it to his pocket. "Sorry. Nothing important."

Lozano rested his hands on his desk. "There have been five robberies, all within the last three weeks, and they've been escalating. The perps hit late at night or early morning, and usually when it's quiet, so we figure they're casing the stores, waiting for a time when there are little to no customers, or when the store's preparing to open. There's usually two assailants, their faces are covered, and they're in and out within a couple minutes."

"Weapons?" asked Daniels.

"They each carry a handgun. Never used them though until the last robbery. The cashier didn't cooperate and reached for his own weapon. They shot back."

"He didn't want to give them money from the register?" asked Daniels.

"Nope. He cursed them out, but they also wanted a certain bottle of scotch. They do it at every robbery. They want a bottle of *Johnnie Walker Gold*. They usually go straight for it, and take it to the register."

"They must case the inside then, too, so they know where to find it," said Rem. "They get a bottle every time?"

"Every time. The latest robbery though, they put the bottle on the counter and the cashier tried to take it back."

"I admire his courage, but that was stupid," said Daniels. "It's expensive scotch, but not worth your life."

"So, we're looking for two perps who like scotch," said Rem. "Do we have a description of these guys?"

Lozano rubbed his neck. "That's the strange part. It's not the same two every time. At first, we didn't think they were connected, until we learned about the scotch request."

"Different perps?" Daniels studied the file.

"The first robbery was two males - one tall and white male and the other brawny and black. The second was two white males, average height and build, the third appears to be the same tall white male from the first robbery and a new person, a woman."

"A woman?" asked Rem.

"Yes," said Lozano. "White, with black or brown hair. It was hard to tell from the grainy video and the witness reports weren't conclusive. She wore a cap that covered her hair and face, but she had a ponytail that ran down her back."

Rem frowned. "We've got multiple perps pulling off these robberies, and they all want the same scotch?" He raised an ankle and put it on his knee. "That's strange."

"What about the fourth and fifth robberies?" asked Daniels. "Same M.O.?"

"Yes. The fourth robbery was two men again, but different from the others, and the fifth was the tall man again, and the woman with the black or brown ponytail. She's the one who shot the cashier."

"She is?" asked Rem. "Could she be the ringleader?"

"Maybe. Maybe not," said Lozano. "She may have just panicked when the cashier wouldn't comply. Either way, it looks like we're dealing with a group of people who are bank rolling their activities with these robberies."

"Any idea who they could be and what their motives are?" asked Daniels.

"None. That's what we were talking about last night with Titus and Georgios. They weren't getting very far. They had a lead on the tall, white guy. Thought they had a source who could give them a name, but the source backed out at the last minute. In fact, everything went cold all of a sudden." Lozano sat back, pulled open a drawer, yanked his tie off and tossed it in the drawer.

"Everything went cold?" asked Daniels. "What do you mean?"

"Our witnesses stopped talking," said Lozano. "The owners of the stores are backing off, saying it's no big deal. The only one still willing to help is the owner of the store where the cashier died, but she wasn't present during the robbery."

"You think someone's threatening them? Telling them to back off?" asked Rem.

"That's my assumption," said Lozano. "Georgios and Titus were doing some digging. Based on the crimes and the descriptions, they researched felons who have a history and could be potentials. One stood out." Lozano pointed. "He's in the file."

Daniels pulled out a mug shot and held it. "Victor D'Mato. Age thirty-five. Six foot two, two hundred five pounds. Convicted of armed robbery and possession. Got out last year." He handed the paper to Rem, who took it.

Rem studied the picture. D'Mato had long, dark hair, a tattoo on his neck, and was unshaven. "Why'd they suspect him?"

"The robbery conviction was a start, and during his trial, a group of followers showed up to voice their disagreement, and they sent threats to the lead detectives. Their notes indicate D'Mato was some sort of aspiring cult leader."

"Cult?" asked Rem. "What is this? The seventies?"

"Koresh was in the nineties," said Daniels. "I suspect it's more common than we realize."

"Before the witnesses got quiet," said Lozano, "Titus and Georgios showed D'Mato's picture around. We figured if he's back to his old tricks, and his groupies were casing the joint first, maybe someone would recognize him or even one of his followers. It was a long shot, but worth a try. There was a worker who stocked the shelves at one of the stores. Titus swears the man's face went white when he saw the photo, but wouldn't say for sure if he recognized D'Mato. Titus and Georgios smelled something fishy. We started surveillance on D'Mato last week, but our boys lost him on the night of the fifth robbery. Brought him for questioning, but D'Mato said he was playing poker with his friends, and his friends backed him up."

"I bet they did," said Rem. He handed the mug shot back to Daniels. "So, you think this guy is involved? Maybe leading this little group that likes to rob liquor stores, and who's now intimidating the witnesses to stay quiet?"

"Seems possible," said Lozano. "D'Mato's cocky. When they brought him in, he didn't act like a man falsely accused. He was smug and overconfident." Lozano shook his head. "He's dirty. I'd bet my wife's apple pie on it."

Rem smiled. "When's the last time you had a piece?"

Lozano leaned back in his chair. "Too long, Remalla. Too long."

"What about video surveillance prior to the robberies?" asked Daniels. "If D'Mato or his group cased the stores before hitting them, they should have been recorded."

"We've looked, but so far, no luck," said Lozano. "It could be he's sending his followers in, who report back. And some stores just have crappy video. It's hard to get a clear photo."

"What about Victor's known friends or acquaintances?" asked Daniels. "You do any surveillance on them? One or two of them must be helping with the robberies."

"We're checking backgrounds, but haven't found one that really stands out well enough to follow up." He sat up. "We think there's more to it, though."

"What do you mean?" asked Rem.

Lozano interlaced his fingers. "Titus talked to an inmate yesterday who shared a cell with Victor before his release. That's what we were talking about last night. This inmate said that Victor has some weird beliefs. Says he believes in the paranormal, plans to stay young and live forever and knows how to do it. Victor bragged about his followers and what they'd do for him, and how, one day, he'd have more power than any cop and would wield his power freely."

"What the hell does that mean?" asked Daniels.

"It certainly makes the cult theory more likely," said Rem. "Guy's a nutcase."

Lozano's brow furrowed. "That's what you two get to find out."

Daniels returned the mug shot to the folder. "Lucky us."

"Any idea where to start?" asked Rem. "This guy seems pretty slick."

"Start at the beginning," said Lozano. "Reinterview the witnesses. Talk to the owners and cashiers. Show D'Mato's picture around. Maybe somebody will talk to you that wouldn't talk to Titus or Georgios. We'll continue surveillance on D'Mato and see if something turns up, which brings me to the next item of interest."

"What's that?" asked Daniels, closing the folder.

"When I talked to Titus this morning, he mentioned something he'd wanted to discuss last night, but Georgios' outburst prevented it." He punched a button on his keyboard and the monitor flickered on. "There's a woman. Her name's Allison Albright." He swiveled the screen toward Rem and Daniels. "You should have this in your email."

Rem saw a picture of a woman taken from a distance as she walked down the street. She wore sneakers, workout clothes and had a baseball cap on her head. Toned and slim, she had olive skin and a long, dark braid of hair that ran down her back. "Pretty lady," said Rem. "I bet she eats more than fruit."

Daniels frowned.

"She's D'Mato's ex. According to the inmate, Victor was crazy about her, but she'd broken up with him before his release. Victor wasn't too thrilled, according to the inmate, and seemed certain they would get back together."

"What are you thinking, Cap?" asked Daniels. "That she could be the lady from the robberies?"

"It's possible," said Lozano.

"But a long shot," said Rem. "A lot of women have long dark hair. God knows who Victor's been shacking up with."

"That's why Titus thought it was worth getting a closer look." Lozano turned the screen back. "This lady might have the goods on D'Mato. And if they are connected, could even be a follower."

"You want us to talk to her?" asked Rem.

"Yes and no." He raised a brow at Rem. "I want you to go under-cover."

Rem straightened. "You want me to what?"

"I want you to get to know her," said Lozano. "If you and Daniels go talk to her, and she clams up like all the rest, then we've gotten no-where. But..." he stuck out a finger, "maybe she'll open up to somebody else."

"You want me to date her?" asked Rem.

Daniels raised his hands. "Hold up. Are we sure this is a good idea? If this woman is involved, you could be putting Rem here into a hell of a mess."

"Last time I checked, Daniels, he's a cop," said Lozano. "That's his job."

Daniels held his chest. "Well, what about me? I'm perfectly capable of going undercover."

"Did you see that photo of D'Mato?" asked Lozano. "Take away the scruffy mustache and beard, and you've basically got your partner star-ing back at you. He's her type." He eyed Rem. "For once, I'm glad you haven't cut your hair."

Rem ran a hand through his own ponytail, wondering about this new assignment.

"Besides," said Lozano, "We'll keep an eye on Remalla. It's a long shot at best, but if Rem can get close, maybe he can get some infor-mation on this guy that might help us catch him. Best case scenario, she's involved and they'll try and recruit him."

Rem bobbed his foot up and down. "That'll be fun. I guess it's better than dating a mortician."

"You sure about this?" asked Daniels.

Rem didn't lie. "No, I'm not sure about it, but I see the captain's point. We've got to try something. Odds are, she hasn't seen Victor in months and wants nothing to do with him, but if there is a chance she knows something, it's worth a try."

"We're watching her," said Lozano, "so we'll look for an entry point. Once we have something, we'll let you know. Also, you better work on that wardrobe of yours. We need you to woo her, not scare her."

Rem scratched at a crack in the arm rest of his chair, thinking about Allison Albright. "How far exactly am I supposed to go with her?"

Lozano tipped his head. "I'll let you be the judge of that. You'll be the one in the middle of it. But I'd suggest you take it slow. See what you find out, then go from there."

"Plus, there's her to think of," said Daniels. "If she's not involved, the sooner you can get out the better."

"But if she is?" asked Rem.

Lozano went quiet and Daniels shook his head. Neither had an answer.

CHAPTER FOUR

Daniels returned to his desk and sat. Rem picked up his coffee, took a seat, and added more sugar to his mug. Daniels stared at the folder Lozano had given him, then tapped a key on his computer and accessed his email. Seeing one from Titus, he clicked on it and opened the attached picture. Allison Albright popped up on his screen, and he studied her.

Rem sat across from him. "Okay. I can hear that brain whirring over there. What's on your mind?"

Daniels looked away from the screen. "You know what's on my mind."

Rem stirred his coffee with a plastic spoon. "Don't worry. We'll probably solve this thing before I have to sacrifice my virtue. Besides, she's likely not involved and hasn't seen Victor in months."

Daniels tapped on the folder. "You don't know that."

"No, I can't be a hundred percent certain, but like Lozano said, I'm a cop. It's my job to figure out what I can about this guy."

"I don't like it. Somethings crawling up my back about this."

Rem took his spoon out of his coffee and tossed it in the trash. "Could be a roach. The other day I saw one scuttle under your desk.

"I'm serious, Rem." Daniels sat back. "You've been through a lot. You could be setting yourself up for trouble. Job or no job."

"What are you worried about? You think I might fall for her?" He sipped his coffee.

"What if you do? What if you like her and she ends up the ringleader? You going to arrest her and put her in jail?"

Rem set his cup down. "With my recent track record, I'd say the odds of me and her hitting it off are slim to none. Besides, I'll be careful."

Daniels rubbed his jaw. "When it comes to matters of the ticker, buddy, you tend to jump first and think later. And if you do like her, you could end up jeopardizing yourself and your career."

"Jeez. Have some faith in me, will you? I'm not a rookie."

"No, you're not. But you've got a big heart, and when you give it to somebody, you'll defend it to the death. And I don't want you killing yourself to prove her innocence and she ends up in prison, or worse, and takes you down with her. Between Jennie, Jill and what Rutger did, you don't need to heap any more crap onto the pile."

Rem sighed. "Listen to you. You've already got me falling for a criminal mastermind and me willing to fall on my sword to save her." He shook his head. "How about we just start with dinner first?"

Daniels waved a pen. "I'm just being cautious. Like I said, something doesn't feel right."

"I hear you, and I appreciate it. I'll be careful, and if I start to feel my heart go pitter-patter, you'll be the first to know."

"You promise?"

Rem raised a hand and held up two fingers. "Scout's honor."

Daniels rolled his eyes. "I told you, it's three fingers."

"Whatever."

Daniels looked back at the picture.

"Hey."

He looked back at Rem.

"Thanks for looking out for me." He hesitated. "To be honest, when Lozano brought it up, I almost declined."

"Why didn't you?"

He studied his coffee. "Because I can't let fear get the best of me. I start doing that, I might as well hang up my badge now, you know?"

Daniels eyed his partner and nodded. "Yeah. I know."

"But don't worry. I'll probably have a few dates with her, it'll go nowhere and we'll be back at square one."

Daniels felt that odd sensation run up his back again.

Rem waited, but when Daniels didn't answer, he shifted the subject. "You want to go to the liquor stores, talk to some witnesses?"

Daniels shook off his reverie. "I will, but you won't."

"I won't?"

"Nope. You need to keep a low profile. If Allison Albright is involved, and someone sees you interviewing people, there goes your cover." He stood and picked up his jacket. "You stay and finish the paperwork on Marcus."

Rem deflated. "Crap."

"I'll go check out the liquor stores and talk to anyone who may know something and flash Victor's picture around. When you finish the paperwork, you can call the store owners and talk to them."

Rem groaned. "All right. I suppose I can do a little digging on Victor and Allison, too. See what I can find. The more we know about those two, the better."

"And you better start thinking about your cover for when you meet Allison. You're going to need a name and a back story."

"I guess so."

Daniels nodded and picked up his green drink. "Keep me posted."

"You, too."

Daniels headed to the squad doors and paused before leaving. "Marjorie's cooking tonight. Making Chicken Marsala. You want to come over for dinner and we can talk about what we learned?"

Rem's eyes lit up. "You had me at Marjorie. Absolutely."

"Okay. See you later."

"And stop worrying," said Rem. "Everything will be fine. You'll see."

Daniels looked back, but all he could do was nod.

**

Rem knocked on the door and waited, eyeing the jack-o'-lantern at his feet, the cobwebs on the windows, and remembering that Halloween was just around the corner. Holding a six pack of beer, he was anxious to pop one open. It had been a long day of finishing reports, talking to liquor store owners, and digging into whatever he could find on D'Mato and Albright. Sighing, he thought back on what he'd learned. He'd hoped to find more than what Titus and Georgios had found, but it hadn't been much. He'd called and spoken with the officers and prosecutors involved in D'Mato's previous cases, and learned that D'Mato was indeed cocky and brash. He'd seemed unconcerned about his arrest, trial and incarceration, laughing and smirking his way through all of it. Rem had even spoken to a guard at the prison who'd remembered Victor D'Mato vividly. The man had quickly attained almost a cult-like status while behind bars, befriending those who could benefit him in some way, and threatening those who couldn't. Victor knew how to handle people and knew how to control them. But what concerned Rem most was how he was able to do it with ease.

The door opened, and Marjorie smiled and welcomed him. "Hey, Rem."

"Hey, Marj. What's shakin'?" He entered and held up the beer. "Thought I'd bring some refreshments."

"Gordon will be happy. He tells me he likes wine, but secretly, I don't believe him."

Rem went into the kitchen and put the beer in the fridge. "Did I beat him here?"

"No. He's upstairs putting J.P. to bed. Should be down soon." She went to the stove and stirred something in a saucepan.

"Smells delicious."

"I know you like my Chicken Marsala. Should be ready soon. Help yourself to one of those beers. You don't need to wait for Gordon."

Rem nodded. "I think I will." He opened the fridge and pulled off one of the beers. He'd kept the six pack in a cooler on the way over so it would stay cold.

"Long day?"

"Yeah. What about you?" He popped the can open and took a swig.

"Not too bad. A lot of meetings." She opened the lid to another pot on the stove. "I hear you got a new case."

"Yeah. We inherited it from Titus and Georgios. You heard what happened with Georgios?"

"Gordon told me. Is he okay? Have you heard anything?"

"Not much. Just that he's at Green Oaks and they're keeping an eye on him." He put his beer on the counter. "You need help with anything?"

"You can set the table."

"I'm on it." He pulled some plates from a cabinet, found the napkins, and grabbed the silverware. Daniels came down the stairs as Rem placed them on the table.

"Hey," said Daniels.

"Hey," said Rem.

"She put you to work already?"

"I offered. Beer's in the fridge if you want one."

"I do. Thanks." Daniels opened the fridge and grabbed a beer. "How's it goin', babe? You need anything?"

"You can pour me some wine," said Marjorie.

"You bet," said Daniels.

A few minutes later, they were sitting at the table as Marjorie brought the Chicken Marsala over. "Dig in."

Rem didn't hesitate, and helped himself. "So, you learn anything new?" he asked Daniels.

"Not much," said Daniels. "Most of it corroborated with Titus and Georgios' reports. I did talk to someone who recognized D'Mato though."

"Really?"

Marjorie came over with a salad and sat. "D'Mato's the bad guy?" she asked.

"He is," said Daniels. "At least we're pretty sure he is."

Rem ate some chicken and sighed. "Delicious as usual, Marjorie."

"Glad you like it." She took a bite of salad.

"What did this person say about D'Mato?" asked Rem.

Daniels took some chicken and salad. "They were right about his effect on people. The guy I spoke with looked scared. Didn't want to speak to me about him, but I used my charm and wits, and got him to talk on the condition of anonymity."

"Since when do you have charm and wits?" asked Rem, through a mouthful of chicken. He took a swig of beer.

"Oh, he has them," said Marjorie. "Just uses them on special occasions." She smiled at Daniels, who smiled back.

"Lucky lady," said Rem. "What'd he say?"

Daniels cut his chicken and stabbed some with his fork. "Said D'Mato creeped him out. He'd seen him once in the store and asked him if he needed any help. Said D'Mato asked where the scotch was."

Rem lowered his fork. "The scotch? Did he mention the Johnnie Walker?"

"No, but it's interesting."

"Sure as hell is. Sounds like the pieces are adding up," said Rem.

"Scotch?" asked Marjorie. Daniels filled her in on the robberies and the burglars' request for scotch. "Can you bring this D'Mato in for questioning?" she asked.

"Titus and Georgios did. Didn't go over well. And unfortunately for us, asking where the scotch aisle is located isn't illegal," said Daniels. "But that's not what creeped the guy I was talking to out."

Rem took some salad and added it to his plate. "What did?"

"Good for you. You're eating something green," said Daniels.

"If you can have charm and wits around Marj, then I can have some salad," said Rem.

"She brings out the best in both of us," said Daniels. Marjorie shook her head.

"That she does," said Rem. "What creeped the guy out?"

"Guy said he told him where the scotch was, but D'Mato hesitated. He asked the guy for a wine recommendation. Something that goes with a beautiful woman and brains."

Rem stopped before he put a forkful of food in his mouth. "And brains?"

Daniels wiped his lips with a napkin. "The guy I was talking to assumed he meant a beautiful woman *with* brains and said so to D'Mato, but D'Mato just smiled. The guy said his hair raised, he got a bad vibe and made a fast exit. He hasn't seen D'Mato since."

"Surely this D'Mato person wasn't suggesting he was eating brains," said Marjorie.

Rem put his fork down. "I may have lost my appetite."

Daniels took a sip of his beer. "Technically, people do eat brains. In some places, it's considered a delicacy."

"I'm sure Hannibal Lecter said the same thing," said Rem.

"Maybe the bigger question is not if he's eating brains, but why," said Marjorie.

Daniels pointed his fork. "That's true. If this guy does have some sort of cult following, maybe it's part of some sort of ritual or ceremony. Or maybe he just likes to shock people, which he successfully did."

"Speaking of cult following, he apparently had one in prison," said Rem. "Victor was a regular Jim Jones." Rem filled Daniels in on what he'd learned from the prison guard.

"Did he say anything about Victor wanting to stay young and live forever?" asked Daniels.

"Didn't mention it."

"Huh," said Daniels. "So, if he is cultivating some sort of cult, the question is why, and for what purpose? Does he really believe all that mumbo-jumbo?"

Rem scooped up some more chicken. "And how do we find his followers?" He ate the bite on his fork.

"I thought you'd lost your appetite," said Daniels.

"I got over it," said Rem.

"Maybe when you sweep Allison off her feet, you can find out," said Daniels. "She may not be dating Victor any more, but she may have been a part of his following in the past."

"Allison?" Marjorie leaned in. "Who's Allison? Someone new?"

"Don't get too excited," said Rem, pushing a piece of chicken around his plate while he chewed.

"Rem's going undercover," said Daniels.

"You are?" asked Marjorie. "When? Now?"

Daniels filled her in on Rem's assignment.

"Seriously?" asked Marjorie. She made a face. "Seems kind of sketchy."

"For Rem or Allison?" asked Daniels.

"Well, both, actually." She put her fork down. "I mean, if she's not involved, then Rem's lying to her to get information."

"And if she is involved?" asked Daniels.

"If she is, then she's not stupid. Don't you think she'd be careful? She wouldn't be spilling her guts to the first handsome fellow who shows a little interest." She swirled the wine in her glass.

"What are you saying?" asked Rem.

She stopped fiddling with her wine and eyed Rem. "I'm saying that if she is guilty, you may have to play house for a while. Are you prepared to do that?"

Rem cleared his throat and sat back. "Officially, it's frowned upon, but we all know how that goes. It's more of a don't ask, don't tell situation." He fiddled with his napkin. "I guess we're about to find out."

"You know you can back out whenever you want," said Daniels. "Now or later. You sense trouble, you get the hell out of there. Investigation be damned."

"I don't think Lozano would agree with you," said Rem.

"Screw Lozano," said Daniels. "Catching a bad guy is one thing, but it's not worth your sanity," said Daniels. "And if Lozano has a problem with that, he can talk to me."

Rem raised his hand. "Okay, partner. Don't get all riled up. Like I said, how about we just start with dinner and go from there."

Marjorie took a sip of her wine. "If she's innocent, and finds out you're a cop, she'll be pissed."

"Yeah, well, I can live with that," said Rem. "God knows I've pissed off plenty of people and lived to tell the tale."

"Let's hope it stays that way," said Daniels.

Marjorie rested her elbows on the table. "What's your cover going to be? Are you going to be a rich oil tycoon, or maybe a cowboy who rides bulls in the rodeo?"

Rem dropped his jaw. "A tycoon or a bull rider? Those are my options? I think you've been hangin' around Daniels too long."

"You want to get her attention, don't you?" asked Marjorie. "That would get my attention." Daniels' face dropped. "Of course, so would a sexy detective, honey." She reached over and patted his hand.

"Uh, huh," said Daniels. He looked over at Rem. "Please tell me you've got something other than an oil tycoon or a bull rider."

Rem held his head. "I was thinking a restaurant owner or an architect. But now you've got me reconsidering."

"An architect?" asked Daniels.

"A restaurant owner?" asked Marjorie. "No. I see you as more of a creative type." She held her chest. "I've got it. You should be a painter." Her eyes rounded. "Or, better yet, a writer."

"Seriously?" asked Rem.

"Seriously?" asked Daniels.

"Yes. Of course," said Marjorie. "Women eat that shit up." She poked Rem in the arm. "What about a name? Do you have a name?"

Rem grinned. "I was thinking Drake Dexler."

"You want her think you're a porn star?" asked Daniels. His brows rose. "That might actually be a great idea."

"Shut up," said Rem. "What's your idea, smart guy?"

Daniels thought about it. "Something simple. How about Tommy Horton?"

"You want her to think he sells insurance?" asked Marjorie. "No, no, no. It should be more romantic, but not too romantic." She squinted. "How about Dominic Remello?"

Rem straightened and Daniels' eyes widened. "That's actually not bad," said Daniels. "You could still be called Rem, but it wouldn't endanger your cover."

"I like it." Rem pointed at Marjorie. "You're good at this."

Marjorie smiled and sipped her wine. "Thank you. I guess I have been hanging around Gordon for too long."

"So, I'm Dominic Remello, the writer," said Rem.

"What exactly have you written, Dominic?" asked Daniels.

"Some short stories, and poems, mostly," said Rem. "And a children's book."

"Really," said Marjorie, resting her chin in her hand. "Do tell."

"Yes, please. Do tell," said Daniels.

Rem launched into the stories he'd written as Dominic Remello, talking about his romantic poems, and lusty short stories, and the story for kids about how to appreciate the differences in others.

"Wow," said Daniels. "I'm impressed."

Marjorie stared at him with starry eyes. "Me, too."

Daniels rolled his eyes. "I think you're about to steal my woman."

Rem chuckled. "Don't worry. I wouldn't take her from you, although it's tempting."

"It's okay, sweetie," said Marjorie to Daniels. "I only have eyes for you."

"That's not what your eyes were saying a minute ago," said Daniels. She rubbed his arm. "Well, let's be honest. Dominic Remello is pretty hot."

Rem felt his face warm. "It seems I have my official cover."

"It seems you do," said Daniels. "If she pulls you up on the internet, though, how are you going to explain your lack of published work?"

"What lack of published work?" asked Rem. "My mom's brother, Uncle Emilio, is a writer in his spare time. How do you think I knew what to say? I'll just tell her it's my pen name. He refuses to use his picture too, because of a botched nose job, and well, his weird chin, which if you ask me, needed more work than his nose."

Daniels shook his head. "Is there anyone in your family who isn't weird?"

"Other than me?" Rem thought about it. "Give me a second."

"Never mind," said Daniels with a smirk. "Let's hope you're right and the author story holds. We'll have to let Lozano know your cover and get your backstory set up in case she does any digging. Hopefully, this will be a short assignment, but once you start, you're going to have to keep a low profile. We'll have to get you a vehicle, too."

"It should hold," said Rem. "It's not like I'm trying to bust a drug ring. I'll talk to her, see what I can learn, and then get out."

"I don't know how she couldn't possibly be interested," said Marjorie.

Daniels grunted. "Let's hope Allison goes for it as well as my wife does."

"If she doesn't, she's crazy," said Marjorie. "Tell Lozano he can thank me by giving Gordon an extra vacation day."

"I'll mention it," said Rem.

They enjoyed the next hour avoiding talk of robberies and under-cover work, and instead discussing J.P. and his walking skills, plus Marjorie's mom's new house, and an upcoming vacation Daniels and Marjorie were hoping to take when time allowed.

Rem leaned back, patting his stomach. "Dinner was great. Thank you."

They'd cleared the table, and Daniels had given Rem a popsicle for dessert.

"You two want any coffee?" asked Marjorie.

Rem shook his head and slurped his popsicle. "I wish, but I need to sleep tonight."

"Me, too," said Daniels, adding a dish to the dishwasher.

Marjorie stood. "Then I'm going to check in on J.P and get ready for bed."

"Give J.P. a kiss for me," said Rem.

"I will." She walked out of the room but stopped at the front entry. "Oh, babe. I forgot. You got a package. I put it out here but forgot to tell you." She brought it to the table and set it down.

"Thanks, hon. I'll get it," said Daniels, wiping his hands on a cloth.

She faced Rem. "It was good to see you, Rem, and good luck as Dominic Remello. I hope it goes well."

"Thanks, Marjorie. I appreciate it," said Rem.

She smiled and headed up the stairs.

Daniels sat at the table and eyed the package.

"You expecting something?" asked Rem.

"Nope." He ripped the package open and pulled out a swath of bubble paper. "It's heavy." He unwrapped it. "What in the hell?" He pulled out a small stone statue. The head was oval-shaped, the carved eyes were round, and the mouth hung open.

"Who sent you that?" asked Rem.

"There's no card." He frowned, but then his eyes crinkled and he chuckled.

"What?"

"You remember that phone call I got? This afternoon in Lozano's office?"

"Yeah."

"It was my cousin Ben. The one who travels everywhere, and then calls to gloat about it."

"Ben? He sent you that?" Rem took the statue and studied it.

"It's something he does." Daniels poked at the statue. "Sends me crazy stuff from the crazy places he goes. Most of it is junk. He once sent me a mug from Japan that disintegrated in the dishwasher. And sent Marjorie a pearl necklace that smelled like dung. Most of the time, we donate his gifts or toss them."

"It's kind of weird," said Rem, eyeing the statue.

"He left a voicemail. Said he was in the Congo, riding an elephant. The reception was terrible." He took the statue from Rem." I suspect this is why he was calling. To rub it in and tell me to expect this."

Rem frowned at it. "You going to keep it?"

Daniels studied it. "I actually kind of like it. It's different."

"That's one word for it," said Rem.

Daniels carried the statue over to the stairwell and placed it on a shelf on the wall. "What do you think?"

The statue's wide eyes seemed to follow Rem. "I think you might want to double-check with Marjorie. It may not be her cup-of-tea."

"She'll love it," said Daniels. He gathered the bubble wrap and the package and tossed them in the trash.

Rem shook his head. "If you say so." He checked his watch. "So, what's on the agenda for tomorrow?"

Daniels joined him at the table. "I'm thinking it might be a good idea to pay a visit to Victor D'Mato."

Rem took the last bite of his popsicle and wiped his fingers on his napkin. "You think that's a good idea?"

"Might as well see what we're dealing with. Size him up."

Rem nodded, but didn't like it. "I'd prefer it if I could go with you."

"I know, but you can't."

"The guy's bad news."

"You have any better ideas?"

Rem huffed. "I wish we could figure out who his groupies are. That would be a great start."

"Maybe if I talk to him, he'll tell me."

"And maybe Lozano will lose twenty pounds, but don't count on it." He tapped his popsicle stick on the table.

"Well, we've got to try something. If you can take the risk with Allison Albright, I can take it with Victor."

"Somehow," said Rem. "I think you're taking the bigger risk."

"Maybe. Maybe not."

Rem's phone rang, and he pulled it out. "It's Lozano." He answered and they talked for a few minutes, and then Rem hung up.

"What is it?" asked Daniels.

Rem sat up, his heart thumping. "Dominic Remello is a go. Allison hangs out at a bar called *Mac Daddy's* on Thursday nights." He put his phone back in his pocket. "Looks like tomorrow, I'm goin' in."

CHAPTER FIVE

Daniels pulled up to the curb and parked along the sidewalk. Double-checking the address, he tapped the steering wheel and stared up at the building. He was in the right place. Victor D'Mato lived on the fifteenth floor in an upscale building with two large trees on either side of the entry where a stone staircase led up to the door.

He got out of his car, squinting in the sunlight and holding his head. Having not slept well, he'd awakened with a headache that had not abated despite the aspirin he'd taken that morning. Trying to shake it off, he crossed the street and entered the building. He found the elevators and rode up to the fifteenth floor. The elevator slowed, the doors opened, and he stepped out. Thinking of Rem, he wondered what his partner was doing. Daniels had suggested Rem not go into work, and instead take the day to prepare for his meeting with Allison that evening. Rem had reluctantly agreed, although Daniels knew his partner would prefer to be here. Since Daniels didn't know what he was about to walk into, a small part of him wished Rem was here too, but he wasn't about to tell Rem.

Finding the apartment, he paused outside the door, took a breath, and knocked. Several seconds passed with no answer, and he knocked again. Another several seconds passed and he was beginning to think no one was home, when he heard the sound of a chain sliding and the door opened.

A statuesque blonde woman with ruby red lips stood at the entry, wearing a skimpy black dress with a glittery belt, and stiletto heels. She was a good inch taller than Daniels.

"May I help you?" she asked in a sultry voice.

"Uhm," said Daniels, momentarily tongue-tied. "I'm here to see Victor D'Mato." He flashed his badge. "I'm Detective Gordon Daniels."

She looked him up and down and turned away from the door. "Babe, there's a detective here to see you."

Daniels heard a chuckle from inside the room, and then a deep voice. "By all means, let him in."

The woman stepped aside and widened the door.

Daniels entered and saw an almost all white room, with big windows that looked down onto the street, and large framed pictures of artwork on the walls, most of which looked contemporary. "Thank you."

A man matching D'Mato's description stood from the couch and the woman shut the door and walked to a side table, where she picked up a pair of flashy earrings and put them on. "You need anything else before I go?"

The man smiled. "No, my dear. I'd say you've earned your keep." He grinned.

The woman straightened, picked up a wad of cash from the table, and a small purse. "Until next time, then."

"Sure thing, sugar," said the man, watching her walk to the door. "And there will be a next time."

She flashed him a seductive smile with her red lips, and left, closing the door behind her. The man made a soft moan, and looked toward Daniels.

His head pounding, Daniels held out his badge. "Detective Gordon Daniels. Are you Victor D'Mato?"

The man held up his hands. He was as tall as Daniels, wore long white silk pants, and his white silk shirt was unbuttoned. The black hair on his muscular, but sinewy, chest set off a big diamond necklace with a diamond letter 'V' that sat around his neck and sparkled in the sunlight streaming through the windows. His wavy dark hair brushed past his shoulders, and Daniels thought Lozano was right. If it weren't for the man's bushy beard and mustache, he'd be a dead ringer for Rem. "Guilty as charged, my friend." He took a few steps. "To what do I owe this lovely visit, Detective Daniels?"

Daniels stood silent, getting a feel for the man in front of him. He definitely gave off a vibe, and he had the odd feeling that Victor had already known who he was and had even expected him. "I wanted to ask you a few questions about some robberies in the area."

"Oh, yes." Victor smiled. "I believe I met a couple of your friends." He tapped his chin. "What were their names?"

"Detectives Titus and Georgios."

"Yes. That's right." He touched his necklace. "Nice enough men, I suppose, although the one named Georgios was a little intense." He turned and walked into the kitchen. "I can only assume he was under a lot of duress. I hear that comes with the job." He opened the refrigerator and pulled out a pitcher. "Can I get you something to drink? Water, perhaps? Or an orange juice?"

Daniels would have usually declined, but his head hurt and his mouth was dry. "Water, please. Thanks."

Victor nodded and pulled out two glasses from a cabinet. "How are you, Detective?" He filled both glasses with water from the pitcher. "I have to say, you look a little stressed yourself." He put the pitcher back in the fridge, closed it and brought the waters over and handed one to Daniels, who took it. "It's not catching, I hope?"

Daniels shivered, and knew he didn't like this man. Something about the way Victor talked made him feel like he needed a shower. "I don't think so."

"Good. Glad to hear it." He gestured. "Have a seat. *Mi casa es su casa.*"

Victor sat on the white couch, and Daniels sat in the white chair beside it, and tucked his badge back in his pocket. "You know anything about five liquor store robberies that have occurred in the area over the last three weeks?"

Victor held his glass and put his arm over the back of the couch. "If you'd talked to your detective friends, you'd know the answer was no. I have no knowledge of any robberies." He sipped his water.

"A man matching your description was present during three of the crimes. You've also been convicted of armed robbery."

He waved a finger. "That's all in the past and correct me if I'm wrong, but the offenders wore masks, did they not?"

"They did."

"So when you say 'matching my description' that's pushing it, wouldn't you say?"

"There are other factors which make you a strong person of interest."

"Really? And what are those?"

His smooth demeanor and confidence gave Daniels a glimpse into why Victor would attract a following. "We know you've been to at least one of the stores in question, and you seem to make an impression when you go. People remember you."

Victor grinned. "I'm a memorable person. No crime against that."

Daniels drank from his water. "Well, if you have no involvement, then it should be easy to prove your innocence. Can you tell me where you were on the nights of the crimes?"

Victor sighed. "I do believe I answered all these questions with your friends. Can't you look at their notes?"

"I prefer to hear it from you."

Victor shrugged. "I'm happy to tell you, but I hate for you to waste your time. Surely you have better things to do?"

Daniels tensed as the first flickers of impatience rose. "I'm trying to solve a crime here, Victor. One in which a man was shot and killed. I'd like to prevent that from happening again." He rubbed his head. "So, if you know something, now would be the time to tell me. Because if this goes further, and more people are hurt, there won't be much I can do for you."

Victor smiled. "Do for me? What on earth do you think you can do for me?"

Daniels took another sip of water and debated how he wanted to play it with this guy. He decided to push a little harder. "Let's not play games here, Victor. You and I both know the deal. You're as dirty as this place is white." He raised a hand at the walls. "Now you can sit there and act all smug and innocent, but your smart-ass charm, white silk pants and flashy necklace don't make me think for one second that you're not guilty of something. The Unabomber looks innocent compared to you."

Victor stared for a moment, then sipped his drink. "The Unabomber? What an interesting comparison. Did you know he was a genius?"

"And his smarts only got him so far. He got cocky, which, I think, is something you're familiar with?"

He flashed his pearly white teeth. "It's one of my more valuable traits, although I suspect you'd disagree."

Daniels set his water down on the glass coffee table and rested his elbows on his knees. "Who are you working with?"

Victor narrowed his eyes. "What exactly do you mean?"

"I'm not stupid, although I suspect you'd disagree."

Victor tipped his head.

"I know you're not the only one involved in this. And something tells me you don't take orders too well, so you must be the one in charge. Only problem is, none of your friends seem to fit the bill as your potential groupies. Which brings us to the big question. Who exactly does? And why are you hitting liquor stores?" He narrowed his eyes. "It can't be to support your need for your pretty furniture and artwork?" He paused. "Can it?" He waited for Victor's reaction. Victor didn't move, but Daniels got the distinct impression Victor's mind was racing, and not in a good way. "Cat got your tongue?"

A quiet second passed, and Victor sat up and put his water glass next to Daniels'. "I like you, Detective. You're so much more interesting than the other two." He held Daniels' gaze. "Where's your partner? Don't you come in twos?"

Daniels didn't hesitate. "He's under the weather. Took the day off."

"Pity. I would have liked to have met him. I can only imagine what a partner of yours must be like."

Daniels shrugged. "Not that impressive really. Thinks he's funny and eats like a goat."

Victor chuckled. "It's not that easy finding someone you can work well with, is it?"

"It can be a challenge. Sounds like you have experience."

He leaned closer. "Oh, I have a lot of experience, but you have no idea with what."

"Why don't you enlighten me?" Daniels sat back. "I've got the whole day, so take your time."

Victor grinned and stared, and Daniels almost squirmed.

"Too bad," said Victor, with a penetrating gaze.

"Too bad what?"

Victor shook his head. "Nothing." After a pause, he stood. "The problem, Detective, is that it's something you couldn't even begin to understand." He walked to the window. "There are things in this world that most have no comprehension of. They aren't willing to take the time to study it, even though it's right in front of their face."

Daniels realized the chair moved, and he swiveled to face Victor. "What is that?"

Victor threw out his hands. "Possibilities. They're everywhere."

"What possibilities?"

Victor pointed. "See? That's where you come up short. Your life is viewed only through your five senses, and that's why you will never be able to fully comprehend the true extent of your nature. Oh, you'll find your man, put him in jail, and move on to your next case, where you'll do it all over again, and one day, they'll put you in a bigger chair with more responsibility as your ass widens, and your arteries harden. Your wife, or your lover, will stand lovingly by your side and you'll raise two point five kids, while your hair goes gray, you get fat, your health declines, and then you're lying on your death bed, regretting most of what you've done with your life." He turned pensive. "Wishing maybe instead of catching the bad guys, you'd actually joined them."

Daniels listened, thinking this guy had lost it, but curious. "You think that's me?"

"You're well on your way."

"But it's not you?"

"No."

"So, you're robbing liquor stores because it's fulfilling and gives you a sense of purpose?"

"You have to think bigger than that, Detective."

"You're not denying that you robbed the stores?"

"I'm saying that it's not about the robberies. It's about what those crimes represent."

Daniels groaned. His aching head couldn't handle this nonsense. "I'm not sure if I should arrest you or get you a shrink."

Victor eyed the street. "I hear Green Oaks has a few good ones."

Daniels shuddered and stood, thinking of Georgios. "What the hell does that mean?

Victor looked back, his eyes flat. "It pays to know your enemies. Wouldn't you agree?"

Daniels took a few steps closer. "Did you have something to do with what happened to Georgios?"

"You're getting ahead of yourself, Detective Daniels. I simply mentioned Green Oaks. As I said, your detective seemed a little stressed. It's not a big leap to assume he'd fall prey to his mental constraints. It happens to the best of us."

Daniels didn't think for a moment that Victor was telling the truth. "Did you spike him with something? Was it drugs?"

He chuckled. "Again, you fail to see the point." He turned from the window. "Your Detective Georgios is only a symbol of the problem. He is what you will be, what all of you will be, because you refuse to see the solution." He stepped closer. "The answers are there, Detective. You only need the courage to take the steps required to find them."

Daniels set his jaw. "And what steps are those?"

Victor's face relaxed and he stepped away, deep in thought. "Do you believe in ghosts, Detective?"

Daniels frowned. "Excuse me?" His mind flashed back to his experiences with his grandfather's house and the Lady of Black River. "What are you talking about?"

"I'm talking about the very thing we all want the answers to. Ghosts, psychics, teleportation, telekinesis. I could go on. There is no end as to what is possible with the human psyche, before, and after death." He raised a hand. "Have you ever bothered to truly explore these things? To really understand the power of the human mind?"

Daniels recalled a few incidents with flying objects on a recent case and Rem's former girlfriend, Jill's, ability to see beyond the obvious and even get inside another's head. "What the hell are you talking about?"

Victor held his stare. "Something tells me you have some experience of what I'm referring to, but yet you still can't accept it, can you?"

Daniels groaned. "I'm just trying to solve a crime here, Victor."

"And I'm leading you straight into the abyss, aren't I?" He raised the side of his lip. "It's a shame really. You have such potential."

"Potential for what?"

"To see so much more." He clenched his fingers into a fist. "Life is fleeting, Detective. You have to grab it by the balls before it's gone."

"You can't live forever, Victor."

Victor's face fell, and he walked over and picked up his water. "Who says?" He took a sip.

Daniels dropped his jaw. "Is that what this is about? What your little cult is about? You plan to live forever?" He scoffed. "And I thought I was dealing with a criminal mastermind. Silly me."

"I wouldn't mock what you don't understand. All it takes is the right ingredients. A little of the dark mixed with the light, plus a sacrifice or two to show you're serious."

Daniels straightened. "Sacrifice? What does that mean?"

Victor opened his mouth to answer, but then seemed to think twice. "Perhaps I've said too much. I'd hoped you'd be one to understand, but clearly I'm wrong."

"Are you some sort of a devil worshipper?" asked Daniels. "You're orchestrating crazy rituals so you can avoid death?"

Victor smirked. "Devil worship is so passé. I'll leave that to rebellious teenagers and bored dysfunctional adults. Besides, the devil is limited in his abilities, if he even exists at all. His power only comes from those who believe in him, and I, for one, do not."

Daniels tried to keep up. "What do you believe in, Victor?"

Victor eyed him, and smiled softly. He put his water down, walked over to a small bar set into the wall, and poured himself a drink from a clear bottle. "I believe in me, Detective." He shot down the drink in one gulp. "Isn't that where anyone's true power lies?"

He set his glass down above a shelf of alcohol which sat below the bar, and Daniels saw a distinctive label and pointed. "Is that Johnnie Walker Gold?"

Victor turned and picked up the bottle. "It is. Would you like some?"

"You like that brand?"

"It's one of my favorites."

Daniels paused, trying to think. When he'd arrived, he certainly had not expected this conversation, and realized Victor was playing with him. He moved closer and put his hands in his pockets. "Understand something, Victor. You can play these games all you want, and pretend with your little cronies that by somehow hurting others, you can outwit death and the devil, and stay young forever, but the truth of the matter is that you won't. You will die right along with the rest of us, old and wrinkled, if you're lucky to live that long. And if I have anything to say about it, you will die in a jail cell, lying above or below your cellmate, wearing your orange jumpsuit, and wishing you'd have figured out all your shit a lot sooner."

Victor swung the bottle of scotch and grinned. "I believe this conversation is over. It's been fun talking with you, Detective, and I look forward to more scintillating discussions."

"Don't get your hopes up."

"Nor should you."

Daniels held Victor's gaze, and that same shiver returned and raced up Daniels' back. Deciding he wasn't going to get much else out of Victor, and not feeling much interest in hearing Victor's false alibis regarding the robberies, he turned toward the door. "You have a nice day, Victor. And enjoy the digs..." he waved at a big painting of a black square with a red dot in the middle, "...while you still have them."

"You, too, Detective." He leaned against the bar. "And I hope that headache gets better."

Daniels opened the door and looked back. Had he mentioned his headache? He couldn't remember.

Victor raised the bottle of liquor as if toasting him, and Daniels walked out.

CHAPTER SIX

Rem sat on a barstool at *Mac Daddy's* and sipped on a drink. He kept an eye on the slowly growing crowd as the work day ended and the bar filled. The music played, and the dance floor was empty, but he suspected that would change soon.

He'd been there for an hour, arriving early since he wasn't sure when to expect Allison and he wanted to get the lay of the land. A few attractive women had smiled at him, but he'd downplayed his interest. It had been a while since he'd sat at a bar with the intention of meeting anyone. He and Jennie had gone out for drinks and dancing a few times, and he supposed some part of him wanted to avoid doing it again since her death. After he'd lost her, Rem had done his best to keep the memories of her at bay, so he'd dived into his work to stay sane, but found it impossible to return to his life before her—when he'd routinely gone out to meet and woo women and have some fun.

Sitting at the bar, though, he let himself think back, and wondered if maybe it was time to step back out into the fray. At the same time, though, the thought of returning to the bar scene felt a little depressing. His interests had changed, and he didn't think he could be that guy anymore.

Sipping on the same drink he'd ordered when he'd arrived, he looked over at a group of women who'd entered the bar, smiling and laughing. Allison was not among them, and he checked the time.

"Can I get you a second?" asked the bartender. It was the third time he'd asked.

Rem debated. He didn't want to get drunk, but he also didn't want to stand out. "Sure. Thanks." The bartender nodded and started on the drink.

Rem smoothed his collar and shifted in his seat. Daniels had suggested he take the day to get ready for his evening, and Rem had reluctantly agreed, realizing he needed time to prepare to be Dominic Remello. He'd gotten up that morning and had gone for a long run. Since Jennie's death two years earlier, he'd let his exercise regimen suffer. A runner at heart, he'd always liked to jog in the mornings and occasionally, Jennie had run with him. Recently, he'd started to make more of an effort, but then he'd met Jill during the Makeup Artist case and they'd spent almost every waking moment working, and their rocky relationship had fallen apart after chasing down Rutger, and then so had he after the revelations that had stemmed from that case. It had taken all Rem's strength for him to get back on his feet again, and any attempts at exercise had been futile.

But now, six months later, some of Rem's motivation was returning, and this unexpected assignment had helped. He was forced to get out there and confront a few demons, and no matter what might happen with Allison Albright, he figured he was benefiting from it. After his morning run, he'd showered, eaten, and headed out to a few retail shops. He'd bought a couple of button-down shirts, and a new pair of jeans, sneakers, and some cologne. He'd even gotten his hair trimmed. If he was going to try and attract a woman, he needed to step up his game. He had no doubt that his lack of care in what he wore and how he looked was directly related to the loss of Jennie, and it was time to deal with that too. He couldn't be a slob forever.

Nursing his drink while he waited for his second, he wondered how long he should wait for Allison. Lozano hadn't given him a timetable, but if he was going to sit there and keep ordering, at some point he would need to eat something. He thought of Daniels and wondered how his meeting with D'Mato had gone. He hadn't liked his partner meeting with that lunatic alone, but realized there was little he could do about it.

The bartender slid his second drink toward him and took his empty glass, and Rem took a sip. Looking over, he caught sight of a woman with wavy, long, dark hair, wearing a red form-fitting dress that stopped at her knee but emphasized her cleavage, and red, strappy heels, walk up to the bar. She placed her small purse on the counter and slid onto a stool. As she crossed her legs, Rem couldn't help but admire the curve of her calf and how her dress hugged her hips. His mouth suddenly went dry, he felt a rush of heat when he studied her, and realized who she was - Allison Albright.

Shit. His thoughts whirled, and he tried not to stare. Gone were the baseball cap, workout clothes and ponytail. The gorgeous woman sitting a few seats down from him made his pulse race. Anxiety crept up, and he studied his drink, feeling self-conscious. How in the hell was he going to approach her? Every man within a hundred feet was already eyeing her. Swallowing, he stilled when he saw a tall man walk up to her, looking like he'd just stepped out of *GQ* magazine, and offered to buy her a drink. Rem waited to see what she'd do and was happy to see her rebuff him. Offering the man a sly smile, she shook her head no, said something to him, and the man frowned and walked away.

Rem sighed in relief, but the doubt surged. If she'd turned that guy down, she sure as hell wouldn't give him the time of day. He held his drink, thinking. *Calm down,* he said to himself. *You're overthinking it. Just relax and smile. If she rejects you, so be it.* But he could only imagine the smack talk he'd hear from his fellow officers when he would have to admit he'd failed.

Taking a deep breath, he took a sip of alcohol for courage, resigned himself to his fate, forced himself to peer over at her, and almost choked on his drink when he caught her looking at him. Without thinking, he looked away and his cheeks warmed. *Get a hold of yourself, Rem. It's not like you've never done this before.* Making himself glance over again, he was encouraged to see her still watching, and she smiled. Her pearly white teeth gleamed beneath her shiny lipstick, and he held her gaze and smiled back, his heart rate doubling. Was she interested, he wondered? In him?

Not sure what to do, and just as confused about his own insecurities, he went back to studying his drink, thinking maybe perhaps Daniels should have been given this assignment. He'd sure as hell be handling this situation with a lot more confidence. Rem thought about it. It was still an option. He could leave now, and they could switch things up and give Daniels a shot, although he suspected Marjorie would not be pleased.

"What are you drinking?"

The voice came from beside him, and he turned to see Allison Albright standing next to him. His voice locked up when he met her gaze. The perfect brow over her left eye arched up, and he could smell her perfume.

"Uhm…a vodka tonic." He almost moaned. Suave he was not.

The side of her mouth raised. "You mind if I sit?" Her voice was soft and sultry, and she gestured toward the stool beside him.

"No, please do." He took a shaky breath. "Would you like one?"

She slid in beside him, crossed her legs again, and he tried not to look. Her dress was sleeveless and he could see the curve of muscle in her shoulders, and her even tan made her skin glow.

"One what?" she asked. "One of you, or the vodka tonic?" She put her purse down.

Rem's heart skipped and for a moment, he couldn't speak and the heat on his cheeks flared. "I, uh, meant the drink. But I'm not going anywhere. At least not until the shrinks realize I'm gone." As usual, when he was nervous, he tried to be funny.

She laughed and he relaxed. "I'd love a drink. A vodka tonic would be great. Thanks."

Waving at the bartender, he ordered for her. Feeling her eyes on him, he swallowed, and said the first thing that came to mind. "You're making me nervous."

She swiveled toward him. "I am? Why?"

Rem decided to be honest. "Because you're the most beautiful woman in this room, and I figured you'd go for the *GQ* guy."

Her gaze traveled over him, and he felt like he was naked.

"*GQ* guys are boring, thinking they can flash their money, their perfect hair and clothes and think I'll fall all over them. They just want something to hang on their arm. Been there and done that."

Rem nodded. "I've never been a *GQ* kind of guy, so I wouldn't know."

The bartender set her drink down, and she picked it up. "I find you far more interesting," she said, taking a sip.

Her full lips sucked on the straw and Rem tried to pull his eyes away, but failed. "Me? Why?" His voice broke, and he grabbed his drink and took a sturdy gulp.

She smiled. "Because you blushed when I looked at you. And you're still blushing now. I don't meet many men who blush." She swirled her drink with her straw.

He fiddled with his napkin. "And I don't meet many women who catch the eye of every person in the room when they enter it."

She put her drink down. "You should have more confidence. You might be surprised who you might attract." She leaned in. "Unless the doctors know something I don't."

Rem chuckled. "Maybe one day, you'll find out." His heart still thudded, but he was happy he'd been able to flirt a little without looking like an idiot.

"Now I'm intrigued," she said. "Just so long as you're not a serial killer. Can I get a yes or no on that one, at least?"

"That would be a no. You're safe on that front." He'd almost told her he'd never killed anyone, but that would not have been the truth, and for some reason, he didn't want to lie to her.

"Good. Glad to hear it. I'm not one either by the way."

"Whew," he said. "Happy to know that. But I will admit to a few flaws. I hate vegetables, tell terrible jokes, and love to watch bad movies in the middle of the night, so there's that."

That perfect brow over her left eye arched again. "I like broccoli, but that's as far as it goes, laugh at stupid jokes when no one else does, and did you catch the Godzilla marathon the other night? I was up till two in the morning."

Rem dropped his jaw. "I was up until three."

Her face brightened, she broke out into a laugh and raised her drink. He raised his and they clinked them together. "My name's Allison Albright."

Rem stilled. The name Dominic Remello was on the tip of lips. His gut twitched and his chest constricted, and he had a thought. His mind whirled as she waited for him to respond, and he wondered if he was doing the right thing, but he'd always trusted his gut before and couldn't stop now.

"Aaron Remalla," he said. "Nice to meet you."

They drank from their vodka tonics, and she put her glass down. "I haven't seen you in here before."

"I've never been in here before," he said. "It's been a while since I've done the bar scene." The music grew louder, and he had to raise his voice.

"Don't tell me," she said. "You been doing those dating apps? I tried them a few times. Didn't care for it."

He shook his head. "No. Not interested in dating apps."

She cocked her head. "Really? I'd think you'd have your pick of women, even if you're a little shy." She raised a hand and brushed a lock of hair off his shoulder. "I think it's the rock star look."

"Rock star?" He shrugged. "That's a first. No..." He sighed. "I...uhm...lost someone. After her death, it took the stuffing out of me and it's been a while since I've dated seriously." He had no idea why he'd told her that, but the words had just spilled out of him.

Her face fell. "I'm sorry. I didn't mean to..."

He waved. "It's fine. It's been a while since it happened, but it's crazy how the mind works, you know?"

She nodded. "I lost someone, too. I mean, they didn't die, but it was an ugly break up. It was hard to get back into the dating scene, and I kind of had to force myself."

Rem wondered if she was referring to Victor D'Mato. "I get it."

"Let's talk about something a little less sad," she said. "I own a gym not far from here. Opened it last year. Do you like to work out?" She scrunched her face and crossed her fingers.

He grinned. "I do, although I've slacked off a bit, but I'm getting back into it. I'm a runner though. Not much of a gym rat. I prefer to be outdoors."

"I hear you," she said. "I like to run outdoors too. I hate the treadmill. But I love to teach classes."

"What do you teach?"

"Yoga, pilates, and a strength training class."

"You must be busy. All that, plus running a business?"

"I barely slept the first year, but business is picking up and I've hired some new instructors, so now my time's freed up a bit." She uncrossed her legs and hooked her heel on the footrest of the bar stool. "What do you do?"

That same constriction returned, and Rem figured he'd gone this far, and he couldn't stop now. He set his jaw, and committed. "I'm a cop, actually a detective."

Her mouth fell open. "Seriously?"

"Seriously."

She rested her elbow on the bar. "I've never met a cop before."

"You can no longer make that statement." His mind raced, and he could almost hear Daniels and Lozano yelling at him in his head. He prayed he knew what he was doing.

"You catch bad guys, like murderers?"

He nodded. "Yup."

Her face furrowed. "Anyone I know?"

"Depends. Do you keep track of murderers?" He considered his history. "You hear of the Makeup Artist?"

Her eyes widened. "You caught him? The serial killer? I didn't want to come out of my house for weeks."

"I helped catch him. I can't take all the credit. It takes a village when it comes to something like that."

"I bet." She shook her head. "I would never have guessed that you would be a cop. I always picture older men with gray hair and big bellies looking rough and tired."

"Rough and tired is true. But I'm trying to prevent the big belly." He patted his stomach.

Unhooking her heel, she swung her foot, and that seductive smile returned. She put a hand on his knee. "Well, so far, you're doing just fine." She moved her thumb over his jeans.

Rem gripped his glass, and his body warmed. This was a bit more than he was expecting, and he warred with himself as to how to handle it.

The music blared as more people arrived and began to hit the dance floor. He realized he'd sucked his drink down to the ice and he held it, wondering if he should ask her to dance. His dance skills were minimum at best though, so he hesitated. "You're making me nervous again."

Her smile grew. "Good," she said. "I like making you nervous."

Shaking his head, he put his glass down. "I can deal with killers and rapists, but you…" He paused. "You might get the best of me."

She trailed her eyes over his face, and his body tingled. *Oh, hell, Remalla*, he thought. *What are you getting yourself into?*

Leaning in, she spoke into his ear. "You want to get out of here? Maybe go someplace a little quieter?"

Rem went still, his body heat indicator spiking, and his heart beating erratically, and questioned his decision making. "I thought you'd never ask."

Looking pleased, she picked up her purse, left her drink, and slid off the barstool. Rem pulled out some money from his wallet, tossed it on the counter and couldn't help but watch her walk as he followed her out of the bar.

CHAPTER SEVEN

Sitting at his desk, Daniels shook out two aspirin into his hand and tossed them in his mouth. He picked up the smoothie he'd bought on the way in to work and took a swallow to wash the pills down. His headache had improved since the previous day when he'd interviewed Victor, but it wasn't completely gone. Add that to a terrible night's sleep and weird dreams, and Daniels wondered if he could slip away at some point and take a nap in the locker room. Rubbing his eyes, he hoped Lozano had some sort of meeting that would get him out of the office so Daniels could close his eyes for a few minutes.

Blinking, Daniels eyed his computer, still thinking about his conversation with Victor. He'd typed it up and planned to tell the captain about it, but Lozano had been on the phone since Daniels had arrived that morning. He had a few thoughts about what to do next, but wanted to run it by the captain first.

Eyeing the empty desk across from him, he wondered for the millionth time how Rem's evening had gone. Daniels had avoided calling or texting him since Rem was undercover, but his curiosity was getting the better of him. They'd agreed that Rem would get in touch when it was safe to do so, but Daniels had expected to hear from him by now. Sighing, he figured his partner had either blown it and was too embarrassed to admit it, or he'd succeeded, and maybe there was a good reason his partner was staying quiet. He was either freaking out, or

Daniels had to consider that Rem could still be with her. The likelihood was slim, but possible.

Groaning and rubbing his neck, Daniels heard Lozano's office door open and saw Lozano step out and approach Daniels' desk. "Anything?" he asked.

Daniels assumed he was referring to Rem. "Not a word."

"What the hell is your partner doing out there?"

"I wish I knew."

Lozano eyed the clock on the wall. "I'm giving him an hour. We don't hear from him by then, go find him."

Daniels nodded. "I was going to give him thirty minutes, but I can stretch it to sixty."

Lozano narrowed his eyes. "You look awful. You get any sleep last night?"

"Not much." He closed his eyes and held his temples.

"You worried about your partner?"

Daniels cracked an eye open. "I admit, he gives me plenty to worry about, but this is just plain, old-fashioned insomnia." He eyed the empty desk again. "To be honest, I half-expected to get a call in the middle of the night from Rem, telling me he'd blown it or backed out entirely."

"Why do you say that?"

Daniels capped the aspirin and put the bottle in a drawer. "In case you hadn't noticed, he's struggled the last six months. Hasn't really wanted to engage. It was like pulling teeth to get him to go out on one date when we were in Dumont, and it hasn't been much easier since."

"Hmm," said the captain. "Well, the last I checked, your partner has a mouth, and he knows how to use it. If he was uncomfortable with this assignment, I suspect he would have said something."

Daniels sat back. "Maybe, probably, who knows?" His thoughts were a jumble.

"Could be good for him. Force him back out there."

Daniels tried to think. "Maybe, probably, who knows?" he repeated.

Lozano raised a brow. "You are tired, aren't you?"

"I'm fine, Cap. Just need a good night's sleep."

Lozano huffed and checked his watch. "You want to go over your talk with Victor yesterday?"

"Whenever you're ready."

He shot out a thumb. "Might as well do it now, while we wait to hear from that irritating partner of yours."

Daniels stood and grabbed his smoothie when the squad doors opened. He stared when Rem walked in, looking relaxed and comfortable in what looked like a new T-shirt, jeans, and light jacket.

"Hey," said Rem. "Good morning." He helped himself to some coffee from the full pot on the shelf behind his desk. "Somebody made coffee for once. Who's my mysterious benefactor?"

Lozano stared, too. "What the hell are you doing here? You're supposed to be undercover."

Daniels slumped. "Don't tell me. Did you scare her off?"

Rem smiled. "On the contrary. I met her, it went well, and we have a date for tomorrow night." He added sugar and cream to his mug.

Daniels frowned. "Then what the hell are you doing here? You're risking your cover."

Rem finished stirring and tossed his straw. "About that…" He hesitated and blew on his coffee.

"About what?" asked Lozano. "Daniels is right. You're supposed to be keeping a low profile."

Rem offered a sheepish grin. "I…uh…kind of…made a right turn at the last minute."

"Right turn?" asked Daniels. "What does that mean?"

"Well…" Rem held up a hand. "Don't freak out, but I kinda told her who I was." He squinted.

"You what?" asked Lozano.

"You told her you were a cop?" asked Daniels.

Rem nodded. "And…uh, my real name."

Daniels dropped his jaw, and Lozano glared. "In my office. Right now." Lozano pointed.

Rem's face fell. "But Cap, I was going to get a jelly don—"

"Remalla," yelled the captain. "Don't start with me." He stomped into his office.

Daniels shook his head. "Could you just once try and follow the rules?" He headed into Lozano's office and Rem followed, holding his coffee.

"I'm telling you," said Rem. "I know what I'm doing."

They entered Lozano's office and took a seat. Lozano sat and expelled a deep breath. "You want to explain to me what the hell you're doing?" he asked Rem. "How the hell do you expect this woman to confide anything to you if she knows you're a cop?"

"You're assuming she's dirty," said Rem.

"You're assuming she's not?" asked Daniels. He picked up on Rem's perkiness, new shirt, and clean jeans. "What exactly happened yesterday?"

Rem told them about meeting Allison Albright, and how she'd walked up to him, he'd bought her a drink, and their subsequent conversation. Then how they'd gone to a restaurant afterward, talked for a few hours, had a nice time, and had gone their separate ways at the end of the evening, making a date for Saturday night.

"That's great," said Lozano. "I'm thrilled you had a nice time, and she's attractive, but none of it absolves her of guilt. If she does have some connection to Victor and has some involvement with his groupies, then she sure as hell isn't going to tell you." He loosened his tie. "Why in the hell did you abandon your cover?"

Watching Rem, Daniels couldn't help but feel a trickle of worry. "What's going on, Rem?"

Rem sipped his coffee and set it on Lozano's desk. "I know it sounds crazy, but bear with me, okay?" He paused to think. "I was sitting there, talking to her and when she told me her name, I stopped. I was going to use the alias, but I held back."

"Why?" asked Lozano.

"Because something told me I didn't need it." He sat forward in his seat. "Think about it. If she's not guilty, then what's the harm if she knows I'm a detective. But if she is…then this could be an opportunity."

"What do you mean?" asked Daniels.

Rem swiveled toward him. "My mind was whirling, and I had the thought that if she is involved, then what could be more perfect than to dangle a potential recruit in front of her, and a disgruntled cop at that?"

Daniels leaned in. "A disgruntled cop?"

Rem nodded. "Yes. Think about it. I drop a few hints about how I hate the justice system, and how corrupt it is, plus how too many perps get back on the street too soon, and we don't get the compensation we deserve, and maybe it's all for nothing and life sucks…" He paused. "You know, the truth."

Lozano grunted. "And you think she'd go for that?"

"Why wouldn't she?" asked Rem. "Can you imagine how valuable I would be to them? To provide them with someone on the inside? Someone who can give them information? Maybe even protect Victor and give them more leeway to commit their crimes?" He stopped and waited for their reactions.

"That's a hell of a long shot," said Daniels.

"You're going to have to give her a lot more than your assurances before they trust you." Lozano leaned back in his chair. "Your partner's right. It's a long shot."

"Maybe it is, and maybe it isn't," said Rem. "But the benefit is, I don't have to hide. I can come in, and do my work. And if they start to show interest, I'll give them something to show my commitment to the cause."

"What exactly would that be?" asked Lozano.

"I don't know, but we can figure it out when or if the time comes," said Rem.

"Let's hope it's not your life," said Daniels. He rubbed his head again, wishing he'd grabbed his smoothie. He stood and pulled a

Styrofoam cup from a dispenser, and helped himself to some water from the jug in Lozano's office.

"You okay?" asked Rem. "You look tired."

Daniels sighed. "I am. Probably because I have an insane partner who does stupid things."

"It's not stupid," said Rem. "I went with my gut. You have to admit, it has more merit than me sitting around and hoping she mentions how she's joined Victor's cult. Maybe this will give her some incentive." He picked up his coffee. "My guess is any involvement she may have had is old news and she's moved on. Plus, she's not the kind of woman who strikes me as a groupie. And if that's true, no harm done. But if I'm wrong, I may get access to Victor D'Mato."

"What you've got access to is a brain malfunction." Daniels took a gulp of water and added some more to his cup. "You could also be setting yourself up for trouble, if she suspects you're yanking her chain."

"She won't suspect," said Rem.

"Why not?" asked Daniels.

"Because I'm good." He flashed a big smile and relaxed against his chair.

Daniels smirked. "You better hope so."

Rem grinned. "After last night, I'd say I'm doing just fine."

Daniels felt a touch of unease and sat.

"What do you think?" Lozano asked Daniels.

"What do I think?" Daniels squirmed in his seat. "I don't think he's left us much choice. It's not as if he can go back and tell her he lied, and oh, I'm really an author who writes smutty short stories."

Lozano waved a pen at Rem. "You better hope you know what you're doing."

"I know what I'm doing," said Rem. "Don't worry. Besides, somebody as gorgeous as her has her pick of men. And I don't see how Victor D'Mato would have any sort of hold on her."

"Don't count your chickens before they're hatched," said Daniels. "I met with the man. He's as cool as an air conditioner in a hot room."

Rem pushed up in his seat. "I've been wondering how your meet-and-greet went."

Daniels filled them in on his conversation with D'Mato.

"I think this cult theory is sounding more and more likely," said Lozano. "The man's got more on his mind than just the robberies."

"He talked about living forever?" asked Rem.

"He did more than talk about it," said Daniels. "He believes in it. Thinks I'm the one who's crazy." Daniels shook his head, but regretted it when his head flared.

"Did he ever deny his involvement in the crimes?" asked Lozano.

"Said he had alibis, but I never got that far," said Daniels. "Figured he'd just lay on some more lies. I'm sure his people will easily vouch for him."

"Doesn't mean it still shouldn't be checked out," said Lozano. "I know Titus and Georgios verified his whereabouts, but another pair of eyes will help. You never know when somebody may decide to turn on him."

"Something tells me nobody's turning on this guy," said Daniels. He thought back to the creepy look on D'Mato's face. "He's got a vibe. I sense bank robberies are the least of his crimes."

"Well, if that's true, the sooner we can find his clan, the better," said Rem. He sipped his coffee and stared off.

"That's a dangerous look. What are you thinking?" asked Daniels.

Rem looked over. "He mentioned that paranormal stuff?"

"He sure did. Talked about it like he'd researched it. He certainly believes in it. Based on his ramblings, I think he believes he can somehow harness that power, and use it as he sees fit."

"He didn't pour you a glass of water with his mind, did he?" Lozano chuckled.

Rem and Daniels shared a knowing glance. "No, he didn't," said Daniels. "But that's not his area of interest."

"Living forever is?" asked Rem.

"I guess," said Daniels. "Wants to stay young. Growing old is beneath him."

Rem shifted his seat. "So, if I'm understanding this, the liquor stores, assuming he's committing the crimes, are some sort of a means to an end."

"If he's big on ceremony or rituals," said Daniels, "which he seems to be, then I think they could be a way to prove a member's loyalty."

Rem nodded. "And once they do it, then Victor's got something on them. They back out, and suddenly incriminating evidence comes to light and they're facing five to twenty for armed robbery."

"Or more, if you consider the homicide," said Daniels.

"If that's the case, then he's got at least five followers," said Lozano.

"At least," said Daniels. "He could be doing other crimes as well, and we just haven't connected them yet."

"Then that's another avenue to explore," said Lozano. "Talk to Research. See if they can find any other crimes that might match with the M.O. on the robberies."

"Probably a good idea," said Daniels. "Something tells me this isn't his first rodeo."

"You mentioned he had the scotch, too," said Rem. "He's playing show-and-tell. Giving us just enough to suspect him, but not enough to arrest him."

"The question is," said Daniels, "where is this leading to? Lozano's right. This is about more than just hitting liquor stores and taking the cash."

Rem tapped a finger on his armrest. "The liquor stores give him power, and committed followers, plus some money, although not enough to support his lifestyle. Something or someone is bankrolling him, if he's living in a fancy apartment."

Daniels rubbed his chin, thinking. "Maybe his groupies hand over all their possessions, plus their life savings to him. They get eternal youth, a new family, plus the stolen cash from the robberies. If they're holed up somewhere in some kind of commune, they need to eat," said Daniels.

"And drink. I suppose they're enjoying some or all of that Johnnie Walker," added Rem.

"Probably a good assumption," said Daniels.

"So they hand over everything to Victor and play by his rules because they think he can offer them eternal youth and vitality? And cheat death?" asked Rem.

"I'm sure that's what he's feeding them," said Daniels. "The promise of never growing old and living life on their terms, since being responsible is so dull and boring."

"Then maybe they're buying into this paranormal stuff too, don't you think?" asked Rem. "Maybe that's how Victor finds and connects with them."

"What do you mean?" asked Lozano.

"You ever check the internet?" asked Rem. "It's got loads of stuff about just what Daniels mentioned. Psychics, telekinetics, ghosts, cryptids, aliens, you name it."

"Sounds like you've looked yourself, Remalla," said Lozano. "You have an interest?" He smiled.

Rem glanced at Daniels. "Let's just say I may have had a passing curiosity a while back."

Daniels kept his mouth shut.

"Somehow, that doesn't surprise me," said Lozano. "But what's your point?"

"My point," said Rem, "is that there are groups that get together to talk about this stuff, plus organizations that research it. Maybe that's a place to start. Look for something around here that might attract that crowd, or find someone who might know more about it. Maybe Victor's made a name for himself in that community. And if he has…"

Daniels pointed. "…then maybe we find somebody who's had more than just a passing interest in Victor."

"Exactly," said Rem. "Maybe we meet someone who got out, or wasn't willing to pass the loyalty test, and who might be willing to talk."

"That's another long shot," said Lozano. "In a case full of them."

"It's worth a try," said Daniels. "We'll do a little digging. See what we can find."

"Well, dig fast," said Lozano. "The rate we're going, they'll hit another liquor store or two before we can say 'boo.'"

"Good choice of words, Cap," said Rem. "Halloween is coming up."

"Just what we need right now," said Daniels. "All the loonies coming out of the woodwork. D'Mato will have his pick of the litter."

Lozano rolled his sleeves up. "Well, take your loony partner here and see what you can find out. And you," he pointed again at Rem with his pen, "better be careful. If that gut of yours is right, and she goes for the disgruntled cop story, you could be faced with robbing a liquor store, or worse, to prove yourself."

"I doubt it will come to that," said Rem.

Lozano narrowed his eyes. "Don't get cocky. If you get the slightest inkling she's dirty, you say something. You got it? You pull some stupid hero shit on this because she's cute, I'll pull your badge so fast, you can join one of those paranormal groups you're so fond of and go hunt for Bigfoot."

Rem deflated. "I hear you, Cap, but I don't think I'll be cryptid hunting any time soon."

"You could guarantee him a close up shot with the big guy that's worth a million bucks, and he wouldn't go," said Daniels. "But Lozano's right," he said to Rem. "You know something, you say something. I don't care if she dresses funny, you tell me."

Rem picked up his coffee and stood. "Okay. Okay. She wears socks that don't match, and you'll be the first to know." He walked to the door. "I'm going to start checking the internet. I have a few thoughts on where I want to look. We good for now?"

"We're good," said Lozano.

Rem nodded and left the office.

Daniels started to follow, but stopped to throw his cup in the trash can.

"You think he's telling the truth?" asked Lozano.

Daniels looked over. "About what?"

"Don't play stupid with me, Daniels. He likes her, doesn't he?"

Daniels hesitated, but the nudge of worry in his belly grew. "Don't worry, Cap. He knows what he's doing."

Lozano huffed. "You better be right. For his sake, as well as your own."

Daniels nodded and left, closing Lozano's door.

CHAPTER EIGHT

Rem sat at his desk with a coffee and flipped on his computer monitor. The screen flickered to life, and he opened a browser window. Daniels returned to his desk and took a seat, but didn't say anything.

They sat quietly while Rem started his search, and Daniels yawned and held his head.

"You get any sleep last night?" asked Rem.

"Yeah," said Daniels. "Probably a full two, maybe three hours."

"You thinking about this case?"

"It's on my mind."

"Well, if you're worried about me, don't." Rem scanned through the results on the screen.

Daniels studied him. "I'm not dumb, you know. I can tell just by the way you walked in here that you like her."

Rem flicked his eyes over and met Daniels' weary ones. "Listen. I like her as a person. Doesn't mean I'm falling for her. Heck. It's been one night, and everybody thinks I'm in love."

"You're right. It's been one night, with plenty more to go." Daniels ruffled through some papers on his desk. "And don't tell me I don't know what I'm talking about. It was like hauling bricks to get you to go out for coffee with Denise in Dumont, and to get you to meet the fruitarian, and now you're all happy-go-lucky about dating Allison, who could be a member of a cult, and you walk in here like you've solved the world's energy crisis. So, yes, I'm thinking you could be setting yourself up for disaster. Even Lozano noticed."

Rem thought of Allison and their evening, and how much fun he'd had and tried to think of how to explain. He swiveled the monitor aside. "I get it. I can see how you might think that, but it's not what it looks like."

Daniels leaned back and crossed his arms. "Then what is it?"

Rem scratched his head, considering how to explain it. "We both know how I've been since Jennie, and what's happened since." He shook his head. "I've been sitting in this pit I wasn't sure how to get out of, and then with Denise and even the fruit lady. I had to face a few fears, but I still wasn't prepared to leave the pit. But last night, I don't know. I was sitting in that bar, with the sole intention of trying to attract someone, and then I did. And not only was she attractive, she was into me."

"Rem..."

"Hold up. Let me finish." He held his coffee, thinking. "We talked, and we got along, and when we said good night, I knew she wanted me to kiss her and I was tempted, but I told her that I wanted to go slow, so nothing happened, but something sort of sparked, and when I went home, I figured out what it was that had me feeling so...so alive."

"What was it?"

Rem rested his elbows on his desk. "It was my first time out of the pit since Jennie. I didn't feel guilty. I didn't feel depressed. I sort of...well...sort of felt like the old me, and I began to think that maybe...maybe there's hope that I can finally find some normalcy again." He paused. "It's been a long time since I felt that way."

Daniels tapped his finger and nodded. "And this woman did this for you?" He straightened. "And you wonder why I'm worried?"

"It's not about the woman. She could call me now and cancel on me, and I could never see her again, and it would be fine. Or we might go on a few dates, I learn she's innocent, but she still ends it. It doesn't matter, because it's not about her. It's about me." He paused. "For the first time in a while, I didn't feel the weight of grief. And it was damn exhilarating." He put his cup down. "I don't know how long it will last, but I'm going to enjoy it while it does. What I do know is that it's a step in the right direction."

"And what happens if the pit caves in again?"

Rem shrugged. "I don't know. We'll just have to see how it goes. Besides, you'll sound the alarm if the dirt starts crumbling."

"But will you listen when I do? I don't know if you realize this, but you're stubborn. You'll be buried in the dirt and fighting for oxygen before you're willing to accept help, and that's what I'm trying to prevent." He picked up his smoothie and took a sip from the straw. "Don't get me wrong. I'm thrilled you've made a breakthrough. I just don't want you to take two steps forward and three steps back. The dark moments fade with time, but they never completely disappear."

Rem understood. He knew Daniels had his own experience with loss. "I know. I'll be careful, and I'll try to be less stubborn, but you know how that goes."

"Don't I ever."

Rem relaxed in his seat. "Besides, I don't anticipate this relationship going anywhere, assignment or not. I'll be lucky if I get three dates out of her. As much as I'd like to think I'm irresistible, this woman is way out of my league."

"You don't know that. I saw Victor. You and he could be brothers. If she's got something for him, then she could well have something for you. Don't get complacent. If she's anything like Victor, she could be dangerous."

"She's dangerous, but not in the way you think. You should see the way she walks."

"Never mind how she walks. Or what she wears, or how she smells."

"Easy for you to say," said Rem.

"You just play your part and act all disgruntled and focus on what happens next. You get distracted, you'll end up naked on some sacrificial table, and I may not be able to save you from that."

Rem grimaced. "Let's hope it doesn't come to that." He cocked his head. "Course, if you're going to sacrifice something, I would be the perfect specimen."

"Rem..."

Rem waved. "I'm kidding. Take it easy. I hear what you're saying."

"Good." Daniels stifled a yawn.

"Why don't you go lie down? You look beat."

Daniels gestured toward Lozano's office. "I'm sure Lozano wouldn't mind me taking a nap during my shift. Bosses love that stuff."

"He won't know. I'll vouch for you."

Daniels rolled his eyes. "You mean like the last time you covered for me when I was late, and you told him I'd joined the circus."

"It was valid. I told him you'd always wanted to learn the trapeze."

"Thanks, but no thanks."

Rem smiled and sipped his coffee. "Seriously, though. If you want to get some shut eye, go do it. I'll tell him you had to run home for something."

"I'm fine. I'll make it." He ran his hand over his papers. "I have no idea what it is I'm supposed to be doing right now."

Rem swiveled his monitor back. "Contact Research. See if they can come up with any other similar crimes to the liquor store robberies."

"Oh, yeah. Right." He sucked down the rest of his smoothie. "What are you doing?"

"Checking out paranormal groups." He scanned the lists of topics, changed his search criteria and kept looking. "When we were dealing with Jill, Jace and Madison, and their woo-woo stuff, I did some look-ing online. Found some interesting info. Pretty fringey, of course, but worth checking out."

"Like what?"

"Well, it's more common than you think. Most people just choose to look the other way, but if you look hard enough, there's all sorts of interesting evidence out there." He clicked on a website and studied a graph. "Get this. When it comes to the paranormal, ancient civilizations, like Atlantis, are the most believable, along with ghosts and hauntings. You know how I feel about those." He raised a brow at Daniels.

"Don't remind me."

Rem eyed the screen. "Then, after that, there's aliens, either ones that visited previously, or are living among us now—"

Daniels snorted.

"What's so hard to believe about that? Have you seen some of the people walking around? The new guy in the cafeteria? He's got to be one."

"Barry? The server? Why?"

"Because he refuses to give me fries unless I order a side salad, too. And have you seen the size of his head?"

Daniels just stared.

Rem continued. "Then after aliens, it's telekinesis, psychics and then cryptids, like Bigfoot. So, there's a whole community out there studying this stuff."

"D'Mato among them."

"But why is he so interested?" asked Rem. "What is it about extra abilities that makes him think he can live longer?" He had a thought. "That's got to be who he's recruiting. I think you're right that he wants to harness those abilities to prolong his life and he needs these people to do it."

"Who the hell knows?" asked Daniels. "The guy's crazy, and his followers likely are too. God knows what they think is possible, or what they believe Victor is capable of?"

"Maybe that's all it takes," said Rem. "Is a little bit of belief."

"You're not buying into all of this, are you?"

Rem peered over at him. "After what we've seen, you're not?"

Daniels pulled an empty bottle out of a drawer and stood. "What we've seen doesn't mean anything. It was a fluke, and we'll likely never see it again. And if you're trying to tell me that Victor has weird abilities, I don't buy it."

"I'm not saying he has them, but he wants them, which is why he's interested. Maybe he's seen flukey things, too."

Daniels filled his bottle from the water dispenser behind Rem. "All of this is pure conjecture."

"Not all of it. You talked to him."

Daniels shrugged and sipped his water. "True. He is odd. And I do think he, at least, has some experience with the paranormal."

"Which is why we need to find the right source to talk to. We go to the wrong group, we're likely to end up with flowers in our hair, singing mantras or going on ghost hunts."

"And what people are those? How do you find a needle in a haystack?"

Rem flipped through the results on the screen. "When I did my earlier research, I found something I thought was interesting. I remember it was a website, with a name and a number."

Daniels stood behind him. "I hope you have more than that to go on."

"I'm trying to find it. It was obscure, but it caught my eye. I had actually called and made an appointment, but we got caught up in our case, and I never made it there." Rem continued to scroll. "Here." He saw the name and clicked on it. The familiar website pulled up.

"That's it?" asked Daniels.

Rem recalled the black screen with one word in large white font, and no additional links. A phone number was listed below it.

Daniels leaned over and read the word. "SCOPE. What the hell is SCOPE?"

"It's here." Rem pointed at the small letters barely visible listed below the larger ones. "The Study of Cryptids or Paranormal Entities."

"These guys need to work on their marketing skills." Daniels shook his head. "How do you know they're not one of those fringe groups with fat guys who have big bushy beards, wear dirty overalls, and search swamps for lizard men?"

"With a website like this? No way. I'm calling them."

Lozano stepped out of his office, and Rem paused as the captain stopped by their desks. "I've got a meeting, then a luncheon with the Citizens against Crime."

"Must be a big lunch," said Rem, holding the phone. "Aren't all citizens against crime?"

"The charity group, Remalla." Lozano slipped on his jacket. "I'll be back in a couple of hours." He eyed Rem. "Try not to do anything stupid while I'm gone."

"Then you better not make that phone call," said Daniels, returning to his seat.

Rem glared at Daniels. "Okay, Cap. Say hi to the citizens."

Lozano grunted and left.

"Now's your chance," said Rem. "Go get some rest. I'll hold down the fort."

"That's what I'm afraid of."

"You want to get some shut eye? Then go for it. But if you'd rather sit here and half snore and stare blankly at the computer, you're welcome to it."

Daniels stifled another yawn. "Fine. I'm going. I'll just lay down in the locker room for a few minutes."

"I'll wake you if he comes back and you're not up."

"Fine. Thanks."

"You're welcome." Rem put the phone to his ear and dialed the number to SCOPE as Daniels walked out of the squad room.

CHAPTER NINE

Rem sat in his car in the parking lot, waiting for Daniels. His partner had called in late that morning and had told Rem he'd meet him outside SCOPE for the appointment Rem had scheduled. Daniels had already talked to Lozano so Rem hadn't needed to cover for him, but Lozano had still asked Rem if he knew what was up. Rem could only shrug because he didn't know. Daniels had not elaborated on the phone.

Checking his watch again, he was about to text Daniels because they were already five minutes late, when Daniels pulled up and parked beside him.

Rem got out and waited on the sidewalk as Daniels emerged from his car. "Where the hell have you been?" It was unusual for his partner to be late. Rem was the one who normally kept Daniels waiting. Daniels had a bandage on his forehead, and he looked wearier than he had the day before, despite his two-hour nap in the locker room. "What the hell happened to you?"

"Don't start with me, okay?" Daniels stomped up beside Rem. "Especially when I wait on your ass all the time."

Rem eyed his partner. His normally gelled hair was askew, his clothes were wrinkled, and he had circles under his eyes. He pointed at the bandage. "What's with your head?"

"Nothing. I'll tell you later. Come on. We're late for this scintillating interview." He headed down the sidewalk, stopped and turned back. "Where the hell is this place?"

Rem bit back a retort. His partner had definitely gotten up on the wrong side of the bed. He shot out a thumb. "This way." He turned, looking at the numbers above the doors on the shops along the street. He was looking for number thirty-three, according to the woman he'd spoken to the previous day. He saw thirty-two, but then the next shop went to thirty-four.

"Great," said Daniels. "Do you even know where we're going?"

Rem spied a door between the shops and, peering through the glass, saw a staircase. He opened the door and saw a small sign with the number thirty-three on it and an arrow pointing toward the second floor. "This way," he said.

Daniels followed him up the stairs. "Where the hell are we going?"

"Up," said Rem. After ascending a flight, he stopped at a black door. The word SCOPE was written in small white letters on a nameplate. "This is it." He opened the door and stepped inside.

They entered a small, red-carpeted room with a desk and a chair, and no windows and nothing on the walls. No one was at the desk, but there was another door along the far wall.

"This is inviting," said Daniels. "You sure they're expecting us?"

"Yes." Rem walked up to the desk. "I talked to someone when I called yesterday." He saw a bell on the desk and rang it.

"Hear ye, hear ye," said Daniels. "calling all cryptid hunters, aliens and psychics. Assemble now or forever hold your peace."

"Would you shut up?" asked Rem. The quiet in the room unnerved him, and he had the strange suspicion they were being watched, although he saw no cameras in the room. "Hello?" he asked. "Anyone here?"

"I'm expecting the fat guy with dirty overalls at any minute," said Daniels.

"Nobody's wearing dirty overalls," said Rem with a glare.

"Care to make a wager on that?"

The back door opened and Rem jumped. A man, about Rem's height, appeared wearing a black cowboy hat, black pants, a button-down green shirt with a tan vest, and boots. He had broad shoulders, a narrow waist and his most distinguishing characteristic was his handlebar mustache. "Detective Remalla?"

"That's me," said Rem. "This is my partner, Detective Daniels." They held out their badges.

The man studied them. "Come on back." He stepped aside to let Rem and Daniels walk past him through the door. Rem noted the bigger space with wooden floors and a skylight. Sunlight brightened shelves that lined the walls, all empty save for one item sitting on a barren shelf in the back of the room. It looked like a small box. A couch sat against one wall along with a loveseat, and another desk and chair with a computer sat against the opposite wall. Another door marked 'Exit' was in the back corner of the room. "Have a seat."

Rem walked over to the couch, and Daniels followed.

The man closed the door and approached. "I'm Mason Redstone." He held out a hand. "Founder and owner of SCOPE."

Rem and Daniels shook his hand and sat on the couch when Redstone relaxed in the loveseat. He threw an ankle over his knee. "How can I help you?" He took his hat off and tossed it next to him. His thick, brown wavy hair was ruffled and long enough to cover his ears.

Rem fidgeted. "I like your mustache," he said.

Daniels moaned.

"What?" asked Rem.

"Thanks," said Redstone, twirling the ends. "My girlfriend hates it, but that's too bad."

"It's not overalls, but it's close," mumbled Daniels.

Rem nudged him in the ribs and Daniels grunted. Rem eyed the room and debated what to say.

"I take it from your phone call yesterday that you're working on a case?" asked Redstone.

Rem nodded.

Daniels leaned up. "I apologize for my partner's non-verbal skills. He gets quiet when he's anxious."

"I'm not anxious," said Rem.

"Then why are you sitting there like a mute?"

"I'm trying to figure out where to start."

"How about the part where you're crazy and this is a wild goose chase?"

Rem argued back. "Or the part where you're in a bad mood and acting like an ass because you're just as uncomfortable as I am?"

"Gentlemen," Mason dropped his foot and sat forward, "perhaps I can help. Obviously, you are having difficulty with this meeting. I can understand. It's not often I meet with policemen."

"Who do you meet with then?" asked Rem.

"What kind of business is this?" asked Daniels.

Redstone smiled. "I am a curator and benefactor of the paranormal community. I am also a medium and researcher which, to answer your question, is where most of my meetings stem from. People have a problem, or an experience, and I can help by answering questions or investigating if needed."

"You mean, if somebody sees something weird, you can help find out if it's real or in their heads?" asked Rem.

"That's one way of putting it," said Redstone.

"You mind if I ask what your qualifications are?" asked Daniels. "How'd you get into this…unusual…profession?"

Redstone grinned. "Let's just say I grew up with it. Thought I was going to end up in a mental hospital for a good part of my youth, until I finally decided I wasn't going crazy. I was just seeing what most people couldn't."

Rem sat on the edge of the couch. "And what's that?"

"Dead people, Detective," said Redstone. "I see dead people."

"Oh, boy," said Daniels, under his breath.

Rem ignored him. "Are you seeing any now?"

"No, but I'm not open right now," said Redstone.

Daniels' brow furrowed. "Open?"

"It's very much like this business. I decide when and where I am available. Otherwise, I'd never get any peace. It can be challenging at times, but I've gotten used to it over the years. Now it's pretty much routine for me."

Rem nodded. "I see."

Daniels rubbed his head.

"Uhm, what about other stuff?" asked Rem. "Are you like a psychic? Can you move stuff with your mind? Do you know aliens?"

Daniels groaned, and Redstone chuckled.

"I don't know the future, nor would I want to," said Redstone. "No. I don't move stuff with my mind, but I believe in it, and I'm aware that aliens live among us. There's more of them than you'd think and they blend in quite well. I wouldn't be surprised if you'd met a few yourself."

"I knew it," said Rem. "Barry is an alien."

"Okay. I think that's it for me." Daniels stood.

Rem grabbed his arm. "Would you relax? We're just having a conversation here. His views don't have to be your views, and we still need to ask about D'Mato."

Daniels blew out a breath and frowned. "Fine." He sat again.

Redstone tensed. "Did you say D'Mato?"

"Yes," said Rem. "You know him?"

"Victor D'Mato?"

Daniels straightened. "Sounds like you're familiar."

Redstone stood, his face serious. He opened his mouth as if to speak, but then hesitated, and began to pace. "I am."

Rem's heart thudded. "Looks like we came to the right place."

Daniels deflated. "Remind me never to doubt your gut again."

"Believe me. I will," said Rem. Redstone moved to his desk and leaned against it, lost in thought. "How do you know him?" asked Rem.

Redstone sighed. "We used to be partners. Best friends, in fact." He shook his head. "It's been a long time, though, since I've seen him. I'd heard he was in prison."

"He got out," said Rem. "Last year."

Redstone cursed and crossed his arms. "I didn't know that."

"I'm getting that impression," said Daniels. "What's the story between you two?"

Redstone stared at the ground. "We met in high school. He was the first one who ever believed me, outside of my family, about my gifts. He encouraged me when everyone else told me to downplay or even hide it. He saw the potential, even when I doubted myself."

"What broke up the friendship?" asked Rem.

"A lot of things, but as I developed my skills, he became obsessive. Wanted to hire me out as some sort of carnival act, and when I refused, he got angry. I told him the direction I wanted to go, and he went with it for a while. We tried to work together, but as my business grew, he became more possessive. I think he envied my abilities. He saw the look of wonder in people's eyes when I helped them, and, well, he didn't like being second fiddle. He wanted the attention. Victor started bringing people in without my knowledge, talking to them about nonsense. Told them how he had access to me and could provide them with the knowledge they sought. He began using these people, telling them crazy things, got involved in drugs, and then it became like some sort of cult. These people began to follow him like abandoned puppies. It was scary, and I began to distance myself."

Rem made eye contact with Daniels.

Then...he went too far." Redstone's eyes hardened. "There was an altercation within my family, and I was forced to sever ties with him. He was furious. Said I didn't know how to really use power, but he did, and he didn't need my abilities to do it." He shook his head. "I haven't seen him since."

Rem eyed Daniels. "What do you think he meant by that?" asked Rem.

Redstone pushed off the desk. "He went off the deep end. Started talking about manipulating the powers of the unknown, and how he could use that power to serve him and his people. Said he could foil death. It was ridiculous."

"If it was so ridiculous, then why worry?" asked Daniels. "Plenty of people start groups and spout crazy things, but are usually harmless. What was different about him?"

"Because," said Redstone. "When I say he didn't have abilities, I meant the paranormal ones, but what he does have is charisma and magnetism. I've never met anyone before or since who could draw people in the way he can. For a while, I needed that. It got me clients and got me started, but I didn't want followers with stars in their eyes who thought I could give them the answers to fill the aching holes in their lives, and then expect them to pledge their loyalty to me with their money and an oath."

"Is that what D'Mato did?" asked Rem.

"It's what he wanted to do. Thought he and I together could be some sort of modern-day paranormal televangelists. I wanted no part of it."

"Looks like we're barking up the right tree," said Daniels.

"Why?" asked Redstone. "What's he been up to?"

"We think he's back to his old tricks," said Rem. "From what we can gather, he and his groupies are robbing liquor stores, and a cashier was killed. D'Mato's a suspect but we can't prove anything."

"I met with him," said Daniels. "He mentioned his appreciation for the abilities you mention." He interlaced his fingers. "And you're right. He's a cool customer. He was unfazed by my presence or my mention of the robberies and his involvement." He ran a hand through his hair and closed his eyes.

"Headache back?" asked Rem.

"With a vengeance," said Daniels.

Redstone studied them. "You two need to be careful. He's not a man to be messed with."

"We're getting that impression," said Rem. He stood. "We're trying to find out what we can about him, plus see if we can find any former followers who might be willing to talk." He pulled out the picture of Allison Albright and showed it to Redstone. "You recognize her?"

Redstone studied the picture. "No. Who is she?"

"Former girlfriend of Victor's. We're wondering if she had any involvement in his group."

"If she was smart, she got out as soon as she could," said Redstone.

"Why do you say that?" asked Daniels.

"Because the repercussions can be fatal if you don't," said Redstone.

Rem frowned, and Daniels looked up from the couch. "What does that mean?" asked Daniels.

"Victor is capable of doing far worse than committing robbery." He walked around to the side of his desk and opened a drawer. He pulled out a bottle and a glass and poured himself a shot. "You gentlemen want some?" He shot back the liquor.

"We're on duty," said Rem.

"I won't tell if you don't," said Redstone.

Daniels stood. "What's he capable of?"

Redstone poured another drink. "Murder, gentlemen." He shot back the second drink and set the glass down. "Cold-blooded murder."

**

Daniels rubbed his bandage and felt his head pulse beneath it. This lousy morning was only getting worse. "Murder? You have any proof?"

Redstone sat at his desk. "I wish I did."

Rem leaned on the edge of the loveseat. "Care to elaborate?"

Redstone took a moment. "It goes back a ways. My family is from Texas, from a small town just outside of Dallas. Before I ever thought of becoming a paranormal investigator, I was a Texas Ranger."

Rem perked up. "Seriously? A Texas Ranger? Did you ride a horse?"

Daniels snorted and rubbed his temples.

Redstone chuckled. "We found cars to be more effective. Plus, they didn't require saddling and the not shitting in the road was a plus."

Rem deflated. "I love those old westerns. It's cool to picture you guys on horses."

"There was a time and a place," said Redstone, "but that's long since passed." He put the liquor bottle back in the drawer. "That time allowed me to hone my investigative skills, but it also made it extremely difficult for me to continue in law enforcement."

"Why is that?" asked Rem.

"Because I was green. Not as a Ranger, but as a medium. I would talk to the families of victims and see their dead loved ones in the room. I wasn't very good at boundaries back then, and I couldn't exactly reveal what I was seeing. It became very difficult to continue. I talked to Victor, who at that time was a car salesman."

"A car salesman? Victor?" asked Rem.

"That doesn't surprise me," said Daniels.

"He was making more money than me," said Redstone.

"That doesn't surprise me either," said Daniels.

"He could sell a fully loaded, jacked-up truck with mag wheels to a little old lady who could barely reach the pedals, but he was bored as hell. Hated the job."

"How'd you end up here?" asked Rem.

"Victor, of course. He knew my family well. I won't go into all the details, but I had a cousin Eddie who I was also close to. Followed me around when I was little and my mother always used to tell me that Eddie idolized me. He didn't have any siblings of his own, so I became his."

"Did Eddie have any abilities, like yours?" asked Daniels, still wondering what to think of Redstone.

"I believe he did, but he was reluctant to pursue them," said Redstone. "It can be difficult for some. But he accepted mine with ease. I didn't tell him about it until I was older, but when I did, he didn't bat an eye. Totally welcomed it. Thought it was cool." He smiled. "Being a Ranger didn't hurt either."

"I bet," said Rem.

"Eddie had moved out here to San Diego and invited me to join him. I have an older brother who lives out here as well, so it was enticing. I'd confided to Eddie my gifts and difficulties as a Ranger by then, and when Victor heard about the idea, he encouraged me. Long story short, I left the Rangers to pursue my true calling. And Victor came along and we began our partnership. I brought Eddie in as well, because Victor could be intense." He paused. "Sometimes, doing the work I do can be draining, and I need time away to gather myself. While Victor saw that only as time and money wasted, Eddie would find ways to sneak me off or would cover for me when I needed to escape. When Victor began to show signs of instability, I relied on Eddie more and more, and it pissed Victor off that I trusted Eddie as much as I did." He shook his head. "I began to realize the direction it was taking and Eddie and I talked about running things together, without Victor. That's where I made my mistake."

"Is this the family matter that caused you to sever ties with Victor?" asked Daniels.

"Somewhat, yes, but there was more to it than that. I didn't really understand what Victor was capable of until he was gone. At the time, I thought he just had different views and he would go one way and I would go another. Considering all I had learned as a Ranger, I was stupid. There were signs, and I overlooked them." Redstone stood and began to pace again.

"Been there. Done that," said Rem. "I'm guessing something happened to Eddie?"

Redstone stopped pacing. "Not long before I broke ties with Victor, Eddie went missing. I called the police, but there was little they could do. No body. No signs of foul play. Plus, his last text message to me was that he'd needed to take care of something and would fill me in later. The police could only assume he'd taken off and would come back in time." He crossed his arms. "But I knew different."

"Why?" asked Daniels.

"Because he came to me," said Redstone.

"Came to you?" asked Daniels. "But I'm assuming he was dead."

Redstone raised a brow. "He was."

"Oh," said Daniels, forcibly not rolling his eyes. "I see."

"What did he say?" asked Rem.

Daniels almost chuckled at Rem's wide-eyed look.

"Not much at first. I was very emotional at the time, so it made it difficult, but I knew Victor was responsible." He paused and cleared his throat. "I couldn't believe it. Part of me questioned the truth of it, but then I learned a few other things about Victor and what he'd been up to, and that sealed the deal. I confronted him the next day."

"What happened?" asked Daniels.

"He denied it, of course. Told me I was crazy. But then went off on how I had entrusted too much to Eddie. That if I'd listened to him, I could have been so much more. I would have learned what true power is." He studied the ground. "They found Eddie's body three weeks later in a culvert down by the wharf. He'd been strangled, and…"

"And what?" asked Daniels.

Redstone swallowed. "A chunk of his skin was missing from his arm. Detectives thought it was just damage from the river, but I pressed them on it. Because I was a former cop myself, they indulged me and did some tests. Found out it was a bite mark."

"A bite mark?" Rem's face paled.

"Someone had taken a bite out of him," said Redstone. "They did impressions, and it was from a human, but there was no other evidence to link anyone to the crime. DNA had been washed away, the body had suffered from exposure, and no one had seen or heard anything. The cops talked to Victor," Redstone eyed Daniels, "but I think you can imagine how that went."

"I sure can," said Daniels, recalling Victor's attitude toward police. "You're sure he did it?"

"I talked to Eddie," said Redstone. "I got it from the source, but that evidence is not admissible in a court of law."

"No, it isn't," said Rem. "Eddie say anything to you about the bite mark?"

"No," said Redstone. "He kept that to himself, despite my asking. Some things are best kept secret, I suppose, or at least Eddie thought so."

"They got impressions. Could they not compare those to Victor's teeth?" asked Daniels.

"They did," said Redstone. "Victor happily allowed it. They compared them, and the bite marks weren't Victor's."

"They weren't? Then whose were they?" asked Rem.

"That's the question. I don't know," said Redstone. "But that's when I knew that Victor's followers were devoted enough to commit murder for him."

CHAPTER TEN

Rem stepped back out onto the street, and Daniels followed.

"Well?" asked Rem. "Pretty fascinating, don't you think?"

Daniels squinted in the light and found some shade. "Don't tell me you're buying all of that?"

Rem stared, unsure what to think about his partner. "You must have knocked your head pretty hard this morning. You're telling me you don't?"

"I'm not saying Victor's not capable of murder, but that whole talking to spirits and Eddie thing? I'm going to need plenty of rope before I make that jump."

"You think he's lying about his abilities?"

"I think he's comfortable with what he believes he thinks he knows, but what he thinks he knows and what's true are probably two different things and not knowable at all."

"Huh?"

Daniels scoffed. "Never mind." He started to head toward his car. "Let's get out of here."

"No, wait." Rem held up a hand, determined to figure out what Daniels meant. "You mean to tell me after all we've seen, heard and experienced, that you can't buy what he's telling you?"

"I don't buy what he's selling, no."

"Why not?"

He stopped and turned. "Have you ever stopped to consider that maybe he's just like Victor? Maybe he's just as fake and just as slick?"

"The guy was a Texas Ranger. You're going to doubt him? Besides, I didn't get that from him at all. I believed him, and we already know that my gut's pretty accurate. You told me so yourself."

"Your gut also likes Taco del Fuego's, hot dogs, and chips with mustard. Forgive me if I question it every now and then."

Rem grunted. "If it hadn't been for my gut, we would have never found this guy."

"I'll give you that," said Daniels, "but I'm not convinced he gave us anything of value."

Rem dropped his jaw. "Nothing of value? The man told us Victor murdered his cousin—"

"Allegedly."

"And that he's got followers who are willing to do his bidding, and that he's power-hungry and has likely fallen so far down the rabbit hole that he's got himself convinced he can live forever. Redstone even said he'd do some digging, and see if he could find out more about Victor and his groupies. How is that not helping?"

Daniels grimaced and held his head. "Have you considered that maybe he's helping Victor? What if they're still working as partners? They grew up together. Those ties can be hard to sever."

"Ah, come on. That's nonsense."

Daniels went to his car. "It's not nonsense and if you'd get your head out of your ass, you'd see it for what it was. I think he's playing us." Running a hand through his unkempt hair, he scowled.

Rem almost yelled back, but stopped. He noted Daniels' fatigue, his slumped posture, and the bump on his head. "What's going on with you? What happened this morning?"

Daniels put a hand on the hood of his car. "Nothing. I'm fine."

Rem walked toward him. "And I'm up for an Academy Award."

Daniels touched his bandage and winced. "I didn't sleep."

"I gathered."

"Had an ugly nightmare. I don't remember much, but I was lying on a table and being burned alive. That much I do recall."

"Yikes." Rem made a face.

"I must have been flailing. Marjorie tried to wake me, but I fell out of the bed and hit my head on the end table. Bled all over the carpet."

"How bad is it? You need stitches?" Rem knew how Daniels hated doctors.

Daniels scowled again. "You and Marjorie. No. I don't need stitches."

Rem chose not to argue with him.

"Because of that, I was in a horrible mood. My head ached, I hadn't slept, and I snapped at Marjorie. We got in a huge fight. J.P. started wailing, and I banged my fist on the table. My coffee cup fell off and shattered on the floor. J.P. was sitting on the ground and a piece of the mug hit him above his eye. His head started bleeding, and he wailed even louder. Marjorie was furious and insisted we take him to the doctor, so I spent the morning at the pediatrician so that he could tell me J.P. was fine and didn't need stitches. He wanted to check my head, too, but I wouldn't let him. Marjorie wouldn't speak to me on the way home." He hung his head and massaged his neck. "And then I end up here." He looked up and waved. "At SCOPE, with you and Mr. I-Speak-to-Dead-People."

Rem studied his partner. "You want to go home? Get some rest? It is Saturday after all."

"No, damn it. I don't want to go home," Daniels yelled. He glared, and then looked away, shaking his head. "What's the point? I can't rest anyway."

Rem tried to decide what to do. Daniels was in no shape to work, but going back to his house didn't seem to be an option. "How about we go get something to eat? Take a break from all of this. Talk about something a little lighter."

"I'm not hungry."

"When's the last time you had a decent meal?"

"Rem—" Daniels pointed. "Don't." He opened his car door.

"Don't what?"

"I'm fine. I just need to get out of here, go back to the station."

"And do what? Stare blankly at the screen while you try not to fall asleep, and feel guilty about J.P.?"

Daniels' eyes narrowed.

"You forget. I know you too well. And you shouldn't feel guilty. You had a moment. You got angry. It happens. He'll have far worse injuries as he gets older. He didn't even need stitches."

Daniels hung an elbow on the car frame. He held his forehead, but some of the anger seemed to drain off of him. "I…I…felt terrible. Blood was running down his face, and he was screaming."

"It was an accident."

Daniels hung his head. "I'm sorry I yelled at you."

"It's okay. It's not the first time, and it won't be the last. And don't worry. Marjorie will forgive you, too."

"I'm not too sure about that. She was pretty pissed."

"Just apologize. She'll give in. That charm of yours gets her every time."

"I seem to have lost it recently."

"It'll be back. You just need some sleep."

"Yeah." Daniels looked up, his eyes hollow. "Listen. I know you believe this guy, but you better be careful. You have to consider the fact that he and Victor could still be in cahoots, and if they are, that puts you in danger." He gestured toward the building. "You showed him the picture of Allison. If Redstone knows her, then she'll know you're on this case."

"I'm telling you Redstone is clean. If he knew her, he'd say so. He wants to help."

Daniels drummed his fingers on the top of his car. "I admire your trust, but you and I both know we've been blindsided before. He could be up there right now, talking to her and telling her you were here."

"Or he could be making some phone calls to the people he knows in a world that we are completely unfamiliar with. We need whatever information he can get for us."

"Just humor me, okay? When you go out with her tonight, keep your feelers up and stay aware and in public. Don't let your blind trust in her and in him put you in a bad spot. And get in touch with me after the date. I want to know when you're home."

"You're worrying too much."

"And you're not worrying enough."

Rem huffed. "Fine. I'll text you."

"Good." He started to get in the car.

"Where are you going?"

Daniels paused with a foot in the car. "I figure I can go in and see if Research came back with that report. Maybe take another nap. For some reason, I seem to sleep better in the locker room."

Rem nodded and started toward his own car.

"What are you going to do?" asked Daniels.

"Goin' back to the station, too. Since you're so worried about Redstone, it can't be that hard to check his story and see what I can learn about Eddie."

"That's a good idea. What time's your date?"

Rem's phone rang and he pulled it from his pocket. Allison's name flashed on the display. "I'm about to find out."

Daniels's brow creased. "Remember what I said."

"I will."

"And don't forget to act disgruntled. The sooner, the better."

"I know. I'll see you back at the station."

"See you." Daniels got in the car.

Rem answered the phone as Daniels pulled out and drove away.

**

Rem laughed and ate the last bite of his mashed potatoes.

Allison took a sip of her wine. "That's when I threw his shoes in the lake. He had to jog home barefoot."

"I doubt he'll ever take a stupid dare like that again."

"If he's smart."

They'd agreed to meet at a casual diner outside of the city that Allison swore served a great steak and homemade pie. She'd been right, and Rem had found the place to be a good location for a second date. It hadn't been crazy expensive or crazy busy. They could sit and talk, be comfortable, enjoy a nice meal and a good bottle of wine.

When she'd arrived, he'd tried not to stare, but her skinny jeans, high heels and light sweater that fell off one shoulder but hugged her hips made it hard not to. Her sexy long legs and toned exposed shoulder were distracting, and he had to remind himself why he was there.

"Sorry. I've been doing all the talking," she said.

"No. It's fine. It's nice to be with someone who can hold a conversation."

She held her wine glass. "How was your day? Are you working on any interesting cases?"

His ears perked up, and Daniels' warning echoed in his ears. "Yes, actually. We may be on the trail of a murderer."

Her eyes widened. "Really? Who did he kill?"

Rem considered how to answer. "He's suspected of strangling a man whose body was found near the wharf. Plus, there was a robbery and an employee was shot and killed." He decided to stick as close to the truth as he could.

"That's awful."

He shrugged. "It's not great."

"How do you take that home with you at night? Don't you find it hard to put it aside when you're not working?"

Rem picked up his wine. "You know, to be honest. It sucks." *Time to act disgruntled*, he thought to himself, and she'd given him the perfect opening. "Sometimes I wonder how much longer I can do it."

She played with her earring. "Why do you say that?"

"It's a tough job. You catch the bad guy and he either pleads out for next to no time, or some technicality gets him off. The people you try to help don't appreciate you. The pay sucks almost as bad as the hours, and half the time, you know who did it, but can't get the evidence you need to get them off the street. It's frustrating and stressful. Not to mention life-threatening." He paused, sipped his wine and put his glass down "Sometimes, I can't help but wonder if it's worth it."

She watched him, and then reached over and picked up the bottle and added more to his glass. "You sound like a man that needs another drink."

"Sorry," he waved. "I'm complaining. I'm sure you'd rather hear how rewarding my job is, and how we always catch the bad guy." He picked up his refilled glass, thinking to himself that he needed to slow down on his alcohol consumption. "Thanks."

She added more to her glass. "What would you do if you weren't a cop?"

He shrugged. "My partner likes the circus. Figure we could pair up and be lion tamers or something."

She smiled. "Does your partner feel the same way you do?"

"He has his moments. But he's always seeing the best in things. It's super irritating."

She pushed her plate back. "You must realize the benefit you serve. If it weren't for you, criminals would run amok. Good people would be hurt." She swirled her drink. "I called the police once on an old boyfriend. If it hadn't been for them, who knows what might have happened?"

Rem's radar went off, and he thought of Victor. "Is this the same boyfriend you had the bad break up with?"

She nodded. "It was. He got rough, and the cops took him in and he sat in jail overnight."

Rem had finished his steak and put his napkin on the table. "Just overnight?"

Allison gripped her glass. "I had second thoughts the next morning. Regrettably, I didn't press charges. In hindsight, I should have stuck to my guns, but he was so damn appealing, and I was swayed by him." She trailed her eyes over Rem and tipped her head. "You remind me of him."

Rem shifted in his seat, her gaze making his heart thump. "Is that a good or a bad thing?"

She slid over in the booth until her leg pressed against his, and warmth spread through his midsection. "I'd say it's a good thing." Facing him, she put an arm over the back of the booth and held her glass with the other.

He held her gaze and his cheeks warmed. "You barely know me."

Putting the glass to her mouth, she took a seductive sip, and he couldn't stop staring at her lips. "I know enough. You're smart and sexy. You have that same charisma, and rugged good looks. And despite your disenchantment with your career, I know it comes from a good place. You're irritated because you can't help others the way you want." She ran the tip of her tongue over her bottom lip and Rem almost fainted. "That's admirable," she said.

Rem considered how to respond. His intentions of making her think he was open to other, less amicable traits, was failing. "I'm not so sure I'm as wonderful as you may think."

"What?" she asked, leaning close, her voice sultry. "Are you trying to tell me you have secrets?"

Rem swallowed and began to wonder if Daniels was right. Was he getting in too deep? "What happened to this guy of yours? I get the impression you were a hard woman to let go of."

She hesitated, and her eyes flared. "He finally got the message and moved on."

"You sure? What if he came back?"

She pulled away. "He's not coming back. I made it very clear that he had no chance with me."

Rem shifted in the booth. "Was he someone who might have had an issue with my profession? I'm sensing perhaps he didn't always stay within the confines of the law." He studied his glass of wine. "Maybe I've met him. Or is he incarcerated?"

Looking tense, she slid back to her side of the booth. "Do we have to talk about him?"

He put his wine down. "Sorry, but I'm curious. I'm a cop and I'm guessing he's a criminal. Makes me wonder."

"Wonder about what?"

Rem decided to dive in. "How different are we really? How do you know I haven't crossed the line a time or two?" He held his breath. If she really wanted nothing to do with the likes of D'Mato, now would be her chance to leave him, and he could order and eat some pie all by himself.

Eyeing her wine, she bit her lip and he sensed her indecision. "What are you saying?" she asked.

"I'm saying I might not be as high and mighty as you think, and you should know what you're getting into." He held up a finger. "Except for the getting rough part. I would never lay a hand on a woman." He could only go so far when it came to playing a bad guy.

She nodded and met his gaze. "That's good to know." She paused, and he could almost see the wheels spinning in her head. She played with her napkin. "Would you like to get some pie?"

It was not the question he was expecting, but Rem settled back, confident that he had her thinking. About what, he couldn't be sure, but she wasn't ready to kick him to the curb just yet. "I would love something sweet."

She smiled and leaned in. "Maybe if you're lucky, you'll get some dessert, plus a little something extra."

He felt her run her toes up his pant leg and almost spilled his wine. He wiggled in his seat. "How about we start with the pie, and we'll go from there."

Sipping from her glass, she moved her foot up to his knee. "Unless you'd rather get the check, and we can go back to my place. I bet I can find you something sweet to eat there." Her seductive smile returned.

Rem sucked his wine down the wrong pipe and choked. He grabbed his napkin and held it over his mouth, still coughing.

Her eyes crinkled with a grin, and she shook her head. "I don't know what kind of rough edges you think you may have, but something tells me I'm going to have fun smoothing them out."

Rem coughed again and wondered if she was right.

CHAPTER ELEVEN

Daniels startled in his bed and cracked an eye open. Sunlight peered through the edges of the curtains and he groaned, wondering what time it was. He knew enough to remember it was Sunday, and he gave silent thanks that he had the day off and didn't have to worry about being late.

The dream still fresh, he pushed back the covers and sat up, recalling most of it, although it was already somewhat fuzzy. Squinting against the light, he leaned over and held his head. His skin was sticky from sweat and that low pulse behind his eyes remained. It wasn't as horrible as the previous day, but it still throbbed and Daniels cursed. His throat dry, he reached for the glass of water beside his bed and took a gulp, thinking of the dream.

Someone was dragging him through the dirt, his clothes dirty and ripped, but his muscles heavy and sluggish, he'd been unable to resist. Hands had grabbed and lifted him and laid him on a table, where his hands and feet had been bound. Desperate, he'd called out for help, but the faces around him were blurred. Looking up at the ceiling, he'd seen wooden rafters and a loft. On the wall had been a large painted image, but its shape had already faded from his memory, although he thought it had been an animal. A hooded figure had approached, carrying a knife, and terrified, Daniels had shrieked, but the figure showed no re-action, and had climbed atop Daniels. The figure's face was a mask of darkness, and Daniels had bucked, trying to knock the figure off, but didn't have enough leverage. The figure had cut away at his shirt, and had brought the tip of the knife to his sternum, where the figure slowly carved a bloody trail down his chest, as a river of red trickled down his ribcage.

"Good morning."

Daniels jumped and held his chest. He turned to see Marjorie standing beside the bed.

"Sorry," she said. "Didn't mean to scare you." She moved closer. "You okay? Did you sleep?"

The dream still echoing in his mind, he nodded. "I'm fine. I slept a little."

She walked to the window and opened the shades. Sunlight streamed in and Daniels shut his eyes. "I would hope so. It's almost noon. I let you sleep in because you've been feeling so awful lately."

"Noon?" Daniels checked the clock beside the bed. He felt like he'd just laid his head on the pillow. His eyes ached and his body felt heavy. "I slept till noon?"

"Yes," she said. "I've just fed J.P. lunch. You want me to fix you a sandwich or get you some coffee?"

After their fight the previous day and his meeting with Rem and Redstone, Daniels had returned to the station, but had not accomplished much. He'd ended up taking another nap in the locker room, and had then gone home, where he'd apologized to Marjorie and explained how he hadn't felt well and wasn't himself. Rem had been right and she'd understood and forgiven him, and he'd taken her for dinner after he'd sat in a hot shower and Marjorie had found a babysitter. They'd managed a nice meal, and Daniels figured his nap had helped. After returning home, he'd played a bit with J.P., happy to see that J.P.'s injury had scabbed over and his son showed no effects from it. His headache returning though, Daniels had gone to bed early, but slept fitfully, his dreams hampering him.

Rubbing his eyes, he tried to think. "Coffee would be great, thanks." The thought of breakfast made his stomach twist and he had no appetite. "I'll get something to eat later."

Marjorie put a hand on his shoulder. "You sure you're okay? You look a little pale."

He forced a smile on his face. "I think I just overslept." He patted her hand. "I'll take a quick shower. That should help wake me up."

She nodded. "Okay. I'll get some coffee started."

"Thanks."

She doesn't love you. She never did. The words were a whisper in his mind, barely audible. He blinked, unsure of what he'd heard. Marjorie left, and he took a shaky breath. It's just the lack of sleep, he told himself. It's temporary. He just needed to get a shower, relax and maybe go to the gym and get in a workout. It had been a while since he'd hit the weights and maybe breaking a sweat would help.

Shaking his head, he thought of the dream again and wondered what it meant, but his fatigue overshadowed his efforts and he stood and went into the bathroom.

After getting cleaned up and dressed, he went downstairs and helped himself to a cup of coffee in the kitchen. His head a little clearer, he took a sip, and eyed J.P. playing in the other room, while Marjorie sat at the table with a pile of papers.

Sipping more of his coffee, he went to the table and sat. His mind returning to the case and the previous day, he went still, thinking of Rem and his date. Rem was supposed to have contacted him to let him know he was okay. Worried, he pulled out his phone, prepared to call when he saw the text message. Rem had sent him a message at eleven o'clock, saying he was fine and to get some rest. Daniels felt relief but then widened his eyes when he saw that he'd responded soon after, giving his partner a thumbs up.

Daniels put his coffee down. He had no memory of responding to the text message much less receiving it. God, had he been that tired and out of it that he couldn't remember a text from his partner?

Gripping his temples, he wondered what was wrong with him. Something was going on, and he wondered whether he should see a doctor, although the thought of it made him grimace.

"You hungry?" asked Marjorie. "I've got some chicken salad. You want a sandwich?"

Daniels put his hand down and stared for a minute. For a brief second, a flash of anger coursed through him. It came and went, but for that second, he had to suppress the urge to yell at her to leave him alone.

Shaken, he kept his cool and did his best to keep his face relaxed. "That would be great. Thanks, babe." He wasn't hungry, but he needed her busy while he tried to figure out what was wrong. *She doesn't love you. She never did.* That small, still voice came again, and he went rigid in his seat.

"Shut up," he whispered to himself.

"What?" asked Marjorie, pulling the chicken salad from the fridge. "You say something?"

"No," he said quickly and gripping his mug. "Just talking to myself."

She nodded. "Did Rem have another date with that woman last night?"

Daniels tried to gather his thoughts, but that voice had him shaking. "Uh, yeah. He did." He held his head.

"How'd it go? You hear from him?"

"No. Not yet. I'll call him later."

"I still can't believe he didn't use Dominic Remello. It was such a great name." She smoothed some chicken salad onto a piece of bread. "I hope he's being careful, especially if she's as good-looking as he says she is." She put the knife aside and added the second piece of bread. "Who knows? Maybe this could turn into a romance, if she's innocent, of course. Rem's a great catch, and I bet she's realizing it." She picked up the knife and cut the sandwich in half. "We should have him over for dinner again soon and pick his brain. I'm dying to know what he's thinking."

Daniels barely heard her. His attention was fully on the knife Marjorie was using. *She loves your partner. Not you.* The quiet voice rattled his brain and he stood. Another flare of anger sliced through him and vanished again, but not before he had the thought of picking up the knife. The voice came again. *Kill her.*

Breaking out in a cold sweat, he stumbled back, and knocked over the chair.

Marjorie stopped, her face falling. "What's the matter? You're as a pale as a ghost."

"I...I...uh...I need to take a walk." Daniels mumbled to himself. Shaking his head, he walked into the foyer, fumbling with his pockets. "Where are my keys?"

Marjorie followed him. "A walk? Now? What about your sandwich?"

Daniels spotted his keys. "Save it for me. I'll eat it later."

"What do you need your keys for if you're going for a walk?" she asked.

He whirled, wanting to snap at her, but stopped himself. "I think, actually, that I'll go to the gym. Maybe some exercise will help me lift this fog." He opened the closet and pulled out his gym bag.

"The gym? Don't you want to change your clothes?"

Looking down at himself, he eyed his baggy sweats, t-shirt, and sandals. "This is fine. I'll wear this." He swung the bag onto his shoulder.

"Gordon, what's going on?"

He hesitated and studied her worried face. "Nothing. I just need to work out. It's been too long."

"Something's bothering you. What is it?" She walked up and took his hand. "Talk to me."

He pulled his hand away. "Nothing's wrong, Marjorie. Stop worrying." Walking to the door, he turned back. "I'll see you later." Feeling the cold spike of annoyance return, he opened the door and left.

**

Rem rounded the corner on the last leg of his run and slowed to a walk as he neared the driveway to his house. Wiping his sweaty forehead with his sleeve, and breathing hard, he thought again of his evening with Allison. After finishing their pie, Allison had suggested a movie. He'd tried to call it a night, but then she'd told him *Night of the Living Dead* was playing at a local dollar theater, and he couldn't say no, and, if he were being honest, he was having fun and enjoying his time with her. Not only was she smart, funny and gorgeous, she was easy to talk to and they had a lot in common. She had almost as many crazy aunts and uncles as he did, plus she laughed at his stupid jokes, so she hadn't been lying about that when they'd first met.

Walking up to his front door, he thought of Jennie and how she'd also laughed at his jokes, and stopped cold. Was he comparing Allison to Jennie? *Shit*, he thought, and chastised himself. *It's only been two dates*, he thought. *Don't get carried away.* He entered his house and went straight to the kitchen, opened the fridge and grabbed a bottled water.

"Hey."

He whirled, almost dropping his water, and saw Daniels sitting at his dining table. He held his stomach. "God. You scared the hell out of me."

Daniels barely looked like he cared. He wore baggy sweatpants, a rumpled t-shirt, and flip-flops, and stranger still, he was drinking a soda. Rem hadn't seen his partner touch a soda in years.

He cracked his water open. "What are you doing here?" Seeing his partner's weary look, he came over and sat. "What's wrong?"

Daniels sat up. "Why does everybody keep asking me that? I'm fine." He rubbed his neck and drank his soda.

Rem raised a brow. Something was definitely up. "Maybe because you show up out of nowhere, drinking that," he pointed at the can, "which any time prior to today, you would have told me how those drinks are gonna cost me a toe or two when I'm older, and it's Sunday when you would normally be spending time with your family, and you also look like hell, although I can appreciate the sweats and t-shirt. Maybe I'm rubbing off on you."

"I'm drinking a soda. Who cares? I picked it up on the way over because I was thirsty. And what's wrong with sweats? They're comfortable. Crap. What is the big deal?"

A hint of concern nudged at Rem, and he sat back and drank some water, wondering how to handle this. "Where are Marjorie and J.P.?"

"They're at home. Where else would they be?"

Rem nodded. "Did you apologize after your fight?"

"Yes, everything's fine. We're fine."

"Then what are you doing here?"

Daniels stood unexpectedly. "Because…"

Rem waited. "Because?"

Daniels paced, his face furrowed. "I had a bad morning, and I had to get out of the house."

"Why'd you have a bad morning?"

Daniels jabbed out a hand. "I don't know. I just had a bad morning. Can't I have a bad morning?"

Rem shrugged. "Sure you can. But you're stringing more than a few together this week." He traced a mark in his table. "What's bugging you? Did you sleep last night?"

Daniels grimaced and held his head. "Stop it," he whispered.

"Stop what?" asked Rem.

Daniels looked over, his eyes haunted. "Nothing. It's nothing." He paced again.

Rem watched his partner, his worry increasing. He'd never seen him act like this. They'd been through stressful cases before and had dealt with a lot worse, but Daniels had always been the rock, and now he seemed more like a pebble being tumbled along the ground in a windstorm. "Is it D'Mato?"

"No, it's not D'Mato."

"Is it me? Are you pissed about something I did?"

"No," he said impatiently.

"Is it something between you and Marjorie?"

He stopped, his face a scowl. "Why do you ask that? Do you know something?" His scowl turned to a snarl and he advanced on Rem. "Have you talked to her?"

Rem had to lean back in his seat. "Whoa." He raised a hand. "Get a hold of yourself, Chief. No. I haven't talked to her. Should I have?"

Daniels went still, and his face softened. He took a step back and look confused.

"Daniels, what the hell is going on?"

"I'm sorry. I'm just..." He put a hand over his face. "I don't know...on edge."

"I can see that."

Daniels paced some more and then sat again. He drummed his fingers on the table. "How was your date last night?"

Rem didn't think for a moment that his partner really cared about his date, but he answered to keep Daniels at ease. "It went fine. We had dinner and went to a movie."

Daniels, his face flat, looked up. "You sleep with her?"

Rem took a second to respond. "You don't beat around the bush, do you?"

"Come on. I know you. If it weren't for this case, you'd be all over her." He snickered.

"Excuse me?"

"Oh, please. You know how you are."

Rem narrowed his eyes. "How exactly am I?" His heart thumped, and he gripped his water bottle.

Daniels raised the side of his lip. "Before Jennie, you slept with everything that moved. I doubt that's changed."

Rem tensed, and if it hadn't been for the fact that he knew something was wrong, he'd have considered getting in Daniels' face and telling his friend what he thought about that comment, but he forced himself to relax. "I didn't know you held me in such low regard."

Daniels sat up and picked up his soda. "Don't get so touchy. I don't blame you. If she were my assignment, I'd have—" He stopped and set his jaw, and his face froze.

Rem swallowed. "You'd have what?"

Daniels closed his eyes and held his head. "Nothing. I'd have done nothing. And forget what I said. You shouldn't do anything either, with her or anyone. Just ignore me."

Rem took a deep breath and debated what to do. "It's okay. And no, we didn't sleep together. After the movie, I kissed her goodnight and came home. Not that I wasn't tempted to go further. The longer I do this, the harder it's going to get. No pun intended."

Daniels didn't laugh. "You'll figure it out," he said, still holding his head.

Rem wanted to say that his partner would help him decide what to do, but now he couldn't be sure. Something was going on with Daniels and he didn't know how to handle it. "Hey."

Daniels looked up and sneered. "Don't look at me like that."

No matter what Rem did or said, it seemed his partner took offense. "Like what?"

"That worried look." He sat back and groaned. "I'm sick of people looking at me like that."

Rem put his water on the table. "Daniels, something is wrong. You're not yourself. So, yeah, I'm sure I look worried. Hell, if I were acting like you, you'd have knocked me into a wall by now, and I wouldn't have blamed you."

Daniels scoffed. "Is that what you want to do? Knock me into a wall?" He chuckled. "That's funny."

Rem was trying to keep up with Daniels' mood swings. "I know you won't like this, but maybe you should see a doctor. You might need some medication."

Daniels' dark gaze pierced him. "I see. You think I need a doctor? What's the next suggestion? A mental hospital?"

"A mental hospital?" asked Rem. "Why would I suggest that?" His phone buzzed, and he took it from the zippered pocket in his workout pants.

"God. A guy has a few nightmares, can't sleep, and suddenly he's ready for the looney bin. Shit. Thanks a lot, partner." He snorted and clenched his eyes shut.

Rem kept his eye on Daniels and glanced at the display. It was Marjorie. "It's your wife." He answered. "Hello?"

Daniels opened his eyes.

Marjorie's anxious voice traveled over the line. "Rem? I'm sorry to bother you, but I'm worried about Gordon. He left this afternoon and was acting strange. He said he was going to the gym, but I think he was lying. And now he won't answer the phone. Have you seen him?"

"He's right here."

He heard an audible breath. "Is he okay? Why won't he answer the phone?"

"He's all right." Rem knew those words weren't true, but didn't know how else to respond. He held out the phone. "It's Marjorie. Said she can't get in touch with you."

Daniels squinted. "That's because I turned my phone off. Tell her I'm fine."

"I think she'd like to hear it from you."

Daniels pushed himself out of his seat. "You sure about that? Or is that what you think I want to hear?"

Rem moaned, not understanding, and shook his head. "It's your wife. She's waiting to talk to you." He raised the phone higher.

Daniels held his head again and mumbled something.

"Are you going to speak to her?"

Daniels turned and snagged the phone from Rem. He spoke a few words, telling Marjorie he was okay and not to worry, then told her he'd be home soon. After hanging up, he tossed the phone back to Rem. "Thanks, buddy. Now I know she calls you."

Rem put his phone on the table and stood. "When she's worried about you, I would hope she would."

"Come on. Don't play stupid. I know what's going on here."

Rem held out his hands. "What is going on?"

Daniels walked to the door and opened it. He turned and pointed. "I...I..." His face fell and the confused look returned. "I have to go."

"Daniels," Rem approached him. "Wait." He tried to stop Daniels, but his partner resisted.

"Leave me alone," said Daniels. "I'm fine. I shouldn't have come here." He headed toward the sidewalk.

"Where's your car?"

Daniels didn't answer and not looking back, he headed toward the street, turned at the driveway and disappeared from view.

CHAPTER TWELVE

Rem sat at his desk on Tuesday morning, reviewing the results of the report from Research. Daniels had received it Saturday, but had done little with it, spending most of his time sleeping in the locker room. On Monday, Daniels had called in sick, telling Rem he wasn't feeling well and needed to take the day. Considering Daniels' surprise visit and strange mood on Sunday, Rem hoped that all his partner needed was a day off, although something told him there was more to it.

Rem had tried to reach Daniels after he'd left Rem's house on Sunday, and had almost driven over to Daniels' place, when his partner had finally contacted him. He'd told Rem he'd returned to his car, which he'd left at a nearby park, and then just driven around for the afternoon. Then he'd gotten something to eat, stopped at the grocery and gone home. He'd apologized to Rem, and told him he'd just needed time to think, and he would see him Monday. Then on Monday, they'd only talked for a minute when Daniels had called in sick. Rem couldn't help but worry, but figured if Daniels needed a day to deal with whatever was bugging him, then so be it.

Rem had spent Monday following up with Redstone's background and his cousin Eddie's murder, plus reviewing the report from Research on possible crimes that could be similar to the liquor store robberies, and murders similar to Eddie's. Lozano had been out most of the day in meetings, and Rem had barely seen him. He'd talked to Allison briefly on the phone. She'd had an instructor out and had been caught up at work, but they planned to get together soon.

Now, sitting at his desk on Tuesday morning, Rem eyed the paperwork on his desk and the clock. It was close to ten a.m. and Daniels was an hour late. Rem checked his phone again but saw no texts or emails. He'd been trying to reach his partner but with no luck.

Lozano came out of his office and approached Rem's desk. "Where the hell is Daniels?" He paused. "He's late, and don't tell me he joined the circus."

Rem would have tried to cover for his partner if he'd known where the hell he was, but that nudge of worry grew. He didn't know what the hell was going on, but was at a loss as to what to do about it. He didn't know if it was a job, marriage, friendship or work problem, and Daniels wasn't talking.

"Well?" asked Lozano. "Have you heard from him?"

"Not yet. Maybe he's still sick and in bed. Probably sleeping through his alarm, and the phone."

"Well, I hope he's getting some rest then, because when he gets his ass in here, he'll be lucky if he's not walking the beat for the foreseeable future."

"I'll try him again." Rem grabbed his phone and sent another text.

"Is that the report from Research?" asked Lozano, pointing at Rem's desk. "Anything interesting?"

Rem sent the text and nodded. "Yes, actually. About six months ago, there were three gas station robberies, all within a ten-day period, over on the north side. Perps wore masks and carried weapons. They never hurt anyone, but the M.O. is similar to our liquor stores, and in fact..." He pulled out a still photo pulled from a video. It was a grainy black and white image of a tall, lean man with long dark hair poking out from the bottom of his cap, holding a weapon on the attendant. "This could be the same guy from the liquor store robberies." He pulled a similar photo that was taken from one of the recent robberies and compared it to the first one. "Think that could be D'Mato?"

Lozano eyed the photos. "It's damn possible. Matches his description." He paused, studying the pictures. "Was he at all three hold-ups?"

"Nope. The other two were different. Our female suspect appears in the first robbery. Same long dark pony tail sticking out from her mask, and similar body type." He pulled a photo out of the female robber at the gas station and handed it to Lozano. "The third robbery had two different assailants."

Lozano raised a brow. "If this is the same crew, then D'Mato's definitely got a following, and maybe a bigger one than we think." He eyed the picture of the female. "You getting any idea as to whether Allison Albright could be this woman in the picture?"

Rem chuckled. "Allison? Robbing liquor stores and gas stations? Unlikely."

"How can you be sure? Did you ask her?"

"Well, no, I didn't ask her."

"Can you account for her whereabouts on the days of the crimes?"

Rem scratched his head. "Well, no."

"Then you can't say one way or the other if she was involved, unless you're thinking with the wrong part of the anatomy."

"Cap..."

"Don't 'Cap' me, Remalla. I've seen pictures of this woman and I've got eyes. I can tell you're having fun with this assignment, but I've been doing this job too long, and I've seen cops get the tables turned when a pretty lady distracts them and they end up getting burned, and sometimes dead." He grunted. "Your partner isn't here to tell you this, but I am. Keep your guard up, and everything else down." He quirked up an eyebrow. "You catch my drift?"

Rem pursed his lips. "It's hard not to."

"And even if she's not involved with the robberies doesn't mean she doesn't still have some association with D'Mato, and could be part of his group."

"I know, I know," said Rem. "I've put out the feelers that I'm not as nice as I look, so we'll see what she does with it, but so far, I haven't picked up on any interest."

"It's still early. Give it a few more dates, and then we'll reevaluate."

Rem nodded.

"And what about that man you went to see, about the paranormal stuff? Was he any help?"

Rem had seen Lozano briefly on Saturday and had filled him in on their meeting with Redstone. "I haven't heard from him yet, but I did do some background checking on his story. He's telling the truth. He was a Texas Ranger with an exemplary record and his cousin Eddie was murdered three years ago. He'd been strangled and had a strange bite mark on his arm. It's still unsolved."

"You think Redstone's the real deal and not involved?"

"I do," said Rem. "And I found something else."

"What's that?"

"When I was pulling records on Eddie Redstone, I learned about another unsolved murder, similar in nature. It happened a year ago. An unidentified man's body was found naked in an alley, in the warehouse district. He'd been bound and strangled and had a bite mark on his arm, plus he had a long cut down his sternum." He waved a paper at Lozano. "The investigating officers said he was a vagrant, and pretty much wrote it off after they found no DNA, no witnesses, and no identification."

Lozano took the paper Rem held. "When did D'Mato get out of prison?"

"Two weeks before that guy bought it."

Lozano lowered the paper, his face serious. "Are you saying D'Mato could be some sort of serial killer?"

Rem shrugged. "I don't know, Cap. If he's not doing the killing, then he could be instructing others on how to do it. There's no way to know until we can find someone who's willing to talk."

Lozano handed the paper back. "This Allison Albright. Even if she's not currently involved, she may have some knowledge of D'Mato's past activities before his incarceration."

"It's possible. She mentioned an old boyfriend who got a little rough. I think she's referring to D'Mato, but she hasn't elaborated beyond that."

"Then keep pushing. If you're not getting anywhere with her, at some point, we may need to bring her in and question her."

Rem rubbed his neck, hating to think of it. "I get it, but let's try my way first. If she is guilty, you're not going to get a thing out of her if you bring her in."

"Then you better work fast, because I get the feeling we're running out of time."

Rem sighed. "Yeah. I know."

A phone buzzed, and Lozano pulled his cell from his pocket. "Lozano," he said. His face furrowed. "When?" He grabbed a pen and a piece of paper from Daniels' desk. "Address?" He scribbled on the paper and listened. "Really? An arrest?" He nodded. "Got it. Thanks." He hung up and handed the paper to Rem. "We've got another liquor store robbery."

Rem took the paper. "Hell."

"Happened this morning as the owner was getting ready to open. Two men in masks with guns. Wanted him to open the safe. He refused and got butted in the head with the gun. We got lucky though. A bystander realized what was going on and called the cops. One guy took off and the other tried to grab the required bottle of scotch, and didn't get out in time. They arrested him in the alley."

Rem stood and grabbed his jacket. "Shit. This could be the break we've been waiting for."

"Go to the store first. Talk to the owner. Find out what happened."

"What about the perp?"

"Let him get processed and booked. I'll try and find your partner and have him meet you at the liquor store. Then go talk to our robber once he's had a little time to sit and think about his future."

"Will do. Hopefully, we'll crack this sucker open. It's about time." He slipped on his jacket and headed for the door.

"And be careful," said Lozano.

Rem waved a hand. "I will."

**

Daniels cracked an eye open, hearing a ringing phone, and tried to remember where he was. Moaning, he blinked, and realized he was sitting in his car, and then recalled his unpleasant morning, and unfortunately, his previous two days.

After his visit with Rem, he'd come home, and told Marjorie he hadn't felt well and spent the rest of the evening in bed, trying to rest and drown out the voices that suddenly wouldn't shut up. She'd brought him some dinner, but he couldn't eat and after a fitful night's sleep where he'd dreamed of hooded figures and bloody knives, he'd awakened to his alarm, his head fuzzy and his mind unsettled. He'd gotten up, prepared for work, and left. On the way though, the strange voices had returned and, disturbed, he'd pulled over at the park. Anxious and worried, he'd called Rem and told him he was taking the day, and then had fallen asleep in his car. After sleeping a few hours, he'd gone to a fast-food place to eat and then to a movie, hoping the distraction would help silence the noise in his head, but he'd fallen asleep at the theatre and he'd woken to the usher poking his shoulder. He'd gone home then, never telling Marjorie that he'd skipped work, and went to bed early again, only to have another restless night's sleep.

That morning though, the voices had gone quiet and, hoping they were over, he'd hastily dressed and left the house, telling Marjorie he wanted to be at work early. She'd given him a quick kiss and then he'd heard the whisper. *She's a liar. She doesn't love you. She never did.*

Frazzled, he'd gotten in his car and parked at the same nearby park he'd stopped at the previous day, trying to collect his thoughts and calm himself. What was the matter with him? Why couldn't he sleep? Why was he so angry? And what were the damn voices? Was Rem right? Should he go to the doctor? Would medication help?

He's lying to you, too. He wants everyone to think you're crazy, so he can have Marjorie. Daniels squeezed the sides of his head. "Shut up," he said aloud. "You're not real. None of that is true." Frustrated, he'd laid his head back on the seat, upset and exhausted, and had quickly succumbed to sleep. It seemed the only time he could get any rest was outside of his home. Hearing his phone buzz, he'd blinked and answered, immediately hearing Lozano's yell.

"Where the hell have you been?"

Daniels tried to get his bearings. "I…uhm, what time is it?"

"What time is it?" yelled Lozano. "You better find a damn watch and start using it. It's after ten o'clock."

Daniels sat up. "Ten o'clock?"

"Yes," said Lozano. "Your partner's been trying to reach you all morning. Didn't you get his texts? Or voicemails?"

Daniels rubbed the sleep from his eyes. "No. Not yet. I…I guess I dozed off." His brain wouldn't work and he couldn't think of anything else to say.

Lozano grunted. "You and I will talk later, but right now, I need you to meet your partner. While you were getting your beauty rest, our robbers struck again this morning. But we got lucky. One perp got away, but one was arrested. Your partner is heading over to the liquor store to talk to the owner. Go join him. I'll send you the address."

A flicker of annoyance made Daniels straighten. "Why not go talk to the guy who was arrested?"

"Because I want you to go talk to the owner first. Find out what happened. Get the details. There's still another perp on the loose. Then you can go question the other one."

"But, Cap, if Rem's talking to the owner, let me interview the guy they caught. Save some time."

"Daniels," Lozano's voice raised. "Last I checked, I was the boss. You two work better together. Go find Rem, talk to the owner, and then you can both go talk to our perp. You got that?"

He doesn't trust you. Doesn't think you can do anything without Rem. Daniels held the bridge of his nose. "Fine." He didn't bother to hide the flare of irritation.

"If you have a problem with that," argued Lozano, "I'm happy to reassign you. A pet store was robbed yesterday. Would you prefer that? You can hunt for Fido instead of a potential cult leader." He paused. "You let me know which you prefer, because I've got no issue with either one."

Daniels could hear the tone in Lozano's voice and knew it would be wise not to push any further. "Sorry, Cap," he said, shaking his head. "I hear you. I'm on my way to the liquor store."

"Good. And keep me apprised, you got that?"

"Will do. Thanks, Cap."

Lozano hung up and Daniels lowered the phone. Eyeing the screen, he saw the missed texts and voicemails from Rem. His irritation grew when the phone buzzed and Daniels received the text from Lozano, giving him the address to the location of the latest robbery. He groaned. Why the hell did he have to go talk to the owner when they'd had one of the robbers in custody? It was stupid. Rem was perfectly capable of interviewing someone without Daniels by his side.

The voice echoed in his ears. *Rem told Lozano you couldn't be trusted. Rem doesn't want you to solve this. He wants all the glory.* Daniels tossed his phone into the passenger seat in annoyance. The hell that was going to happen. He fumbled with the car keys and turned the ignition. Rem could handle the owner, and he'd go talk to the man in custody. He'd text Rem and let him know later. With Daniels' initiative, they'd get the answers they needed and hopefully crack this case wide open, and Daniels would get the attention and recognition he deserved.

Not his partner. Checking the traffic, he hit the accelerator and headed down the road.

CHAPTER THIRTEEN

"I can't believe this," said Mr. Adelpho, holding a cold pack over a bloody bandage on his head. His shirt was covered in blood, and he pointed at Rem. "What do my tax dollars pay for? Where are you guys when we need you?"

Rem eyed the dried blood on the owner's face and neck. "Are you sure you don't want to go to the hospital, Mr. Adelphi? You may need stitches."

"It's Adelpho. And no, I don't want to go to the hospital. I've already got to deal with all of this, and now you want me to pay a hospital bill, too?"

"I'm just checking. You could have a concussion."

"A concussion is the least of my worries. Somebody tried to rob me today. Don't you care about that?"

Rem shook his head, questioning whether he should have interviewed the perp first and saved himself some time. "Can you tell me what happened?"

"I already told the officers. Now I have to tell you, too?"

"It helps to hear it from the source." He checked his phone again, but there were no messages from Daniels.

"Am I keeping you from something?" asked Mr. Adelpho. "Don't tell me. Is there another robbery going on that you guys can't do anything about?" He waved a hand. "I mean, we're talking about people's livelihoods here."

"I understand. Which is why I'm here." Rem waited. "Just tell me what occurred."

Adelpho sighed. "Fine. Yes. I was preparing to open. The next thing I know, there're two men with a gun in my face."

"Was the front door open?"

"No. They came in through the back. I'd taken out the trash, and suddenly they were there. They wanted me to open the safe, but I refused. They seemed a little ruffled, but then one of them got angry. I told them I'd open the register. I always keep sixty dollars in it, and I did. I gave them the sixty bucks, but they weren't satisfied."

"Where's your safe?" asked Rem.

"In my office. In the back."

"How did they know you had a safe back there?"

"Your guess is as good as mine."

Rem nodded and pulled out a small pad of paper and wrote on it. Daniels normally wrote down any details but it would be up to Rem on this one. "You have any employees who might have done this?" he asked. "Anyone fired recently?"

Adelpho shook his head. "My son and my nephew work with me, and I have a maintenance man. I trust all of them. And no one's been fired."

"Who else would know about the safe?"

Adelpho squinted and adjusted the cold pack over his injury. "I don't know. I had repairmen here last week. Maybe they saw it?"

Rem handed the pad and pen to him. "I need names of your current employees, plus anyone you can think of who might be aware of the location of the safe."

"Are you serious?" asked Adelpho.

"It's what your tax dollars are paying for."

"But they arrested one of the robbers. Won't that help?"

"They caught one. Not the other. Any information you have will be beneficial, especially if you want us to prosecute the man involved. The more we know, the better."

Adelpho groaned. "Fine." He lowered the ice pack, and Rem could see the dark blood on the bandage. "I'll write it down. It'll be easier if we go to my office." They'd been standing up near the front by the register since Rem arrived, and Rem followed Adelpho toward the back. "I need to go there anyway to check on things. I'm sure there's fingerprint dust everywhere. It's probably a mess."

"I know this has been a tough morning, Mr. Adelpho," said Rem, "but I promise, we'll do our best to get out of your hair as soon as—"

Adelpho opened the door to his office and stopped. Rem caught sight of a man of average build, wearing a mask, squatted beside the safe, attempting to open it. The back door was open and a paper flew off the desk when a breeze blew.

Adelpho pointed a shaky finger. "That's him. That's him."

The man jumped up and raced out the door.

Rem threw down his pad and paper. "Call nine-one-one." He raced through the door.

Adelpho responded. "Again?"

The man with the mask ran down the alley, moving at a fast pace. Rem kept up, glad he'd been exercising recently, but the guy was quick, and Rem picked up his speed.

"Stop. Police," he yelled.

The man kept going, staying in the alley, but as he approached an upcoming street, he attempted to dodge a dirty, discarded couch and tripped on a piece of wood as he ran around it. He tumbled and fell, and Rem caught up and jumped on top of him.

"Stop. You're under arrest." He struggled to get leverage, but the robber of average height and weight didn't move in an average way, and he twisted beneath Rem, kicked out, and knocked Rem off his balance. Rem fell sideways, and the man wiggled out of Rem's grasp and was up on his feet in seconds, but instead of running from Rem, he turned and faced him.

Rem rolled and stood, staying nimble on his feet, and pulled his weapon. He didn't want to use it because he needed this guy alive, but not having a choice, he hoped the man would relent and go quietly. Before Rem could aim, though, the man swiveled, kicked out, and made direct contact with Rem's gun, knocking it loose. The gun fell and skittered along the ground.

Breathless and cursing, Rem considered his options, which weren't many. The man continued to face him, a sneer on his face, and Rem realized the guy planned to stay and fight. Rem prayed Adelpho had called nine-one-one, and raised his hands in a defensive posture. "You sure you want to do this?"

The man continued to smile through his mask, bounced on his feet and began to circle Rem.

Rem took a deep breath and went back to his training. It had been a while since he'd been in a fist fight, and he hoped his skills were up to the challenge. If Daniels had been there, they'd have cuffed this guy by now, but that ship had sailed. If they were going to catch this man, it would be up to Rem.

"Listen," said Rem, trying to catch his breath from the chase, but his heart and adrenaline were pumping. "Right now, it's just armed robbery. But now we're talking assaulting a police officer. That's adding a few years to your incarceration. You might want to consider that."

The man raised his fists and said nothing, but continued to dance around Rem.

"Think long and hard, friend," said Rem, circling the man. "It's not worth it."

The robber smiled, but remained quiet, and Rem tried a new tactic. "You working for D'Mato? You think he's got your back? Because you're an idiot if you think he does."

The soft sound of a siren could be heard in the distance, and Rem said a silent prayer of thanks that help was coming, and maybe he would survive this.

At the sound of the siren, or maybe it was D'Mato's name, the man shot forward and tackled Rem, knocking him backward and onto the ground. Rem grunted and twisted, and the man punched Rem in the side. Rem punched back and kicked with his knee and hit the man in the ribs. He heard a crack, and the man made a grunt and rolled away. Moving fast, the robber jumped up and stood before Rem could even get to his knees.

Hearing the wail of the sirens, Rem started to stand, but before he could, the man whirled, and with a primal yell, threw out a leg in a roundhouse kick, and hit Rem in the head with his foot. The impact knocked Rem sideways and the concrete reared up at him. The world tilted, and everything went black.

**

Daniels sat in the small cell, waiting to see the man who'd attempted to rob the liquor store, who'd been identified as Tyler Bodin. After signing in and checking his weapon, Daniels sat at a square table, and listened to the sounds around him. Doors clanging, men yelling, buzzers sounding, and his own head throbbing. The damned headache had returned.

Footsteps echoed, and Daniels looked to see a guard leading a man in an orange jumpsuit, his hands cuffed in front of him, toward the cell. The guard opened it and guided Bodin toward the chair and sat him on it. Daniels thanked him and the guard left, closing the cell door behind him.

Tyler eyed Daniels, and Daniels eyed him back. Tyler was a skinny, young white kid with stringy brown hair and a painfully thin mustache.

"Tyler Bodin?" asked Daniels.

Tyler didn't answer; he just stared.

"I hear you like to rob liquor stores, or at least you like to try and rob liquor stores."

Tyler didn't respond.

"I also hear you had a friend who helped you. Care to identify him? You do, and this might go more smoothly for you. It'll show the prosecutor you're willing to work with us. Might mean less jail time."

Tyler leaned back in his seat and sighed as if bored.

Daniels narrowed his eyes, wondering how to get him to talk. "Who put you up to this? You can't tell me you're the brains of the organization. I'd find that hard to believe."

Tyler smirked, but didn't answer.

Daniels drummed his fingers on the table. "Let me take a wild guess. Is it Victor D'Mato?"

The man's eyes flickered with recognition, but he didn't answer.

"That's right. We know who your boss is. He's been calling the shots, but not for long. His time's running out, and I think he knows it. The question is, are you going to take the fall for him? Because that's exactly what he wants."

Tyler shifted in his seat and stared at the floor.

"He'll leave you holding the bag and you'll do the time, while he runs around in his pretty apartment and pajamas, recruiting new guys just like you, who do his dirty work for him."

Tyler studied a nail, his handcuffs clinking together.

"You think I haven't seen guys like you before, all under the spell of some supposed guru, who end up in prison or worse, while their leader gets the high-powered attorney, avoids a long sentence, and his pretty boys do the time and are left with nothing?" He leaned forward. "Be smart. Tell us how you got involved, who recruited you, and about Victor. I'll talk to the prosecutor and we can likely get you immunity. You might walk away scot-free."

Tyler shook his head.

"You're only going to have one shot at this. I leave and your chances go with me. Especially if we catch your friend. He talks, and it's all over." He pointed. "Or any one of your groupie friends for that matter. Whoever talks first, wins."

Tyler looked up, his eyes glittering, and he spoke. "You have no idea who you're dealing with."

Daniels shrugged. "Oh, I think so. He's not as scary as you think, Tyler. He's just a guy like you. Not that tough, no matter what you may think, or what he may tell you." He rubbed his aching temples.

Tyler chuckled. "You'll find out soon enough."

Daniels dropped his hand. "Find out what?"

Tyler smiled, and relaxed against his seat. "In due time, Detective. In due time."

A flare of anger rose, and Daniels scowled. "Tell me what you know, Tyler, or you're going to rot in prison for a nice long time, and when you get out, you'll have wished you'd played this game differently."

"You have no idea what the game is," said Tyler. "You're the one who's playing with the wrong deck, and by the time I get out of here, which will be soon, you're going to know exactly who's holding all the cards."

Daniels resisted the urge to grab this guy by the neck, but his ire grew. "You listen to me, you little punk—"

There was another clang and footsteps traveled. A male voice echoed down the corridor and bounced against the walls. "Tyler Bodin. Don't say another word."

Daniels looked to see a short man with dark spiky hair and a round belly wearing a rumpled suit and tie, approach the doors with another guard, and Daniels cursed as Tyler smiled.

"I'm his attorney," said the man through the bars, "and you cannot speak to him without representation." The guard opened the doors and the man entered, holding a briefcase. "Now, if you don't mind, I'd like to talk to my client."

"Have a nice day, Detective," said Tyler, his grin growing.

Daniels set his jaw, but knew his time was up. He stood, his eyes on Tyler. "Sure thing, Counselor. He's all yours." He pointed again. "But don't think we're done here, Tyler."

"Thank you, Detective. I'll take it from here," said the attorney. "You can talk to him later, while I'm present, assuming we have something to say."

"Somehow, I suspect you will," said Daniels. He approached the doors, which stood open as the guard waited, and walked through.

"Hope you feel better, Detective," said Tyler. "And say hi to your partner." Tyler chuckled.

"That's enough, Tyler," said the attorney, setting his briefcase down.

Daniels raised a brow and watched through the bars as the guard shut the cell door.

**

Lozano hung up the phone, angry as hell, and wondering how to handle this fiasco. His office shades were open, and he saw Daniels enter the squad room and sit at his desk. He stood, stomped to his door, and flung it open. "Daniels," he yelled.

Daniels held a disposable cup with a long straw and a bag, which he tossed on his desk. "I was about to eat lunch, Cap. Can it wait?" His eyes were weary and his skin looked sallow.

Lozano fought to stay cool, but was losing the battle. "Get your ass in here. Now."

Daniels sighed, grabbed the bag, and stood. Holding his cup, he took his time walking toward the office.

Lozano returned to his seat. "Shut the door," he said as Daniels entered.

Daniels shut it and sat. He put the cup on the desk and opened the bag. He pulled out a hamburger and french fries, and ate a fry. "What do you need, Cap?"

Lozano tried to comprehend what he was seeing. His normally responsible and trustworthy detective with impeccable health habits was unkempt, acting cavalier and eating junk food. "How was your morning?"

Daniels shrugged and spoke through a mouthful of burger. "Not as successful as I'd hoped." He sipped on his drink and swallowed.

Lozano leaned in. "I thought I told you to go to the liquor store. Did I not make that clear to you on the phone this morning?"

"I know, Cap. I was going to go, but then I thought better of it." He picked up another fry.

"You thought better of it?"

"Yeah. Rem can handle an interview. He's good at it. I figured why not go talk to Bodin? Not that it did any good. His attorney showed." He popped the fry in his mouth. "I doubt it mattered, though. The guy wouldn't say a word. Just sneered at me. I don't think he's going to be much help when it comes to D'Mato."

Lozano put his hands on his desk and kept his voice low. "Well, maybe if you'd gone to the liquor store with your partner, you might have caught his accomplice."

"How would we have done that?" asked Daniels, sipping his drink.

Lozano glared. "Because your partner walked in on him robbing the safe. The guy returned to finish the job, and your partner chased him down an alley."

Daniels froze as he prepared to take another bite. "What?" He sat up, his face looking paler.

"Now it seems I have your attention." Lozano raised his voice, as he considered what might have happened to one of his detectives. He stood. "Too bad I didn't have it this morning when I *told you to go to the damn liquor store.*"

Daniels sunk in his seat, before lowering his burger. "How's Rem? Is he okay?"

Lozano jabbed out a finger. "He was punched in the stomach, kicked in the head, and lost consciousness. Thankfully, the owner called nine-one-one and a patrol car arrived and the perp took off, which is damn lucky, because he could just as easily have killed your partner."

Daniels went still. "Shit."

"You're damn right, shit," yelled Lozano. "If you'd done as I'd asked, we'd have this guy in custody, and not a cop in the E.R." His anger got the best of him and he kicked at his chair. It slammed into the back wall with a thunk. "Next time I tell you to do something, you do it. You understand?" He ran a hand over his head, and took a deep breath.

Daniels put the burger on Lozano's desk. "He's in the E.R.? How serious is it?"

The door to the office opened, and Lozano turned to see Rem standing in the doorway. His forehead and chin were scraped, his shirt was ripped and his right eye was swollen and bruised. Lozano glared again. "What the hell are you doing here?"

**

Rem had heard Lozano yelling from the moment he'd entered the squad room. Seeing his partner in the office, he walked over. Neither Lozano nor Daniels noticed his presence until he opened the door.

"Thought I'd see what all the fuss was about." He eyed the food on Lozano's table, noting the burger and fries, which his partner never ate. "How nice. You didn't think to get me any, especially after my crappy morning?"

"You're supposed to be in the hospital," said Lozano.

"I checked myself out. Figured I'd do better out here than in there."

"Did they say you had a concussion?" asked Lozano.

Rem shrugged. "Mild. No big deal. I'll live." He rubbed his aching head. His eye throbbed and his belly hurt where he'd been punched, but the doctors had told him there was no serious damage. They'd wanted to keep him overnight for observation, but he'd declined.

"Rem," Daniels stood, looking uncertain, with that same confused look. A french fry fell from his lap. "I'm sorry. I...I...thought..." He shook his head.

"You thought what?" asked Rem. "That you'd just ignore all my texts? Not call me back?" Feeling a little wobbly, Rem took a seat in the office. He'd had plenty of time to process Daniels' absence, and he'd been working hard to not assume anything. "You just felt the need to ignore me?"

"I didn't ignore you," said Daniels.

"Then what would you call it?" asked Rem.

"I...I...fell asleep. I didn't hear the phone." He held his temples, and grimaced. "Then I talked to Lozano...and..."

"And what?" asked Rem. Nothing Daniels was saying was helping Rem's mood.

Daniels sat again and hung his head. "I went to talk to Tyler Bodin. The guy who was arrested."

"And how did that go?" asked Rem.

Daniels pressed his thumb and forefinger deeper into his temples. "Not great." He shifted in his seat. "His lawyer showed."

Rem touched his swollen eye, feeling it throb. "Which would have happened either way." He rubbed his tender belly. "It would have been nice if you'd been at the liquor store to help me out." He paused, angry but trying not to be. "But no, you decided to go it on your own." As much as he tried to understand, he couldn't get the picture of his assailant's foot swinging out at him and feeling it connect with his head. If that man had gone for Rem's gun instead of running, he'd be dead now.

"If you'd listened to me," said Lozano to Daniels, his voice tight. "That man would be in custody along with Tyler, and your partner wouldn't have a concussion."

Daniels dropped his hand and stared off, his eyes unfocused and a mixture of emotions crossing his face. He squeezed his eyes shut and shook his head as if to clear it. When he opened his eyes again, his lost look was gone. "You don't know that, Cap. That guy might have taken us both out." He waved a hand. "Rem's fine. What are you so worked up about?"

Lozano went quiet, and Rem studied his partner. "What the hell is the matter with you?"

Daniels frowned. "Nothing's the matter with me. I'm just tired of being second fiddle around here."

"Second fiddle?" asked Rem, sitting up.

"To who?" asked Lozano.

"To him," said Daniels, jabbing a hand at Rem. "He's perfectly capable of handling himself, and he did. I did my job. I went and talked to Bodin. It's what we do, it doesn't mean we always have to do it together."

Lozano leaned over his desk, his palms resting on top. "I gave you an order. You were supposed to follow it." He cocked his head at Rem. "Your partner needed you today, and you weren't there."

Daniels stood, his posture rigid. "Rem needs this and Rem needs that. Hell. Why don't you throw him a party every time he walks into the squad room?"

Lozano froze, and Rem tried to fathom his partner's startling transformation. He stood and faced Daniels. "What's going on with you?"

"Nothing's going on with me. Maybe for the first time, I'm seeing things clearly." Daniels narrowed his eyes at Rem.

Rem had no idea how to respond.

Lozano spoke quietly. "Remalla. Take the rest of the day. Go home and take it easy."

"Cap...," said Rem.

"Don't argue with me," said Lozano, his face furrowed. "I've had enough of that for one day. Just go, and I'll see you tomorrow. Daniels and I have some things to discuss."

"Great." Daniels smirked and looked away.

Completely at a loss for words, Rem gave in and nodded. "Okay."

"And keep me up to speed on Albright," said Lozano. "Let me know your progress."

Daniels looked back, his face clouded. "Cap, I can—"

"Be quiet, Daniels," said Lozano. "You'll be lucky if you can ticket a speeder after today. Now, *sit down.*"

Rem grimaced at the sound of Lozano's voice, walked to the door and opened it.

Daniels swiveled, his hand out. "Rem, I—"

"Forget it," said Rem. He walked out and closed the door behind him.

**

Daniels sat and tried to focus, but his mind wouldn't cooperate. Rem had left and Lozano was yelling at him, but he couldn't process any of it. *Let Rem go. He's not your friend. He never was.* The voice wouldn't be quiet. *This is good. Now he knows how you really feel. The only person you can trust is yourself.*

Lozano was asking him something but Daniels wasn't listening.

Maybe next time, he won't be so lucky. He'll get what he deserves and then so will you. Daniels rubbed his face. "Shut up," he said.

"What did you say," said Lozano.

"Shut up, shut up, shut up," whispered Daniels. Some measure of clarity returned and he'd realized what he'd said and done.

"Daniels," yelled Lozano.

Daniels stood. "Give me a sec, Cap. I have to talk to Rem. Then you can yell at me." He ran out of the office but Rem was gone. He raced out the squad doors and took the stairs down two at a time. "Rem," he yelled, certain his partner couldn't have made it out yet. He turned the corner and headed down to the ground floor.

Rem stood near the door and was saying something to Shorty, the tall officer at the front who handled visitors and issues at the entrance.

"Rem, wait." Daniels got to the bottom just as the door to the station opened and a woman walked in.

She saw Rem and smiled. "Rem," she said. She wore yoga pants that hugged her toned legs and a short jacket that covered her fitted workout top. Her muscled midriff was exposed, and her long, dark, hair hung down from a ponytail. He realized it was Allison Albright and felt the collective pause as every man in the area stopped and looked.

Rem stilled and saw Daniels but then turned toward Allison, his eyes widening. "Allison? What are you doing here?"

Daniels stayed where he was, but was within feet of them.

She came over and hugged him. "I'm so sorry to bother you at work." Her eyes rounded. "What happened to your face?"

"Nothing. Just part of the crappy job. Comes with the territory." He sighed and Daniels knew he was playing the part of the man who hated his work, but suspected his partner wasn't currently acting. "Did I miss something? Was I supposed to be somewhere?"

Two patrol officers walked by Daniels, heading toward the stairs, and Daniels overheard their conversation. "How'd Remalla get so lucky?" asked one, eyeing the exchange between Rem and Allison.

"Thinks he's hot as shit," said the other. "Look at her. That chick's nothing but trouble. He'll find out soon enough."

The other one chuckled, and they disappeared up the stairs.

"No," said Allison. "I was in the area. I can't stay long. I have to go teach a class, but I thought I'd drop in and say hello." She glanced over at Daniels, who was staring at them.

Rem looked over, his face flat. "Oh, this is my partner, Gordon Daniels."

She nodded at him. "Hello. I've heard a lot about you. It's nice to meet you."

"Nice to meet you, too." Daniels' head spun a bit, and he blinked.

"Listen," she said to Rem. "I was wondering if you'd like to have dinner tonight. At my place. Thought I'd make something simple, like spaghetti, open a bottle of wine, and we can relax." She carefully touched his eye. "If you're up for it."

Rem flicked a glance at Daniels. "I'd love it." He flinched a little at her touch. "And it's not as bad as it looks."

She moved closer. "If you want, I'll kiss it for you. Maybe even give you a nice shoulder massage." She giggled and whispered something in his ear.

He blushed. "Well, how can I say no to that?"

"Great." She moved back.

"I'll bring the bottle of wine," he said. "What time?"

"How about six?" she asked.

"Perfect."

"I'll see you then." She paused for a second, before moving close again and kissing him on the cheek, and as she did, she eyed Daniels and smiled, her gaze like a hawk's who had a hold of its prey. Daniels' head swirled again. *She's more important to him. He cares more about her than you.*

She stepped back and Rem waved. "See you later."

"Bye," she said to Daniels, and left.

Daniels fought the voice in his head and seeing Rem head for the exit, he raised a hand. "Rem, wait."

Rem hesitated as he reached the doors, but then turned. "What?"

Daniels walked over. "Listen, what I said…" His head throbbed and he paused. "I…I…shouldn't have…" *He's the enemy. Don't trust him.*

"Shouldn't have what?" asked Rem.

"I just…I got frustrated…" The whispered voice raised in volume. *He wants you out. He and Lozano both. He's more interested in Allison…and Marjorie.*

"Frustrated? Is that the word you want to use?" Rem put his hands on his hips. "If anyone should be frustrated, it's me."

Daniels gripped his head. He'd come down here to say something, and now he couldn't remember what it was. *Marjorie. He wants Marjorie. He'll take her from you.* Daniels gritted his teeth. "I don't like Allison. Something's not right about her." He didn't know why he said it, but it just came out of his mouth.

Rem held his gaze, and then scoffed. "Listen, Daniels. I don't know what the hell is going on, but you're mad at me, you're mad at Lozano, and you're mad at Marjorie. I can't get through to you, and you don't seem to have any desire to talk. And then, when I almost get killed today because you appear to be more interested in following your own advice, you're more concerned about a woman who's about as dangerous as you when you're sleeping in the damn locker room." His raised voice echoed through the room, and Daniels could feel the stares from Shorty and others in the area.

"Rem, just let me explain…" He tried to say something helpful, but no words emerged. He debated telling Rem about the voices, but they bellowed inside his head. *He'll take everything from you. He's not your friend. You can't trust him. You can't trust anyone.* He shut his eyes.

"You've had your chance, partner. If you want to explain whatever the hell is going on here, you know where I am." Rem expelled a harsh breath, and rubbed at the scrape on his forehead. "But now I'd like to go home and rest, because I have a date tonight. Your sorry ass, and your recklessness today, aren't going to keep me from it." He paused and his eyes narrowed. "Unless that's what you want."

He'll take it all from you. Your wife. Your kid. Everything. At the thought of J.P., everything seized up inside Daniels and his anger blazed. "I don't want anything from you. You want to go on your date, so be it. But if she turns out to be a murderer, then too bad. You thought you were on you own today? Just wait till she gets a hold of you."

Rem stilled, his jaw set. "That's it, isn't it? You're jealous. I have what you want, is that it?" His eyes flashed. "You have it all. The fabulous wife, the cute kid, the nice house, the best friend, and what? You see me with a beautiful woman, who might be perfect for me, and you can't stand it." Rem took a step closer. "You've gotten a little too comfortable with me being right where you want me to be. And you can't stand that someone else may have my time, attention and interest."

"That's absurd. You want to hang out with the Grim Reaper, then do it. I won't stop you. I couldn't give a shit what you do with your time."

Rem snickered. "Thanks a lot, best friend. I'm more than happy to take your suggestion and hang out with whomever I please. I already know after today that I'll have to fend for myself anyway." He turned away and yelled. "From here on in, you can take your advice, and your supposed friendship, and shove 'em up your ass." He pushed on the door, flung it open, and walked out, leaving Daniels alone in the lobby.

Breathing hard and livid, Daniels waited for a moment at the empty doorway. When Rem didn't come back, he turned, seeing Shorty and several other concerned faces staring back at him.

Frustrated, he stared back. "What are you looking at?" he shouted, before racing back up the stairs.

CHAPTER FOURTEEN

Remalla took the last sip from his glass of wine, and Allison smiled, stood, and went into the kitchen. "I'll open another bottle."

They'd finished the wine Rem had brought and had enjoyed a delicious meal of spaghetti. "You make a tasty meatball," said Rem.

She picked up another bottle from the counter, and an opener. "I can't take credit. I bought them on the way home and heated them. I'll tell you another secret, I'm not much of a cook." She popped the cork, came over and picked up their glasses.

Rem relaxed in his seat. It had been a nice evening, and the wine had helped him forget about his argument with Daniels that afternoon. After leaving the station, he'd gone home and taken a long, hot shower. He'd tried to nap, but couldn't get the conversation out of his mind. Something was eating at his partner, and if Rem didn't figure out what it was, or Daniels refused to deal with it, then Rem had to wonder if their partnership was at risk.

Figuring he was worrying too much, and that eventually things would sort themselves out, he'd decided to focus on the case and had come to Allison's for dinner. Watching her now, as she refilled the wine glasses in the kitchen, he still wasn't sure what to do. They'd had a nice evening, and he'd told her about his day, leaving out the details about Daniels, but telling her about his encounter in the alley. Voicing his frustrations about his job, and even his partner and captain, he waited to see how she would react, but she'd only offered sweet consolations and advice. By all accounts, she seemed genuine and concerned, and it was getting harder for him to see her as a groupie, much less someone involved in armed robbery.

His emotions jumbled, he debated probing further, but also didn't want to risk completely turning her off. It became obvious then that some part of him wanted to continue seeing her once this assignment was over. That realization bothered him. Was his interest in her jeopardizing the case? Should he take himself out before he got in too deep?

Normally he'd ask his partner for advice, but that wasn't an option. He recalled his words to Daniels. *A beautiful woman who might be perfect for me.* Is that what he thought?

"Penny for your thoughts?"

He looked up to see her standing beside him, holding a glass of wine. "Sorry," he said, taking the glass. "Drifted off for a second."

She brought her glass to his and clinked it. "Here's to no more injuries or near-death experiences."

"I'll drink to that." He took a healthy sip, and so did she.

She took his hand. "How about we have a seat on the couch. Get more comfortable." Guiding him, she walked over and sat on the sofa. She wore a flowy short skirt with a halter top and she crossed her long legs. "Obviously, you're still thinking about work." She sipped from her glass.

Rem sat beside her, and shifted to face her, resting his elbow along the back of the couch cushions. "Is it that obvious?" He took another sip. "This is good."

"I bought it when I got the meatballs. It better be good because I didn't go cheap."

"You chose well."

"I'm glad you like it."

He relaxed against the cushions and debated what to say.

"How's your eye?"

He touched his swollen brow. Thankfully, his eye hadn't taken a direct hit when he'd landed on the pavement. "It's okay." He took another sip. "The wine helps." He told himself to slow down so he could keep a clear head and drive home safely. He checked his watch. "I'll have to stop with this glass, though. I've got work tomorrow."

"Hmm," she said, sipping from her glass. "What's your rush?"

"No rush," he said. "But I need to keep a clear head. Especially around you." He raised his glass and clinked it against hers.

"Don't do me any favors." She smiled and took a drink. "Tell me something," she said, tracing the seam of a pillow. "If your work is so unpleasant, why not do something else?"

Rem considered his response. "I guess because of the investment. I've spent a lot of years getting to where I am and I don't want to start over. Plus, every once in a while, we get the bad guy, and he goes away for a long time, so it's not all bad." He drank some more wine. "Plus, sometimes I wonder..."

"Wonder what?"

Rem swirled his glass. If he was going to go for it, now would be the time. "Whether or not I could use it more to my advantage."

Her eyebrow quirked up. "What do you mean by that?"

He shrugged. "Just that I know of other cops who look the other way and get paid well for it. I always wondered where they got the guts. Now, I think I understand." He waited to see how she would respond.

She held her glass, her eyes wide. "You're that jaded?"

He sighed. "Maybe I am. If the right offer came along at the right time, I'm not sure what I would do." He held her gaze. "Does that bother you?"

Her eyes glittered in the lamp light, and she studied him.

Rem held his breath. "I mean let's be honest. I get the impression your ex may have treaded in some dark waters." He paused. "What if I did, too?"

"My ex?" she asked, putting her glass on the coffee table. "Why bring him up?"

"I'm just curious. What exactly was he into anyway?"

Sitting back, she cocked her head. "Bad things."

"Bad things? That sounds sinister." He smiled and took another sip of wine.

"Things I'd rather not go into, at least not at the moment." She shifted and leaned forward. "But maybe later, I can give you all the gory details." Moving up close, she took his glass from him and placed it with hers, then sliding up next to him, she whispered a heavy breath into his ear. "Since you're so jaded, you might enjoy it." He went still when she brought her face to his, and her eyes darkened. "Feel like having some dessert?"

Her breath tickled his cheek, and he swallowed. "What's on the menu?" He tried to think, but everything felt foggy, and he couldn't catch his breath.

"Take a wild guess, Detective." She touched her nose against his, lingering, and then she brought her lips down over his. Her mouth was hot and wet, and she kissed him with passion and ardor, her tongue meeting his and her teeth nipping his lips.

Rem tried to hold back, but his body was quickly choosing not to. His mind whirled with how to respond. He couldn't deny he was attracted to her, but something about her response to his question about her ex made him itch, although for some reason, he couldn't think straight enough to figure it out. Her lips slanted over his again and again, and he kissed her back, but some nudge of warning told him to slow down and he pulled back. His head briefly swam, but he blinked and everything righted itself. "Hold on," he said. "Are you sure we're not moving too fast here?" He broke out into a cold sweat and fought to control his breathing.

She slid closer, her body pressed against his, and ran a hand through his hair. "In case you haven't noticed, I've been wanting to do this since I met you." She kissed his cheek and peppered kisses down his jaw and his ear, where she nibbled on his lobe. "You turn me on, Detective," she said breathlessly. "And I want you." She brought her hands to his chest and rubbed them over his shirt. "And if you haven't figured it out…" She rose up and straddled him, one knee on either side of his legs, and lowered her face back to his and slid her hands around his neck. "Bad boys turn me on."

Rem moaned as she slanted her lips back over his and rocked her hips against him. He brought his hands to her waist, intending to slow her down and push her back, but a wave of dizziness hit him.

Breaking the kiss, she pushed him back against the couch when he made a feeble attempt to resist. "Just relax," she said. "You're going to feel really good, real soon. Just let me do all the work." Her lips found his again, and she tasted like wine and spaghetti and Rem fought to think. His mind warred with him, telling him to get out while he could, but his limbs would not comply. Her body moved against his and everything reacted, and he wanted to tell her no but his lips were covered by hers. Her hands continued to travel and they found their way under his shirt, where she ran them up his chest. Dragging her lips from his, she trailed them down the hollow of his neck, where she sucked and kissed him, while her hands moved lower.

He managed a trembling breath. "Wait. Hold up. Maybe we should take a minute." Blinking as his vision blurred again, he was surprised he'd spoken clearly. Everything was happening so fast, he could barely keep up.

She ripped at his shirt, and it opened, buttons popping off, and then her lips were on his ribs. "God, you're so sexy," she said, between kisses. Her hands moved to his belt.

"Allison," he said, but it sounded slurred. "I think maybe I've had too much wine." Her lips on his body made it hard to grasp what to do. He wanted her, but then realized it was wrong. All of this was wrong.

He tried to push up, but she pushed him back. "Take it easy. You're all wound up. Just relax and let yourself go." Her lips returned to his, and he couldn't help but kiss her back. She felt so good. Her tongue slid over his, and he moaned. Somehow, his hands came up and cupped her face, then one slid behind her neck, and he increased the intensity of the kiss. In his mind, it was like he was watching a movie. His limbs acted on their own.

She briefly broke away. "There you go. That's what I'm waiting for. I told you you'd feel better." Her hand on his belly slid lower over his jeans, and he arched against her and sucked in a breath. "See? I know you want me." She moved against him. "Tell me you want me." Her mouth covered his again, and Rem's mind went blank. Everything was a haze of heat and movement. Some random thought broke free of the fog, and told him to stop, but he couldn't.

She took one of his hands and moved it to her breast. "Touch me," she said breathlessly, and she kissed him again.

Rem moaned into her mouth, and he couldn't pull his hand away, and her other hand was doing things to him that made him shudder.

"That's it," she said, against his mouth. "Tell me."

He couldn't breathe, and some infinitesimal part of him tried again. "No…I don't…" Then the dizziness returned, and so did her mouth on his lips, and her hand slid beneath his jeans. "Oh, God," he cried out, pressing against the pillows.

She pulled back from the kiss, breathing hard, lips swollen and her eyes smoldering, and she smiled. Something in that smile told him he was screwed, literally and figuratively. Her body was like liquid fire, and he was a moth to the flame. She brought her lips down to his neck, his chest, his belly and then trailed them down to follow her hand.

Rem thought he was losing his mind. He'd never felt so conflicted, but he couldn't stop her. Moaning, and his head spinning, he hated to admit that she was winning this battle, and worse, he was going to let her.

After touching and kissing him intimately for what seemed like an eternity, she paused and looked up at him, then seductively pulled her top off. Her beautiful breasts reflected the light, and Rem wanted to touch them, but held back. "Tell me," she whispered. She ran her hands up his legs and hips, and Rem whimpered, hating his weakness, but desperate for her touch. "Tell me," she said again.

"Allison, please…" His voice faltered when she trailed her fingers over his lower belly, teasing him, and Rem caved. Everything swirled, his body tingling and his muscles heavy; he couldn't fight her anymore. Catching his breath, he met her gaze, even though her face blurred for a second before sharpening again. Something shifted inside him, his mind dulled, and then her insistence didn't matter anymore. "I want you," he whispered in defeat, and she smiled again, and resumed her teasing, only now with her lips instead of her fingers. Allowing her to continue what she'd started, Rem let out a moan of pain and pleasure, leaned back, and resigned himself to his fate.

**

Daniels sat at the bar, nursing another drink, and stared at the other patrons, some dancing, some playing pool, and some sitting at the bar like him, getting drunk. A basketball game was on the TV, and music played from a juke box. Resting his head in his palm, he thought back on his afternoon and his argument with Rem. There was a brief flash of remorse, but then it was quickly replaced with anger. *It's not your fault. It's his. You don't need him. You only need yourself.* Daniels groaned in frustration, and knocked the rest of his drink back. He waved at the bartender, who came over.

"One more," he said, waving at his glass.

"I think you've had enough," said the bartender. "You should go home, Detective."

Daniels scoffed. "I'm fine." He banged the glass on the counter. "Just one, and I'll go." He leaned in. "And how do you know I'm a detective?" His words slurred.

The bartender put his hands on the counter. "Because you and your partner have come in a few times. I'm Sergio. Remember?"

Daniels squinted, and a memory flickered. He and Rem had come in and had drinks on more than a few occasions, and notably one – the night after Jennie's funeral, when they'd closed the place down, and Sergio had called a car service to get them home.

"Sergio," he said, pointing. "That's right. How've you been?"

"Fine." Sergio wiped at the counter with a cloth. "Haven't seen you in here recently. How's your partner?"

Daniels glowered. "I don't want to talk about him."

Sergio stopped wiping. "You two have a falling out?"

That flicker of anger spiked. "I said I don't want to talk about it."

Sergio frowned. "You okay, Detective?"

Daniels cursed, stood and wobbled. "Never mind."

"Can I call someone to take you home? You shouldn't drive."

Daniels fiddled with his wallet, trying to take it out of his pocket. "I didn't drive. I walked."

Sergio watched him fumble. "You walked? Why?"

"Because I wanted to," said Daniels, his voice rising. He recalled his argument with Lozano after the ugly altercation with Rem and leaving the squad room in disgust. He'd driven back to that stupid park, not wanting to go home, and trying not to think about Rem, or Marjorie, or the whole repugnant mess. He didn't have the patience for it. The voices had continued to echo in his mind, telling him how unfair it all was, and how no one appreciated him and his gifts, and he'd fallen asleep in the car again. He'd woken a few hours later to his ringing phone. It had been Marjorie, and he'd lied to her and said that he and Rem would be hanging out that night and to not expect him until later.

She'd hesitated, and he'd barked at her, telling her it was no big deal. She'd shouted back at him in response and then he'd hung up.

The touch of remorse returned, and he stumbled and almost fell into the bar. Finally accessing his wallet, he pulled out some bills and tossed them down. "My car's at the park. I'll walk back and sober up."

"You sure?" asked Sergio. "I can call a service."

Daniels waved him off, the feeling of remorse still flickering. "Sorry I snapped at you. I..." He rubbed his forehead. "I...haven't been my-self."

"You want me to call your partner?"

The remorse vanished. "Hell, no." He shoved off the counter. "He's the last person I want to see." He thought of going somewhere else to drink, but some measure of logic told him he'd had enough. At this point, he'd have to sleep in his car again before he could drive home. "I don't want his or anyone's else's help." He thought of Rem on his date with Allison. "And he doesn't need mine."

Sergio took the money. "You be careful, Detective."

Daniels snorted. "Always am, Sergio. In fact, I'm the only one who's careful, and it's getting old." The voices whispered, and he nodded in agreement, waved and left the bar.

**

Rem cracked an eye open, unsure of the time. Everything was dark, and he didn't recognize where he was. The room was wrong, and the bed had the wrong color sheets. Shifting, he moaned when a slice of pain shot through his skull. He held his head and sat up, trying to think. How much wine had he drunk, and where was he?

Movement beside him made him flinch, and in the darkness, he saw Allison, naked in the bed. Everything came back in a flash. The dinner, she'd filled his glass, the couch, her kiss, her mouth on his body, moving lower, his cries of pleasure. Rem clenched his eyes shut, remembering what had happened next. It was as if his body had not been his own. She'd been the aggressor, and he'd let her take command.

After the couch, they'd had sex on the dining table, tossing the plates, silverware, and everything else, onto the floor. His body had been on auto pilot, and he couldn't stop touching her, and she'd teased him with her mouth, her fingers, and anything she thought would drive him wild, and he'd let her, until he'd taken her wherever they'd found themselves. On the table. On the couch, and on the floor, until she'd pulled him into the bedroom, where she'd ravaged him more, telling him what to do and how to do it, and in his mind, he sensed he was not himself. Something was wrong, but he was powerless to stop it. She had complete control, and he felt helpless, yet at the same time, he wanted her, needed her and begged for her. It was as if she were a puppeteer and he was the puppet that needed the strings to be pulled, and desperate when she denied him.

Holding his head, he watched her sleep, feeling the echoes of despair in his mind, and the guilt. What had he done? He hadn't planned on this. The shock coursed through him as he recalled his overconfidence. He'd believed he'd had control over the situation, but clearly, he had not. He'd failed, and now she'd gotten into his head, and he wasn't sure he could get her out. Did he want her? Had he fallen for her? Had he simply lost all reason, and let her do what she pleased? Was he that guy, that couldn't control his needs and had let himself do what he knew was wrong?

But was it wrong? They were two adults, attracted to each other, who were capable of saying no. He paused, thinking. But had he been capable? A vague recollection of his slurring speech and blurring vision made him wonder. Had she drugged him? Had she coerced him into having sex?

Rem shook his head, and regretted the movement when another crack of pain flared. He tried to remember how much wine he'd had. Certainly not enough to have this kind of hangover, or had he? Everything seemed hazy and his fuzzy mind wouldn't settle.

Slipping out of bed as she slept, Rem moved quietly through the apartment, finding his clothes, and wanting to get out of there as soon as possible. Thinking about their night together, he suddenly felt dirty, but stupid at the same time.

It's nobody's fault but your own, Remalla. You set yourself up for this. You wanted the fire and you got it. The accusatory thoughts came hard and fast, and suddenly he had a vision of Jennie, and his heart sunk. What would she have thought of him? Finding his jeans by the couch, he slid them on, and stopped when a memory hit him from the night. They'd been in bed, Allison straddling him, and Rem had closed his eyes, feeling her move against him, and some distant voice telling him it's not your fault, and he'd opened his eyes, and seen Jennie's face instead of Allison's. His stomach had clenched and his body had frozen, and he'd tried to stop and pull away, but Allison wouldn't let him. She'd leaned over and held him down, her eyes like lasers, and her body moving faster, and then Jennie's face had faded, and she'd become Allison again, and Rem had lost his fight and his will. Nothing made sense. It felt like Allison had taken everything from him - body, mind and soul.

Standing in the living room, feeling lost and confused, he almost crumpled to his knees when a wave of regret and anguish washed over him, but he wouldn't let himself falter. He found and put on his shoes, and after finding his ripped shirt, grabbed it, picked up his wallet and keys, and quickly left the apartment.

CHAPTER FIFTEEN

The sound of the phone bore into his skull, and Rem opened his eyes. Quickly surveying the room, he was relieved to see it was his own. Sluggish and his head still hurting, he reached for his cell and groaned when he saw it was Lozano.

He answered. "'Lo?"

"Where the hell are you? Do you have any idea what time it is?"

Rem tried to wake up and seeing the amount of sunlight coming through his windows, he knew it was later than he'd hoped. He pushed up in the bed. "No, I don't." He figured at this point, honesty was his best defense.

"First your partner. Now you?" yelled Lozano. "What the hell game are you two playing?"

"No games, Cap." Rem squinted at the light. "I got in late last night. Guess I didn't set the alarm. I'm up now. I'll be there in thirty minutes."

"Just get your ass in here." The line went dead.

"Shit." Rem hung up. Images of the night before reared up, but he pushed them back, and he jumped out of bed.

Thirty minutes later, just as he'd promised, he walked into the station, threw his jacket over his chair, and headed straight for the coffee machine. He hadn't had time for a cup before the leaving the house, and his stomach rumbled. Whatever had been in his system seemed to be fading; his head was clearer and his appetite was kicking in.

"Remalla."

Rem turned at the sound of Lozano's voice and saw his captain standing outside his office door. "I'm here, Cap. Getting a quick cup of coffee." He gave silent thanks that someone had made a pot and poured some into a mug. He eyed Daniels' quiet desk, and wondered where he was.

Sipping from the cup, he saw Lozano standing and waiting and figured his captain wanted to talk. He headed over. "Morning. Sorry I'm late."

Lozano gestured toward his door. "Have a seat. I can't wait to hear your excuse."

More images flickered from Rem's night and his stomach clenched, but he pushed past it. He took a seat in Lozano's office, and Lozano closed the door and sat behind his desk.

"You look tired. How much sleep did you get?"

Rem did the calculation in his head, trying not to think of what little sleep he'd had at Allison's. "I'm thinking maybe two, three hours." He rubbed his eyes.

"Did you see Allison Albright last night?"

Rem gripped his mug and blew on the hot brew. "Yeah. How'd you know?"

"Because your partner told me she showed up downstairs, before I kicked his ass out of here yesterday."

Rem sipped his coffee. "He did, huh?"

"The question is, why didn't you tell me?" asked Lozano. "You're on assignment. I need to know where you are, and what's going on, especially now with your partner acting like a damn fool." He paused. "Is that why you were late? Because of your date?"

Rem fidgeted in his seat, and a memory of Allison kissing his chest, and more, made his stomach lurch. He debated what to say. "It went a little later than I thought, and I had a little too much wine."

Lozano waited, his eyebrow raised, and he leaned back in his seat. "Anything else I need to know? Did she talk about her ex? Did you dangle any potential indiscretions in front of her?"

Rem studied his coffee, trying to think how to answer. "I told her I'd be open to possibly turning a blind eye to certain things, and making some extra cash. She told me her ex had done some bad things, and that she might be willing to discuss them with me." He studied his coffee, wondering if he could still drink it.

Lozano leaned in. "Really? It sounds like you're making some headway and she might know something. You think after another date or two, you might get her to talk?"

Rem froze up at the thought of seeing her again, but nodded anyway. "Probably, maybe. It's hard to know." He caught the slightest tremble in his fingers and lowered his cup out of eyeshot of his captain. He cleared his throat. "Listen, Cap…"

Lozano wrote something on a piece of paper. "Yes? What is it?"

Rem fumbled for words. "I…uh…I'm not sure I should see her again."

Lozano put his pen down and paused. "Listen, Remalla. I get it that this assignment isn't easy. I can imagine how difficult it can be to be with a beautiful woman, trying to keep your personal feelings aside while you try to get information from her. It can be a difficult balancing act."

Rem touched his swollen eye and looked away.

"How's your face?"

"It's okay." His face was the least of his problems.

"Just hang in there a little bit longer, okay? If she doesn't crack soon, then maybe we'll talk about bringing her in instead."

Rem nodded and decided not to say anymore. "Sure thing." An image of Allison clutching at him and moving on top of him made him squirm. *God, what is the matter with you, Remalla? It was just sex. You obviously wanted it just as much as she did.*

"I know it's hard without your partner, and he'd talk you through this, but you're going to have to survive without him for the next couple of days."

Glad for the change in subject, Rem took a breath and forced away the flashback. "Why is that?"

Lozano picked up his pen. "Because his attitude bought him two days unpaid leave, and I'm still debating making it a week for his insubordination and dereliction of duty."

Rem sat up. "Cap, I'm sure he's just stressed. It's been a tough week." Despite their argument, Rem couldn't help but back up his partner.

Lozano aimed the pen at him. "You better hope that's all it is, because he owes you and me an apology. I don't care how much stress he's dealing with, when his actions threaten another, especially his own partner, I'll show his ass to the door. This job is hard enough without a fellow officer making it harder."

Rem nodded. "I hear you."

"And since you're partnerless for the next two days, see what you can find out about Tyler Bodin and any known associates. And then you can go talk to him with his attorney present. It's worth a shot to see what he has to say."

"The guy will probably be out on bail by the end of the day, if he isn't already. Something tells me D'Mato takes care of his people, which is why they are loyal to him."

"Regardless, we still need to talk to him. And those bodies with the bite marks. Don't forget to follow up on those. And what about Redstone? You hear anything from him?"

"Not yet."

"Well, call him. See if he's got any information."

"Will do." Rem sipped some coffee, glad that his hands had stopped shaking. "Anything else?"

"I'm sure there is, but let's start there and, hopefully, your partner will get his act together, and get his sorry ass back in that chair."

Rem stood, wondering whether he should call Daniels. Their argument flashed in his mind, and he doubted if Daniels would even take his call. "I hope so." He walked to the door.

Lozano huffed and sighed. "Between Georgios and Daniels, and Titus taking some time off, I'm gonna run out of detectives."

Rem stopped, a flare of insight sparked, and a chill ran up his spine.

"Go on. Get to work," said Lozano, focusing back on his task.

Rem nodded, but his mind was whirling. He left the office and went back to his desk, but his thoughts returned to the night that Georgios had lost it. What had he said? Rem sat in his chair and put his mug on the desk. Georgios had been holding the gun, and had complained about voices, and lack of sleep, and had even blamed Titus for something. What was it? Not getting the credit he deserved? Rem shivered, remembering Georgios turning the gun on himself, Daniels tackling him, and the loud boom of the gun. Closing his eyes, Rem tried to think, and snapped them back open when he had a clear vision of Daniels holding the gun on himself, instead of Georgios.

Something clicked in Rem's brain. Georgios' worn and disheveled look, the despair and anger in his eyes, Titus' confusion as to what was going on and Georgios' anxiety, accusations, and hypersensitivity. Rem sat forward. It almost mirrored Daniels' issues exactly.

He jumped up and ran into Lozano's office. "Cap?"

"What is it?" Lozano looked up from a file.

"It's about Daniels."

"What about him?"

Rem stepped into the office. "What you said about him and Georgios. Don't you think it's a little odd that two detectives would lose it in the same week?"

"What do you mean?"

"Think about it. Georgios was working the same case, and he suddenly falls apart and tries to kill himself. You give the case to us, and now Daniels is going crazy."

Lozano put down his pen. "You think there's something more going on? A connection between the two?"

Rem thought back on Daniels' decline. "Daniels hasn't been sleeping. He's been having nightmares. He's short-tempered and argumentative." He narrowed his eyes. "Has he said anything to you about hearing voices?"

Lozano's brow furrowed. "Nothing directly." He paused. "But when he was in here yesterday, after you left, he kept mumbling to himself. He even told me to shut up, but it was under his breath."

Rem's heart thudded. "Could it be he was actually talking to himself, and not you?" Rem recalled Daniels mumbling when he'd shown up after Rem's jog.

"Maybe. It's possible," said Lozano.

"Shit," said Rem, starting to leave.

Lozano stood and yelled. "Where are you going? You think D'Mato has something to do with this?"

Rem hesitated at the door. "I don't know, but I sure as hell am going to find out." He pointed, anxious to leave. "I want to talk to Titus. You have his address?"

Lozano took a moment and then accessed his computer. He punched a few keys, grabbed some paper and wrote on it. Rem stepped in, and Lozano ripped off the paper and handed it to him. "His phone number and address."

"Thanks," said Rem, running out of the office.

"Let me know what you find out," yelled Lozano.

Rem yelled back an "I will," as he grabbed his jacket and raced out of the squad room.

**

Daniels moaned and held his head, as fingers poked him in the shoulder. He raised an arm and batted them away.

"Gordon." The fingers poked again. "Why aren't you up? You're supposed to be at work."

Marjorie's voice penetrated his haze, and Daniels opened an eye, seeing her sitting on the side of the bed and looking annoyed. "What time did you get in?" she asked. "And why are you in here?"

He eyed the room, and realized he was in the guest room. Recalling coming home the previous night, he had a brief memory of walking in here and collapsing on the bed. He still wore his clothes and shoes, but his head was quiet and he heard no voices. He took a second to appreciate it. "I didn't want to wake you." He rubbed his eyes. "What time is it?"

"You should have been at work an hour ago." She frowned at him. "You and Rem should know better."

His argument with Rem flashed in his head and so did Lozano's suspension. He recalled snapping at Marjorie on the phone. "I took the day off." A flare of annoyance poked at him. Why was she interrogating him? He pushed it back, not wanting to argue.

"I didn't know that. I'd have let you sleep." She stood. "I'm late. I have to get J.P. to daycare and get to work."

His annoyance grew, and he wanted to snap at her again. He'd actually been sleeping, and she'd interrupted it. Taking a deep breath, he held back, and some clarity returned. "I'm sorry I was short with you last night."

She stopped and looked back. "You've been like this all week. What is going on?"

She doesn't care. She's pretending. He held his head in frustration. "Nothing. It's just been a tough case." He tried to think. "Rem and I argued."

"You argued? About what? You two rarely fight." She studied him. "Did you argue at the bar?"

He bit back the urge to yell at her to leave him alone and let him sleep. "No. It doesn't matter. We'll figure it out." His head throbbed and he waited for her to leave.

"I hope so," she said. "You two arguing is like J.P. losing his favorite toy. Nobody's happy until he gets it back."

"Yeah," said Daniels. *She's glad you and Rem argued. Gives her a reason to talk to Rem.*

"I've got to go. You get some rest. I'll call later and check in on you."

He nodded, and squinted at the light coming in through the blinds. "Sure."

She hesitated at the door. "You sure you're okay?"

She doesn't care about you. Never did. Daniels forced himself to ignore the voice. "I'm fine." He laid back down, pulled the covers back up and closed his eyes.

**

Rem pulled up to the coffee shop, parked and got out of his car. Entering, he smelled the coffee and heard the whir of a grinder. Normally, he'd be first in line, but he had no interest. Seeing Titus wave from a nearby table, he walked over and sat across from him. "Hey, Titus. Thanks for meeting me."

Titus drank from a cup. "Not a problem. What happened to your face?"

Rem touched the scrape on his head. "It's nothing. Ran into a tree."

Titus squinted, but then shook his head. "I have to admit, I'm curious. What's so important that you had to meet immediately. Something with the case?"

"I think so. How's Georgios?"

Titus stared at his coffee cup. "Better. He's been getting some sleep and is acting normal again. He's getting out of Green Oaks tomorrow. Then we'll see."

Rem nodded. "How are you?"

Titus' brow raised, as if surprised Rem would ask. He sat back. "I've been better. Seeing your partner almost kill himself messes with your head."

"I bet."

"I'll be back at work next week, though, so I'm hoping that will help."

"What about Georgios?"

Titus chuckled sadly. "Coming back to work? Right now, I'd say it's a long shot. I guess it depends on how he does once he's home, and if he sees the shrink." He tapped his cup on the table. "He's got some work to do." He sighed and looked out the window.

Rem considered his next words. "What if I told you there might be some explanation for his behavior?"

Titus looked back. "What do you mean?"

Rem thought of Daniels. "When did you first notice something was off with Georgios? Was it recent? Did it come out of nowhere?"

Titus rested his elbows on the table. "It was sudden, but not all at once. One day he was fine, and then he got surly. Said he couldn't sleep. It went downhill from there. Told me he had ugly nightmares. A couple of times, he had to take a few naps in the locker room just to get through the day."

Rem held the bridge of his nose. How had he missed this?

"He started getting on me, acting like I had it in for him, and he had issues at home, too. Started yelling at his wife and kids. It scared Phyllis enough to ask him to leave the house. I think that was the night before he lost it in Lozano's office."

"I heard him say something about voices. Did he ever say anything to you about hearing them?"

Titus sighed. "Not directly, no, but he would mumble at himself, and I swear it was if he was talking to someone. I wrote it off as fatigue and stress. God knows I've talked to myself more than once."

"Did this start when you took over the liquor store robberies?"

Titus pursed his lips. "Let me think." He rubbed his head. "Near as I can remember, that's about the time he stopped sleeping. Right after Lozano put us on the case. Probably within two days of it."

Rem nodded, certain that he was on to something.

Titus leaned in. "What's going on? You think someone is messing with Georgios' head?"

"I'd almost guarantee it."

"How do you know that?"

Rem shifted in his seat. "Because guess who just got himself two days suspension without pay because he disregarded an order and got in Lozano's face?"

Titus' face fell, and then his eyes widened. "Daniels?"

"He's basically Georgios' twin. Lack of sleep. Mood swings. He's angry at everybody, including me. He went against Cap's orders yesterday and all hell broke loose."

"Shit," said Titus.

"I agree."

"But how do we prove it?" asked Titus. "What's causing it? How do you get inside someone's head like that enough to cause a complete personality change in such a short period of time?"

"I don't know, but I plan to find out. You planning on seeing Georgios any time soon?"

Titus nodded. "Yeah. This afternoon."

"If his head's clearer and he's feeling better, then that likely means whatever they've been doing to him or giving him has stopped, at least for now. He might be able to tell you something. See what you can find out. There had to have been some change in routine, or some sort of trigger that started all of this. Maybe he'll remember something."

"What are you going to do? Talk to Daniels?"

Rem smirked. "Unlikely. He's right in the middle of it. We argued yesterday. I doubt he'll talk to me."

"Be careful," said Titus. "Whenever I tried to talk to Georgios, it only made him madder."

"I'm gettin' that. I screwed up. I should have known something was wrong."

"How the hell were you supposed to know?" asked Titus. "Hell. My partner's in a psychiatric ward on suicide watch. I didn't know either."

Rem watched a dad at a table wipe his toddler's face and thought of J.P. "It seems like whatever this is starts with sleep." He hoped Daniels was okay. He'd left him a message on the way to the coffee shop, but his partner hadn't called back. "What if it's something at home? Maybe drugs in their coffee or a common food?"

"Then why doesn't the rest of the family have an issue?"

Rem's head throbbed as his worry increased, and he rubbed his neck. His body still felt heavy after his night with Allison and lack of sleep. "I don't know." He thought of Georgios' wife. "But if it is starting at home, maybe his wife knows something. You have her number?"

"Phyllis? Sure." He pulled out his phone and gave Rem the number.

"Do me a favor," said Rem, standing. "Contact her and tell her I'd like to meet with her. I'll give her a call but I don't want her thinking I'm crazy when I ask her weird questions about her husband. The woman's probably stressed enough as it is."

"I'll call her now."

"You talk to Georgios and I'll talk to her, and hopefully, something will come to light."

Titus held up a finger as he dialed and waited. Phyllis must have answered because Titus started talking.

Rem listened and stifled a yawn. He debated getting a coffee and wished he had some aspirin.

Titus hung up.

"Well?" asked Rem.

Titus stood. "She said to come right over. Here's the address." Rem pulled out his phone and added it. "I'm going to see Georgios now," said Titus. He eyed Rem wearily. "Let's hope we find our smoking gun soon, before we both lose a partner."

Rem smacked Titus on the arm. "Thanks, Titus. I owe you." He turned to leave.

"You find out what the hell is going on here, and we're even," said Titus, as Rem waved and left.

**

Rem pulled up to the small two-story brick house and parked in the driveway. Eyeing the neighborhood, he got out and walked up to the front door. It opened before he could knock, and saw a short woman with shoulder-length brown hair, round brown eyes with glasses, and wearing jeans and a blouse.

"Detective Remalla?"

He nodded and showed her his badge. "Phyllis Georgios?"

She widened the door. "Please. Come in."

Rem entered the house. It was clean and tidy, save for laundry on the couch and a bike leaning against a wall. "Thank you for talking to me on such short notice."

"I hear you want to discuss my husband?"

"I do. I have some questions about his...condition."

She eyed him, her eyes wary. "I suppose that's one way of putting it. Come into the kitchen. I put some coffee on when I knew you were coming. I know how detectives like their coffee."

"Bless you, Mrs. Georgios. I could use it."

"Phyllis, please. If we're going to talk about my husband's sanity, or lack thereof. You should use my first name."

He smiled. "Okay." He followed her into the kitchen and sat at the breakfast table. "I hope I didn't come at a bad time."

"Bad time?" She pulled down a mug and filled it from the full pot on the brewer. "It's been a bad time since Paul started getting sick." She brought the mug over and set it, along with a spoon, in front of Rem. "I'd say at this point, anything you have to say couldn't make it much worse." She pointed. "There's sugar and cream on the table."

"Thank you." He helped himself to some cream and a solid helping of sugar.

She gestured toward him. "Looks like you had a bit of a scuffle."

"Oh," he touched his eye. "It's nothing. Fell off a skateboard."

She made a dubious face, walked back into the kitchen, picked up a plate, and brought it over. "I have some cookies, too. I know it won't stick to your bones, but it's all I have on short notice. Would you like some?"

Rem sighed. "If you weren't married, I might be tempted to propose." He grabbed a cookie and winced when his headache flared. "I don't suppose I could trouble you for some aspirin?"

She offered a knowing smile. "We have it on auto-ship, right along with the coffee."

"Sounds like Georgios and I have more in common than I thought."

She walked to a cabinet and pulled out a bottle. "I think we met once, at the policemen's picnic. It was maybe two or three years ago. I don't know if you remember." She doled out two pills and brought them over.

"It's possible," said Rem, taking the pills. "You are a little familiar."

"You were with a pretty lady. I think her name was Jennie, if I recall. It's why I remember. She was very sweet. You two were an attractive couple."

Rem paused before popping the pills. "Thank you."

"I heard about what happened to her. I'm very sorry."

Rem took the pills and swallowed them with a sip of his coffee. Jennie's face flashed in his mind, and then Allison's took its place. He grimaced. "I appreciate that."

She put the pill bottle away and returned to sit beside him. "How can I help you?"

Rem took a bite of his cookie, and Phyllis handed him a napkin. He halfway felt like he was sitting at home with his mom, who was equally as good at giving him things before he could ask for them. "I'd like to ask about your husband. I know what happened at work, but I was wondering if you would mind telling me what happened at home?"

Her face fell, and she played with her wedding ring. "I wish I knew, or could explain it. My kind, caring husband turned into Jekyll and Hyde. I couldn't figure it out."

Rem tried to wrap his head around the kind and caring side of Georgios, but failed. "How did it start?"

She swallowed. "I remember he started waking up in a bad mood. Cranky and mean. He'd snap at me and the kids. Then he'd apologize just as fast. Tell us he hadn't slept well. Then it just progressed from there. I couldn't understand it because I slept next to him, and he seemed to be sleeping fine, but then the nightmares started, and he'd flail around, and I'd have to wake him. He'd have no recall once awake, though, or at least that's what he told me." She sighed heavily and looked away.

"Take your time," said Rem, taking another bite of cookie and a solid gulp of the needed caffeine, and put his cup down. "What happened after that?"

"It just got worse. He'd get angry over nothing. And if I tried to figure out what was going on, he'd get furious." She shook her head. "He even went so far as..."

Rem waited. "As what?"

Her eyes shimmered. "He accused me of sleeping with Adam, his partner." She picked up a napkin and dabbed her eyes. "It was horrible, and I was horrified. We got in a terrible fight, and he screamed at me and the kids, who'd done nothing wrong. I could have lived with that, but..."

"But what?"

She gripped the napkin. "It was the look in his eyes that truly terrified me. I saw something there I'd never seen before."

Rem held his breath, and his coffee. "What was that?"

She sniffed. "Hatred. Pure hatred. I think...I think...that maybe in that moment, he considered hurting us." Her eyes filled. "That's when I told him to leave." She held the napkin against her mouth. "It was awful."

Rem debated what to say. Could Daniels go that far with Marjorie?

Phyllis lowered the napkin, and continued. "But in a split second, he blinked, and it was like he was himself again. He couldn't apologize enough, but I'd seen too much. If that look returned, and I knew it would, I couldn't be sure he would be able to stop himself. He had to go." She shook her head. "I think he knew I was right. He understood something was wrong, but was powerless to stop it, and worse, whatever had a hold of him prevented him from asking for help."

Rem set his mug down. "What do you think had a hold of him?"

Her gaze met his, and her eyes didn't waver. "Evil, Detective. Pure evil."

CHAPTER SIXTEEN

Daniels sauntered down the stairs, tired and annoyed. He'd fallen asleep again after Marjorie had left, but he'd been plagued with horrible nightmares where he'd fought with Lozano and Rem after they'd conspired behind his back, and Marjorie had joined them, and then he'd caught her cheating on him with Rem, and they'd laughed. A knife had appeared in his hand, and he'd swung it, and the sound of her screams had woken him. Opening his eyes in a sheen of sweat and his head aching, he'd thrown off the covers and tried to shake off the dream. Then he'd showered, put on some clothes, and gone downstairs.

With Marjorie at work, and J.P. at daycare, the house was quiet. Daniels stopped at the kitchen table, and rubbed the side of his head. Even though his headache was still there, he had a moment of peace with no voices, and remembered Marjorie's worried face that morning. Angry at himself for his behavior toward his wife and best friend, he swore he would do better, and would handle his emotions. Whatever it was that was tormenting him, he would figure it out.

They're lying to you. They're all lying to you. You should be angry. The soft whisper returned, as it did each morning not long after he woke. He dug his fingers into his temples, intent on drowning them out. "I'm not listening to you," he said out loud.

He opened the fridge and stared at it, but none of the heathy food appealed to him. He wanted something sweet, like a donut or a soda, but Marjorie never bought sweets. His anger percolated. *She doesn't know what you need or want. Only you can take care of yourself.* "Oh, shut up," he yelled, slamming the refrigerator door closed.

He pulled his cell out of his pocket and checked the time. It was almost noon, and he had a voicemail from Rem. He considered running out and getting some fast food, and debated whether to listen to Rem's message, recalling their angry words the previous day.

Who cares what he has to say? He can't be trusted. He's gone. Marjorie's gone. They're together. Right now.

The kernel of disgust in his belly blossomed, and his chest constricted at the thought of Marjorie cheating on him. He recalled his dream, and curled his hands into his fists. Were they together? Was this Rem's plan? To get Lozano to suspend him, so that he could get Daniels out of the way and spend time with his wife?

He punched at the wall, knowing in some part of his brain that it didn't make sense. His wife and best friend wouldn't betray him.

You know it's true. You know it's true. You know it's true. The voice insisted and the nugget of anger exploded into rage, and he swiped at a bowl of apples on the counter. The bowl fell and shattered and apples rolled across the floor. Breathing hard, and his mind whirling with images of Rem and Marjorie together, he eyed the knives in the block on the kitchen counter.

Just then, he heard the key in the lock, and Marjorie opened the back door. Seeing him, she smiled. "Hi, babe. How are you feeling?" She closed the door behind her. "I thought I'd come home for lunch and check in on you." Stopping near a fallen apple, she eyed the mess. "What happened?"

Daniels turned, his rage growing, and glared at her.

**

Rem expelled a deep breath, understanding Phyllis' fear. "Do you honestly think he would have hurt you?"

She wrung her hands. "I have no doubt in my mind. Whatever state he was in, kept him from seeing me. It was like he was staring at a piece of wood, and he wanted to smash it into pieces."

Rem swallowed, his throat suddenly dry, and his heart pounding. "Do you have any idea where this may have come from? Was he having any personal issues? Any family history of mental problems?"

"Nothing outside the ordinary, and his family's weird, but not that weird."

He shifted toward her. "Did something in his routine change, other than his personality? Did he start eating or drinking something different? Did someone show up that you didn't know? Did he get anything in the mail?"

She clenched her eyes, frustrated. "No. I don't recall anything like that. He was—" She stopped, her eyes opened, and she held the edge of the table. "Wait a minute…"

Rem straightened. "What is it? Do you remember something?"

"I…he…got something." She stood and ran out of the room.

"Phyllis?" he asked, wondering if he should follow her. He heard her from the other room. "I hated it, and wanted to get rid of it. But he was so protective of it."

Rem stood. "What?" He waited, curious.

She ran in. "This…this thing. I don't even like to hold it."

Rem dropped his jaw, and a shudder ran through him. Phyllis held a small stone statue, with a round head and eyes and an open mouth. It was the same statue Daniels had supposedly received from his cousin. "Where did he get that?"

"I don't know. It came in the mail. Paul liked it and put it on a shelf in the living room. He wouldn't let me near it. Didn't even like when I dusted it." She set it on the table.

Rem stared at it in disbelief. Could this be the cause of Georgios' and Daniels' decline in such a short period of time? A cold chill ran through him just looking at it. "When did he get this?"

"Right before he started going nuts."

Rem didn't even like looking at the statue. His mind racing, he made a few decisions. "I don't know how or why, but I think you may be on to something. You mind if I take it?"

She chuckled. "If I weren't married, I'd be tempted to propose. Please do."

Rem was unsure if he wanted to touch it, although he'd already touched the one sent to Daniels and figured if he was cursed, he would have known by now.

Phyllis left the room. "Hold on." She came back with a shoe box. "Here. Put it in this."

Relief coursed through him. "Thanks." He took the box and used his napkin to quickly pick up the statue and place it inside. Just holding it made his skin prickle and his hair raise. He closed the box and picked it up.

"You think that's what's causing all of this?" she asked. "Could that be possible?"

He wasn't sure what to say. "I don't know, Phyllis. You've been living with it. What do you think?" He thought of D'Mato and his belief in the paranormal. Is that what they were dealing with? Could D'Mato have that kind of power?

Her eyes widened. "All of this started after he put that statue on the shelf. It's not good, whatever it is. I can feel it." She stood straight. "I want my husband back. He comes home tomorrow, and I don't want that thing here when he returns."

Rem tucked the box under his arm. "Then consider it gone."

"And my husband won't know a thing about it?" she asked with a little worry.

"I was never here," said Rem. "But you'll have to tell him something when he sees it's missing."

"You let me worry about that." Her shoulders relaxed. "What are you going to do with it?"

Rem picked up his coffee and drained it. "As you said, let me worry about that. The less you know, the better." He set his cup down. "Thanks for the coffee."

"You be careful, Detective. Something tells me you're dealing with forces here better left alone."

Rem nodded and had to assume she was right, but Daniels' life was at stake. "Maybe so, but these forces have messed with your husband, and now my best friend. Because of that, they're about to deal with something they should have left alone." He secured his hold on the box. "When I find out who's responsible, they're gonna wish they'd stuck to basket weaving."

She smiled softly. "I can see it in your eyes. Whatever evil this is, it won't survive in the wake of love. I know that much." She moved closer and touched his elbow. "Take care, Detective."

Rem expelled a breath, hoping he knew what he was doing. He had an idea though, and that was to trust his gut. "I will."

She reached for the plate on the table. "Have a cookie for the road. I think you might need it."

He couldn't help but smile and took a cookie. "Thanks." He turned, headed through the house, and she opened the front door for him. "I'll be in touch," he said.

"Actually, no," she said. "Unless you have something I need to know, I'm going to be fine without knowing another thing about…that." She gestured toward the box. "I will anticipate clear roads ahead for me and my husband." She paused. "Maybe I'll see you at the next picnic, though. Let's leave it at that."

He understood. "Then you have a nice day." He popped the cookie in his mouth.

"I'll say a prayer that you do, too, Detective."

"I appreciate that." Chewing his cookie and holding the box, he left.

CHAPTER SEVENTEEN

Rem took the stairs two at a time, holding the shoebox beneath his arm, and reached the door to SCOPE. It was locked and he pounded on it. "Redstone." He banged on it again. "Redstone. Answer the door." Rem had called SCOPE on his way over, but it had gone to voicemail. He needed answers fast and Redstone was his best and only source. He prayed the man was here.

He pounded again. "Redstone. It's Detective Remalla. We need to talk." He raised his arm, prepared to hit the door again, when the locks turned and it opened. A woman stared back at him, looking irritated. She was in her mid-to-late twenties, petite, with pale skin, stubby bangs, and straight reddish-brown, purple-streaked hair that reached her shoulders. She wore all black, her eyes were ringed with black liner and she had a piercing in the left side of her nose. She put a hand on the frame. "What the hell do you want? You need to make an appointment."

Rem yanked out his badge, and held it out, trying not to drop the box. "The time for appointments has passed, lady. I need to talk to Redstone. It's urgent."

Her face furrowed and she opened her mouth, when Rem heard another voice. "Mikey. It's okay. Let him in." Redstone appeared behind her.

Rem pushed on the door and entered the small front office. "Sorry to interrupt, but we need to talk. Now."

Redstone crossed his arms. Wearing a fitted blue t-shirt, and a pair of khakis with socks on his feet, he looked decidedly less put together than he had the previous day. The shirt emphasized his muscular chest, arms and shoulders, and despite his casual attire, he held an air of confidence about him which Rem supposed came with being a former Texas Ranger.

"Mason, who is this guy?" asked the woman. "You made your rules for a reason. How the hell do you know he can be trusted?"

"I'm a cop, Mikey," said Rem, using the name he'd heard Redstone use.

"Good for you," said Mikey. "Having a badge doesn't make you Superman." She eyed Redstone. "If nothing else, Mason, you should be even more careful."

Redstone raised a hand. "It's okay, Mikey. Not everyone is a bad guy."

"I hope you're right." Looking Rem over, she shut the door. "Something about him is off, though. He feels weird." Rubbing her arms, she shivered. "Like he took a bath in fetid water." Mikey stepped back. "You sure about this?"

Redstone stood quiet, and Rem put his badge away and held out the box. "I've got something you need to see."

Redstone eyed what Rem held, his face tense. "It's not him you're feeling, it's whatever's in the box."

Mikey stepped further back. "It's bad. I don't like it."

Rem erupted. "This thing is killing my partner. I don't care if you don't like it. I need your help."

Redstone hesitated and tipped his head. "Bring it back." He walked to the door that led to the other room, and Rem followed, with Mikey keeping her distance behind him. They entered the area with the empty shelves, couch, and desk. Rem spied a pillow and blanket on the couch. "Put it here." Redstone picked up his computer and set it on the floor and moved anything else on the desk to the side.

Rem set the box down and opened it. The statue rolled slightly and slowed to a stop with the face toward them, as if staring.

Mikey kept a wide berth. "Hell. What is that thing?"

Redstone stared at it and took a step closer. "Did you touch this, Detective?"

Impatient, Rem ran a hand through his hair. "I used a napkin to put it in the box. I touched the other one, though."

Redstone froze. "Other one?"

"There's two?" asked Mikey.

Rem pointed. "This statue was sent to a cop I work with, who almost killed himself a week later. Now my partner, Detective Daniels, has one just like it, sitting beside his wedding photos at home, and he's currently losing his marbles, and I'd like to prevent him from losing any more."

Redstone eyed the statue. "Your partner has one of these?" He walked to his desk, opened a drawer and pulled out oven mitts.

"What the hell are those?" asked Rem.

"They come in handy in my line of work." Redstone leaned over the box and picked up the statue.

"Careful, Mason," said Mikey. "That thing has some bad mojo on it."

Redstone held it up and studied it. "Fascinating."

Rem wanted to scream. "I'm glad you're so taken with it. Maybe you can buy it dinner later, but right now, I need to know what the hell it is. Why is this stupid thing wreaking havoc on the people it's sent to?"

Redstone turned the statue, checking all around it. Then he set it on the desk, squatted and stared at it. "I've heard of this before, but never actually witnessed it." He took the mitts off and tossed them on the floor.

"Mason, you're too close," said Mikey.

Redstone went still. "I think we're okay. It's not targeted at us."

"Doesn't mean it's not dangerous," said Mikey.

Rem almost audibly moaned. "What the hell is it?"

Redstone rubbed his chin, his eyes narrowed, then he reached out and touched it.

"Mason, don't…" said Mikey.

Redstone ignored her and closed his eyes. Rem waited, hoping Redstone knew what he was doing. If he turned out to be some kooky witch doctor who started speaking in tongues, he didn't know what he would do.

The room was quiet along with Redstone. Rem swallowed, trying his best to stay calm, but he knew his partner was out there devolving while Redstone played with this stupid stone.

"Mason," whispered Mikey, after several seconds passed with no reaction from Redstone.

Rem was prepared to say something a little louder and less productive, when Redstone sucked in a breath, opened his eyes, and pulled his hand away. Shaking his fingers out, and looking pale, he stood.

"What is it?" asked Rem.

"You okay? What did you see?" asked Mikey.

Redstone took a deep breath. "My suspicions are confirmed. It's some sort of curse, probably with a spell to create madness. Whoever did it, knew what they were doing. It's potent stuff." He shook his head as if to clear it and stepped back. "You say your partner has one of these in his house?"

Rem nodded. "Yes. I was there when he got it in the mail. He loved it and put it on a shelf, and he's slowly been losing his mind ever since."

"I can imagine," said Redstone. "It's designed to attract his interest, and when it's in the home, it wreaks havoc on the mind. What are his symptoms?" he asked Rem.

Rem ran through all of Daniels issues.

"Voices? He's hearing voices?" asked Redstone.

"I think so," said Rem.

"Then it's fairly progressed, but there's still time." His voice dropped. "Has he hurt anyone?"

Rem's heart dropped. "Hurt anyone? No. He'd never do that."

"Don't be too sure. I'm sure your partner has a good heart and well-intentioned belief system. His love for his family and friends will help him and slow the process, but it's not foolproof. At some point, if he doesn't hurt them, he'll hurt himself."

Rem thought of Georgios and shut his eyes, praying he still had time. He expelled a shaky breath. "What do I do? I'm not going to sit back and let a stupid statue take my partner's mind, and possibly his life."

Redstone continued to study the statue. "Who sent it to him?"

"Had to be D'Mato. He received it right after we were assigned the case."

Redstone stiffened, and Mikey swiveled toward Rem. "What?" she said. "You mean Victor D'Mato?"

"The one and the same," said Rem.

She aimed a glare at Redstone. "Did you know about this? About Victor?"

That caught Rem's interest. "You must be acquainted. I hear he's quite the charmer."

Redstone deflated. "Remalla and his partner were here a few days ago to talk about a case involving Victor."

Her face darkened. "And you didn't tell me?"

"There was nothing to tell, Mikey."

Mikey's jaw fell. "Nothing to tell? That son-of-a-bitch is out there, and obviously doing something to attract the interest of the cops, and you don't think that's pertinent?"

"Can you two deal with your personal issues later?" asked Rem. "Let's focus on the damn statue. How do I get my partner back?"

Mikey huffed and shook her head, and Redstone regarded Rem. "It won't be easy, but it can be done." He put his hands on his hips and turned. "Let me think."

"Well, think fast, because time is short."

Mikey approached the statue. "How the hell did Victor get the ability to do this?"

"He likely had help," said Redstone. "This type of energy is focused and deliberate. One of his followers probably has knowledge of hexes and spells. If they know what they're doing, combined with Victor's maniacal will, they would be a powerful ally."

Mikey crossed her arms. "I can't believe this."

"You and me, both," said Rem. "Redstone...?" He tossed out a hand, waiting.

Redstone paused and then nodded, his face determined. "The first thing we need to do is get it out of his house."

"I can do that," said Rem.

"It may not be as easy as you think," said Redstone. "He'll be protective of it. If he's home at the time, he's not going to let you take it."

Rem considered that. "I'll figure it out. I'll find a way to get it." He thought of Marjorie. "Maybe his wife can help."

"That's another thing. Until you can get rid of it, cleanse the house, and your partner, it's better if his loved ones get out of harm's way. He'll be unstable and angry, and there's no point in bringing him back from the brink if he has to live with the guilt that he's hurt someone he loves. You have training and know how to handle him. I'm sure his wife loves him, too, but for her own protection, she should go somewhere safe."

Rem shook his head in disbelief. "Okay. I can make sure she gets out of the house."

"Good. The sooner, the better."

"What do I do with the statue once I have it?" asked Rem.

"Bring it here. I'll know what to do with it. I have some experience dealing with evil artifacts." He flicked his eyes toward the back of the room.

Rem followed his gaze and saw the strange box sitting on the shelf.

"Mason, that was different," said Mikey.

Redstone shrugged. "Different in some ways, not so much in others. Evil is evil."

"That thing was...is...haunted," said Mikey, gesturing toward the box. "You knew what to expect. This thing..." she waved at the statue. "...is some sort of curse, probably involving black magic. You don't have experience with that."

"Maybe not," said Redstone. "But I do have access to information that most don't."

"Please don't tell me you're going to have to read a bunch of books," said Rem.

"I'm not talking about books, Detective." Redstone quirked his brow. "Don't forget who I am, and what I can do."

Rem groaned, finding it hard to believe he was having this conversation. "Well, then, talk to whatever dead person you need to, but hurry."

Redstone nodded and paused again, staring off. After a few seconds, his focus returned. "Once you get the statue out of the house, you're going to have to smudge the whole home."

"Smudge?" asked Rem.

"Yes. With sage," said Redstone. "I'll explain later. Then clean everything your partner has touched. The house. His clothes. His sheets. The plates, cups, counters, floors, basically a thorough cleaning. Hire someone if you have to."

Rem's heart thumped. "Okay. What about Daniels?"

"That will be the true test," said Redstone. He twisted the end of his mustache, deep in thought.

"I'll do whatever it takes," said Rem.

"What about the rite of exorcism?" asked Mikey.

"Oh, shit," said Rem, sighing deeply.

"No. He doesn't need a priest. This is not a haunting. D'Mato doesn't deal in devils and demons. This is different."

"Then what?" asked Rem, with a small amount of relief.

Redstone eyed the statue. "The first and best thing is getting rid of the object, but the longer he's been exposed to it, the trickier it becomes to pull him out of his mental pit. He won't trust you, and he'll resist your help. But, if you can get him to see reason, if you can pull out the evil and bring to light the goodness in him, he'll hopefully do the rest, and he'll find his way back." He stepped away and walked toward the back of the room. "You'll need help, though."

"Where are you going?" asked Rem.

Mikey watched Redstone. "Give him a sec. I think I know what he's getting."

Redstone disappeared behind a door in the room that Rem had not noticed on his first visit. After a few seconds, he returned, holding a box. He brought it over, set it on the table beside the couch, and opened it. Inside was what looked like several dried skinny twigs with leaves bound together, a candle, two small bags – one that looked like a bag of sand and one a bag of salt, matches and a necklace. He pulled out the twigs. "This is sage. Light the candle, and let it burn in the house. Light the sage with the candle. It will smolder and smoke. Take it through the entire house once the statue is removed and wave the smoke throughout, including all over your partner's things. That's what smudging is. Do it to yourself too, and once you find your partner, smudge him also. Use the sand to put out the sage."

"You're serious?" asked Rem.

"I couldn't be more serious. If this were my family, I'd do exactly what I'm telling you to do."

Rem nodded. "What else?"

Redstone picked up the necklace. "This is an amulet. It's been blessed and is highly protective. You need to get him to put it on and keep it on, until he gets past the worst of it and feels safe."

Rem studied the necklace. It was hammered metal in a square shape with a swirling design in the middle of it. "Fine. Okay. What's the other bag?"

Redstone raised it. "Salt, plus a few other minerals and herbs. Once he's through it, have him bathe in it. Use the whole bag."

Rem swallowed, imagining how he was going to explain all of this to his partner. "If you say so."

Redstone returned the bag to the box and closed it. "I say so."

Rem's phone buzzed, and he grabbed for it, hopeful it was Daniels, but it was a text from Allison, and his stomach clenched.

I missed you this morning, handsome. Call me. It was followed by a blushing smiley face emoji.

His fingers trembling, he put the phone away.

"Not your partner?" asked Mikey.

"No," said Rem. He focused back on the box. "After I do all of this, Daniels will be Daniels again?"

"If you're able to reach him, and complete all of the other steps, yes. He should be fine," said Redstone.

"How will I know?" asked Rem. "Will there be a sign, or an indication that I've succeeded?"

Redstone nodded. "Oh, you'll know. He'll either get worse – his rage will grow and he'll fight every instinct he has to push past the darkness, or he'll acknowledge the evil presence, confront it, and force it out. The sage and necklace will help, plus having someone there to guide him. If he does that, then you'll know you've won."

"How long will it take?"

Redstone picked up the box. "I don't know, Detective. It takes as long as it takes. Could be an hour, twenty-four or longer. Depends on how stubborn he is."

Rem took the box. "Great. Then count on it being at least a week."

"Hang in there," said Redstone. "If his ties with you and his family are as strong as you believe, he may snap out of it faster than you think. Use that. It will be his weakness, so to speak."

Rem sighed. Allison's text flitted through his head, and he told himself he'd deal with it later. Trying to think, he figured his next step was to find his partner.

"What about the man who received this one?" asked Mikey, pointing at the statue. "How is he?"

Rem moaned. Shit. He had to think of Georgios, too. "He's been in a psychiatric unit for the week. He goes home tomorrow."

"If he's been away from the statue for several days, and the item is no longer in his home, then that will help. But his home should be smudged, as well," said Redstone. "If he's made it this far, then that might be all he needs, so long as the object stays gone. I could get you an amulet and salt for him, too."

Rem figured he'd have to be getting in touch with Phyllis sooner than she'd hoped. "I can talk to his wife, but right now, I need to find Daniels."

"I agree. He's your bigger concern," said Redstone.

Mikey chuckled, her eyes wide. "Are you seriously expecting him to do all this by himself, Mason? He's supposed to find the statue, remove it, clean and smudge the house, do the laundry, find his partner, smudge him, pull him off the ledge, and somehow have him wear the necklace, oh and move the family at the same time?" She eyed Rem. "Maybe you do think he's Superman."

Rem wanted to curl up on the couch. The aspirin he'd taken had barely thwarted his headache, and his fatigue and emotional turmoil from the previous night were catching up. His muscles ached and his eyelids were heavy. "I'll manage." He massaged his neck. "I don't have a choice."

His phone rang and he tensed, worried it was Allison. He grabbed his phone and tensed for a different reason. It was Marjorie.

He answered. "Marjorie?"

"Rem?" Her voice was high and shaky. "I...I need your help. It's Gordon. I...I...don't know what to do. Oh, God." She was crying and could barely keep it together.

His heart leapt into his throat. Was he too late? "What happened?" he asked. "Are you and J.P. okay?" He said a silent prayer that Daniels hadn't hurt her. "Where's Daniels?"

Breathless, she made a stuttered sob. "I don't know. He left." Her voice caught and he heard her gulp in air. "I came home for lunch, and he was…was so angry. I tried to talk to him, but he wouldn't listen. He said horrible things. He grabbed me and I screamed…" Another sob erupted. "I'm so scared. I don't know what to do." She was so upset that Rem could barely understand her.

"Stay there. I'm coming over. Lock the doors."

"He has a key, Rem." Her raised voice broke. "Oh, God. What is happening?"

"Where's J.P.?"

"He's at daycare."

Rem let out a relieved breath, grateful that J.P. had not been home. "Okay. Stay calm." He tried to soothe her. "He's not going to hurt you. I promise." He couldn't bring himself to believe that Daniels would ever hurt Marjorie or J.P., no matter what influence he was under. "I think I may be able to get through to him, but we're going to have to do a few things first." He made eye contact with Redstone, who looked as worried as Rem felt.

"What are you talking about?" She sobbed again. "What's wrong with him?"

"I'll explain more when I get there. I'm coming right now. Keep an eye out, and call me if Daniels comes back."

"O…O…Okay. Hurry." Her voice quaked. "Please."

"I'm coming. Right now. Try not to worry." He heard her take a shuddered breath. "I'm going to hang up, but I'll be there soon."

"Tell her to start cleaning the house and his laundry. If he's out of the home, then take advantage. It will keep her busy. Help with the fear," said Redstone.

Rem relayed the message to Marjorie, and to her credit, she accepted what he said, didn't question it, and he hung up. "I have to go. Daniels is going downhill fast." Holding the box with the items Redstone had given him, he headed for the door.

"Wait a minute," said Mikey. "You're not going alone." She followed him. "I'm coming with you."

"What?" asked Rem.

"What?" asked Redstone.

Mikey whirled on Redstone. "Are you seriously going to let him do this by himself? Isn't this what you do? Help people in exactly this position?"

Redstone looked flummoxed, but Rem didn't have time to wait. "If you want to help, Mikey, I'll take it. But we have to go. Now."

Mikey held her ground. "Well, big brother? Get your ass in gear. How often do you get to experience something like this?"

Redstone's face turned from uncertainty to determination. "Let me get my shoes. You two go. Send me the address, Mikey. I'll be right behind you."

CHAPTER EIGHTEEN

Rem pulled into the driveway of Daniels' home, and had the car door open before coming to a complete stop. Mikey followed, holding the box Redstone had given Rem.

Marjorie threw the door open before they could knock. "Rem," she said. Her eyes were puffy and red, and she started crying the moment she saw him.

Rem pulled her close, and she buried her head in his neck. "It's okay," he said. "He'll be okay. We'll figure it out."

She pulled back and sniffed. "I haven't heard from him. He won't answer the phone." Dabbing her eyes with a rumpled tissue, she looked around him at Mikey. "What's going on, Rem?"

Holding her shoulders, he guided her to a kitchen chair and sat her in it. "I'll do my best to explain, but right now, I need to find him. Do you have any idea where he went?"

Holding the tissue to her mouth, she shook her head. "No. I don't." She gripped Rem's wrist. "What's wrong with him? And who is she?" She pointed at Mikey, who had laid the box on the kitchen counter and was opening it.

Mikey pulled out the items in the box and put them on the counter. "My name's Mikey Redstone, Mrs. Daniels. I'm here to help. I'm going to light this candle and then help you finish cleaning the house. My brother, Mason, is right behind us. He'll be helping out with the smudging and the removal."

Marjorie eye's widened. "Smudging? Removal?"

Rem pulled up a chair and sat beside her. "You have to trust me, okay? If we want to get Daniels back, then let her do her work."

Marjorie watched as Mikey lighted the candle. "Where are your cleaning products?" asked Mikey, putting the matches down.

Marjorie's brow furrowed.

"Mrs. Daniels." Mikey came close and squatted in front of Marjorie. "I know a lot is happening right now, but he's right." She gestured at Rem. "You have to trust us. We know what we're doing." She paused. "Did you start cleaning already? Have you started his laundry?"

Marjorie sniffed and dabbed at her nose. "I cleaned our bedroom, and threw a load of his clothes in the machine."

"Good," said Mikey. She put her hand on the edge of the table. "I'll start on the kitchen, but I'll need something to clean with."

"Marjorie," said Rem. "You with us?"

Marjorie stared and then closed her eyes and shook her head. "Yes. Okay. Uhm. Under the sink, there's some stuff you can use, and in the utility room, over the washing machine."

"Good. You're doing great," said Mikey. "I'll get started." She stood and turned toward the kitchen.

"Rem, what is this all about?" She took his hand. "What does this have to do with Gordon?"

He tried to think of how to explain. "This case we're on, the one we talked about the other night…"

"The one where you're undercover?"

He nodded. "The man we're after, he sent something to Daniels. The statue." He gazed over at the stairwell and saw it sitting on the shelf. "The one Daniels thought was from his cousin."

"That thing?" She followed Rem's gaze. "I hate that thing." She stood and walked toward the stairs and the strange statue. "It makes me uncomfortable. I tried to move it, but he wouldn't let me. Said it was special."

She started to go up the stairs, but Rem stopped her. "Leave it. Someone's coming to get rid of it. He'll take it out of the house. The less contact you have with it, the better."

"Are you saying that…that…ugly piece of stone is causing all of this?"

"I am. You remember what happened to Detective Georgios? In the squad room?"

Her face fell. "He's the one who tried to kill himself?"

Rem nodded. "Someone sent him a similar statue, and he'd been on this case before us, and Daniels has been showing all the same signs as Georgios." He hesitated, but told her the rest. "The statue is cursed. It causes madness. It starts with lack of sleep and progresses from there."

Her eyes welled. "Are you saying he…Gordon…he's going to…to…do what Georgios did?"

"No. That's not what I'm saying." He had to keep her from thinking the worst and tried to guide her back to the chair, but she resisted. "We can help Daniels by getting rid of the statue, cleaning and smudging the house, and all of Daniels' belongings, so that when he returns, all of that mojo from the statue will be gone. That's important if we're going to beat this thing."

"But what about him? What about Gordon?" She wiped her eyes.

"I'm going to help him, too," said Rem. "But I have to find him first."

She hugged herself. "Oh, God. I don't believe this."

"Tell me what happened when you came home."

She sniffed. "He…he…was angry the moment I arrived. There was a broken bowl on the floor, and I asked him what was wrong. He just stared at me, and his eyes…his eyes were just wrong." Another tear slipped down her cheek. "He asked me where I'd been, and I told him at work, but he didn't believe me. Said I was lying to him." Her fingers shook, and her tissue was ripped and torn.

"Sit back down." He brought her back to the chair and found another tissue for her. "Where did he think you'd been?"

"Oh, God." She held her head, her eyes clenched. "He accused me of being with you. Said you and I were both lying and sneaking around behind his back." She took a shaky breath and blew her nose into the tissue. "I told him that was pure nonsense. I had no idea where that was coming from. I told him to call you, but he just sneered at me."

Rem grabbed another tissue and gave it to her. "Did he leave after that?"

"No." She dabbed her eyes. "He kept yelling at me. And then he'd do this weird thing where he'd stare off and then mumble, and then he'd tell me to shut up. I didn't understand any of it. I wondered if he was on drugs and I asked him. It just made him angrier." She fumbled with the tissue. "And then…then… he started to yell at me about J.P. Told me I was a bad mother. That he would take J.P. away from me." Fresh tears spilled over her lashes. "Threatened that I would never see him again. I lost it and I…I… I got in his face, and he grabbed my arm and yanked on me. I yelped and something in him froze, and he blinked, and for a moment, I think whatever had a hold of him, faded or went quiet. I don't know. He let go of me, and I moved away, terrified, and he…he…said he was sorry. He kept repeating it, and said he would never take J.P. from me, and then he left."

"He said nothing about where he was going?"

"No, Rem. He didn't. I called the daycare and told them not to let J.P. go home with his father, and to call me if he showed. They said that J.P. was fine, and they'd call." She gripped Rem's arm. "We have to find Gordon. We have to help him."

He caught sight of her bare arm, and saw the dark bruises starting to form above her elbow. "Did he do that?"

She touched her injuries. "Who cares about my arm? It's fine. It will heal. But Gordon needs help."

Rem could only imagine the guilt that would be gnawing at his partner. "I'll find him. I promise." Movement caught his eye, and he saw

Redstone standing at the open front door. Rem wondered how much he'd heard. "Come on in."

Redstone entered, holding a bag, and came over to Marjorie. "This is Mason Redstone," said Rem. "He's going to get rid of the statue."

"Hello, Mrs. Daniels." He spoke to Rem. "Where is it?"

"On the shelf by the stairs," said Rem. "Stay here, Marjorie."

Marjorie stood. "No. I have to do something. I can't just sit here." She wrung her hands.

Mikey spoke from the kitchen while wiping down the counters and cabinets. "Then start cleaning. Every room in this house has to be sparkling, plus all his clothes. Then we'll start smudging."

Rem waited, hoping Marjorie would be able to hold it together, and after a second, she straightened and wiped her face. "Okay. I'll start in the living room, and then I'll do J.P.'s room and his toys."

Mikey nodded and Marjorie walked past Mason, but stopped. "You're going to get that thing out of here?"

"I am," said Mason, turning toward the stairs.

"Good," said Marjorie. "The sooner, the better. I want my husband back."

Rem thought of Phyllis, and admired both women's strength in the face of evil. "I'm going to help Redstone," he said. "And then we'll find Daniels."

She nodded, her face red, and left the room.

Redstone walked to the stairs and climbed them, until he neared the shelf with the statue. He studied it, his face serious.

"Well?" asked Rem.

"This one is even stronger than the other. Whoever created the curse, is getting better at it." He spoke low, probably to prevent Marjorie from hearing.

"Wonderful," said Rem. His own tension on high alert, he stretched his neck. "What does that mean for Daniels?"

"Hard to say, but based on what his wife said, he stopped himself before he went too far. There's still some sense of decency and light within him, so that's a good sign." He eyed the statue, reached out and touched it. He went still for a moment, before removing his hand. "Just like the other one. Only more powerful. It's a good thing we're here. Another day or two, and…well…it might have been too late."

Rem groaned. "Can we get it the hell out of here?"

Redstone dug into the bag he held. "Before we do, we need to smudge." He pulled out another bundle of bound twigs and leaves and went down the stairs. "I brought a second one since I suspected we might need it." He lit the sage from the candle in the kitchen and handed it to Rem.

"How's it going?" asked Mikey, mopping the floor.

"Just peachy," said Rem, holding the sage that began to smoke.

Redstone lit the other bundle on the counter. "I'm going to remove the statue."

Mikey moved the mop back and forth. "You have fun with that. I'm going to hit the upstairs after this."

Redstone's sage began to smolder. "Turn around," he said to Rem.

Rem frowned. "Turn around?"

"Yes," said Redstone. "Arms out and feet wide."

"He's going to smudge you," said Mikey. "It won't hurt. I promise." She smiled.

Rem hesitated, then turned. "Just don't set me on fire." He held out his arms.

"I'll try not to," said Redstone.

Rem got a glimpse of Redstone waving the sage around his limbs and torso and then over his head and feet.

"You're good," said Redstone. "My turn."

Rem turned back, and Redstone faced the other direction and held his arms out. Rem stood, holding his sage, uncertain what to do. "You sure I'm qualified?"

Mikey set the mop aside with a smirk. "I'll do it."

"Thanks," said Rem, and she took the sage from Rem and waved it over Redstone.

"Okay," said Mikey. "You're done." She gave Rem the sage back.

Redstone swiveled. "You, too. Everyone needs it who's been in this house. Tell Marjorie." He started to smudge Mikey.

Rem called in Marjorie, who gave Redstone a weird look, but she didn't ask questions. Redstone smudged her after Mikey, and she went back to work.

"Okay," said Redstone. "Let's go get that statue."

The house filled with a light aromatic smoke, and Rem hoped the smoke detectors wouldn't go off. "Should we open the windows?"

"Yes," said Redstone. "It will help air out the house, and the smoke." He yelled at Mikey to open the windows when she finished with the kitchen and she said she would.

Redstone approached the statue and waved some sage over it, then handed his sage to Rem, plus the bag he'd carried with him when he'd arrived. "Hold this. I'm going to put it in here."

Rem held both his sage and Redstone's and managed to open the bag and keep it open, eager to get this done. The statue with its open mouth and big eyes seemed to stare at him and a chill ran through his body. "I'm ready when you are."

Redstone reached for the statue and carefully lifted it. He brought it to the bag and lowered it inside. He let go, and Rem closed the bag, and handed it to Redstone. "It's all yours. I hope you and Mr. Wide Eyes have a happy life together."

"Oh, we will." Redstone took the bag. "After I cleanse it, he'll sit on my shelf, along with his friend."

Rem wanted to ask him if he was crazy, but didn't really want to hear the answer. Redstone took the bag and carried it down to the front door, where he set it on the front patio. He returned and took his sage from Rem. "Start smudging the house. You do the upstairs and I'll do the down. Go into every room and wave it in each corner. Do a double dose in your partner's bedroom and closet. Might as well open the windows while you're up there."

Rem held his sage, wondering what Daniels would think of all this, and thought of Lozano. Now that the statue was out of the house, he had to focus on finding his partner. He headed upstairs, pulled out his phone, and called his captain, who answered on the second ring.

"Remalla? What'd you learn?"

Rem didn't mince words. "It's definitely D'Mato. It's a long story, but he's involved with Georgios' and Daniels' sudden mental break-downs. Daniels is escalating and needs help, but I've got to find him first. I need an APB on him." He entered J.P.'s room and waved the sage.

"You're serious?" asked Lozano. "It's that bad?"

"It's that bad." He smudged J.P.'s closet and headed for Daniels' and Marjorie's bedroom. He considered where his partner may have gone. "If I don't get to him soon, I'm afraid he might hurt himself." His heart thumped at the thought. "I don't think we have a lot of time."

"Okay. I'll issue it."

"But add in that no one is to approach him," said Rem. "If Daniels is unstable enough, it could be disastrous if an officer tried to apprehend him."

"What do you want them to do? Take him to lunch?"

"Just have them call it in. Then I'll take it from there." Rem entered the master bedroom and began to smudge it. "It's important, Cap."

Lozano grunted. "I hope you know what you're doing."

"I'm just following my gut. It's led me to some crazy places…," he swirled the sage and the smoke curled up the far wall and he went into the bathroom, "but it's usually right."

"Okay. I'll let you know if I hear anything."

"Thanks, Cap." He hung up and went into the closet, spending a little extra time on Daniels' side, then returned to the bedroom and finished there. He smudged the hallway and the guest room and returned down-stairs. "Upstairs is done." He put the sage out in the sand Mikey had put in a plate.

Redstone entered the kitchen. "So's the downstairs."

Marjorie joined him in the kitchen. "The living room is clean and I've done most of J.P.'s toys. I need to add another load of laundry and finish the upstairs."

"I'll help you," said Mikey. "We'll have this place knocked out in no time."

Rem fidgeted. Daniels was out there and he had no idea where to look.

"Have you heard anything?" asked Marjorie.

"I called Lozano. They're looking," said Rem. He rubbed his shoulders, trying to think. If Daniels was getting worse, there's no telling where he could be, but if he was fighting his demons, and was trying to put some distance between him and his family to protect them, he'd go someplace where he'd be more isolated and where he'd pose less of a threat. But where was that?

"Why don't you sit?" asked Marjorie. "You look like you're about to fall over." She took his arm and guided him to the chair she'd sat in earlier. "Have you eaten anything today?"

Rem held the bridge of his nose. "Two cookies."

She eyed him with concern. "I'm beginning to wonder if I should be as worried about you as I am about Gordon." She turned toward the kitchen. "I'll make you a sandwich."

Mikey came out of the utility room holding a bucket of supplies and wearing gloves. "I'm going to start upstairs."

"Thanks, Mikey. I'll be up in a second." Marjorie opened the fridge.

Redstone waved his sage around the kitchen and then put it out in the sand. "I'm going to take the statue back. Get it out of here, in case he returns."

"Good," said Marjorie. "Will he come looking for it?"

"Hopefully, if I can locate him and get him through whatever mental hell he's in," said Rem, "he won't even care it's gone."

Redstone blew out the candle and put everything back into the box. "Bring all of this with you when you find him. Don't forget."

Rem almost laughed. "How could I?"

Marjorie put some lunchmeat on the counter. "I'm going with you."

Rem sat straight, his headache flaring. "I appreciate that, but no, you're not."

Redstone put the box on the table beside Rem, and stood, listening.

"He's my husband, Rem. I can help. He'll need me."

"I get that," said Rem, "and I know you want to help, but it's too much of a risk."

"Risk?" she asked. "He could hurt you just as well as he could hurt me."

"And if he comes at me, I'm better equipped to handle it than you are, and he would never forgive me if I put you in harm's way."

She grabbed a loaf of bread. "I signed up for this. I want to come." She opened the bag and pulled out two pieces of bread.

"Marjorie…"

"Don't argue with me, Rem." She smacked some mayonnaise on the bread.

Redstone cleared his throat and they both looked at him. "I'm sorry to interrupt, Mrs. Daniels, and I understand your concern, but it's better if you don't go."

Marjorie stopped in the middle of making the sandwich. "What do you mean?"

Redstone crossed his arms. "I'm not good at beating around the bush, so I'll be blunt. Your husband is under extreme stress and emotional upheaval. His mind is not his own. I know you mean well, but if Detective Remalla can reach him, then it's better he does it alone."

"But why?" asked Marjorie.

"Because he's dangerous," said Redstone. "If he should lash out or fight, he might very well succeed in hurting himself or Remalla. Right now, the less stimuli, the better. If he truly believes what the voices that he's been hearing are saying, and he were to see you two together, it could very well reinforce the belief that you are lying to him, and that's the last thing you want. If that happened, and you were there…well…I'd hate to think of your son being parentless."

Marjorie's jaw fell open. "He would never—"

"You saw him today," said Redstone. "Can you be sure?"

Marjorie went quiet, her face uncertain. "You think he's hearing voices?"

"Based on what I've heard, almost certainly," said Redstone.

A new worry flickered in Rem's mind. "Did he have his gun?"

Marjorie looked over. "I…I don't know. I didn't see it on him when he left."

"I'm not talking about his service weapon. Lozano would have taken that."

"What for?" asked Marjorie.

"Because Lozano suspended him for two days."

"He what?" she asked. "Gordon told me he took time off."

Rem stood. "If he doesn't have his weapon, then that will be a big relief and one less thing to worry about. Unless he took his personal one." He gestured toward the front closet. "Can you check the safe?"

Marjorie left the sandwich and wiped her hands on a towel. She raced to the closet and opened the safe. Her face fell. "Shit. It's gone."

"Hell," said Rem.

"Which is exactly why you should stay home, Mrs. Daniels," said Redstone.

Rem's phone rang and seeing it was Lozano, his heart raced. He answered. "Anything?"

"Nothing on the APB, but I just got a strange call."

Rem tried not to get too hopeful. "Was it Daniels?" Marjorie's eyes widened.

"No. It was my alarm company," said Lozano. "From my cabin on Secret Lake. The alarm was triggered, but it was turned off. They called me, just to check that everything was okay."

Rem's brain clicked as the pieces fell into place. Lozano's cabin, where he and Daniels had spent a few long weekends, and even solved the murder of Madison Vicker's husband. It was quiet, secluded, and the perfect place to go to be alone. It was also a good place to be if you wanted to kill yourself, but Rem forced that out of his mind. "That's it. That's where he is."

"You want me to call the sheriff?" asked Lozano.

"No," Rem almost yelled. "Don't." Rem recalled working with the local sheriff. Involving him would seal Daniels' fate. "I'll go find him. I don't want anyone else there."

"You're sure?"

"Very. Let me talk to him first. Trust me, Cap. It may be his only way out."

"All right. You do what you have to do. Just be careful. And keep me up to speed."

"I will. Thanks, Cap." He hung up. "I know where he is."

"Where?" asked Marjorie.

"I'm going there. You stay here. Finish the house, and I'll call you, or he'll call you, as soon as it's possible."

"Rem. No. Please. Let me help." Marjorie held her chest. "I have to do something."

"You can," said Redstone. He eyed Rem. "Once you get there, and you talk to him, you can call her." He tipped his head at Marjorie. "Let him hear her voice. Better yet, do a video call. Let him see her. It's the next best option other than her being present. She'll be safe, but talking to her could bring him around if he resists."

Rem nodded. "That's a good idea. You up for that?" he asked Marjorie.

"Yes. Of course," she said. "I'll keep my phone by my side."

"And may I suggest that you make arrangements for your son to be elsewhere tonight," said Redstone. "Just in case by some small possibility, your husband returns, and he's...not himself."

Marjorie's eyes rounded and shimmered. "I'll call my sister. She can pick him up and keep him."

Rem took a breath, and steadied himself. "It's just a precaution, okay? I'll get through to Daniels. I'll bring him back safe and sound. He'll be just as annoying and cranky as ever, but in a good way."

Marjorie bit her lip and straightened, and he admired her courage. "I believe you. If anyone can do it, you can." She wiped the tears from her eyes and returned to the kitchen, finished adding the lunchmeat and put the sandwich in a plastic bag. She pulled out a bottled water from the fridge, put them both in a paper bag and handed it to Rem. "For the road."

Redstone grabbed the box from the table. "Don't forget this."

Rem took the bag and the box. "Do me a favor," he said to Redstone. "I need you to contact Phyllis Georgios for me. She's the wife of the man who received the first statue. I'll send you her contact info. Tell her I sent you and let her know what she needs to do. Her husband comes home tomorrow, and I want her prepared."

Redstone nodded. "I'll call her as soon as I have the number."

"Thank you." Rem put the lunchbag and box in one hand and gave Marjorie a hug. "I promise. I'll get through to him. He's got a lot of love to come home to and he'll beat this," he whispered. Feeling his own emotions rise, he set his jaw. He refused to consider failure.

She nodded against his chest and pulled back with a sniff. "I know you will." Fighting back tears, she patted his shoulder. "Now go get my husband."

CHAPTER NINETEEN

Daniels sat on the couch, his gun on the cushion beside him, and stared out at the lake. It was quiet this time of day, and the only thing that moved were the trees when the wind blew. He was grateful for the peace, because it seemed he'd been at war with his mind for too long, and he needed it to stop.

He'd stopped for food on the way over, and the fast-food bag, along with a few scattered french fries and a can of soda, were on the table, but none of it had satisfied him. He still felt as empty as he had that morning when he'd come downstairs. Shutting his eyes, he tried to burn the memory from his mind of Marjorie's fear of him. He'd grabbed her arm, and she'd yelped in pain and pulled away, her face a mask of terror.

Something had ripped through him in that moment. The pain he'd caused his wife twisted his gut, and he knew then that he could never return. Tormented, he'd left, and with nowhere else to go, he'd come to Lozano's cabin. It had the calm he required, and he could do what he had to do with no interruptions and no witnesses. His mind on overdrive, he thought of Marjorie and J.P., and wondered how it had all fallen apart so fast. Marjorie's smile and J.P.'s laugh, their times together as a family, and Daniels' love for them, was over. He couldn't trust himself, and he couldn't live with that, nor could he live without them.

Eyeing his gun, he reached over and touched it, hoping he'd have the courage to do what needed to be done. He thought of Rem, and prayed his partner would not be the one to find him. But then he recalled their argument, and that crazy anger returned. *Rem started all of this*, he thought. *It's his fault, not yours.*

He leaned forward, his head in his hands, desperate to stop the whispers in his head. "Please stop talking," he said, his hands trembling. "I can't do this anymore." His voice broke and he thought again of his family, and Rem, and in his head, he told them goodbye as his eyes filled and a tear escaped and ran down his cheek. He reached for his weapon.

The creak of the door stopped him, and he turned to see Rem through the glass, entering the cabin. He gripped the gun and held it in his lap. Sniffing, he wiped his face and composed himself.

Rem stepped inside, carrying a box and a bag. He poked his head around the door. His face showed a brief moment of worry, but then he smiled. "There you are. I've been looking all over for you." He spoke softly, but his eyes were alert and his gaze fell on the gun.

Daniels didn't answer, but sat back against the couch. The anger welled up and consumed him. "What are you doing here?"

Rem closed the door and walked inside, facing Daniels on the couch. "I, uh, heard you were up at the lake. Thought you'd like some company." He set the bag and box on the small dining table and opened the box.

"You thought wrong." Daniels rubbed his thumb over the handle of the gun.

"Looks like you had lunch," he said, "Wish I could say the same." Rem pulled out a candle. "You mind if I light this?" He looked around. "It might add a little atmosphere."

Daniels eyed the candle. "I couldn't give a shit what you do." He clenched his eyes shut, trying to fight the rush of ire, and the sudden urge to raise the gun, but that twist in his gut stopped him. Taking a breath, he opened his eyes, and glared.

Rem nodded, still projecting calm in that irritating way of his. "Okay. Good to know." He set the candle in a holder and lit it with a match. 'There. That's nice, isn't it?" He pushed the candle to the middle of the table.

Daniels didn't respond. He stared off through the windows, angry that Rem had interrupted him. If he hadn't, he'd be dead by now, and all this pain would be over.

"You mind if I sit?" Rem gestured to the loveseat next to the couch.

"Do you recall what I just said?" Daniels spat.

"Sorry. That's right. You couldn't give a shit." He took a couple of slow steps and sat, his elbows on his knees. "Pretty day."

"Fuck the weather." Daniels sneered and debated how to get rid of him.

Rem's shoulders raised. "That seems a little harsh."

"What are you doing here?"

Rem studied his hands. "Thought I'd check on my partner. See how you were doing." His gaze returned to Daniels and the gun. "My guess is not too hot."

"Like you give a shit about me. I know…" His head swum, and an image of Rem and Marjorie together bubbled up. "I know what you did."

"What did I do?"

"Don't sit there acting all stupid." He stood, furious. "You lied to me. Marjorie lied to me. You took her from me." He waved the gun.

Rem stayed in his seat and held out his hands. "No, I didn't. I would never do that to you, and neither would Marjorie. She loves you, just like I do, and she's worried sick about you. She wants you to come home."

Daniels aimed an evil stare at Rem. "You saw her?"

Rem hesitated, his face pale. "She called me in tears. I went over, trying to find out where you went. She's scared to death about what's going on with you."

"What else did you do while you were there, huh?" He imagined them together in his bed.

"Not what you're thinking, that's for sure." Daniels could see the strain on Rem's face. "When you're feeling better, I'll give you the full scoop."

"I feel fine."

Rem looked him over. "You do? Because you're not looking like the Daniels I know. You kind of look like me, on a bad day."

Daniels scrutinized himself. His hair hung in his eyes, his clothes were rumpled and dirty and he smelled like fast-food and cold sweat. "Who cares what I look like?"

"You do. Or at least you used to." He waved at the table littered with fries. "And you sure as hell never used to eat this stuff."

"What I choose to look like or eat is none of your damn business."

Rem smirked. "That's true, and if I thought you'd really started to hate your veggies, and that this was your actual fall fashion choice, I'd be all for it. But I know it isn't, and I suspect you do too."

Daniels faced him, gripping the gun. "You don't know what the hell you're talking about."

"Yes. I do. I know you better than anyone. This isn't you." He paused. "And I know why you're not sleeping, having nightmares, and hearing voices."

Daniels went still. "How do you know…" His head flared, and he grimaced.

"How do I know you're hearing voices?" Rem watched him with worry. "Remember what happened with Georgios last week? Your problems are the same as his, and there's a reason why you two suddenly went from two sane adults to falling apart in such a short period of time."

Daniels chuckled harshly. "You're comparing me to Georgios? That's funny."

Rem sighed. "You're the one standing there with the gun. What's so funny about it?"

"You don't know what you're talking about."

Rem sat up. "Yes. I do. What's happening to you has a real source. This is not by accident and this is not permanent. You can get better. You remember that statue you thought came from your cousin?"

Daniels swiveled, his body rigid. "What about it?"

"It's not from your cousin. It's from D'Mato. He sent it to you to drive you mad, and to probably distract us from chasing him, which is working rather well. He targeted you and Georgios. Georgios had the same statue in his house."

"That's ridiculous. My cousin sent it to me. I even talked to him."

Rem's brows rose. "You did? What did he say?"

Daniels recalled his cousin returning the phone call Daniels had missed. "He said he never sent me anything, but he's lying too."

"So, everyone's lying? Is that it?" asked Rem.

"Yes, damn it," yelled Daniels. "I know what you're trying to do. You're trying to confuse me." He blinked and touched his head.

"It's the statue, partner. It's messing with your head. But we can fix it." Rem stood. "Let me help you."

"I don't want you to help me." He waved the gun. "I don't need anyone's help. Leave me alone."

Rem didn't back down. "This is D'Mato's fault. He's the cause. If you want to get angry at someone, get mad at him."

"I want you to leave." Daniels shook his head, trying to make sense of everything.

"I can't do that."

Daniels faced Rem, and raised the gun. "Yes. You can."

**

Rem eyed the weapon, his stomach churning. When he'd entered the cabin, and seen Daniels with the gun, he'd had the urge to throw up. His partner was a mess and his torment was written all over his face. Rem figured he'd arrived just in time, but couldn't help but wonder if his partner could still be reached. Daniels held the gun on him with a shaky grip, and Rem worried Daniels would fire just from sheer tension.

Rem stood there, his hands raised, and his body shaking, but wouldn't give up. He would either pull Daniels back from the brink, or they'd both die in Lozano's cabin by the lake.

He spoke calmly. "What are you going to do? Shoot me?"

A myriad of emotions ran over Daniels face. "If I have to." But confusion clouded his features and the gun shook in his hand.

"And what happens then? You shoot yourself?"

Daniels face hardened. "Yes."

"Why? What for?"

"Because I have to."

"No, you don't. What about Marjorie and J.P.? They need you."

He shook his head. "No, they don't. I...I..."

Rem took a steady breath. "They love you. Don't you know that? You love them, too."

"I can't protect them," he yelled. He moved the gun off Rem and put it toward his head.

Rem's heart almost beat out of his chest. "Don't. Please don't."

Daniels' voice trembled. "I have to. I...I...can't live like this."

"Then shoot me first, because if you make me watch, I'll want to die, too. I won't be able to live with it. So, put the gun back on me."

Daniels' hesitated, his eyes filling. "You'll be just fine. You'll move on, just like everyone else."

"Would you listen to yourself?" asked Rem, desperate. "Your family will be devastated. I'll be devastated. I barely made it through Jennie, and now you want me to live through this? You're a cold-hearted bastard." He didn't know what else to say.

Daniels made a groan and lowered the gun slightly, although it was now aimed at his neck. "You don't need me, just like you didn't need Jennie. The only person you care about is yourself."

The words hit Rem in the gut, and he had to remind himself that this wasn't Daniels talking, but some madman that had taken his place.

"How can you say that?" Frustrated and scared, he tried a new tactic. "You were there when I lost her. You remember? If it hadn't been for you, I would have never survived it. You were my rock. I needed you and you were there for me, just like I'm here for you now."

Daniels made a guttural noise and lowered the gun. "You didn't need me."

Rem swallowed. "Didn't need you?" He paused, and he thought back. "Did you know I thought about taking my own life? Not long after her death? I was on the brink, and I had my gun, and I was just staring at it, wondering if it would be worth it, just to end the agony of her loss. And then you came over, and you stayed with me. I never told you what I'd been thinking, but somehow, I think you knew. God knows what would have happened if you hadn't shown that night." His voice wavered. "And it's not just me. You've been there for Marjorie, as her husband, and J.P., as his father. And on the job, too. I remember going out on a call not long after we became partners, and we met a woman who we knew was being abused, and she wouldn't talk to us, but you gave her your card, and told her to call you at any time if she needed help. And she did. On a Sunday night at midnight. And you didn't hesitate. You rushed over to help. Got her and her kid out of the house. And that's just one story of many. God knows how many lives you've touched and the people you've helped. So don't stand there and tell me that I, or anyone else, didn't need you, because we did. We do." The memories of losing Jennie swirled along with his terror, and his emotions bubbled over and a tear ran down his cheek.

Daniels went rigid, as if determined to fight Rem's help, but at least he'd lowered the gun and pointed it at the ground. "Nice try. Especially the crying."

Rem sniffed. "I'm not trying anything. I want to reach you."

"You can't reach me. It's too late. I'm dead inside." His shoulders sagged and his face fell and it was the first sign of the real Daniels since Rem had arrived.

"That's just temporary," said Rem. He wiped his face on his sleeve. "We got rid of the statue. You'll start to feel better soon, if you'll let go and let me help you."

Daniels' anger sparked. "You got rid of the statue?" He took two steps forward and Rem took two steps back.

"You're damn right I did," said Rem. "With Redstone's help. He said it was evil."

"Redstone?" yelled Daniels. "You involved him?"

"I didn't have a choice," Rem yelled back. "I needed him. We were losing you and had to get you back. That damn statue started it, and I got rid of it."

Daniels raised the gun again on Rem. "You had no right."

"I had every right," said Rem. "If it means saving your life, then I'd remove a million statues, but thankfully there were only two."

Daniels groaned, then cursed. "I hate you."

"You don't. You just think you do."

Daniels held the gun, his arm taut, and then lowered it again. "Damn it. Why can't I shoot you?"

Rem expelled a relieved breath. "Because the Daniels I know is still in there, and he won't let you." He took a step closer. "C'mon, buddy. Talk to me. I know you want to do what's right. I know you want to go home. I know you want your life back. Let me help you."

Daniels stepped away. "And I told you, I don't want your help."

"You're just going to give up? You're not even going to try?"

"Go away," he yelled.

"No," yelled Rem. Daniels turned and walked to the window, looking desolate. Rem considered tackling him and taking the gun, but didn't want to risk it. He walked up behind Daniels, but didn't get too close, since his partner got fidgety when Rem encroached on his space. "I'm staying until I get through to you. I made a promise to Marjorie that I would bring you back safe and sound, and I intend to keep it."

"Then you're going to end up lying to her, too." He looked back, his expression smug, as if he had a secret ace up his sleeve. "Just like you did with Jennie, and with Jill."

Rem steadied himself. Daniels was bringing out the big guns to get him out of the cabin, so he mentally prepared himself. "I didn't lie to any of them, just like I'm not lying with you."

Daniels smiled, and an ice-cold shiver creeped up Rem's spine. "Yes, you did. You made them think they were getting this stand-up guy. Mr. Perfect. Mr. Jokester who makes everyone laugh." He faced Rem, his knuckles white from his hold on the gun. "What they didn't know was what they really had – a pathetic, whiny, emotional asshole, who puts his needs and wants first. Your relationships were doomed from the start. If I'd had the guts, I would have told them myself."

Rem swallowed and took the hit, his stomach rolling, but steeled himself. "Is that all you got? And I thought you were trying to be mean." He stepped closer. "If you want to get rid of me, you're going to have to work a lot harder than that."

Daniels' eyes flashed. "And what about that poor girl Allison? You're lying to her, too. Pretending to be someone you're not, while you're falling for her. I hope she gives you what you deserve. A broken heart."

Rem's chest tightened, and he forced himself to breathe, his encounter with her flashing in his mind. "Don't get your hopes up."

He snickered. "What happened the other night, huh? Did you finally get what you wanted? Did you get in her pants?"

The urge to throw up returned. "I don't want to talk about Allison."

"Why not?" He tipped his head, and Rem knew Daniels could sense Rem's sensitivity. "Did you screw it up? Not the big Romeo you thought you were? She was disappointed, wasn't she?"

"Shut up. I said I don't want to talk about it."

"Well. I do. Tell me, partner. Did she scream your name in pleasure, or regret?" He pouted his lips. "I'm guessing the latter."

The memories Rem had been trying to shove back, reared up and he fought not to retch, but then the self-doubt returned, and the crushing weight of stupidity. He raised his trembling hands. "Please. I don't want to…" He cleared his throat. His partner was winning this battle and he had to fight back. He took a second to center himself. "You want to talk about me? What about you with Marjorie? Huh?"

Daniels' look of superiority faltered. "What do you mean?"

"You weren't honest with her either." Rem squared his shoulders, hoping this tactic would not back-fire. "You told her how much you loved her. How much you cared. But now I know the truth."

Daniels' face shifted to one of pure hatred. "What do you mean? I never lied to her."

"You told her you were a good guy. That you'd care for her, till death. You took an oath with her. And look at you. The first sign of trouble, and you cave." He stepped closer and carefully pulled out his phone. "You owe her more than that, don't you think?" Daniels looked confused, and Rem punched some buttons. "If that's true, then you ought to stand up and be a real man. If you're going to turn your back on her and J.P., then have the courage to tell her yourself."

He hit the speaker and heard the call go through. Marjorie picked up on the first ring and her face lighted up on the screen. "Rem?" she said, her face furrowed with worry. "Is he there?"

Rem turned the phone toward Daniels.

CHAPTER TWENTY

Daniels went white and backed up until he hit the window.

"Babe?" asked Marjorie. Her voice quivered. "Oh, God. Are you okay?"

Rem walked closer, holding the phone out.

"Put it away," said Daniels.

"No," said Rem. "Talk to her. Tell her your decision."

Daniels shook his head.

"Honey, please talk to me," said Marjorie. "I love you and I need you. Please don't do anything stupid." Rem could hear the pain in her voice and heard her sob.

"Marjorie…" Daniels's face crumpled. "I can't…"

"Yes, you can," said Marjorie, her voice strengthening. "I know you. I know the man I married. You can do anything. You're the strongest person I know. You'd do anything for your family, and I'm asking you now to fight. Fight for me and J.P. and for yourself."

Daniels raised a hand and covered his face. His other hand held the gun but it hung loosely by his side.

"Listen to Rem, baby. Do what he says. He loves you, too. We want you back. Please." Her voice caught and Rem could imagine the tears running down her face.

His partner hung his head and moaned, his own voice cracking. "I don't think I can do it. I…I…don't want to hurt you."

"You won't hurt me."

Daniels sucked in an agonized breath. "I hurt you today. I grabbed you. I was so...so mad."

"Honey, I'm fine. And it wasn't you. It was whatever had a hold of you. But that's over now. It's all over. You're strong enough now. The house is safe and you can come home." Rem heard the hitch in her breath. "I want you to come home."

Daniels squeezed his head and clenched his eyes shut. "I can't think. Nothing makes sense."

Rem eyed the gun, and was close enough to reach out and take it, but worried it was too soon.

"Listen to my voice. I'm right here. Rem is there. We'll do it together. We can be strong for you. Please." She expelled a drawn-out breath. "I can't lose you."

Daniels' legs began to falter and he slid down the wall, and Rem followed, ensuring he could still see and hear Marjorie. Rem's muscles were so tight with tension, he had to consciously lighten his hold on the phone. The last thing he needed was to drop it or accidentally disconnect and lose the thread that was holding Daniels together.

Daniels moaned and opened his eyes. They were bloodshot and shimmered with tears. "Marjorie..." His face tightened, and something shifted, and he let go of a sob. "I'm sorry."

Rem held his breath, praying this was the breakthrough they needed.

"Don't be sorry, Gordon. Be strong." Her voice rose. "Fight for me. Don't give up." She paused and tears ran down Daniels' face, and Rem's own eyes welled with tears. "Gordon," said Marjorie, her voice steadier. "Where's the gun?"

Daniels' chest heaved, and he wiped his face. "I have it. I'm holding it."

"Give it to Rem, honey. Right now. Give it to him."

Since sliding to the ground, Daniels had laid the gun down but still held it. "What if...what if..." Daniels could barely get the words out. "I'm still dangerous?"

"You're not. I know you," said Marjorie. "Trust me. I wouldn't tell you to do it if I didn't know it was right. Give it to him. Trust him." Her voice broke, but she kept talking. "If not for me and your son and your friend, then for you. You have to believe in yourself, baby."

Daniels bit his bottom lip and made eye contact with Rem, who was trying to keep the phone still, but his hand wobbled with fear and anxiety.

"You give me the gun, and I'll give you the phone," said Rem in a whisper. "Deal?"

Daniels' shoulders shook as a wave of tears surfaced, and he slid the gun over and Rem took the phone off speaker and video and handed it to him, allowing him some private space with his wife. Taking the gun from Daniels, Rem sat back on the floor, emotionally and physically exhausted, as Daniels broke into sobs and spoke to Marjorie.

Rem couldn't stop his own tears from falling as Daniels finally released the mental torture afflicting him, allowed Marjorie to break down his defenses, and started to find his way back again.

Getting a hold of himself, Rem took a breath, releasing the enormous pressure and realizing how close it had come for both him and Daniels. His muscles ached, his head throbbed, and he could barely keep it together. Watching Daniels, and feeling more certain that his partner had survived the worst of it, he stood, and removed the clip and bullet in the chamber from the gun. He set the gun on the table and put the clip and bullet in his pocket. Spying the box and the sage, he figured while his partner talked to Marjorie, he could do something useful and calm himself at the same time.

Still talking, Daniels whimpered, held his head, and cried softly. Rem went into the bathroom, found some tissues and set them beside Daniels, and then picked up the sage and lit it. Smoke bloomed and began to softly curl and rise, and Rem waved it through the air and around Daniels, who didn't even look up. He walked through the cabin, smudging every corner as Redstone had instructed, and then returned to the living area. Daniels spoke softly into the phone, but his sobs had lessened and he held a rumpled tissue in his hand.

Rem put out the sage, pulled out the necklace and laid it on the table. Daniels sniffed and listened to Marjorie, and Rem went to the couch and sat, drained and weary, but thankful his friend was back. Holding his head, his stomach rumbled. He'd never touched Marjorie's sandwich and it sat on the table, but Rem wasn't sure he had the strength to eat it, or even walk over and get it.

Several minutes passed as Daniels and Marjorie spoke, and Rem heard more tears, but he let Daniels and his wife have their space. He debated leaving the room, but didn't want to go too far in case Daniels needed him. Thinking of what they'd been through, he shuddered, Daniels' angry words echoing in his mind.

After a few more minutes, he heard Daniels sniff and whisper. "I need to talk to Rem." He moaned softly and let go of a breath. "I love you. So much." He paused. "I know. I will. I promise." He took another shuddered breath. "I'll call you back. Soon. Don't worry." He paused. "Okay. Bye."

Rem remained where he was, the room taking on an eerie quiet. Hearing Daniels put the phone down, he looked back. His partner's face was red, his eyes swollen and wet, but it was Daniels, and not some evil caricature of him. "You okay?" Rem asked.

Daniels sat still, his back against the wall, and looked over, his face dejected. "I don't think I can get up. I'm not sure my legs will hold me."

Rem stood, his own legs weary, and walked over, his hand out.

Daniels, his eyes wet with tears, took Rem's hand. Rem hauled him up, and Daniels got to his feet. He wobbled, but Rem held on until he stabilized. They stood there, Rem ensuring his partner didn't fall, and Daniels hung his head. He spoke, his words strangled. "I'm sorry."

Rem fought back his own tears. "Don't. There's nothing to be sorry for."

Daniels' gaze met his. "I said and did horrible things." More tears welled and ran down his face. "How can you forgive me?"

Rem guided him to the couch before he fell over. "Sit," he said. "I'll get you some water."

Daniels let himself be guided and took a seat on the couch. Rem went into the kitchen, filled a glass from the faucet, wet a dishtowel and brought both over. "Drink." Daniels took the glass with shaky hands and drained it. He handed the glass back to Rem. "I'll get you some more," said Rem. "Take this." He handed the wet towel to Daniels who held it against his face. Rem returned to the kitchen and refilled the glass. On the way back, he picked up the necklace. Setting the water on the coffee table in front of Daniels, he held it out. "Put this on. It will help."

Daniels lowered the cloth and stared at it.

"It's an amulet. Redstone said it will help protect you. Keep it on until you feel stable enough to take it off."

Daniels took a second, but then took it and slipped it over his head.

"Good. You need anything else?" He sat beside him.

Daniels put the wet towel back against his face. "You haven't forgiven me yet."

Rem bit his lip, wondering what to say. "There's nothing to forgive."

Daniels lowered the cloth. "Don't do that. Don't sit there and act like this is no big deal. I held a gun on you for God's sake. I was…I was…" He gripped the cloth in a fist. "I wanted to kill you," he whispered. "And I almost did." His tears returned.

"But it wasn't you," said Rem. "I can't blame you for being under the influence of something you had no control over."

"Well, I sure as hell can." He sniffed, wiping his face and nose again with the towel. "I should have stopped myself. I should have realized something was wrong. How could I…" His words caught. "How could I have hurt Marjorie…and you…" A sob escaped. "God. I accused the two of you of having an affair." He cursed. "And you could have been killed in that alley because I wasn't there." He tried to catch his breath. "And what I said about Jennie and Jill, and you." He hung his head. "What the hell happened? What did he do to me?" He held the towel back over his face and whimpered. "I'm not sure how I can get past this."

Rem put a hand on his friend's shoulder, doing his best to keep his own emotions in check and trying to find the words to provide the solace his partner needed. "Go easy on yourself. You've been through hell and back. Your mind was poisoned by some crazy cursed statue intended to malign and destroy you. Give yourself time. It won't happen overnight, but you'll get back to being the Gordon Daniels we all know and love."

Daniels dabbed his nose. "My mind's a wreck."

"I'm sure it is. You're going on no sleep and not much food." Rem's stomach grumbled again.

"I can't believe I ate that crap." He lowered the towel. "But it was like I couldn't taste or smell or even hear right." He clenched his eyes. "And those voices." He put his head in his palm. "If I hear any more, I think I'm going to lose it."

"When's the last time you heard one?" asked Rem.

Daniels opened his eyes, and his shoulders dropped. "Not since you arrived." He expelled a breath. "Thank God."

"Then I think you've made it to the other side of the mountain. You're over the worst of it."

"How can you be sure?" asked Daniels, his voice uncertain. "What if it comes back?"

"It won't. The statue is gone, and we've cleaned and smudged your house. And I smudged you and you've got the amulet. The only thing left is for you to take a bath in some salt Redstone gave me, and to wash those clothes you're wearing. Then get some good, uninterrupted sleep and a decent meal. Then I think you'll feel a lot better."

Daniels raised his head. "Smudging? What the hell is smudging?"

Rem chuckled. "You have no idea the things I've learned from Redstone. I'll tell you about it later, but first, I think we need to focus on cleaning you up, food and rest."

"You're forgetting something." Daniels looked over. His crying had slowed, but his voice still trembled. "You need to forgive me."

Rem sighed. "I told you, there's nothing to—"

"Then just humor me, will you?" He laid the cloth on his knee. "Just because I'm improving doesn't mean I've lost my memory. I almost killed you and said things meant to hurt you."

Rem recalled the pain, but refused to blame his friend. "It's okay."

"No, it's not, damn it." His voice rose, and Rem flinched without thinking, unable to help himself.

Daniels' energy evaporated. "You see?" He softened his tone. "Don't tell me you aren't affected by what I said and did. I can see it on your face."

Rem touched his swollen eyelid, which throbbed along with his head. "What do you want me to tell you? That your words hurt? That it was like being stabbed in the heart? It wasn't pleasant, and I know you didn't mean any of it, but if you need to hear me say the words, then I will. I forgive you."

Daniels wiped his eyes. "What I said about Jennie, and Jill, and even Allison…"

Rem shriveled at the sound of Allison's name. "It's done. It's over. Let's move on." He stood. "I think Lozano's got a robe in the closet. I'll run a bath and throw the salt in, you get cleaned up, toss your clothes out in the hall, and I'll throw them in the machine. Marjorie made a sandwich but we're going to need more than that. I'll order us some pizza. By the time we eat, your clothes should be clean."

Daniels eyed him, and Rem hoped he wouldn't pursue the topic about the women in his life.

"You sure you're okay?" asked Daniels. "No hard feelings?"

"No hard feelings."

Daniels sighed deeply. "Okay." He ran a hand through his messy hair. He grimaced. "What kind of pizza?"

"Don't worry. Yours will be loaded with veggies. Mine will be a double pepperoni."

"I told Marjorie I'd call her back."

"No problem." Glad his partner had changed the subject, he headed toward the bathroom, grabbing the bag of salt on his way. "Stay put. I'll start the bath and let you know when it's ready."

**

An hour later, the pizza arrived, and Daniels walked out of the bathroom wearing the robe from the closet and looking more like his old self. Rem had thrown his clothes in the dryer and sat down on the couch to eat. "Feel better?" he asked.

"You have no idea." He touched the amulet. "I left this on."

"Good. Leave it on until you're ready to take it off." Rem handed him a napkin. "Now sit and eat. Did you talk to Marjorie?"

Daniels nodded, looking weary. His eyes had dark circles beneath them, but they were at least alert and less bloodshot. "Yes. I told her we'd be a while longer."

Rem looked through the windows. The sun was setting, and he recalled waking up that morning after only a few hours of sleep, and a memory flashed of his previous evening. Had that been just twenty-four hours ago? "What'd she say?"

"She's just happy I'm better, and not about to shoot myself. She's going to pick up J.P. from her sister's and bring him home."

"Good." Rem took a bite of his pizza when his phone buzzed. Chewing, he pulled it out and saw the text message from Allison.

Everything okay? I'm worried. I'd hoped to hear from you today.

He stopped chewing.

Daniels picked up his pizza. "Something wrong?" he asked and took a bite.

Rem debated what to do. Answer Allison? Answer Daniels? His mind spun. He was still on the case and technically, still seeing her. *Give it another day. You'll be fine*, he told himself.

Before he could talk himself out of it, he typed out a quick message, trying not to think of the previous night or what would happen if he saw her again.

Had a crisis to take care of. Will call tomorrow.

He hesitated over the Send button, but then punched it, his stomach knotting. He put his pizza down. "No. Nothing," he said to Daniels. He wiped his fingers on his napkin, and tried to think of something else.

Daniels blinked with fatigue, and Rem wondered how much longer his partner would be able to stay awake. "How's your pizza?" he asked, hoping Daniels would not ask him more questions he wasn't ready to answer.

"Good. How's yours?"

Rem made himself eat. "Good." He took a bite and watched Daniels yawn. "You know, I think you may need to tell Marjorie we're going to stay the night. I doubt you're going to make it past your next bite."

Daniels chewed and waved. "I'm okay." He swallowed and sighed. "Did you talk to Lozano? Am I still employed?"

"Called while you were in the bathroom. You still have a job. He told us both to take the day tomorrow, and then we'll hit the case full force when we come back."

"What about Georgios? How's he?" He yawned again.

Rem filled him in on what he knew about Georgios and how Redstone was contacting Phyllis and telling her how to prepare for Georgios' return.

Daniels nodded, and Rem wondered how much his partner had actually heard. His eyes were half slits and he could barely hold his head up. They ate quietly until Daniels closed the lid on his pizza.

"Why don't you go lie down for a second? You look like you're going to fall over," said Rem.

"I think I just need to rest my head. Once my clothes are dry, wake me, and we can head out." He tossed his napkin on the coffee table, laid sideways on the couch, and closed his eyes. He was asleep before his head hit the pillow.

Rem watched his partner for a second, then picked up his phone, called Marjorie, and told her everything was fine, but he and Daniels would be crashing at the cabin that night, and would come home in the morning. They talked for a bit, and she thanked him for all that he'd done, wished him a good night, and they hung up.

Rem stood, put the leftover pizza in the fridge, found a blanket, and draped it over Daniels, who softly snored. Then he sat in the loveseat, hooked his legs over the edge, and lay back against the cushion. There was a blanket hanging over the back and he pulled it over himself. He thought about going into the bedroom, but wanted to ensure Daniels slept. Thinking he'd relax for a minute, and then go lay down, he rested his head back, and was asleep within seconds.

CHAPTER TWENTY-ONE

Jennie's face hovered above him, and Rem moaned with pleasure. Smiling, she touched his chest and ran her fingers over his skin. Her touch was electric, and Rem sighed and ran his hands up her thighs, relishing in the feel of her as she rocked against him. The nightmare of her death jangled in the back of his mind, but he ignored it, wanting only to immerse himself in the moment, and be with her.

Sighing in relief, he closed his eyes, her body moving against his, and said a silent prayer of thanks that she was back, and they were together again.

Hearing a laugh, he opened his eyes and froze, dread seeping through his body, when Jennie's face morphed into Allison's. "Hi, handsome," she said. She lowered her head and kissed his chest. "You're mine," she whispered against his skin. "All mine." She grinned.

Seeing her, Rem fought to get away. "No," he said. "No."

Allison pushed him back. "You'll feel fine in a second. Just relax." Her voice faded and she rocked her hips. "Tell me you want me," she whispered.

Rem scrambled back. "No. Stop." He flailed, and hands shook his shoulders and he heard a voice.

"Rem. Rem."

He opened his eyes in a cold sweat, and saw Daniels looking down at him. Breathing hard, he tried to orient himself.

Daniels stood beside the loveseat. "You were having a nightmare." His brow furrowed. "You okay?"

Rem sat up, his back protesting, and shook off the dream. His throat was dry and he blinked. "Yeah." He swallowed, still seeing Allison's face. "I'm fine." He noted the sun coming through the windows. "What time is it?"

"It's seven o'clock. We both crashed and slept through the night. I woke up when I heard you calling out."

Rem massaged his temples. His headache had subsided, and he felt more rested than the previous day, but his stomach curdled again.

"You sure you're okay?"

Rem pushed up and flipped his blanket back. He needed to shower, brush his teeth, and lie in his own bed where he could pull up the covers and hide. "I'm fine. Just a bad dream."

Daniels studied him, and Rem plastered a smile on his face. "It's nothing." He suspected what Daniels was worried about. "It wasn't about you, if that's what you're thinking."

The furrow between his eyebrows remained, but Daniels nodded. "I should call Marjorie."

Rem shoved his hair back and stretched his back. "I called her last night when you fell asleep. Told her we'd be home this morning."

Daniels relaxed. "Thanks. The last thing I need is to worry her some more."

Rem looked over his partner. "How are you feeling this morning?"

The creases and circles beneath Daniels' eyes had faded and he appeared more present than he had in days. "Finally had a solid sleep. No dreams, and no voices." He fiddled with the amulet around his neck. "I think I'm back."

Rem sighed in relief. "Thank God."

"You and me both, buddy. Now I just want to see my wife."

"I don't blame you." He eyed Daniels' robe. "Your clothes should be dry, although wrinkled."

"Can't be any worse than yesterday." He fiddled with his sleeve. "I'll get 'em. And we'll head out." He paused. "If you're good, I'll buy you breakfast."

Rem chuckled, and his stomach unknotted as the dream faded. "I could go for some pancakes."

"I figure I owe you that much." He hesitated. "Last night's a little fuzzy, but I want to be sure I thanked you for what you did." His face softened. "I'm fairly certain you saved my life."

Rem smiled, grateful to have his partner back. "No thanks needed, but you're welcome."

Daniels stood for a moment, then nodded and left to get his clothes.

Rem slowly stood, trying to get his bearings. Sleeping on the loveseat had not helped his posture and groaning, he kneaded his muscles, and wiped the sleep from his eyes. He had a faint memory of using the restroom in the night, and wondered why he hadn't gone to one of the bedrooms to sleep instead of returning to the loveseat. His body would have thanked him for it.

Eyeing his phone, he doubted he had any battery left since it hadn't been charged. It came to life though, when he picked it up, and saw an unread text message from Allison.

Hope everything is okay. Can't stop thinking about you. I want you again...and again. Can you come over tomorrow? It was followed by an emoji blowing a kiss.

Everything clenched, and it felt like a white-hot poker sliced into his gut. He threw his phone onto the couch, remembering the dream and unable to prevent the anxiety and fear he'd felt during and after his night with her from rearing up. Shutting his eyes, he shook out his hands, trying to erase whatever the hell she was putting him through. What kind of game was she playing?

"What's wrong?"

Rem turned and opened his eyes. Daniels stood there in his wrinkled, but clean, clothes. "Nothing. Nothing's wrong." He inwardly groaned when he realized his mistake. He'd spoken too quickly and with little confidence.

His partner instantly frowned. "You sure about that?"

Rem made himself relax and slapped on a smile. "Just tired, I guess. That loveseat wasn't too comfortable."

Daniels eyed Rem's cell and studied him. He pointed. "You were on your phone."

"Just checking messages." He straightened his shirt, and smoothed his hair, trying to ignore his partner's stare. "You ready?"

Daniels opened his mouth, paused and Rem could sense his doubt. "What's going on?" asked Daniels.

Rem sighed, eager to leave. "It's nothing. Can we go?"

"Is it me? You still pissed?"

Rem waved him off. "No. I told you. It's nothing important. Come on." He moved to leave, but Daniels stood his ground, his eyes narrowed, and Rem knew his partner's mind was whirling, trying to figure it out. "Would you relax? You worry too much." He halfway wished his partner was still out of it because he would have been easier to distract. "Let's go. Marjorie's waiting and I'm hungry."

"Hold up," said Daniels. "We both know what I've been going through the last few days, but I have no idea what you've been up to." His partner tipped his head. "How was your date with Allison?"

Rem stilled, his heart starting to thump, and he mentally cursed. His partner was too damn smart and could read him too well.

"I remember she came by the station the day you were injured, and we argued. You were going to see her that night. How'd it go?"

Rem tried to collect his thoughts but wasn't succeeding. "It was no big deal. We had dinner." The discussion forced him again to recall his night with her, and his breathing picked up. "That's about it. C'mon."

Still frowning, Daniels pointed again. "You going to leave your phone?"

Rem realized his cell was still on the couch. "Oh." He chuckled. "Thanks." He picked it up, slid it into his pocket, and started to walk out.

"What happened after dinner?"

Rem stopped and groaned. "Nothing. Can we go?"

"Nothing? You didn't talk? Did you make any progress? Did she say anything about Victor?"

Frustrated, Rem raised his voice. "I really don't want to talk about it." He instantly deflated and raised his hand. "Sorry. I'm sorry. I just…"

"Just what?" Daniels' expression shifted to one of concern. "What are you not telling me?"

Rem shook his head, realizing Daniels wasn't going to let him out of this conversation. He scrambled for a way to deflect. "I'm telling you. It was—"

"Nothing," finished Daniels. "I heard. You've said that about ten times now. But I don't believe you."

"Please," said Rem. "Can we just go?"

**

Daniels watched his partner, noting the tension in his body and face, and hearing the slight waver in his voice, and knew something was wrong. His near mental breakdown had prevented him from keeping up with Rem and the case, but now he planned to catch up. He held his ground. "We're not going anywhere until you tell me what is going on."

Restless and agitated, Rem sighed and faced the window. "It's no big deal. It…uhm…didn't go the way I thought, and I'm just…just… struggling with it, but I'll be fine."

"What exactly are you struggling with?" He remembered Rem telling him how Allison might be perfect for him. "Did something happen between you two?"

Rem mumbled under his breath, and turned back toward Daniels, but wouldn't look at him. "You could say that."

Daniels' concern grew. It wasn't often his partner had trouble talking, especially about a woman. "So talk to me. Whatever it is, I'm sure we can work it out."

Rem leaned back against the window, his face flat, but he fidgeted. "It's really not that big of a deal."

"Then it shouldn't be that hard to tell me." Daniels waited.

Rem groaned under his breath. "Fine. I went over for dinner."

"And?"

Rem shut his eyes. "We ate spaghetti and finished a bottle of wine, and she opened another one." He opened his eyes and ran his hands through his hair, and Daniels detected the slight shake in his fingers. "And we sat on the couch and talked. I sipped on the wine and told her I was unhappy as a cop and was considering looking the other way if I could make a little money from it. And I asked about her ex and if he had a criminal history, wanting to see if she'd talk. She said something about maybe telling me more about him, and I thought I was getting somewhere, but then…"

He went quiet. Daniels started to worry, and his heart rate picked up. "Then what?"

"She…uh…slid up next to me and started kissing me. Told me she'd been wanting to do it since we met."

Daniels let Rem take his time and stepped closer. "What'd you do?"

Rem hesitated. "I…uh…kissed her back. I mean, it was nice, but…" He sighed and cleared his throat. "…she got more aggressive."

"Aggressive how?"

Rem put a hand on his head. "Do we really have to talk about this?"

Daniels' chest tightened, but he tried to keep the concern out of his voice. "Aggressive how?"

"I...I...didn't expect it." He closed his eyes again. "She straddled me, and I thought we were going too fast. I told her we should slow down, but..." He opened his eyes. "I was having trouble."

"What do you mean?"

The pitch of his voice rose. "I...I...couldn't think. Everything was fuzzy. My vision was swirling, and my mind was jumbled. My tongue felt thick, and she was all over me. I told her to stop, and I think I was slurring. She kept going though, and I...I...was reacting to her. It felt good, but it also didn't. I knew something was wrong and I tried to...wanted to...pull away, but I couldn't do it. It was like my body didn't want to listen to me but wanted to listen to her instead. And then...then..."

Daniels took a slow breath. "Then what?"

Rem set his jaw, and Daniels knew he was trying to hold it together. "Her mouth was on my body, and she moved lower, and I...hell...I couldn't stop her, and she made me say I wanted her, and I said it." He swallowed and held his stomach. "Afterward, she got on top of me, and it didn't stop there." He paused and took a shuddered breath. "I...I...uhm...think I tried to get away, and told her no, but she just pushed me back. Told me to relax, and that I would feel good soon." He squeezed his temples as if wishing he could forget. "And she was right. Something shifted, everything blurred, and I couldn't say no." His forehead creased. "We had sex. On the couch, on the floor, it went on for a while, and that whole damn time I felt like I was some pathetic character in a video game. She was manipulating all the buttons on the remote, and I was totally at her mercy...and she kept saying how much she wanted me and made me say how I wanted her."

Allowing Rem to finish, Daniels tried to keep his fury under control.

"And that...wasn't even the worst of it," Rem's voice caught. "...we were in her bed, and she was back on top of me, and she morphed into Jennie, and I thought I'd lost it. It scared the hell out of me, and I tried to leave but she kept telling me to relax, and to give in, and...and..." He hung and gripped his head, his knuckles white with strain. "...Shit.

I did. I gave in. Again and again." Releasing a fractured breath, he looked up, finally looking at Daniels with haunted eyes. "And the next thing I remember, I woke up in her bed, naked and disoriented, with her sleeping next to me. My head throbbed and I thought I was going to throw up." He paused, composing himself. "I just grabbed my clothes and got the hell out of there. I went home and took an hour-long shower and got a few hours of sleep. And I've been struggling ever since to either try and forget it or figure out what the hell happened."

Daniels stood in disbelief and clenched his hands into his fists, mad at himself for not being there to help and furious with Allison Albright. "What the hell happened?" His attempt to soften his voice failed. "It's called sexual assault, partner. That bitch drugged you and forced herself on you. That's what happened." He turned and paced. "I can't believe this."

"I…I…let her. I could have…should have left."

Daniels whirled. "She drugged you, Rem. You were impeded, and couldn't say no. That's called non-consensual sex."

"That's not…she didn't…" Rem struggled to explain.

Daniels pointed. "You're bigger and stronger than she is. I've seen you fight and bring down violent offenders, and you're telling me you couldn't leave? Whatever the hell she gave you prevented you from leaving. You were assaulted."

Rem thought back. "But I…I…participated. I responded. I…my body…complied."

Daniels argued back. "You talk to any cop working sex crimes and you know exactly what they would say. The body reacts, Rem. It does what it's designed to do. You get touched, and you get aroused. That's normal. But your mind didn't comply. You were screaming for help, and…and…" He swiped at a picture of the lake on a bureau and knocked it to the ground. "…shit…you couldn't do a damn thing."

"This isn't anybody's fault but my own. I walked in there. I knew the risks."

"Don't do that. You couldn't expect this. No one would expect this." He stopped and took a breath. "This is not your fault."

"I...I...should have known. I should have tried harder. Plus, I'm a guy..."

"So what?" said Daniels. "If you switch the two of you around where you're the one who drugged her, and you had sex with her, you think we wouldn't be looking to arrest you? Does that somehow make it better or worse? Just because you're a man doesn't mean you can't be a victim."

Looking worn and exhausted, Rem went to the couch and sat.

"Did you tell Lozano?"

"No."

"You should. We ought to haul her in on charges."

"On what grounds? My denial? I didn't report it or get a drug test, and she could sure as hell say it was consensual." Rem shot out a hand. "Besides, she keeps texting me, wanting to see me, and I'm still on this case. Lozano wants me to meet with her again."

Daniels erupted. "The hell that's going to happen. If he wants her to talk, I'll personally walk her ass to the station and we'll talk, but you are not going to see her again. Screw her damn texts. Consider your assignment over."

Sighing, Rem rubbed his face. "I'm not going to argue with you."

Daniels paced again. "Damn it. I knew something was up with her. The way she looked at me when she was at the station..." He put his hands on his hips. "But I was too damn messed up to figure it out."

"This isn't your fault either. You were going through your own hell. D'Mato made sure of it."

Daniels considered that, and sat across from Rem. "You think he was a part of this? Maybe they worked together. She got to you, and he got to me?"

Rem rested his head in his palms. "I have no idea. I didn't get the impression she was the type, but obviously my gut isn't foolproof. I didn't see this coming from a mile away."

"We still need to tell Lozano."

"No."

"Rem..."

Rem held up his hand. "I'm still reeling from this, okay? I'm not ready to walk in and tell my captain that I was..." He stopped. "...God, I can't even say it. I'm still not sure I believe it." He stood and paced with frenetic energy. "I mean, I was attracted to her. I was interested."

"I don't care if you were sitting on her couch wearing nothing but a fig leaf, nothing gives her the right to do that except your clear-headed, open, honest, and willing agreement. She knew what she was doing, and she deserves to be punished for it. If she's done it to you, she's probably done it to others."

"Well, the odds of her arrest aren't exactly in my favor." He put his hands in his pockets and stared at the ceiling. "I told her I wanted her."

"I don't care what you said. If you were drugged, it doesn't matter. Stop blaming yourself."

Dejected, Rem returned to the couch and sat. "It's kind of hard not to. I feel so stupid."

"When we get back, I'm going to talk to Lozano."

Rem's eyes widened and Daniels held up a hand. "I won't tell him anything if you're not ready, but I'll let him know you won't be seeing her again."

"What about the case, though? She may be our best lead."

"Then we'll find another way. If she doesn't respond to questioning, we'll tail her. It may be a long shot, but it's worth a try."

Rem blew out a heavy breath. "Chalk one up for Remalla. Goes undercover and gets assaulted. That's one for the books."

"Don't do that."

"It's true, isn't it?"

"It happened. I hate it and so do you, but we'll figure it out. If you can save me from a curse, then we'll get you through this."

He sunk into the couch. "I see more shrink visits in my future. Lucky me."

"Yeah, well. I see a few in mine too. We can compare notes."

They sat quietly for a moment before Rem sat up, looking like he'd just pulled himself out of a well, but slipped at the last second and fallen back in. "Well, we're not going to accomplish anything sitting here."

Daniels paused, disgusted at what had happened and angry at himself for missing the clues, but tried not to upset his partner. "Thanks for telling me. I know it was difficult."

"I dreaded it."

"I can imagine." He eyed his friend, worried about his mental state, but Rem, although frazzled, seemed to be holding it together. "You still want that breakfast?"

Rem paled. "I'm gonna take a raincheck. I think I'd just like to go home, curl up in front of the TV, and get some sleep."

"You sure you're okay?" Although Rem seemed to be composed, Daniels knew how good his partner was at masking pain.

Rem stood slowly. "I'm as good as I can be for the moment, but God knows where I'll be tomorrow, or the day after that. Time will tell." He grunted. "And God help the next woman I date. She's going to need it."

Daniels stood, too. "You know where I am, if you need to talk."

Rem nodded, his face pinched. "Same goes for you." He picked up the picture from the ground and returned it to its place on the bureau, picked up the box with the items Redstone had given him, and walked toward the door. "The rest of the pizza's in the fridge. You want it?"

Keeping an eye on Rem and still not convinced about the stability of his partner's mental state, he went to the kitchen. "I'll get it." He grabbed the pizza from the fridge. "You want yours?"

"I'll pass. Just toss it." He hung by the door. "C'mon. Before your wife starts calling, wondering where you are."

Knowing Rem would never throw away leftover pepperoni pizza, Daniels tried again. "Why don't you stay at our place for a night or two? You know you're welcome." He didn't like the idea of Rem being alone. His experiences the last few days had taught him how dangerous a dark mind could be if left unchecked.

"Nah. You and Marjorie need some time, and I'd rather be in my own space." Rem opened the door. "I put your gun in the car by the way, while you were cleaning up last night. Didn't want to take any chances."

Daniels hadn't even thought of his weapon. "Probably wise." He walked out and Rem locked the knob and closed the door. "You call if you need anything. Don't wallow in it if it rears up on you," said Daniels.

"Don't worry. I'll be okay, but you better do the same. You hear one voice…"

"You'll be the first to know."

Rem headed to his car which was parked behind Daniels. "Tell Marjorie she's a trooper. She's the toughest lady I know. If anyone saved your ass, it was her."

"I know and I'll tell her." Daniels suspected his partner was trying to divert the subject so Daniels wouldn't worry, and he sighed, wishing there was more he could do. "I'll call you later. Get some rest."

"Believe me. I will. You, too. I'm not the only one recovering." Rem paused at his car door. "And thanks."

Daniels nodded. "You're welcome." And he watched as Rem got in and drove away.

CHAPTER TWENTY-TWO

Rem uncurled from the couch, noting the time and thinking he should just go to bed. It was eight p.m. and he'd basically spent the day lying in front of the TV. Once he'd come home, he'd taken a shower, gotten comfortable, eaten some food and settled in for a day of nothing. His mind attempted to wander back to his night with Allison, especially when he'd texted her back to tell her that he would be unable to see her, but outside of that, he'd managed to keep himself distracted. He'd caught up on the latest TV series he'd been watching and now, *Sharknado* was playing quietly on the screen. Even by Rem's standards, the movie was awful, but it required no thinking at all, which is what he needed.

Daniels had called an hour earlier and checked in. Rem had told him he was fine, and Daniels said his house felt ten times lighter and he'd even taken a solid nap, with no dreams or voices. Marjorie and J.P. were exactly what he needed to finally feel like himself again. Rem was pleased to hear it, and although he knew Daniels was worried about him, Rem reassured him that he was okay and not sitting in some dark mental pit. After agreeing to get back to the case first thing in the morning, they'd hung up.

Stifling a yawn, he stretched. Seeing the dirty plates and cup on the coffee table, he picked them up and brought them to the kitchen, and then rinsed the pile of plates in the sink, put them in the dishwasher, and flipped it on. He dried his hands, thinking he'd watch the end of the movie and then hit the hay, when the doorbell rang.

He stilled, wondering who it could be, and walked to the door and checked the peephole. His blood rushed in his ears when he saw Allison. Stepping back, he debated what to do. Answer or ignore her?

She knocked and spoke. "Rem? Are you there?"

Rem paced, and hated his reaction. He'd done nothing wrong. If anyone should be embarrassed, it should be her. And then he realized the amount of shame he was carrying, and got mad. She rang the bell again, making him madder, and he walked over and opened the door.

She stood in front of him, wearing slim jeans and a red blouse with a loose jacket, and she smiled, but seemed nervous. "Hey," she said.

Rem didn't move. "Hey." He waited to see what she would say or do.

She hesitated. "You mind if I come in?"

Rem debated, but told himself that confronting her would be good for him, and stepped back. "If you want." He made a mental note not to let her near the kitchen.

"Thanks." She came inside, and he closed the door, feeling that disturbing discomfort rise up, but he took a breath and calmed himself. She wouldn't be able to get to him again, that much he knew.

She turned. "Sorry to bug you, but I…I…just wanted to be sure everything was okay."

A thought occurred to him. "How'd you get my address?"

She pulled something from her pocket. "You left this at my place." She held out his driver's license. "I thought I'd drop it off and we could talk."

Rem eyed the license and took it from her. Had it actually fallen out of his wallet or had she taken it? There was no way to know. He dropped it on the entry table. "What do you want to talk about?"

She looked around the house. "Nice place."

"I like it."

She nodded and fidgeted. "Can we sit?"

He gestured toward his living room, and she walked further in, but stood beside the couch. She ran her fingers over it and faced him. "Is something wrong?"

He widened his eyes in disbelief. "Is something wrong?"

"Yes," she said. "You seem distant. I thought after our night together that...that...I don't know...that maybe we had a spark or something..." She played with her fingers. "But I'm getting the impression you're avoiding me."

Rem stared at her, unsure how to respond. "A spark? You think we had a spark?"

"Yes, I did." Her face fell. "Didn't we?"

Rem narrowed his eyes, his heart racing. "What the hell are you talking about? You know what you did to me, and you think we had a spark?" He shook his head. "Who the hell are you, lady?"

Her jaw fell. "What do you mean?"

He yelled at her. "You drugged me. You put something in my wine, and you're going to stand there and act like you're some sort of girl next door?"

Her face paled. "That's what you're mad about? I thought you liked it."

"Liked it?" he yelled. "You thought I'd like being in a stupor, unable to resist, while you did whatever the hell you wanted?" His mind raged.

"It...It... was only supposed to help you relax," she argued back. "You seemed uptight, and well, a little shy, so I thought I'd speed things along, help you unwind."

Rem couldn't believe what he was hearing. "Unwind? Is that what you're calling it?"

"What are you talking about? Are you saying you didn't want me?"

"Not like that, I didn't. How dare you give me something without my knowledge. I could arrest your ass for what you did to me."

"Oh, come on," she yelled back. "Don't give me that crap. You had plenty of fun if I recall, and if you didn't want to do anything, then why didn't you say so?"

"Because I couldn't," he yelled. "And any resistance I did put up, you pushed back, and wouldn't listen."

She sneered at him. "Oh, really? Little ole' me held down you? You couldn't simply stand up and walk out the door?" She scoffed. "I'd like to know what judge would buy that story."

Her words hit him hard, and he questioned himself. Was she right? Could he have tried harder? Did he allow her do whatever she wanted because, deep down, he really wanted it? It took a second before he rejected all of it. None of this was his fault.

He walked closer. "You can stand there and act all innocent and pretend this is on me, but I know the truth. You slipped something in my drink without my knowledge. You knew exactly what you were doing. If you were interested, then you should have had the courage to say it, and take the risk of rejection, instead of numbing me enough to get what you wanted without me being able to resist." His voice shook and he took a second to get his bearings. "If you'd been straight with me, hell, I probably would have gone for it, but for some sick reason, you thought you'd get your kicks by messing with me. And now you're going to stand here and act like it was no big deal. Well, I'm not drugged now, and I can say exactly what I want. You're sick and you need help." Breathing hard, he stepped away. "And I think you need to leave."

Her eyes wide, she sat on the armrest, looking confused and hurt. "I'm sorry. I didn't realize. I...I...thought...I don't know. I thought you'd enjoy it. You kept talking about how fed up you were, and hated your life, and I...I thought it would help."

"Why would that help?" asked Rem. "How could you do that?"

"Because I didn't think it was harmful. I didn't know you weren't having fun. Because you certainly didn't show it."

His doubts tried to surface again, but he shoved them back. "You were all over me. What exactly did you think would happen? I didn't have a choice but to react, but my mind never caught up to my body. I told you we should slow down, that I thought I'd had too much to drink. You ignored all of it."

She straightened. "Oh, please. Most men who go out with me are all over me by the first date, and if not, then certainly by the second. You told me you wanted me. What did you expect?"

"You told me to say that."

"Now I'm in control of your voice?"

"When you put a chemical into my body that I have no knowledge of, and God knows how much of it, then yes, damn it. I did what you asked, because I could barely think straight."

She made a derisive snort. "It's so easy for men, isn't it? If you were all over me, I would have been expected to have sex with you, but when it's the other way around, suddenly you're the injured party."

"I would have never done to you what you did to me, and if you'd been the slightest bit hesitant, I would have stopped and checked in. I don't take advantage of any woman in that situation. If you're not into it, then neither am I. Period."

"Well, aren't you Mr. Perfect?"

He bit his lip, realizing the conversation was going nowhere. "I think you need to go."

"Fine." Crossing her arms, she sighed. "If that's what you want." Pausing, she studied the ground and kicked a sock on the rug. "I didn't mean for it to be that way. Victor and I..."

Rem held his breath. Hearing her mention Victor, his self-doubt rose again. Could she still be of value in this case? "Victor?" he asked. His heart pounded harder. He didn't want her to stay any longer, but if she could offer some information... He sighed as the cop side of him warred with the personal side.

"My ex," she said. She put her hands on her hips. "He...uh...used the drug on me, and I used it on him. He got a kick out of it."

Rem deflated, now even more uncertain. Had Victor messed with her the way she had with him? Conflicted, he hesitated. Now what did he do? "Allison, did he...Victor...assault you?"

She faced him, her face furrowed. "No." She shook her head, but Rem sensed her discomfort. "We were into it. That's why I assumed you would like it, too." She stared off. "I obviously thought wrong."

"That drug is dangerous. You shouldn't be using it on anyone."

"I guess...I don't know." She hesitated. "I thought you liked me."

He moaned. "That's just it. I did like you. Why couldn't you have just told me, instead of knocking me out of my senses?"

"You were so uptight. I wanted you to enjoy yourself." She traced a finger along the couch. "I'm sorry. I screwed up."

Some of the tension in Rem's shoulders dissolved and his heart slowed. "I'm sorry, too, but I still think you should go." He knew he was losing the chance to learn more about Victor but couldn't handle being around her. His stomach still twisted at the memory of what she'd done.

Nodding, she sighed. "Okay. I understand."

He hung his head and waited, and she headed for the door. Following her, she reached for the knob. "If you change your mind..."

"I won't."

Her shoulders drooped, and she pulled the door open, and then stopped abruptly. Rem looked to see three men standing at his entry. One tall and dark-haired, and two shorter men on either side of him. They pushed inside, as Allison stepped back. "Victor," she said, her face stricken.

Rem went rigid. It was D'Mato.

"Hello, Allison. You're looking lovely today." Victor walked in, and the two men followed. He wore slim, pressed brown pants and a purple shirt with half the buttons undone, leaving his dark chest hair visible. A diamond V necklace sparkled from around his neck. "How nice to see you."

Rem thought of his gun, which was in his bedroom, and his cell, which was on the couch. His mind whirled and his heart rate soared.

"What...what are you doing here?" asked Allison. "How'd you—"

Victor smiled. "It's called following you." His gaze ran over her. "You think I don't know where you are at all times?" His gaze went to Rem. "Detective Remalla. How nice to meet you. I believe I had the pleasure of meeting your partner. Smart man, but a little overbearing."

Rem tried to breathe. "What are you doing here?"

He nodded at his men, who closed the door. "I thought it might be nice to talk. Get to know each other better." He smiled at Allison, who wrung her hands. "I mean, you are dating my lady. Or at least, that's what she thinks."

"I'm not your lady," said Allison. "And what do you mean?"

"You need to leave," said Rem.

"Or what? Are you going to call that intimidating partner of yours? I hear he's had a rough few days. I doubt he'd be much help." He waved toward the living area. "Why don't we get more comfortable?" His two thugs grinned, and one of them seemed familiar, but Rem couldn't place him.

"I'm leaving," said Allison, moving around him.

One of the thugs blocked her exit.

"Not yet, you're not," said Victor. He walked into the living room and sat on the couch as if he owned the place. "Cozy, if you like this sort of décor." He waved. "Please, join me."

Rem kept an eye on Allison and the two thugs. One of the thugs had dirty blond hair and the other brown. The one with brown hair sneered at him.

"Don't keep me waiting," said Victor. He raised a brow. "You know how I can be when I get impatient." He eyed Allison.

Allison looked at Rem and he nodded, hoping to reassure her, although it was clear they were not in a good situation. She walked forward and he followed, the thugs behind him.

"Excellent," said Victor, as they entered the room. "I don't suppose you have any scotch, do you? Maybe some Johnnie Walker?" He smiled.

Rem neared the couch. "I'm all out." He stayed present to his surroundings in case an opportunity presented itself to get out.

"Too bad. Guess I'll have to make do." He picked up a pillow and held it. "Have a seat, my dear. It's been too long." He patted the couch.

"What do you want, Victor?" asked Allison, staying where she was, her voice shaky.

Victor shook his head at the TV. "Pure trash. No wonder this world is going to hell." He picked up the remote and turned it off.

"Then maybe you ought to go elsewhere, since you find my tastes so disagreeable," said Rem.

"Not all of them," said Victor, looking at Allison. "You and she have been getting to know each other better." He rested his arm on the back of the couch. "Did she tell you anything about me? Or did she hold back?"

Allison's eyes flared. "Leave him alone."

Victor sat forward. "You realize what he's after, don't you? You think you met him by accident? He's a cop."

"I know that," she said.

"He's investigating me. He knows you and I dated. He's hoping you'll lead him to me. It's the oldest story in the book. How you missed it is surprising." The side of his mouth rose. "Or was it that you were distracted. I mean, look at him." He gestured at Rem. "He's almost as good looking as me." He leaned toward her. "Tell me. Did he please you as much as I did?" He paused. "Did he find those special spots that make you scream?"

"Shut up," said Rem.

Allison looked away.

"Looks like I hit a soft spot, Detective," said Victor. "I guess the answer is yes." His face brightened, and he cocked his head. "Unless it's the other way around. Did she find your special spots? Allison is very talented in that area. Maybe you were the one screaming, instead of her?"

Rem gritted his teeth. How was he going to get this man out of his house? One of the thugs behind him snickered.

Victor watched them both and stood. "I guess I'm not going to get an answer. Pity. It could have been a scintillating conversation."

"Please, Victor…" said Allison. "Leave us alone. If you think you're protecting me in some weird way, don't. I know what he's after, and I know what he wanted."

Rem swallowed, wondering if that was true.

"Really?" Victor walked over and ran a tendril of her hair through his fingers. "You knew all along? And you didn't tell him anything?"

"What was there to tell?" asked Allison. "Other than you're insane, with insane beliefs."

Victor shrugged. "This is true. I am somewhat unique." He cocked his head. "But you knew things. Still do. It's why I can't take the chance."

"What chance? I didn't tell him anything," she said.

"You knew about the liquor store robberies?" Rem asked, trying to buy time.

"Liquor store robberies? What robberies?" she asked Victor.

Victor chuckled. "You haven't seen me recently. I've added some new recruits. They had to prove their loyalty, just like you did." He touched her hair again and she flinched.

"That's what they're doing?" asked Rem. "Your goons rob stores so they can show how much they care?"

"It's quite effective," said Victor. "Although Allison proved her loyalties in other ways." He ran a finger down her shoulder, and she pulled away.

Rem thought of the drug she'd given him, and sensed Allison had more experience with it than she'd admitted.

"Leave her alone," said Rem.

Victor dropped his hand and glowered at Rem. "Oh, Detective. I admire your courage. It makes sense why you and your partner get along so well. What you did for him, and how you got rid of that statue, was impressive. You even located Redstone." His eyes glimmered. "He was a good friend once. His family and I go way back."

"He said you two had a falling out. I can't imagine why," said Rem.

Victor held his stare, as if recalling something. "That's another story, for another day." He tipped his head. "But you still found him, which I admire. That, and," he walked closer and Rem fought not to step back, "this strange resemblance you and I share. It's quite remarkable. Although," he touched the sleeve of Rem's sweatshirt, "you could work on the wardrobe."

"You ever want to borrow something, let me know," said Rem. "I got a set of ripped jeans you're welcome to choose from."

Victor chuckled. "I can see why Allison likes you." He frowned. "But I sensed I interrupted something. Did you two have a spat?"

"How about we cut to the chase," said Rem. "It's getting late, and I've got to be at work early tomorrow." He flicked his eyes over Victor's shirt. "So stop trying to act all mysterious and tough, with your big fancy V and chest hair, because it's been a long couple of days, and I could use some sleep." He didn't know which was better, encouraging Victor to leave or trying to draw out the conversation. Either way, he said a silent prayer that he'd get out of this mess.

"Thank you, Detective. I appreciate your directness. You want to get to the point? Then let's get to it." He spoke to his men. "Take her to the car."

Allison froze. "What?" The two thugs walked up beside her and took her arms.

"You hurt her, you'll answer to me," said Victor, and the thugs loosened their grip.

"Let her be," said Rem. "She's not yours anymore. Let her go."

Victor shook his head. "You have no idea what you're talking about. She will always belong to me." He stuck out a finger. "Go. You know what to do."

"Victor, wait," said Allison, breathless. "What are you doing?"

"Exactly what I want, as I usually do. And you'll go, unless..." He smiled at Rem. "You want him to get hurt."

Rem tried to stay calm. "Don't worry about me, Allison. I'll be fine."

"Will you, Detective?" asked Victor. "I do believe you've already tried once with Thomas here, and I believe you lost." He gestured at the dark-haired man, who grinned at Rem.

"How's your head?" asked Thomas.

Rem's stomach dropped. It was the man from the alley.

"Too bad I didn't have more time," said Thomas.

"How are the ribs?" Rem glared back. "And you could work on your safe-opening skills. Is that why you're here now? Still trying to prove yourself?"

Thomas' grin faded.

"Enough," said Victor. "Take her to the car."

Allison held back. "What are you going to do with him?" she asked, looking at Rem.

"We're going to talk," said Victor. "No harm in that. Unless you choose to argue with me. And we know how that normally ends, don't we?"

Allison's eyes rounded when the dark-haired man pushed her forward, and she reluctantly started walking. "Just do as he says," said Allison.

"Don't hurt her," said Rem, helpless to do anything to stop Victor. If he chose to fight, it could put both him and Allison at greater risk, especially if he lost.

"That's up to you," said Victor. He eyed his men. "Go."

The man with dirty blond hair shoved her, and she walked with them to the door and disappeared from sight.

Rem took a deep breath. "Now it seems it's just you and me."

"Very true," said Victor. "But sadly, there can only be one."

Rem stayed cautious, in case Victor pulled a weapon, but Victor surprised him when he returned to the couch and sat, looking relaxed. "I need you to change. I can't take you anywhere looking like that."

A shiver ran up Rem's back. "We going somewhere?"

Victor picked a piece of lint from his pants. "We are. I need you, Detective."

"I appreciate that, but I'm busy. Go need somebody else."

Victor met his gaze, his expression unchanged. "Change your clothes. Jeans is fine. I don't need anything fancy. You have two minutes. And if you make any attempt to reach out for help, or try to fight, she'll pay the price." He resumed his lint-cleaning.

"What?"

"You heard what I said. You're coming with me. Get dressed. Contact no one. If you don't do exactly as I say, she'll suffer for it." He aimed a steely gaze at Rem. "And if you think I'm kidding, try me. I'll haul her in here, and yank out a fingernail, and you can watch."

"You just told your men not to hurt her."

"I did, but I can do whatever I want."

"You are insane," said Rem. "What do you need me for?"

Victor sighed as if bored. "It's a very important time of year, Detective, and I have an important ceremony coming up, and I need a suitable, shall we say, stand in." He rested his elbows on his knees, his eyes laser focused. "And you're the perfect fit."

"The hell that's going to happen," said Rem, his heart rate tripling as he tried to think of a way out.

"It is going to happen, whether I have your compliance or not. I just thought I'd offer you the chance to do it the easy way. If you'd rather do it the hard way, we can do that too, but it will be painful."

Rem stared, his mind whirling. He thought of his gun. Could he get to it in time?

"And if you don't care about Allison, then consider your partner. You make any attempt to resist and find that weapon of yours, I'll find him and his family, and that pretty wife and child of his will face a terrible fate." He put a hand on his knee. "I suspect another statue would be a welcome relief, which I could easily provide again, should he need it."

Rem's breath caught, and his body trembled.

"You have a minute left," said Victor, checking a nail. "I suggest you get moving."

CHAPTER TWENTY-THREE

Daniels tapped his finger on a file folder on his desk, eyeing the time. He'd been at work for thirty minutes and had been able to talk with Lozano about his last few days. Rem had already explained some things, and Daniels had explained the rest. The captain found most of it shocking and unbelievable but was happy to have Daniels back and up to full speed.

Daniels had expected Rem to arrive during their talk, but he still hadn't shown, nor responded to any voicemails or texts. Recalling their phone conversation the previous evening, he hadn't detected anything out of the ordinary. Rem had seemed fine, considering, and had suggested that he would even try and come in early. Checking the time once more, something nudged at Daniels and he tried to call again.

Lozano poked his head out of his office. "You hear from him?"

Daniels listened as the call went to voicemail. He hung up. "No."

"You think it could be Allison Albright? Could he be with her?"

Daniels had not told Lozano about Rem's assault. "No."

"You seem pretty sure. I got the impression he liked her."

"Not anymore, he doesn't." He stood and grabbed his jacket. "I'm going over there."

"You sure? He's probably sleeping through his alarm, like he did the other day."

Daniels knew Rem had spent their day off lying in front of the TV and planned to go to bed early. There would be no reason for him to be sleeping through any alarm. "Well, if he is, I'll wake him up."

Lozano grunted. "All right. Let me know."

Daniels nodded and headed out, the nudge growing stronger.

Thirty minutes later, the nudge became a shove when he pulled into Rem's driveway and saw Rem's car. Either Lozano was right, and Rem was sleeping through his alarm, or...Daniels' heart thudded, imagining Rem injured or worse. He ran up to the door and tried the knob. It was unlocked and the door opened.

Now he knew something was wrong. Rem would never leave his door unlocked. Pulling out his gun, he pushed the door open slowly and peered around the edge. Hearing nothing, and not seeing Rem, or anyone else, he stepped inside, gripping his weapon. His breathing picked up. "Rem?" he called, but there was no answer. Rem's driver's license was sitting on the front table, and he glanced at it before checking the kitchen and living area and poking his head into the bedroom. The bed was unmade, but that wouldn't be unusual. Rem was not a bed-maker. He ran upstairs, but no one was home.

Worry turned to fear, and he holstered his gun, and started looking more closely. He went into Rem's bedroom and found his wallet and car keys sitting on a side table. Telling himself to stay cool, he went into the living room, and froze when he saw Rem's phone on the couch. *Shit*. He started to call Lozano when he thought of Rem's weapon. He ran back to the bedroom and opened the closet, seeing the gun safe on the floor. Squatting, he reached and opened it. It was unlocked and Rem's gun was inside.

Daniels' fear bloomed. His partner was out there somewhere with no wallet, cell, or gun. What the hell had happened? Running out of the bedroom, he grabbed his phone.

"Detective?"

Daniels whirled near the open front door, reaching for his weapon, and saw a woman. Her eyes widened and she stepped back. He recognized her. It was Rem's neighbor, Mrs. Wilson.

He lowered his hand. "Mrs. Wilson?"

She put a hand on her chest. "Did I come at a bad time?"

Daniels shook his head, eager to call his captain, but not wanting to scare her. He'd met Mrs. Wilson a couple of times since Rem had moved in. She'd been a friend of Rem's Aunt Audrey, who'd since moved to assisted living. Rem thought she was a sweet lady, but a little nosy.

"I'm sorry," he said. "I'm looking for Rem."

She held up a bag. "I was just stopping by to bring him some of my blueberry muffins. I know how much he likes them. I saw him come home yesterday morning, and he looked, well, sad. I know the crazy hours he keeps, and I thought it would cheer him up. I was going to stop by last night, so he'd have them for this morning, but he had friends over, and I didn't want to disturb him."

Daniels straightened and scowled. "Friends? What friends? When?" He stepped closer and joined her on the patio.

"Oh, uhm, I think it was around eight o'clock. I was watching my favorite reality show on TV with Ed. You know, the one where they try to match strangers up to find true love. It never works, but it's fun to watch."

"And what did you see?"

"Well, this woman cheated on her man with the man's brother—"

"No, no, no. Last night. Who'd you see at Rem's?"

"Oh, sorry," she said, with a chuckle. "Well, I'd seen his light on, and I packed up the muffins once they were cool, but when I looked out again, there was a car out front, and then another one showed. Three men got out and went to the door. I figured he was hosting one of those poker games he likes, so I went back to my show." She waved. "Ed hates it when I keep him waiting. Gets all impatient."

"How long were they there?" Daniels had no doubt she'd been watching.

"Well," she stared off, "the show ended, and I looked again. I saw a woman walk out with two men. Pretty girl. And they sat in the car and waited. Ed yelled at me to come back, and I was about to when I saw Aaron leave too, with the other man. It was odd because once they got to the car, that man got in with the woman and the two men got out and drove off with Aaron. I figured they were going out for food or something. That's why I came over this morning with the muffins, but I guess he's still out. He must be having fun."

"The men," said Daniels. "What did they look like?" He already suspected the woman was Allison Albright.

"Oh, I didn't see them very well. It was getting dark. But the one that walked out with Aaron was taller than the others, and he wore something sparkly around his neck." She pointed. "And you know, I thought he looked a lot like Aaron."

Daniels' heart fell. Rem had left with Victor D'Mato.

**

Daniels pulled his car to a screeching halt in front of D'Mato's building. After talking to Mrs. Wilson, he'd called Lozano, and Forensics was currently dusting Rem's place for prints, although Daniels already knew who he was dealing with. After talking to Lozano, he'd driven to Allison Albright's apartment, but she wasn't home either, and none of the neighbors knew where she was, and she hadn't shown up at work, so she was technically missing, too. His next stop was D'Mato, and he eyed the building, recalling his last visit. Could Rem be inside?

Lozano had sent officers to question Tyler Bodin, the man who'd been arrested at the latest robbery. He'd made bail, and likely wouldn't talk, but they had to try.

Daniels got out of his car and ran up to the front of the building. Hopping on the elevator, he thought again of Rem, praying he was okay and sending out a silent message to his partner, telling him to hang in there; he would find him.

The elevator dinged at the top floor, and Daniels headed toward D'Mato's door and banged on it. "Victor D'Mato? Police. I need to speak with you."

Lozano had put out an APB for Rem and D'Mato, and had wanted to send officers with Daniels, but Daniels had told him no; he needed to go on his own. Based on his last visit, he knew D'Mato would relish talking to Daniels, and maybe Daniels could use that to find Rem, but if other cops were thrown into the mix, Victor would shut his mouth and not say a word. Mrs. Wilson's testimony as a witness was shaky at best, and Daniels realized it wouldn't be enough to hold D'Mato. He banged again when there was no answer. "D'Mato?"

Another few seconds passed, and Daniels wondered what the hell he would do if no one answered, when he heard the locks turn, and the door opened. Another woman stood there, just like before, only this one was different. She was short with blonde hair in a pixie cut, with big round blue eyes. She eyed Daniels. "Can I help you?"

Her words came out slowly, and Daniels noted her dilated eyes. "I need to see Victor." He held out his badge. "I'm Detective Gordon Daniels. He knows me, and he knows what it's about."

She smiled and leaned against the door. After a few moments, she widened it. "Come on in."

Daniels kept an eye on her, certain she was on something, and stepped inside, seeing the familiar white walls, contemporary décor, and fancy art.

"My name's Cindy." She closed the door behind her. "Victor said you might be stopping by."

The hair on his neck rising, Daniels turned. "Where is he?"

She giggled. "He's not here. He's busy." She walked to the couch and sat. A large glass of orange juice was on the table in front of her. "You want something to drink?"

Frustrated, Daniels ran a hand through his hair. "No."

"You sure? You look like you need to relax." She picked up the juice. "I have just the thing for that."

"I don't need to relax. I need to find Victor."

She shrugged. "I'm not expecting him anytime soon." She sipped her juice.

Daniels frowned. "Listen, Cindy. This is urgent. It involves a missing detective. My partner. And I think Victor knows where he is, so if you know something, now's the time to tell me, otherwise, you could be arrested as an accessory if something happens to that officer."

Cindy put the juice down and sat back against the cushions. "Oh, Detective. You worry too much."

Daniels wanted to reach over and grab her. "Do you know where he is?"

"Come." She patted the couch. "Sit next to me."

Daniels warred with himself. Play nice, or get mean, he wondered. Considering Cindy's state, he figured playing nice might work best, although in his current mood, getting mean would have felt better.

Watching her, he walked over and sat beside her. "Cindy. This is important. Can you focus long enough to answer my questions? Victor is into something bad, and you could get caught up in it. If my partner is injured or worse, you could end up in jail for a long time."

She crossed her legs and twirled a short piece of hair around her finger. Her gaze held his and she shifted to face him. "You're really cute."

Daniels let out an audible moan. He was getting nowhere. "Cindy, please..."

She reached over and put a hand on his knee. "Care to make it interesting?" She wet her bottom lip with her tongue.

He wanted to grab and shake her, but instead, gritted his teeth, and put up with it. "What'd you have in mind?"

Sliding up close, she ran her hand up his leg, and whispered in his ear. "I want you."

Daniels went still and put his hand on her wrist to prevent her fingers from moving up any further. "What are you on, Cindy?"

She grazed her lips over his cheek. "Do you want me?" She sighed softly. "Tell me you want me."

Her words stopped him cold, recalling what Rem had told him. Allison had said the same. "Cindy…"

"I promise, you'll have fun. Just lie back and relax." She tried to move her hand, but he held on.

The words echoed in his head. Cindy was repeating the same words Allison had said to his partner. "I'm a cop, Cindy. I'm not here to have fun. I need to find Victor."

She pushed up, and he let go of her hand. "Don't cops need love, too?" She brought her hand up to his cheek. "I'll make it worth your while."

He shoved her back. "You're not hearing me."

Swiveling, she reached and picked up her juice. "Have some. It'll help."

"I don't want any damn juice." He began to wonder what exactly these people were taking and how often they were taking it. Allison wasn't the only one caught up in Victor's web.

"You sure?" She waved it at him. "I hear your partner really liked it."

His scalp prickled, and playing nice went out the window. He stood, took the juice, slammed it on the table, grabbed her by the arm and hauled her up. "What do you know about that? Do you know Allison? Did you talk to her? Where is she?"

"Let go of me." She tried to pull away, but he held on.

"Understand something, Cindy. Right now, I'm pissed. My best friend is missing, and I intend to find him. Obviously, Victor has messed with your head, and Allison's too, and God knows who else's, but there's nothing I can do about that. But what I do know is that if something happens and my partner winds up dead, I'm coming for you." He pointed at her. "And if I found out you knew something, and didn't tell me, there's not a jury or judge alive that's going to keep you out of a dirty, small prison cell for the rest of your life, and then you can sit on your lumpy cot and dream about your precious orange juice, because the only fun you'll be having is staring out your barred window." He let go of her and shoved her back onto the couch.

Cindy's face creased and she shot the finger at him. "You're an asshole."

He leaned over and got in her face. "Where is Victor? Where is Allison? Where is my partner?"

She rubbed her arm where he'd grabbed her. "I don't know," she screamed. Whatever haze she'd been in when he'd arrived, faded, and her eyes flared. "Victor just told me to stay here. Said you'd be coming by, and to try and keep you busy, and if I did…"

Daniels waited, but she clammed up. "If you did what?" He paused. "You'd be rewarded?" His mind raced. "Is that what he expects? For you to prove your loyalty to him?"

She laughed at him. "You're so stupid. You think you know everything. But you don't know shit."

"Then tell me," he said. "Maybe I can help get you out of this mess. Get your life back. Be a normal person."

She sneered. "Why would I want that? So I can walk around like a zombie, like most do? So I can get old and fat and gray, wondering what the hell I did with my life?" She shook her head. "I'd rather die in your stupid jail cell."

"You think Victor can give you what you want? And you call me stupid? He's using you, Cindy, like he uses everybody. And when he's done with you, he'll toss you out like a piece of garbage. He doesn't care about you. The only thing Victor takes care of is Victor. And if something does happen to my partner and hell rains down on you and any other of Victor's followers, how much you want to bet that Victor will happily let you take the fall."

She stood. "You're just like everybody else. Blaming all your troubles on everyone, especially on people like Victor. Because you don't understand he's different. He can offer what you can't, no matter what you threaten."

"And what's that, Cindy? Please tell me because I could use a good laugh."

Her eyes shot daggers at him. "Life. He offers life. And once I'm higher up, I'll experience it myself, just like those who've proven themselves will do tonight." She narrowed her eyes. "At the ceremony."

Daniels went still. "What ceremony?"

She shrugged. "Sorry, Detective. That's all I know, other than your friend will play an integral part in it."

"What do you mean?" Daniels fought to stay in control.

She put her hands on her hips, knowing the power she had, and using it. "The veil is thin, Detective, this time of year. One must take advantage."

Daniels stared, trying to think. Then it hit him. Halloween. All Soul's Eve. It was the next day. So much had happened over the last week that he hadn't even thought about it. "What's Victor planning? What ceremony?"

"The one where he prolongs life, Detective, for him and his proven followers," she paused, "by taking the essence of one and giving it to another."

Daniels wasn't sure he heard right. "What are you saying?"

She retrieved her orange juice. "Your partner." She took a sip. "Victor will take his life to lengthen and empower his own, and those who pledge their loyalty to him."

It took everything inside Daniels not to grab Cindy and throttle her. If she was telling the truth, then Rem only had hours to live. "When?"

"Sometime after dark, but before midnight. You never know with Victor. But don't bother asking where. I'm not privy to that information."

"Then who is?" he yelled.

"Only those who rank high enough to know, and all of them are with Victor, preparing." She took another sip of her juice, looking satisfied.

Daniels grabbed the juice and hurled it. The glass shattered and the orange liquid splattered against the walls. He grabbed her elbow. "Somebody knows, and I'm going to find out who."

Instead of fighting him, she smiled, and pushed up against him, her hand tugging on the collar of his shirt. "Good luck, Detective." She giggled again. "You're going to need it." She tried to kiss him, but he shoved her back, and she fell onto the couch and started to laugh.

**

Daniels sat in Lozano's office, bouncing his knee and staring at the ceiling. He pulled on his hair, trying to figure out what to do next. Where would D'Mato take Rem? They'd checked every known location with no luck. Cindy's laughter echoed in his ears, and he groaned.

Hearing the door open, he saw Lozano return. "Mel and Garcia are interviewing Cindy," said Lozano, returning to his seat. "Hopefully, whatever she's on will start to wear off, she'll stop flirting with them, and we can get something out of her."

"Don't count on it," said Daniels. "She's trying to prove her worth to D'Mato." He sat up. "What about Tyler Bodin? Any luck with him?"

"None. He's not talking either."

"Shit," Daniels stood and paced. "Why the hell didn't I insist he stay with me and Marjorie last night?"

"If he had, it could have been much worse. You don't know what D'Mato would have done. If he wanted to get to Remalla, he'd have found a way, and it might have been through you and your family."

Daniels had informed Lozano of Allison's assault on Rem. Normally, Daniels would have kept Rem's confidence, but with Rem missing, Lozano needed to know what they were dealing with. Daniels shook his head. "Still...I wish...he shouldn't have been alone."

"You're not a mind reader, Daniels, and until you are, you have to work with what you've got." Lozano grunted. "What about Albright? You think she's involved in this, or is she a victim, too?"

Daniels grunted. "No idea. Based on what Mrs. Wilson said, it's hard to know if she was there with Victor or not. Hell, according to her, Rem left willingly with D'Mato."

"You know he wouldn't have done that if given the choice."

"No, he wouldn't." Daniels stilled. "Unless D'Mato threatened him, or maybe Allison."

"Or maybe you. Did you forget he tortured you with a supposed crazy statue? Don't you think he could use that against Remalla?"

Daniels' heart sunk. His partner would walk off with a monster in order to protect the ones he loved. He dropped his head. "Damn it."

"Stop feeling guilty and let's think. There's got to be a way to figure out where he is." Lozano scratched his head. "We've got APBs for Remalla, Albright and D'Mato. We're talking to Tyler and Cindy. I've got a team going through the cases of the unidentified dead vagrants with the bite mark, plus that friend, or is it cousin, of that paranormal fellow. What's his name? Redstone? Maybe they can find something connected to D'Mato. If we can get Cindy to stop hitting on our officers and float back to earth, maybe she can give us some names of other followers. If we can find someone else who's willing to talk, maybe we'll get somewhere."

Daniels stared off, barely hearing the captain.

"Daniels? Are you listening?"

"I'm an idiot." He headed for the door and opened it.

"Where are you going?"

"Redstone, Cap. He knew D'Mato. He might be able to help me find him."

"You think? It's a long shot. I thought he hadn't seen him in years."

"We're running out of time, and if there's a possibility, I'm going to try."

Lozano sighed. "Okay. I'll let you know what's happening here and let me know what you get out of Redstone."

Daniels nodded and ran out.

**

Daniels charged up the stairs, and reached the door marked SCOPE. He banged on it. "Redstone? Mason Redstone? Police." He tried the knob and knocked several times. "I need to talk to you." Not wanting to take the time to find the phone number, Daniels hadn't called before arriving. He prayed Redstone was there and banged again. "Redstone?"

The door opened, and Redstone stood there, wearing jeans and a t-shirt with socks on his feet. "Don't you guys know how to make an appointment?"

Daniels pushed his way in. "I need your help."

Redstone squinted. "It's not another statue, is it?" He closed the door.

"No. It's my partner. He's missing, and D'Mato has him."

Redstone went quiet. "What? Detective Remalla?"

"Yes." Daniels was breathing hard and did his best to stay calm. "One of his followers told me D'Mato's doing some sort of ceremony tonight, and Rem's involved. Something about taking one life to pro-long another. I don't know much more than that." He clenched and opened his eyes. "But it's tonight. I've got to find D'Mato, and I'm running out of options."

Redstone's face paled. "A ceremony? Tonight?"

"Yes," Daniels nodded. "If you know anything about how to find D'Mato or Rem, you need to tell me." He pointed. "I don't care who you have to talk to, or if they're dead or alive. I'll take whatever I can get."

Redstone tipped his head, his eyes wide. "Come on back."

Daniels followed Redstone into the next room. His gaze traveled to the empty shelves with the small box, but now a plexiglass container sat beside it and inside were two statues, both small and round with wide eyes and open mouths. Daniels stopped short.

Redstone noticed. "Don't worry. They're harmless, although I'd ad-vise you to keep your distance."

Having a brief flashback, Daniels touched the amulet around his neck.

"I'm glad you're wearing it," said Redstone. "Best to keep it on a while longer." He went over and sat on the couch. There was a pillow and a blanket on it, and he shoved them aside. "Have a seat."

Daniels shook off the frightening memories. "You don't think...D'Mato wouldn't use that..." It was almost too scary to put into words.

"Use a statue on your partner?" asked Redstone. "No."

Daniels released a relieved sigh and pulled his gaze from the shelf. "Then what's he up to, and how do I find him?"

Redstone leaned over and put his elbows on his knees. "You need to prepare yourself, Detective."

Daniels felt the bile rise in his throat. "What do you mean?"

Redstone gestured. "You should sit."

Daniels wanted to argue and yell but composed himself and forced himself to sit across from Redstone. "What is it?"

"I'll be straight with you." Redstone interlaced his fingers. "Victor won't use a statue, because he doesn't have the time, but he can break your partner down in other ways. He's good at it. He knows how to scare someone, whether it be through drugs or mind games. I suspect that's how he's built his following over such a short period."

Daniels set his jaw and went rigid, thinking of Rem walking off and willingly getting into a car to face God knows what. "But he only took Rem last night. And this ceremony is today."

"It doesn't matter. I know Victor. He likes fear. It turns him on." He studied his hands. "He'll work his followers up into a frenzy, all feeding on the terror of another. And when it reaches its peak..."

Daniels cursed and stood. "Then the sooner we can find Rem, the better." He gripped the back of the chair he'd been sitting in. "Where would Victor take him?"

Redstone pressed his fingertips together. "He'd need someplace quiet, where he could have upwards of maybe twenty or thirty people involved, and not be interrupted, and certainly not draw any unwanted attention. It would likely be outside the city."

Daniels groaned. "We've looked. Victor doesn't own or have connections to, any place like that, and what he does have, we've checked."

"It's probably connected to one of his followers, or he used a different name. He wouldn't have used his own."

"We can't find any of his followers, either, and the ones we have, won't talk." He dropped his head. "There's got to be something."

Redstone got up and went to his desk. He sat and tapped on his computer keyboard. "I did some checking, after I first talked to you and your partner. I went back and reviewed my cousin's case, looking to see if anything stood out."

Daniels straightened, hopeful. "Did you find anything?"

Redstone clicked his mouse. "His body was found down near the docks, with that strange bite on his arm." He read something on the screen. "He had bruises on his wrists and ankles, likely from being tied down, his clothes were ripped, and had cuts on his body—"

Daniels held his head. "This isn't helping."

"Sorry," said Redstone. "But what was interesting is that he had sand on his skin and clothes."

Daniels looked up. "They found him down by the docks."

"The docks, Detective. Not the beach. I never understood it."

"So he was killed elsewhere and dumped."

"It seems so."

"You think they're doing this ceremony on the beach?"

"Maybe," said Redstone. "It's a good way to wash away the evidence if the tide comes in and takes it all away."

"But where are you going to have a private ceremony on a beach?"

"There's miles of coastline in this state, Detective."

"But not miles where you could safely kill someone without being watched."

Redstone sat back. "Keep in mind. This is just a theory. There are other ways to get sand on you without being on a beach. They could start at the beach and then move elsewhere. Or maybe there's sand involved in this ceremony. There's no way to know."

Daniels cursed, feeling the weight of his worry and fear.

"You know anything about the ceremony itself?" asked Redstone.

"Uh, yeah." He relayed to Redstone what Cindy had told him.

Redstone leaned an elbow on the desk. "He's thinking he can take the life force of another and make it his own. Probably thinks he'll live longer or grow stronger because of it." He shook his head. "The man's insane."

"Why my partner though?" asked Daniels. "Why Rem?"

"There's a myriad of reasons, but I suspect he's attracted to his energy, his chi, which is strong. Your partner is also on the side of good. He fought for you when you were declining rapidly, and he fights for others. Plus, he's not afraid to stand up to D'Mato. And there's that strange resemblance they share. It's an attractive package to take from someone and give to yourself, which is what Victor thinks he's doing." He paused. "It's also an effective way to stick it to you."

Daniels cursed again and paced. "What the hell am I going to do? How do I find him?" He stopped. "Somebody out there knows something, damn it." He kicked at the chair, dejected. "I can't let this happen."

Redstone expelled a breath, and Daniels looked over, noticing Redstone's far-off stare. "What? You thinking of something?"

Redstone hesitated. "It would mean betraying a confidence."

Daniels walked up and rested his palms on the desk. "My best friend could die a horrible death tonight. I don't give a shit who you're protecting. If you know something that might help, you have to tell me."

Redstone met Daniels' gaze, his face conflicted.

A door slammed from up front, and then the inner door opened. A woman walked in, wearing all black with black boots. She had a piercing in her nose, and her straight reddish-brown hair with purple streaks brushed her shoulders. One eye was bruised and almost swollen shut, and she had a fat lip.

Redstone stood. "Mikey. What the hell happened to you?"

She threw the jacket she was carrying into the chair, her face contorted in anger. "Victor," she said. "Victor happened to me."

CHAPTER TWENTY-FOUR

Hearing a squeak and the scamper of tiny claws, Rem pressed back against the wall. Sitting in total darkness, he had no idea where he was or who he shared the space with, but judging by the noises, it seemed his roommates were a couple of mice. At least he told himself it was mice, and not rats. But the longer he sat there, the more his mind assumed the worst, and he swallowed, telling himself to stay calm.

After leaving his house with Victor, he'd been driven off by Victor's thugs, who'd covered his head with a hood, secured his hands behind his back, and made him lie down, threatening injury to Allison or Daniels if he did not comply. Victor had taken off with Allison and he hadn't seen either of them since. The men had driven for a while and then they'd stopped, and he'd been led to this room, where his hands had been untied, and they'd closed the door and left. He'd slid the hood off but couldn't see a thing. Not a speck of light permeated the darkness. Not the biggest fan of the dark, he'd made a concentrated effort to not lose it, and had tried to explore his new digs. His mind imagined horrible things, but he did his best to push through the fear. He could tell the area was small and the floor was dirty. He'd jumped when he'd touched something soft and damp, but probing further, he'd determined it was a mattress - an old and decayed one if what he felt was any indication. He wouldn't have been surprised if that was where the mice were making their home.

Exploring more, his fingers bumped into cold metal, and he realized it was a bucket, which he guessed had been provided in case he needed to use the facilities. He found the door, too, but it was locked and when he banged on it, all he heard was quiet. Sensing the emptiness around him, he'd sat back against the wall, feeling alone and scared. His only companions were the one or two mice – not rats - who occasionally skittered across the floor.

Chilly, he pulled his jacket around him, strangely grateful that Victor had made him change, and tried not to think what might happen next. Refusing to touch the mattress, he'd done his best to get comfortable in a corner and, as the hours had passed, he'd dozed on and off, having no idea how long he'd been there.

Now, awake and trying to orient himself, something crawled over his ankle, and he jumped and shrieked. Cold, thirsty, and hungry, he blinked, pulled his legs up and wondered what time it was. It could have been three a.m. or three p.m. and he wouldn't have known the difference.

Resting his head on his knees, he thought of Daniels, assuming that his partner had, by now, realized he was missing and would have the whole force out looking for him. He said a silent prayer that they would find him. Shivering, he huddled around his legs and remembered what Victor had said. That he needed Rem for something, and Rem didn't think it would be for anything good.

Sighing a shaky breath, and hearing another squeak in the room, he couldn't help but worry about what Victor's people would do when they came for him.

**

Daniels approached Mikey, not sure he heard correctly. "Did you say Victor?"

She eyed him. "Who's this guy?" she asked Redstone. "I thought you didn't have any appointments today."

Redstone stood. "This is Detective Daniels. Daniels, this is my crazy sister, Mikey." He gestured at Mikey. "What happened to you?"

"Daniels?" she asked. "Remalla's partner?" She looked at Daniels. "You're the one with the statue?"

Daniels took a step closer. "That's me."

"Where's your partner?" she asked.

"He's gone," said Daniels. "Victor took him, and I'm trying to find him."

Mikey's face froze. "What? Detective Remalla? With Victor?"

"What did you do, Mikey?" asked Redstone. "What happened to your face?"

Mikey touched her swollen eye. "Are you sure?" she asked Daniels.

"Yes. I'm sure," said Daniels. "If you know where Victor is, you need to tell me." He prayed she'd have the information he needed.

"Did you see him?" asked Redstone. "Did you see Victor?"

Mikey paced. "Shit. What is Victor up to?"

"Mikey. What is going on?" yelled Redstone.

Mikey glared. "Yes. I saw him." She put a hand on her hip. "When you told me he was back and active, I decided to confront him. After what he did…"

"Are you serious? You know how dangerous he is," said Redstone.

Mikey whirled. "So am I. I couldn't just sit back and act all meek and afraid. I've had years to deal with his abuse and its aftereffects. I'm angry. He deserved to know."

"Where is he?" asked Daniels. "How did you find him?"

"I know Victor," said Mikey. "I know his spots and where he hides himself, and he's a creature of habit. I was under his thumb for a while, but not anymore. After I helped your wife get your house clean, I started looking for Victor, and I found him."

Daniels didn't know how Mikey knew his wife, but that would be a question for another time. His heart raced when he realized Mikey could lead him to Victor. "Where?"

"I can't believe you did that. How unbelievably stupid. You could have been killed," said Redstone. "And by the looks of it, you almost were."

"I confronted him, Mason. I had to do it. We fought. He was his usual smug self, but I didn't cower to him. I told him what I thought, but he didn't give a shit."

"How long ago was this?" asked Daniels, his impatience growing.

"I don't know. Two hours?" Mikey shook her head. "I had no idea about Remalla. How long's he been gone?"

"Since last night," said Daniels. "Did you see anything when you were with Victor?"

"Nothing to indicate he was holding someone, but Victor isn't stupid. He'd keep Remalla away from prying eyes. Some place where no one would look." She eyed Mason. "We argued, and I got in his face. That's when he hit me, but I hit back, and didn't leave without making a few marks of my own. But at least I said what I had to say."

Daniels stepped over. "You need to tell me where he is. Rem's life depends on it, and we're running out of time."

Mikey nodded, her face serious. She picked up her jacket. "I'll do you one better. I'll take you to Victor."

"Don't be ridiculous," said Redstone.

"Don't tell me what to do," said Mikey. "Besides, it's a long drive. It's a remote place near the beach." She raised a brow at Daniels. "And if you want to get there fast, I'm your best bet."

"The beach?" asked Redstone. He made eye contact with Daniels.

Daniels thought of the sand on Redstone's cousin's body. "You want to go, fine, but when we get there, you let me deal with him."

Redstone grabbed some shoes sitting along the wall. "I'm coming."

**

Daniels drove down a dirt road outside of the city along the coast, and Mikey pointed. "There. Turn there."

Daniels almost passed a rutted and overgrown driveway. He slowed and turned. The driveway was long and bumpy, with big trees alongside it and, resisting the urge to speed up, he went slow, but his mind and eyes remained alert to anything that might indicate Rem's or Victor's presence.

"Here. This is it," said Mikey.

A small bungalow came into view, looking almost as overgrown as the driveway. Daniels stopped behind a beat-up jeep covered in dirt and sand. "Is that Victor's car?"

Mikey nodded. "I don't know if he owns it, but it was here earlier, so I think that's the car he's using."

Daniels undid his seatbelt. He'd informed Mikey of the circumstances surrounding Rem's disappearance, so she knew the deal, but she didn't have any insight into the upcoming ceremony or what Victor had in mind for Rem.

Redstone sat in the back seat and eyed the house in silence. "You sure you want to go in there by yourself, Detective? You don't want to bring him in for questioning?"

Daniels had debated that same question but knew what had to be done. "All I've got is an eyewitness that said Rem got into a car with Victor and his friends. Nothing forced, and Rem hasn't even been missing twenty-four hours. Plus a couple of followers who are either high as a kite or won't talk. A good attorney will walk Victor right out of the station." Daniels popped the door open. "This is what Victor wants. He'll expect me to beg him to save Rem. If I bring him in, he shuts up, but maybe if I talk to him one-on-one, I might make some progress."

"And what if he doesn't talk?" asked Redstone. "If he's planning some ceremony, you think he'll just give your partner up?"

"I don't know," said Daniels. "I doubt he expected Mikey to show, and maybe me finding him will throw him off his game. I can only hope he'll realize we're closing in fast, and he'll have no choice but to give Rem up. If I have to, I'll take him in and find some reason to hold him. Mikey, you'd come in handy for that if you accuse him of assault. If I can get him off the street, I can use that time to find Rem. Then we'll go from there."

Mikey unbuckled her seatbelt, as well. "You're right about Victor. He loves mind games. He'll try and twist you into a pretzel, so don't be surprised if he uses Rem to get to you. He expected you to be out of the picture by now because of that statue, so you might be able to get him to think twice, especially if you arrest him for what he did to me, but regardless, expect the unexpected."

Daniels thought that was good advice. "You two stay here."

"You sure?" asked Mikey. "I can come with you."

"Mikey, you are not moving from this car. I'll hold you down myself if I have to," said Redstone. He eyed Daniels. "I'll keep my ears open, though, in case you need anything."

Daniels recalled Redstone's background as a Texas Ranger. "I'd appreciate that. If something should happen, contact Captain Frank Lozano. He'll know what to do."

Redstone nodded, and Mikey bounced her knee. "Be careful," she said.

Daniels nodded. "I will." He slid out and closed the door.

Approaching the entry, he pulled his gun and held it at his side. He knocked and listened but didn't hear anything. "Victor D'Mato? It's Detective Daniels. I need to speak with you." He knocked again, but there was no answer. "Victor?"

Trying the doorknob, he found it was unlocked. He opened the door, it swung open, and he waited, standing outside, and listening. Hearing and seeing no one, he took a step inside. "Victor? It's the police." There was no response.

Taking a few steps, he noted the cozy interior which was more inviting than the exterior. An oversized, cushioned fabric couch faced a large stone fireplace and picture windows that overlooked sandy dunes and wispy grass which blew in the wind. Walking further in, he saw a sparse kitchen and hallway, which led to a back bedroom. "Victor? Hello?" He gripped his gun and entered the kitchen. A plate was in the sink and there was a half-filled pot of coffee on the counter. He walked down the hallway and checked the bedroom, finding a rumpled bed, but nothing else.

Heading back toward the front, he spied a back door between the windows. Moving closer he could see a long walkway that must have led to the water. Assuming Victor was outside and possibly on the beach, Daniels opened the door, his gaze darting around the property, looking for any possible place where Rem might be held, but seeing nothing, he stepped onto the porch and then onto the walkway. Sand-covered and wooden, it creaked as he moved down it. The wind picked up and tossed his hair, and he could hear the sound of ocean waves. The sand dunes on either side sloped up and the walkway rose until he reached the high point, and he could see the bottom of the dune at the end of the wooden path, and beyond that, the ocean.

Moving slowly, he stopped cold when, in the distance, off to the side of the next dune, and just before the sand flattened out, he saw what looked like someone lying face down on the ground. Too far to tell yet if it was a man or a woman, he picked up his speed and stopped again, an icy chill running through him, when he got close enough to see that it was the body of a man with wet, long, dark hair plastered against his skull.

CHAPTER TWENTY-FIVE

Rem sat in the darkness, holding his head. The hours had merged into one long unending nightmare of brief periods of dozing, the skittering of rodents, and the sound of his own breathing. He figured he'd be doing better if he could at least see something, but his lack of sight created irrational fears. What if they never came for him? What if Daniels never found him? What if the rodents became bolder and more aggressive? Had there been others locked in this room? Had they died here, screaming for help as their terror became real, and the animals feasted on their bodies?

He forced himself to stop thinking and to focus on the positive. Daniels would find him and Victor and his goons would be arrested, and maybe even Allison would find her own way out of whatever hell Victor had created for her.

He thought of Lozano and Daniels and knew they were looking. Someone would talk and they'd locate him and get him out of there. Rem might not be sleeping in any dark rooms for a while, but he'd be free of this hellhole.

Something furry brushed his ankle, and he sucked in a breath and whimpered. He just wanted to get out of there. He tried to swallow, but his throat stuck from thirst. He'd been given no food or water since being dumped there. His mind drifted. *What if they never come back, and you're left here to die from dehydration and exposure, and they'll find your body half-eaten by rats?*

He held his head. *Stop it. Just stop it,* he said to himself. *This is exactly what Victor wants. Don't give him the satisfaction. Daniels will find you. You will survive.*

Rubbing his eyes, he heard another squeak, but this time it wasn't the rodents. Raising his head, he listened, and felt fairly certain he heard the hum of an engine and the sound of an approaching vehicle. Tensing, he sat up as the noise grew louder. Someone was coming.

**

Daniels stepped off the walkway and approached the body lying on the side of the dune. Thinking of Rem, his belly shriveled in despair. His partner was lying dead in the sand. Daniels had failed, and Victor had won.

But the logical part of him noted the clothes the man wore. They weren't Rem's usual outfit of blue jeans and a t-shirt. This person wore tailored clothing and—

Daniels saw a flash of a reflection from the man's neck. "No," he whispered. He squatted and took the man's pulse, not expecting to feel anything. His skin was cold and, as Daniels suspected, there was no heartbeat. Taking hold of a shoulder, he pulled the man toward him. Blood stained the sand beneath the body, and Daniels stared in shocked disbelief when he saw the sparkling V shining up at him. The dead man was Victor D'Mato.

**

Rem listened as more cars seemed to arrive. He could hear doors open and close, but no voices. If someone was out there, they weren't talking. He called out, hopeful that someone could hear and help him. Banging on the walls, he yelled, but no one responded, and no one came to find him. He blinked, wishing he could see something, and he kept banging until the sounds ended and the silence returned.

His mind raced with frightening scenarios. Was he in some sort of soundproof room? Had they left him here, doomed to die, while people came and went, never aware of his presence? What if he was never found? Breathing hard and terrified, he bit back the panic and forced himself to calm down. None of those things would happen. He was freaking out, and he had to control his fear if he was going to get out of this mess. Instead of sitting again, he paced, trying to stay active, but after several minutes, his lack of food, sleep and water caught up, and he sat again, telling himself to conserve his energy. Rem took several deep breaths, and tried to think rationally, because there was another scary possibility to consider; one where he hadn't been forgotten, and whoever had arrived wasn't ignoring him, but was preparing for him instead.

Moaning, Rem hung his head and said a silent prayer.

**

Daniels eyed Victor's body, still in shock, but grateful it wasn't his partner. Trying not to think about Rem, he went into detective mode. If Mikey had been telling the truth, then Victor had been murdered not long after Mikey had left him. Had the killer been present when Mikey had been here? Did Mikey know the killer? Or, had Mikey killed Victor and lied about their encounter?

Looking at the body, he saw that Victor's bloody shirt was open, exposing his chest. A long thin cut had been sliced down his sternum, and his throat had a puncture wound. A heavy pool of blood darkened the sand and ran down his chest, neck and ribcage. His wrists and ankles were raw and red, so he had to have been tied down. Checking the area, he saw depressions in the dune that might have been created from several footsteps, but it was hard to be certain.

Standing, he caught sight of Victor's exposed shoulder when a gust of wind blew Victor's shirt open, and Daniels saw a tattoo. Something about it made him take notice and he stared. It was of a colorful bird with tear drops falling from its eyes, as if the bird were crying. A flicker of a memory stirred, and he tried to recall where he'd seen the tattoo before, but he couldn't grasp it.

Noting the time of day, he snapped out of his reverie. The shadows were growing long and with Victor dead, his partner's chances for survival had just plummeted, and he didn't have time to waste. He raced back to the house, calling Lozano on his cell and telling him about Victor and to send the appropriate teams. He didn't mention Mikey's possible involvement, because at this point, she was his last lead, and he needed her.

Getting off the phone, he saw Mikey and Redstone standing by the car as he approached. Determined, he walked over to Mikey. "Tell me exactly what happened when you met with Victor."

Mikey's eyes widened. "What do you mean? I told you. We argued. He hit me, and I hit him back. Then I left. Why? Where's Victor? Did you talk?"

"Where'd you hit him?" asked Daniels.

"What's this all about?" asked Redstone.

"Where?" asked Mikey. "Why does that matter?"

Daniels studied her face, trying to detect if she was lying to him. "Because he's dead."

Mikey's face drained of color. "He's what?"

"He's dead?" asked Redstone, looking just as pale.

Daniels pointed, angry. "He's lying on a sand dune with his throat cut. Which means you're the last one to see him alive, and if you're telling the truth, he was murdered not long after you left. Or you're lying, and you killed him."

Mikey shook her head. "I didn't kill him. He was alive when I left."

"Mikey wouldn't kill anyone, Detective," said Redstone.

"You sure about that?" asked Daniels. "She was pretty angry, and from what I gather, she had a reason to hate Victor." He stepped closer to Mikey, looming over her. "Are you playing some sort of game here? Do you know where Victor is hiding Rem? Did you have something to do with Victor's death?" He shot her a dirty look. "Because if I find out you're involved in this, you're going to be spending a nice chunk of the rest of your life behind bars."

Mikey dropped her jaw. "I had nothing to do with this. I didn't kill him."

"That's enough, Detective," said Redstone.

"No, it isn't," said Daniels, facing Redstone. "Because my only lead is dead, which means so is Rem, and if she knows something, she better say something. Now."

Mikey held her chest, and her eyes welled with tears. "I swear it on my brother's life. I didn't kill anyone."

Daniels studied her, gauging her truthfulness. "Was there anyone else here when you arrived or left?"

"No," she said. "At least, I didn't see anyone. But I didn't check the house, and I wasn't here that long. I suppose someone could have been on the beach, or in the bedroom. I don't know."

"Damn it," said Daniels. He clutched his neck and shut his eyes.

"If he's dead, then maybe there's no ceremony," said Redstone.

Daniels opened his eyes, recalling the crime scene. The more he thought about it, the more ritualistic it appeared. The lacerations on Victor's wrists and ankles, the disturbed sand, the puncture on his neck, the cut down his sternum. "No. I think there was a ceremony, Redstone, and somebody held it here. It looks like Victor somehow became a victim of his own madness."

"You think they chose to kill Victor, instead of Rem?" asked Mikey.

Daniels stared up at the trees, trying to think. "I don't know. But something went wrong. Something Victor didn't see coming." He thought of Allison. Was she involved, or was she a victim, like Rem?

He didn't think for a second that Rem was out of the woods. He eyed the time. It was getting darker.

"Was there anything else about the scene?" asked Redstone. "Anything that might help point you in another direction? Anything in the house?"

Daniels hadn't searched the house, but since it was a crime scene, he technically needed to let the Crime Unit go through it, but if that was his only option, he wouldn't hesitate. Something else bugged him, though, and he thought of the tattoo. "Victor has a tattoo on his shoulder, of a crying bird. Does that ring any bells for you?"

"He's had that for a while now," said Mikey. "Why? Did you recognize it?"

"It doesn't ring any bells for me." Redstone studied him, his brow rising. "But it does for you. Where have you seen it?"

Daniels ran a tense hand through his hair, wishing he could just slow down and think, but that lingering sense that Rem's time was short wouldn't abate. He had to move fast. "I don't know, but it's familiar."

"I think you do know," said Redstone. "Come here." He took Daniels' arm and pulled him over to the base of a tree. "Sit."

"I don't have time to sit, Redstone," yelled Daniels.

"You want to find your partner? That tattoo is nagging at you for a reason. Give it a second to reveal itself. Five minutes of going quiet is a lot better than an hour of running in circles. Now sit."

Daniels wanted to resist but had to acknowledge that he didn't have any other options, so he sat.

"Good. Get comfortable. Try and relax. You're as tight as Mikey when she can't pay a bill."

"Hey," said Mikey, swatting Redstone in the arm. "I told you I'd pay you back."

Daniels ignored them and took some deep breaths. Redstone was right. Every muscle was bunched, and he shook with adrenaline. He forced himself to calm down and focus.

"Good," said Redstone. "Keep breathing. And think of the tattoo. Just bring it up in your mind's eye. Don't try to force anything."

Daniels did as Redstone instructed, feeling silly, but willing to give it a shot. He brought up the picture of the crying bird and continued to breathe. His shoulders came down and his mind slowly stopped swirling.

"Take your time," said Redstone. "Give it a moment to surface but stay relaxed."

Daniels did his best to do as Redstone asked, but he was acutely aware of the passing minutes. His partner was in trouble, and he was out here meditating. Feeling anxious, his heart rate began to pick up again. "This is ridic—"

An image popped into his head, and he frowned.

"What is it?" asked Redstone. "What do you see?"

Daniels' heart thudded harder, but for an entirely different reason. He was back in one of his nightmares, when his mind was playing tricks on him, sleep eluded him, and the voices spoke to him. He swallowed, recalling the vision.

"Let it play out," said Redstone, speaking softly. "Allow it to unfold. You're not there, Detective. You're just a bystander."

Daniels' mind drifted, and he stiffened. He was being held down. There were people watching. He recalled the knife, lowering and piercing his skin. He'd been desperate, fighting to get loose, but failing. The knife had cut his skin along his sternum, like Victor, the blood spilling and rolling down his sides. At this point in the dream, he'd been flailing, but he wouldn't let himself out, because there was something else. The location. Daniels detached from his fear and focused. He was in a warehouse, old and no longer in use. There was a loft above, and on the side of the building was a painted image. It was the crying bird. He opened his eyes and saw Redstone squatting in front of him with Mikey behind him, watching.

"What is it? Did you see the bird?" asked Redstone.

Daniels replayed the vision in his head. "It was from a nightmare, from when..." He found it hard to say.

"...the statue affected you," said Redstone. "Where was the bird?"

"I was...the bird was...on a building...no...wait. On a wall. It was painted on the side of a wall."

"Where?" asked Redstone.

Daniels straightened. "It's a warehouse. An old warehouse. There were people inside, and I was lying on a table...or something cold. They were watching...." He thought of Victor on the beach and stood. "Does Victor own a warehouse?"

"I don't know," said Redstone.

Mikey stared off. "Wait...hold up."

Daniels itched to do something. "What is it? Does he own one? I don't recall anything in his background that says he did."

"Could be owned by someone else," said Redstone. "What do you remember, Mikey?"

Mikey held her swollen eye. "Before Victor went to prison, back when I was...well, under his spell and I thought I was smart and everyone else was stupid..."

"I recall those days," said Redstone.

"I...I...," she crossed her arms, "I was one of his favorites." She swallowed, as if the memories were painful.

Redstone's face fell. "Mikey..."

"It's okay," she whispered. "That was another time, but I remember he was comfortable around me. He said things."

"What things?" asked Daniels, acutely aware of the ever-encroaching darkness.

"His plans. His goals. His crazy theories and beliefs. But I remember once when I was with him, he was talking to someone about a warehouse. A place where he could be private with his followers, where no one could interrupt."

Daniels' adrenaline coursed through him. That had to be where they were holding Rem. "Where? Do you remember where?"

"They never discussed where. And this was years ago. He said something about family. I think he was purchasing it from a family member, or at least that's what it sounded like. I never heard anything about it since, and then he did his stint in prison, and I got out."

Daniels tried to think. They'd found nothing in their investigation that linked Victor with an old warehouse, but could his family own one or have a connection to one? Could Victor have purchased one under another name? "We have to find that warehouse."

"It would have to be nearby," said Redstone. "He'd want to be able to travel easily to it, especially if his followers have access. There's the old warehouse district in the city."

"No way it would be there," said Daniels. "Too many people. It would have to be away from the city. If it's old and out of use, it could be anywhere."

"Maybe not," said Mikey. "There are old warehouses in the city, especially in the industrial section. It could be there."

Daniels raced for the car. "Come on." He jumped into the driver's seat and Redstone and Mikey followed. He grabbed his phone.

"You're thinking to start checking old, abandoned warehouses?" asked Redstone.

"Yes," said Daniels. "If Lozano can pull up a list of possible places that may no longer be in use, we can start sending out patrols. There can't be that many that are secluded and abandoned. Rem's got to be in one of them. And we can do another check on Victor's family. See if any of them ever owned a warehouse. And we can do a search for the image of the bird itself. If it's tattooed on Victor and painted on a wall, then maybe it means something."

"It's a lot to check in one night," said Redstone.

"You have any other ideas, you let me know," said Daniels, throwing the car into drive as Lozano answered the phone.

CHAPTER TWENTY-SIX

Hearing a noise, Rem jumped. He'd been sitting against the wall for a while, and may have dozed, when he heard a bang. Sitting up, he waited, his heart thumping when he heard approaching footsteps. His anxiety ramped up and, breathing hard, he heard the steps grow louder, and then he heard a door open in the distance, and a small sliver of light blossomed through a crack of wood.

Hopeful that he may have been found, he stood. "Hello?" he yelled. "Anybody there?"

Another door opened, this one much closer, and he held his breath when someone walked up just outside his door. He held his stomach. "Please. I need help. I'm a police officer."

No one spoke, but a small, square plate at the base of his door screeched and rose up, and muted light entered his room. A plastic bag with a sandwich in it was slid in and then a bottled water followed. Then the plate fell back into place, and the muted light vanished.

"Wait," said Rem, running to the door and hitting it. "Don't go. Get me out of here."

No one answered, the distant doors slammed, one louder and one softer, his one trickle of light disappeared, and the darkness returned.

**

Daniels drove fast down the highway, talking to Lozano on his cell, and getting updates as fast as Lozano had them. They'd dispatched patrols down to the industrial area, and were doing checks on any possible old, secluded warehouses that could belong to Victor. Lozano was checking on the image of the bird, but so far, had not had any luck. And they were still checking Victor's family connection but had found no one connected to Victor that owned a warehouse. Forensics and a coroner's unit had arrived at the bungalow, and they were searching it for clues.

After Lozano had updated him, Daniels hung up, frustrated. The sun had descended, and he recalled Cindy's words regarding the start of the ceremony. *Any time after dark.* He hoped and prayed that Victor's death might somehow prevent Rem's, but something told him that Victor's little group had no intention of stopping now. Cursing, he smacked the steering wheel with his palm.

"I'm guessing it's not good news," said Redstone.

"No," said Daniels, trying to focus on the road. "It's not."

"We'll find him," said Mikey, who sat in the front seat. "We've got to." She rubbed her head. "Think, Mason. Of all of us, you knew him best. Where would Victor get hold of a warehouse?"

Daniels heard Redstone sigh. "I wish I knew. I haven't seen Victor in years, Mikey. That's a lot of time to buy a piece of real estate." He sat forward and leaned toward the front seat.

Mikey looked back at him. "What about his family? Have you been in touch with them at all?"

"I've spoken to his mother, but even that's been a while. His brother lives in New York and last I heard, they were still estranged, which is why it's odd you heard Victor speak of family. He barely spoke to his. If he was close to anyone, it was—" He sucked in a breath.

Daniels glanced back. "What? It was what?" His skin broke out in chills when he saw Redstone's face.

"Mason? What's wrong?" asked Mikey.

"Oh, shit," said Mason. He sat back and Daniels eyed him through the rearview mirror. "He was closest to us." Redstone's eyes rounded. "Maxwell," he said.

Mikey turned in her seat. "Max? What does he have to do with this?"

"Who's Maxwell?" asked Daniels, gripping the steering wheel.

"Our older brother," said Mikey.

Redstone leaned in again. "Victor wasn't talking about his family. He was talking about ours."

"What do you mean?" asked Mikey. "He's not our family."

"Not anymore, he isn't. But one of the reasons Victor and I moved out here was because of Max, remember?" Redstone held the back of Mikey's seat. "Max couldn't stop talking about it. He owned property and was doing well for himself."

Daniels' shifted nervously in his seat. "What property? Did Max own a warehouse?"

Redstone closed his eyes. "God, it's been a while, but I remember when I first visited, Max took me around town, showed me the sights." He opened his eyes, his face sullen. "He took me out of the city limits, to an isolated area. It used to be an old farm, but the area had been used to manufacture something, I don't remember what. It had a big building on it that was falling into disrepair. He thought the real estate value would go up, so he held onto it. I remember him telling me later that he had an interested buyer who wanted to stay anonymous, and he was planning to sell it."

Daniels took a steady breath. Could this be the clue they needed? "Where?"

Redstone held his forehead. "That's just it. It's been years."

"Call Max," said Mikey.

"He's out of the country. In Indonesia, I think. Won't be back until next week," said Redstone. He shut his eyes again and held the bridge of his nose. "Let me think."

Mikey pulled out her cell. "I'll try to reach him."

"Come on, Redstone. Do that relaxing thing you told me to do," said Daniels. "You've got to remember where that property is."

"Back then, it was a more secluded area," said Redstone. "The city's grown since then, but it was decent acreage with a lot of trees and overgrowth, so it would serve Victor's purposes."

"Think," said Daniels.

Mikey listened on her phone. "Hell. It's going to voicemail." She left a hurried message and hung up. "Focus, Mason. If anyone can remember, it's you."

Daniels thought of Lozano. "I can call my captain. Give him your brother's name. They can look for a record of sale." He pulled out his cell, praying they would have enough time.

Redstone went quiet as Daniels dialed. Lozano answered, and Daniels gave him Maxwell Redstone's name. Lozano said he'd find out what he could and hung up.

Daniels waited and watched as Redstone sat quiet in the backseat, and jumped when Redstone suddenly opened his eyes, grabbed the back of Daniels' seat, and pointed. "Take the next exit."

Daniels didn't hesitate and, tires screeching, left the highway.

**

Rem held the bottled water. He'd sucked down half of it before telling himself to slow down because he had no idea when he'd get another one. The sandwich sat untouched. He'd opened the bag, but the smell of the food made him queasy and based on the squeaking he was hearing, his mice roommates were enjoying a nice feast.

Holding the water, he tried not to think the worst. At least he hadn't been forgotten. Someone knew he was here and had fed and given him something to drink. That gave him hope. The darkness pulled at him though, and the thought of spending another night out here made him want to cry. In fact, his emotions were swirling, and his chest hurt from the tension. Raising a hand, he rubbed his eyes and clasped his hands together when he felt his fingers begin to shake. His body tingled, his movements slowed, and his tongue began to feel thick.

Something cold slid through him. *No,* he thought to himself with dread. *No, not again.* He recognized the symptoms from his night with Allison. His head became foggy, and he found it hard to think. Tightening his grip on the water, he opened it and emptied the remains on the ground. It had been tampered with, and he'd been drugged. Even though he couldn't see, his head swam, and he moaned in despair. Gripping at the wall, he tried to stand, but his legs wouldn't hold him, and he slid back down. Resting his head against the wall, he blinked, but the dark played tricks on him, and he thought he saw someone in the room with him. The figure morphed and lunged at him, and he pushed back against the wall with a shriek. The vision faded, and Rem fought to stay calm, but his body began to tremble, and his teeth chattered.

He wrapped his arms around himself, saying soothing words, and doing his best not to lose it. His head spinning, he reached out to hold the wall, certain he was falling, and thought of Daniels. Guilt swept over him when he realized he wasn't going to make it. He would die alone in this black room, going stark raving mad. The sadness and panic bubbled up, and he couldn't stop the sob that erupted from his core.

Holding his belly, which swirled almost as much as his head, he heard a noise. It was the same sound as earlier. A door was opening. Listening, he tensed when he heard the second door open, and then loud footsteps approaching.

He tried to talk, but his vocal cords locked up, and he froze when the door to his room opened. Two men stood there, one holding a flashlight, and Rem squinted, barely able to see. They approached him, dropped a hood over his head, grabbed his arms, and dragged him out of the room.

**

Daniels stopped at a light, his fingers rapping at the steering wheel. "You sure you know where we're going?"

"We ate at a restaurant," said Redstone, "about two blocks up. It was called Max's which is why I remember it. It's gone now, but I can use it as a starting point. I don't think it was far from there."

The light turned green, and Daniels hit the accelerator.

"Do you remember any distinguishing characteristics about the property?" asked Mikey. "Was there an ornate gate or a fancy mailbox?"

"It was your standard gate. Nothing special, although it had a padlock at the front. And the entry was wrought iron. There were vines growing all over it. You almost couldn't see the iron."

"What about a sign? Was there a name?" asked Daniels.

"Not that I recall." Redstone looked out a window. "Here. The restaurant was here." Daniels slowed as he passed an office building. "Keep going straight," said Redstone.

Daniels kept driving. "What about neighbors? Did you see any?"

"I don't recall," said Redstone, staring out as Daniels drove.

"Did Max say anything about the place?" asked Mikey. "Why did he buy it? What did it process? Who owned it before him?"

"It was purely an investment," said Redstone. "That's all I know."

Daniels passed more buildings and moved into a residential neighborhood. "Are we close? This doesn't look like anything close to farms."

"I know," said Redstone. "I told you. It's been a while. This area has been developed since I was here, but there are some things that are the same. If Max sold the property to Victor, though, then Victor would have no reason to change it. He'd leave it as is to keep prying eyes away."

They kept driving, and the homes became sparser, but larger and with more land. "Ringing any bells?" asked Daniels. He began to wonder if they were on a wild goose chase, but they had nowhere else to go. If this didn't pan out, and the warehouse was not found, he didn't know what he would do. He kept going and tried not to think the worst.

**

They dragged Rem out of his hellhole, and he felt the coolness of fresh air on his skin. The cloth on his head made it hard to breathe, and he tried to get his feet under him, but his drug-induced disorientation made it hard to stabilize himself. He heard the swell of crickets and knew he was outside. Wanting to scream for help, he opened his mouth, but all that emerged was a squeak. He couldn't summon the energy to do it. They continued to half-pull, half-drag him and the ground went from what sounded like pebbled rock to grass, and then to a hard surface. The pressure around him changed and it felt like he'd been moved inside. Hearing the reverberations of his movement against a structure, he was dropped to the ground, where he landed on all fours. His palms slapped against a dirty floor and his knees hit hard. His vision swam and his stomach rebelled, and he fought to stay up. He wanted to stand but didn't have the balance. Shivering, he felt the slickness of the sweat on his skin.

Footsteps encroached, and someone yanked off his hood and pulled off his jacket. Bright lights made him clench his eyes shut, and breathing hard, he wondered where he was. No one spoke, but he knew he wasn't alone.

He heard the crackle of fire, and once his eyes adjusted, he opened one, and saw a torch. He opened the other and got a look at where he was kneeling. Four torches illuminated a square area with a raised stone platform in the middle. Men and women stood around the square, spread evenly apart, all watching with no expressions. Scanning the area, he saw he was in the center of an old building with high ceilings that were falling in and which stretched out in a wide expanse around him. There was a loft above, but the shadows prevented him from seeing anything in it. The crackle of the burning torches echoed throughout the building, and he tried to catch his breath.

"Where am I?" he managed to whisper, but no one answered him. They just continued to stare like bored sentries looking out over a quiet countryside. "What do you want?" he asked but got no answer.

More footsteps neared, and he saw two men approach, dragging another figure—a woman. They dumped her beside him, and he blinked, trying to clear his vision. The woman groaned and pushed up.

"Allison?" he asked. He tried to sit up but fell back against the stone platform.

Her gaze met his. She looked tired and frazzled. "Rem?"

He tried to reach out but was having trouble directing his limbs. "Are you okay?"

Tears sprung into her eyes. "I'm so sorry," she said. She crawled over to him. "Are you hurt?"

His thoughts were a jumble, and he couldn't help but stare at the men and women staring back at him. "I think they gave me something." His voice sounded slurred.

Raising her hand, she touched his cheek. "This is my fault. I'm sorry."

Rem tried to move but was finding it increasingly difficult. "Any idea what to do now?" he managed to ask. "Looks like they're waiting for something." His heart pounded against his chest. "Is Victor about to make his big appearance?"

She laid her head against his chest and squeezed his wrist, and he heard her sob.

"Hey, don't cry," he said, trying to instill some confidence into his voice. "I've been in worse pickles than this." He managed to move his hand to her arm to assure her, although he wasn't feeling too confident. "We'll get out of here."

She nodded and sniffed against his shoulder. "I'm scared," she said.

Rem swallowed, watching the people around him, and shaking from his own fear. "I know. Me, too."

She kept crying, and a man walked up to them. He grabbed Allison by the arm and pulled on her.

"No," said Allison.

"Leave her alone," said Rem, reaching for her. He pushed up and the man kicked him in the stomach. Rem rolled into the dirt, retching, and trying to find his lost breath.

"Please," Allison screamed. "Let me go." But the man yanked her back, and another walked up and took her other arm as Allison struggled. "Don't. Please."

Rem watched, helpless, as they pulled out a knife, and using it to cut her clothes, they stripped her until she stood naked. Tormented, he watched as she cried, and they brought out a dark cloak, put it over her head, and it fell over her body, covering her, including a hood on her head. All he could see was the firelight reflecting from her face and eyes as she stood in the robe.

The men let go of her, and she stood still, watching him, and he wanted to scream at her to run, but his own terror stopped him because he expected that he would be next. The men would grab and strip him, and he would be forced to wear the same heavy cloak. Attempting to get away, he struggled to get his arms beneath him, but everything ached, and another intense round of vertigo hit him, and he fell back into the dirt, his fingers clawing at the ground to stop the spinning.

Fighting back his own tears, he almost yelped when he felt a hand on his shoulder, and a soft voice in his ear. "Relax," it said. "Don't fight it. You'll feel better if you just relax." The hand moved down and caressed his back and his insides curdled as his mind flashed back to his night at Allison's. "Let me take care of you," said the voice. "Like I did before."

Whimpering, he turned his head, and saw Allison smiling down at him.

**

Redstone sat forward. "Avocados. I remember now. It was an old avocado farm."

Daniels glanced back from his seat, his eyes alert as the scenery became heavier with trees and foliage. "You're sure?"

"Yes." Redstone pointed. "I remember this place." Although it was dark outside, they passed a sprawling estate with a large sign sporting a green avocado lit up in neon. "Keep going."

Daniels hit the accelerator, trying not to go too fast, but knowing they had to hurry. He refused to believe they would be too late.

"There," said Redstone. "That grocery store. Maxwell pointed it out to me when we were here. Turn left at the next light."

"I hope you're right," said Mikey.

Daniels turned, and once they made it past the busy corner, it went quiet. The road was dark, and it turned to one lane. He slowed the car, hoping and anticipating that they were close. "Anything? Are we nearby?"

Redstone groaned. "I'm not sure. I don't recall how long we were on this road."

The lack of light didn't help. If there was a fence with an overgrown wrought iron entry, it would be almost impossible to see.

"Right side or left?" asked Mikey.

"Right," said Redstone. He sighed. "I think. But I know it's on this street."

Daniels fought to stay cool. If they ended up being within a mile of Rem only to find him dead, Daniels would never forgive himself. He kept driving, looking for anything that might be a driveway leading to an old farm. They passed the occasional mailbox, but they looked well maintained, so he didn't stop. They moved slowly down the road; it curved slightly and when he rounded it, he stopped when the road came to an end. He cursed in frustration.

Mikey gripped the dash. "It's a dead end, Mason. Are you sure we don't turn off somewhere earlier?"

Redstone didn't answer.

"Redstone," yelled Daniels, ready to pull his hair out and yank out Redstone's handlebar mustache at the same time. "Where the hell are we?"

Redstone popped the door open. "I think we're here."

Daniels held his breath. He looked out the windshield, but his headlights illuminated only the vegetation in front of him where the road stopped.

"Here, where?" asked Mikey. She opened her door and got out.

Daniels turned off the ignition, but left the headlights on, and exited the vehicle. The area was dark, and all he could hear were crickets. The moon was out, but he could see no entry to any farm. "There's nothing out here."

"You have a flashlight?" asked Redstone.

Daniels popped his trunk and grabbed one. He flipped it on.

Redstone headed across the street, and Daniels followed, holding the light. Mikey walked with them. "Look for a fence," said Redstone. "If it was overgrown then, it would be more so now."

Daniels couldn't see anything resembling a fence but continued to scan the area with the light.

"Over here," said Mikey. "Look."

Daniels searched for her and found her on the other side, across from him. He ran over.

"Shine the light," she said pointing.

He did and saw it. A pebbled dirt road, leading into foliage, with what looked like recent tire tracks. Redstone joined him. "This is it." He raced through some vines, and Daniels went with him, and stopped when they almost ran into a padlocked, wrought iron gate.

CHAPTER TWENTY-SEVEN

Rem tried to scramble away. Sharp stones on the ground cut at his palms, and he pushed with his feet, but his body felt like dead weight. His mind fought to understand what was happening to him. What was Allison doing?

The hand on his back lifted, and he heard her speak. "Secure him."

Footsteps approached and hands gripped his arms and legs. They lifted him, and although he struggled to free himself, they were stronger. His back hit something cold and hard, and his limbs were pulled tight. His wrists were tied to the corners above him, and his ankles to the corners below, and he was staring up at the ceiling, lying spread-eagled on the stone platform, unable to move. He pulled, but didn't budge, and although he didn't believe it was possible, his terror notched up higher.

Allison appeared beside him, standing in her cloak, and sliding her hood back, she looked down at him.

Rem's heart was racing so fast, he wondered if he'd have a heart attack right there and die. He wondered if that might be the better option. "Please," he managed to whisper. "Let me go."

She smiled down at him, then took a couple of steps up, and stood over him. Squatting, she lifted her robe, straddled, and sat on his waist, her bare knees revealed and her hands resting on his chest. He hadn't thought he could be more frightened, but he'd been wrong.

"Did you like my performance?" she asked, leaning over him. "Was I suitably scared?"

Rem moaned. What was going on?

She trailed her hands down to his stomach. "I'm impressed with how you tried to reassure me." Her eyes twinkled in the firelight. "It confirms that we chose well."

Rem tried to pull it together and struggled against his bindings, but they held tight. "What are you doing?" He hoped he was making sense because his words sounded jumbled to him. "Why am I here?"

Her gaze traveled over him. "You wanted to get to know me, didn't you? You wanted to see if I was involved with Victor or would tell you something about his followers?" She ran her hands over his chest. "Are you suitably informed, Detective?"

Rem's stomach twisted and cramped. Had she known Rem's motives the whole time? Had she fooled him that easily? "At my house," he said. "You were scared." He didn't know if he should engage with her or not.

"Victor and I thought it would be fun to mess with you." She ran a fingernail down a rib. "Victor likes his games."

Rem gritted his teeth at her touch and fought to stay present. "Where's Victor?" Talking was his only option, although he realized all it would do was delay the inevitable.

Her smile grew. "He's dead."

Rem took a deep shuttered breath, shut his eyes, and prayed for help.

"Mere hours ago," she said. "It was unfortunate, but necessary. He'd become a burden, but, as it turns out, also a benefit." She trailed her finger up to Rem's neck and jaw. "He'd served us well, but it was time."

Rem kept talking. "You killed him."

She ran her finger over his lips. "After he went to prison, I found his people looking to me for guidance. I took advantage of the void. Victor had taught me a lot, but I learned much more while he was gone. After his release, he was…hesitant to accept any changes that weren't directly his." Her palm cupped Rem's face, and she stroked his cheek with her thumb. "His teachings and beliefs were still as brilliant and enthralling as ever, but the means to them had suffered. His assumptions were flawed and old. He still believed in the need for human flesh to accomplish our desires, but that was unnecessary. Blood is more effective and far simpler." Her thumb stroked Rem's bottom lip, and he turned his face away from her touch. "And then Victor made a fatal error." She pushed Rem's hair back and ran her fingers through it. "He wanted to choose."

Rem tried to keep up, but the combination of her fingers, her words, and his anxiety made it hard to comprehend. "Choose what?" The words trembled as he spoke them.

Her hands returned to his chest, and she slid them down to his waist. "Between the darkness and the light, my love. When we found you, he chose the light, but I knew the truth. True power would come from sacrificing both."

She raised her hand, palm up, and someone stepped forward and put a knife in it. Something shifted in Rem's core, and he stifled a sob when she held the knife over him. He knew then he was going to die.

Allison put the tip of the knife at the top of his shirt. "I saw clearly that Victor was the dark, and you were the light. It was perfect. He was cruel and maniacal, and you, well you fought so hard to save your partner, and you tried to be such the gentleman with me. You two were the opposite sides of a coin. It was destined." With a flick of her wrist, she sliced the knife through his t-shirt, and cut it open to the hem, exposing Rem's chest. She rested a palm on Rem's quaking belly. "I promise. I'll make it quick, but I can't promise it won't hurt."

Rem whimpered and hot tears rose and fell from his eyes.

**

Daniels handed his phone to Mikey. "Call Lozano. The number is in the contacts. Tell him what's going on. He can track me through GPS. You stay in the car and don't move until back-up arrives. You got that?"

Mikey took the phone. "What are you going to do?"

Daniels pulled his weapon and checked it. "I'm going in."

"Are you crazy?" asked Mikey. "By yourself?"

"No," said Redstone. "I'm going with him."

Daniels looked over. "You sure about that?"

Redstone leaned down, yanked up a pant leg, and pulled a gun from an ankle holster. "I always come prepared." He checked the gun. "I'm a licensed P.I. in this state, and with my background, I believe you'll find me helpful."

"Mason, seriously?" asked Mikey.

"Do as he says, Mikey," said Redstone. "Go back to the car, call his captain, and wait for the cavalry. Do not, under any circumstances, follow us in. You'll be risking your life, as well as ours and Remalla's. Do you understand?"

Mikey stood, her expression a mixture of worry and fear. "Promise me you'll be careful."

Redstone paused, put a hand on her shoulder, and nodded. "I will. Don't worry. Now go to the car." He slid the gun into his waistband.

Mikey's gaze darted between them, her face furrowed, and she turned back.

Daniels eyed the fence, looking for a way in. "You realize what we're walking into?"

"We could always wait for back-up," said Redstone.

Daniels shook his head. "Something tells me we're out of time. But if you want to wait, there's no judgement from me." He tossed the flashlight over, found a handhold, grabbed it, and pulled himself up and over the fence. He landed hard in the dirt, and then waited, listening.

He heard a rustling, and a grunt, and then Redstone landed beside him, swiping at his pants. Daniels grabbed the flashlight and aimed it into the brush.

"Let's go find your partner, Detective," said Redstone, and Daniels took off into the trees.

**

Rem eyed the knife Allison held, and another sob erupted. "You're going to kill me." He clenched his eyes shut as another wave of dizziness hit him and everything spun. He felt her lean over him.

"Did you drink all the water?" she whispered.

Rem expelled a pained breath and opened his eyes. "No."

Her fingers trailed down his chest. "It would have gone better for you if you'd finished it." Her gaze followed her fingers. "You are a magnificent specimen." She kissed him along his collarbone, and down his sternum, and he squirmed to pull away, but only succeeded in pulling his bindings tighter. His hands and fingers were going numb from the pressure.

"Don't," he whispered.

She raised her head. "You didn't mind it before." Her fingers played with his chest hair. "As I recall, you had a good time, as did I." She grinned. "Better than any time I had with Victor." She loomed over him and lowered her lips near his. "For old time's sake." Her mouth descended over his, and she kissed him hard.

Rem wanted to pull away, but he let her kiss him, hoping in some crazy way it would help if he didn't resist. Her tongue probed his mouth, and his stomach lurched in protest, and he couldn't help but turn his head and break the connection. He groaned in desperation and dread.

Rising up, she ran her fingers down his chest, her nails scratching him. "I'll remember our time together with fondness. You gave yourself to me then, just as you will tonight, and your sacrifice will serve us all, and I thank you. Your offering will not be wasted. Take heart in that."

Rem fought to clear his head, and some of the swirling abated. He hated to ask, but wanted to know, so he forced the words out. "What are you going to do?"

She continued to stroke his skin, and her body rocked against him. "If we only had more time, we could have some fun."

Rem fought the urge to throw up, and almost did, but someone approached and distracted him when she stood beside Allison. He tried to focus, and saw a woman with long, dark hair staring down at him. Her average features did not stand out from any of the other followers, save for her striking blue eyes.

She put her hand on his head and pulled on his hair. Rem swallowed, trying not to be sick. "You're right," said the woman. "He is special." Her voice was bitterly cold and low, and, to his ears, it sounded like a growl. She leaned over. "Perhaps we could both have some fun."

Allison stilled and sneered. "Return to your place. Now."

The woman narrowed her eyes, and Rem could almost feel her enmity, but whether it was for him or Allison, he didn't know. The woman's icy gaze met Allison's. "I created the statues. Victor said they bought us critical time. He told me I would be rewarded." She pulled on Rem's hair again. "This is what I want."

Allison stopped roving her hands over Rem, but her eyes flickered with distaste in the light. "Then you will be the first of many to taste what is offered." She held the dark stare with the woman, her face flat. "Now go."

The woman hesitated and, after a few seconds, she let go of Rem, stepped back, and not saying a word, disappeared back into the group.

Allison frowned with annoyance, but returned her attention to Rem. "While it is enticing to spend more time with you, Victor was right about making haste. Time is short, and the veil is very thin tonight. It has been all week." She looked up, and Rem did, too. He could see a sliver of moon through a hole in the ceiling. "It's a good night to celebrate the darkness…" she looked back at him, "…and the light." She held the knife over him. "You want to know what I'm going to do?"

Seeing the knife glitter in the light of the moon, Rem regretted his question. He pulled against his restraints without success.

Placing the knife tip at the top of his sternum, she pressed it against his skin and he sucked in a whimpered breath. "I am going to reward loyalty. All of us here have earned our place in the circle."

Rem bit his lip in revulsion and bile rose in his throat.

"We have tasted the blood of the dark and received its power and vitality." Holding the knife, she pulled the tip down his sternum, drawing blood, and Rem gritted his teeth, the pain slicing through him, along with the panic. "And now we will taste the blood of the light and receive its beauty and vigor." She ran the knife down to just above his stomach, and Rem refused to cry out as the steel burned into his skin, but he couldn't stop the tears from falling.

She raised the knife and held it. "And we will all benefit. Your sacrifice will provide us with the long, healthy, and youthful lives we crave, while everyone else grows weak, tired, and sick." She touched the tip of the knife with her finger, wiped the blood from it, then put it in her mouth and sucked it off.

Rem grappled with the pain. His chest ached, and he could see rivulets of his blood trickle down his chest to the stone beneath him. "You're crazy," he whispered in gasps, but her torture had helped sharpen his senses. Catching his breath, he blinked and felt sweat drip from his forehead. "The only thing my blood is going to get you is an upset stomach. And if you drank Victor's, you better make a doctor's appointment."

Allison removed her finger from her mouth. "They will come, one by one, and take what they wish." She touched a drop of blood from his chest. "But this amount is meager." She ran her finger down his side. "We'll need more."

Rem's breathing escalated, and he fought for more time. He wasn't ready to die. "They'll find you. You're killing a cop, and you killed Victor. They'll come for you."

"Which is why, after tonight, I will disappear, as will anyone who wishes to join me, and the others will scatter, until it's time again and those beyond will call us back to reconvene, and taste again, the dark and the light."

Rem groaned and fought to ignore the pain slicing through his chest. "Those beyond? Who are they? Another set of pathetic groupies?" His body trembled, and his voice shook.

She ran another finger through his blood. "No, Detective. The ones who call me, who speak to me." She waved a hand. "These people are not the only ones present. We are being observed from the other side. They revel in this sacrifice as much as we do."

Rem blinked when her face blurred, and then righted itself. "I'm not particularly enjoying this."

She licked her finger and waved the knife. "I am."

Rem heard a weak mewling sound and realized it was him. "Please. Let me go."

"You have a contingent here as well," she said. "From the other side." She stared off, as if listening. "They're fighting for you. Wanting me to free you." She cocked her head. "It's two women. Both strong and courageous, determined to help." She played with the tip of the knife. "Too bad there's little they can do, except welcome you when you cross over." Allison sighed softly. "I believe one of them is your former lover. Pity she left so soon. Perhaps a ceremony such as this would have saved her."

Anger bubbled up and trampled his fear. "Fuck you," he said. "And your miserable little group. You're all going to die as tragically as you lived, and you'll be lucky if anyone gives a shit when it happens."

Allison's eyes flared, and she gripped the handle of the knife. "A spark of courage. Good for you. Not even Victor showed that." Leaning over him, she raised the knife to his throat. "I think the time for talk is over." She placed the tip against his jugular. "Shall we begin?"

**

Daniels raced through the trees, the flashlight bobbing over the thick foliage, and Redstone followed. He stayed on the drive of pebbled rock, but off to the side and out of sight of anyone who might be standing watch. After a minute or two, but what felt like more than an hour, he spotted an open area, and the drive stopped in front of a structure. It looked like an old house. It was dark and not in use, and as he approached, he saw what looked like a small shed beside it. The door was open, and as he neared, he swiveled the light toward it. Inside was a small, murky room and as the light brightened it, he saw another door and room beyond it.

"What is it?" asked Redstone behind him.

Taking a step inside, Daniels shone the light, and within the inner room, he spotted a grimy mattress, an empty water bottle, and two rats, who scattered when the light beam hit. He saw a chewed bag and the remains of what looked like a sandwich. "Shit." He couldn't imagine anyone being left in that space, much less his partner. "Come on."

He ran toward the rustic house, and he and Redstone quickly entered, but saw no one and nothing. It looked like an old office space that nature was quickly reclaiming. Daniels' fear climbed when he didn't find Rem.

"Daniels. Look," said Redstone, who'd found a back door and stood outside of it.

Daniels ran over and joined Redstone. In the distance, toward the rear of the property, was the warehouse from his nightmares. Sucking in a sharp breath, he saw the cars parked in front, and the flicker of firelight from within the windows. "That's it," he said. "That's where they're holding him."

He took off in a sprint, racing toward the building, with Redstone right behind him. Nearing the structure, Daniels stopped behind a car, and Redstone joined him. One end of the building was open to the air. It was dilapidated, and Daniels wondered if the doors would even close any more. Listening, he heard nothing. The crickets didn't even chirp.

"You see what's on the wall?" asked Redstone, breathing hard.

Daniels squinted and froze when he saw a bird with teardrops painted on the side of the building. Goosebumps rose on his skin. "I see it." He ducked back down.

"How do you want to do this?" asked Redstone.

Daniels spied a second open area to the side. "I'll go in the front. You take the side."

"You know there'll be more than one of them."

"I'm guessing. But I'm not waiting." Daniels gripped his gun, eager to move. He eyed Redstone, who nodded at him.

"I'm ready when you are," said Redstone, holding his own weapon. "I hope your captain is on his way."

"Me, too," said Daniels, and he took off toward the building.

CHAPTER TWENTY-EIGHT

Rem thought of Jennie, the only hope out of the darkness that he could see at that moment and felt a moment of peace when he realized he would see her soon. But then he thought of Daniels and agonized that his partner would find him dead in this ugly building on this stone slab, with his blood drained and his body marred.

"I'll make a small puncture, right here," said Allison, and Rem felt the sharpness of the blade against his neck, and could barely breathe, expecting to feel the slice against his skin. "Your blood will spill onto the stone, and they will have their fill." She whispered into his ear. "And while they do, I will breathe your final breath, as yours slows and stops, and your essence will become mine, as will your life force." Her lips grazed over his jaw. "It's a remarkable experience. So much more sensory than Victor's silly bite marks." She moaned into his ear. "And so much more potent." Nibbling his lobe, she pulled on it with her teeth.

Rem did his damnedest to be brave, but his heart raced, his chest ached, and his breathing was coming in rapid and shallow gasps. His terror swelled when, from the corner of his eye, a line began to form as the group of followers prepared to take their turns. "I hope you burn in hell." It was the only thing he could think to say.

Allison shifted above him. "Hell is not the issue, my love." She placed the tip of the knife against his throat and began to press. "Life is."

**

Daniels raced into the warehouse, seeing a group of people standing quietly around a stone platform, some in a line, but his gaze settled on the woman, kneeling over someone, and holding a knife to their neck. His heart stopped when he realized it was Allison straddling Rem, and he raised his gun and yelled at the top of his lungs. "Police. Nobody move or I'll shoot."

A flicker of movement to his right caught his eye and he saw Redstone run up from the other side, his gun raised. "Everybody stay where you are," Redstone yelled. "Don't move."

The faces in the group turned, as if waiting for something. He took a few steps closer, his gun trained on Allison. Breathing hard, and his adrenaline surging, he saw his partner was tied down, but appeared to be alive. "Get away from him."

Allison glared, her eyes reflecting the blazing torches in the room. Still holding the knife, she pulled it back from Rem's neck.

Daniels moved closer, his gun unwavering. "I said get away from him." He noticed Rem's shirt was open and there was blood dripping down his chest.

Redstone moved inward as well, and kept his gun trained on the followers, who hadn't moved or spoken.

"You're a brave man, Detective," said Allison. "For someone who's outnumbered." She pointed the knife at Rem. "One word from me, and they'll rush you. You can't take them all before I take your partner."

Daniels blood boiled, and his face heated. "My first shot goes right through your head, lady. They may take me, but I'll take you first." He aimed his gun. "How you doin', Redstone?"

Redstone never faltered. "I'm aiming for these two." He nodded toward two of the bigger men. "And if I'm lucky, I'll get that one, too." A third man of larger stature tensed and his eyes rounded. "That's right," said Redstone. "I'm looking at you, big man."

Daniels kept his sights on Allison, whose expression shifted from one of smugness to one of uncertainty. "You not feeling lucky?" asked Daniels. He could see Rem's fingers clench and unclench and his chest heaving, and assumed his partner was conscious.

Allison wavered, her eyes flitting to Rem and the knife. Daniels moved closer, ready in case she attacked. "Don't do it."

She scanned her followers, who all seemed ready to do her bidding, when there was a loud wail of a siren and a police car rammed into the front side of the building, taking part of the siding with it, then there was a rush of footsteps and yelling, and Daniels saw a sea of blue enter the area, guns drawn.

Relief washed over him when he realized Lozano had sent the cavalry and Mikey had shown them where to go. At the first sign of their entrance, the followers lost their nerve and began to scatter, and Daniels didn't hesitate. He ran over to Allison, who was distracted by the chaos, and grabbed her. He pulled her off of Rem and yanked her to the ground, taking hold of her wrist which held the knife. As he drove his knee into her back, she fell face down into the ground. "Drop it."

She hesitated but let go and the knife fell. He yelled at a passing officer to cuff her and get her out of there, and bag the knife. The officer took over, and Daniels holstered his gun and ran over to Rem.

His heart stopped when he saw his partner's cut shirt and the wound in his chest. Rem's eyes were glazed, and his breathing was shallow and erratic. "Rem? Can you hear me?"

His partner couldn't seem to focus. Redstone ran up next to Daniels. "How is he?"

"Not good. Help me get him untied."

Redstone moved to Rem's ankles and Daniels undid Rem's wrists. The skin was raw and abraded, and Daniels squeezed Rem's fingers, trying to get the blood circulating, and brought Rem's arms back down to his sides. He tried again to get Rem to look at him. "Rem? It's me, Daniels."

Rem blinked, and made a whimpered moan, and Daniels noticed his eyes. They were as wide and dilated as Cindy's had been.

"Shit," said Daniels. "He's been drugged. Help me get him up."

Redstone helped Daniels get Rem into a sitting position and then came around to the side. Daniels put one of Rem's arms over his shoulders, as did Redstone. "Be careful of his chest," said Daniels. "Let's get him out of here."

They carried him out of the building into a sea of swirling and blinking lights. The scene was chaotic as followers were being led in cuffs to police cars, and cops ran around the scene, checking and securing the area.

Daniels found a quiet spot away from the confusion and sat Rem down, his back against a large tree, and squatted beside him.

Rem rested his head back, but his body shook with tremors. Daniels spotted an officer he recognized. "Carl. I need a blanket. Hurry."

Carl eyed Rem, nodded and ran off.

Daniels checked the cut in Rem's chest, but it didn't appear to be too deep and the bleeding seemed to have stopped. "Rem," he spoke softly and took his wrist. "Can you talk? Are you okay?"

Rem grimaced, and his face paled until he turned white and began to retch.

"Help him lean over," said Redstone.

Daniels got behind him and supported his partner as Rem vomited into the leaves, although nothing came up. It took a few minutes until Rem, completely spent, finished, and Daniels pulled him back into a sitting position. Getting him situated, he saw Carl bring the blanket. He took it and wrapped it around Rem, who continued to shake and stare off with an awful blank gaze.

Daniels wondered what to do, and gently patted Rem's face, trying to get him to come around. "Rem? Buddy? It's me. Talk to me. Please."

"It's the drugs," said Redstone. "He's out of it."

Rem's cheeks began to gain more color, and he blinked again. His eyes drooped, and his gaze darted around in confusion, and then he finally focused on Daniels.

"Hey," said Daniels. "There you are. Look at me, partner."

Rem's eyes filled. "Daniels?" he whispered, his voice cracking.

"It's me." Relief flooded him. "You're safe. You're okay."

Rem scanned the area again, as if not trusting him, and then settled his gaze back on Daniels. He lifted his hands and curled them into Daniels' shirt, then fell forward and crumpled. Daniels heart broke when he heard his partner begin to sob.

Daniels held Rem's head, which was buried in his shoulder. "It's over, buddy. It's all over. She can't hurt you." He let Rem cry out his anguish and fear into his shirt and debated what to do. His partner was an emotional and physical wreck. "Just relax."

Rem immediately tensed and tried to pull away, but Daniels held on. "Hey. Take it easy. You're fine. Relax." Rem went rigid and stiffened.

"Don't say that to him." Mikey appeared beside him and squatted.

"Mikey? What are you doing here?" asked Redstone.

"You said wait until the cavalry arrived," she said. "And I did."

"What do you mean?" asked Daniels. "Say what?"

"Don't tell him to relax," said Mikey. "It's like a trigger word. She likely said it to him, too."

Daniels cursed to himself, wondering what mental torture Allison had done to his partner. "Sorry, buddy." He pulled Rem back. "Don't be scared. You're safe. I've got you. Nobody's going to hurt you."

Rem eased up and fell back into Daniels' shoulder. His crying had slowed, but he held onto Daniels' shirt like a lifeline, and his body still shook.

"We need to get him to a hospital," said Redstone.

Daniels felt Rem stiffen again. "No," said Rem, whispering. "No hospital. Please."

Daniels warred with himself. His partner needed medical help. "Rem, listen. You need to see a doctor. You've been drugged and injured."

Rem dug into his shirt. "I can't." His voice broke and his shoulders trembled.

Daniels rubbed his back, trying to assure him.

"It's better if you can avoid a hospital," said Mikey, her face somber. "If they've given him what I suspect, he's highly sensitive to stimuli right now. You throw him in an ambulance with people poking at him, and trying to stick him with needles, and you're going to double his recovery time, if he recovers at all." She reached out and took Rem's wrist and squeezed it. "He needs quiet. A place where he can come out of it at his own pace, where he feels familiar and safe." She sighed. "If you can find a doctor that can come to him, that would be better."

Daniels heard footsteps and saw an EMT approach. "Let me look at him." The EMT squatted and grabbed a stethoscope.

He touched Rem and Rem sucked in a shuttered breath, lurched away, and yelped. "No. Don't."

Daniels knew then what he had to do. "Leave him. I'll take care of it."

The EMT widened his eyes. "He needs medical attention. I'll get him in the ambulance, and we'll get him to the hospital."

Daniels heard Rem whimper. "I said I got it. I'll take full responsibility. I'll sign whatever I need to."

The EMT paused and shrugged. "Suit yourself." The EMT picked up his gear and walked away.

Daniels swallowed, thinking. "Mikey. Go get the car. Bring it down here. We'll bring him home. I know a doctor I can call who can check him out."

Mikey nodded and ran off.

"You sure about this?" asked Redstone.

Daniels felt Rem tremble against him, rubbed his partner's shoulder and nodded. "I've never been surer of anything in my life."

CHAPTER TWENTY-NINE

Daniels sat beside Rem on the couch while Doc Martin did his best to examine him, although Rem would barely let him move the blanket. Daniels had called Lozano and the doctor on the way to Rem's, telling them both the situation, and Martin had agreed to come over. Daniels had met Doc Martin after being injured during the Jace Marlon case, and the doctor had taken a quick interest in his and Rem's careers. Having always had an interest in police work, he was fascinated and had offered to help whenever needed. They'd used him once when Marlon had required medical help and would not go to a hospital.

Rem sat huddled on the couch, his knees up and the blanket around him. He'd refused to lie down and wouldn't drink any water. Still shaking, Rem would only allow the doctor near him as long as Daniels stayed beside him.

Finishing up, the doctor nodded at Daniels, who nodded back. Daniels stood, and leaned over Rem. "I'm going to talk to Martin. Stay put, okay?"

Rem looked up with haunted and worried eyes, his pupils still dilated.

"I'll be right over there," said Daniels. "You need anything?"

Rem pulled the blanket closer and dropped his head.

Daniels patted his shoulder and stepped away to talk to the doctor. "How is he? Does he need a hospital?" He didn't know what he would do if Martin said yes.

Martin put his stethoscope in his bag. "Ideally, yes, but in his current mental state, I agree that this might be the better option. I'd like to get an IV in him, but he won't let me near him with a needle. If you could get him to drink some water, that would help." He pulled out a prescription pad. "Keep him warm. His vitals are okay but could be better. I don't know what they gave him, so the best thing to do is wait it out. I'll prescribe something to help with the anxiety and maybe help him sleep, but he shouldn't take it until whatever's in his system is gone. I'd do a blood test, but we know how that will go."

"How's his chest?" asked Daniels.

"Not terrible. The cut is not too deep. He can live without stitches. I cleaned the wound as best I could, but if you could get him in the shower, that would help. I didn't see any other serious physical issues other than his wrists. They're bruised and raw, but they'll heal."

"How long do you think he'll be like this?"

"It's hard to say. If he could rest and drink plenty of water, I'd hope by morning he'd be better, but I can't be sure." He scribbled on the pad. "If he begins to decline – spikes a temperature, has shortness of breath, or starts hallucinating, call an ambulance, and bring him in. You'll just have to deal with the mental repercussions later."

Daniels watched his partner and rubbed his eyes. "Okay. Thanks, Doc."

Martin pulled off the paper and handed it to him. "And call me if you have any questions. Doesn't matter what time it is."

Daniels set the prescription on the front table still covered in fingerprint dust from forensics dusting it that morning. "I will. Thanks. We owe you. Again."

"Happy to help. I'll follow up in the morning. See how he's doing."

Daniels nodded and saw him out.

Mikey approached. She and Redstone had been waiting in the kitchen. "Well?" she asked.

Daniels expelled a deep breath and massaged his neck. "We need to get him to drink some water. Let's start there."

Redstone came over, and Daniels filled him in on the doctor's advice. "Listen," said Daniels. "I've got this. You two can head home."

Mikey had disappeared and returned with a glass of water. Redstone lifted a brow. "Try telling her that."

Daniels followed Mikey into the living room. Daniels sat next to Rem on the couch, and Mikey sat on the coffee table, facing Rem, and holding the water.

"Hey, partner," said Daniels. "Doc says you need to drink something. You're dehydrated."

Mikey held the water out.

"I don't want it," said Rem, his voice low. He gripped the blanket, and his fingers trembled.

"The doctor says you need it. You wouldn't take the IV. You'll feel better if you drink it, and maybe you can get some rest," said Daniels.

Rem hugged his knees. "No. I don't want to rest."

Mikey held the water out. "Hey, Remalla," she said. "It's Mikey. Remember me? Mason's sister?"

Rem glanced up at her and then looked away.

"Listen. I know you're scared right now," she said. "And that maybe they drugged your water, and that's why you don't want this. But it's okay. It's safe. I got it right out of the tap unless you consider tap water dangerous."

"I would," said Redstone, who stood behind Mikey.

Daniels berated himself. He hadn't considered that Rem would be afraid to drink the water. He recalled the empty water bottle in that horrid room and shivered.

Rem set his jaw, and his eyes settled on the cup. Daniels imagined his partner had to be thirsty, and how awful it would be to want the water and be too frightened to drink it.

Daniels reached and took the cup from Mikey. "The water is safe. I promise. You trust me?" He held it out.

Rem's gaze darted from the cup to Daniels, and he moaned.

"It's not drugged. I swear. We wouldn't do that to you," said Daniels. "Just take a sip. Can you do that much?"

Rem swallowed, his expression a mixture of desire and despair. He studied the cup, and Daniels moved it toward Rem's hands. Rem clenched his eyes and then opened them, and with shaky fingers, took the glass.

"There you go," said Daniels. "You're doing great."

Rem raised the glass and sipped from it. His face froze for a moment, as if the water was distasteful, and Daniels thought he'd hand the cup back, but then he took a bigger sip, and then lifted the glass and gulped it down. Daniels sighed in relief and took the cup back.

"You want some more?" asked Daniels.

"I'll get some," said Mikey, not waiting for a response, and took the glass from Daniels.

Rem pulled the blanket close again, and Daniels recalled Martin's advice to keep Rem warm. "Redstone. There's a closet around the corner. Can you get him another blanket?"

Redstone turned and walked away.

"You want to lie down in your room?" asked Daniels.

"No," said Rem. "I want to stay here."

"You want me to turn out the lights?"

Rem jolted and tensed. "No. Please. Leave the lights on." His voice fell to a whisper. "I don't want to be in the dark."

Daniels recalled that room again and could imagine why. "Not a problem. The lights will stay on."

Mikey returned with more water and handed it to Rem. He stared up at her with wary eyes but took it from her and drank it. Daniels considered that a success. Rem had drunk the water, but also taken it from someone other than Daniels. It was a baby step, but one in the right direction.

Redstone brought out another blanket, and Daniels wrapped Rem in it, ensuring his comfort, and nodded at Redstone and Mikey to follow him.

They walked into the entry. Daniels took the cup from Mikey, grabbed his keys, and handed them to Redstone. "Why don't you two go home and get some rest. Take my car. It's going to be a long night, and there's no point in all of us staying up."

Redstone nodded. "You're sure?"

"I don't mind staying." Mikey eyed Rem with concern.

"I know you don't, and I appreciate it," said Daniels. "I owe you both for your help tonight. If it hadn't been for your memory, Redstone…" he looked back at Rem wrapped in blankets on the couch, "…this would be a very different outcome. And Mikey, your understanding of all he's been through, has been a big help."

"I'm coming back tomorrow. You'll need to get some rest, too," she said. "And don't even try to tell me no."

Daniels didn't have the strength to argue. "I won't. And if you want to help, I won't stop you."

"You take care, Detective," said Redstone. "You've been to hell and back yourself. Try not to overdo it."

Daniels almost chuckled. The weight of the last three days sat on his shoulders like a giant barbell, but at least the heaviness of Rem's absence was gone, and he knew the rest would improve with time. "I'll try. Go get some sleep."

He saw them out and closed the door behind them. Turning, he eyed Rem, who blinked with fatigue but seemed determined not to sleep. Daniels returned to the couch and sat beside his partner.

**

Hearing a quiet knock, Daniels cracked an eye open. Soft sunlight filtered through the windows, and he blinked the sleep from his eyes. The knock came again, and he sat up in the chair across from the couch.

He'd moved off the sofa when he'd gotten up to use the bathroom in the night and had returned to find Rem lying on his side across the couch, finally succumbing to sleep. Daniels had adjusted his blankets and put a pillow under his head, and Rem had barely moved. Daniels moved to the overstuffed chair, where he could keep an eye on Rem, and had dozed off.

He stood and moaned, his muscles protesting, and checked the time. If his brain was calculating correctly, Rem had only been asleep an hour. He walked to the door and saw Mikey through the peephole. He opened it. "Mikey?"

She walked in, carrying bags of groceries, and headed into the kitchen. He followed her. "What are you doing?" he asked, still trying to wake up.

"I'm restocking the fridge. There's nothing to eat in this house, and you and your partner are going to need some food." She began to empty the bags.

He blinked and yawned. "Did you get any rest?"

She looked him over. "More than you. That's obvious." She nodded toward the living room. "How's he doing?"

"Finally went out about an hour ago."

"Stubborn, isn't he?"

"You have no idea."

She put bread and peanut butter in the pantry. "You're officially relieved. Go home."

He frowned. "I'm what?"

Holding a bag of chips, she stared. "Look at yourself, Detective. You almost look as bad as he does. You need to go see your wife and kid, get cleaned up and get some shut eye. You can't be there for him if you fall apart yourself."

Daniels held still. His stomach grumbled, and his eyes hurt from exhaustion. He'd called Marjorie last night, but he had heard the worry in her voice.

"You're just barely out the woods yourself. You know your partner would agree with me. Besides, if he just fell asleep, he'll probably be out through the afternoon. By then, you'll be back, and you can take it from there."

Daniels had to admit she was right. He was running on empty. "Okay. I hear you." He watched her put a carton of eggs in the fridge. "I'll go. But if he needs anything…"

"I'll handle it. I have some experience with this. But I'll call you if it's warranted. Don't worry. He'll be fine. Here." She reached into her pocket. "Your car keys."

He took them, still hesitant. "Thanks. You're sure about this?"

"I am. Now go."

"If you need transportation, Rem's car keys are on the table in his room." He scribbled his phone number on some paper from the kitchen and slid it toward her. "My cell."

"Great, but I doubt I'll need it or the car." She scribbled her own number, and he took it. "Say hi to Marjorie."

He frowned, still wondering how Mikey knew his wife, but decided he'd ask about it later. "See you soon." He turned, did a last check-in on Rem, who still slept comfortably, and left.

CHAPTER THIRTY

Later that afternoon, Mikey hung up with Daniels. He'd done what she'd asked and gone home, seen his family, and gotten some sleep, but called her the moment he'd woken, and she'd assured him that Rem still sleeping on the couch, and not to rush back. She'd heard the relief in his voice, and he'd said he'd clean up, grab a few things, and head over.

Eyeing the living room, and seeing Rem asleep, she turned back to her magazine and flipped through it, sipping from her coffee. She'd made a pot earlier and had eaten a sandwich, periodically checking on Remalla. Although he slept peacefully, she stayed alert, knowing all too well that the ugly nightmares would come.

She considered calling Mason, since she knew he wanted an update, and was about to when the doorbell rang. Not wanting the sound to wake Rem, she ran to the door and opened it.

**

Daniels backed out of his driveway and onto the street, on his way back to Rem's, when his cell rang. He saw it was Lozano, and answered, prepared to tell him the latest.

"Hey, Cap," he said.

"Daniels? You at Rem's?" asked Lozano.

"No, but I'm headed that way. Why?"

"Is he by himself?" asked the captain, sounding concerned.

"No. There's someone with him." There was a brief pause on the line. "What is it? Is something wrong?"

"We're talking to the followers we picked up from last night. Most of them have clammed up, but one of them is talking. Wants a deal to prevent jail time."

"I bet he does. What's he saying?" He nudged on the accelerator.

"Told us about the robberies. We were right they were designed to prove their loyalty. Said Victor told them that the sacrifices would prolong their life and their youth, and they used drugs to maintain control. Said Allison was with him from the start. He also told us about the ceremony. They did it the night before Halloween because all the crazies come out on Halloween. Can you believe that?"

Daniels stopped at a light. "Strangely enough, yes."

"There's something else, though. He's filling us in on Allison Albright and Victor D'Mato, but he also mentioned another woman, who he believes is just as dangerous. Another follower who wanted what Allison had. I want you to be careful."

A sliver of anxiety made his stomach clench. "Who?" asked Daniels, waiting for the light to change. "Has she been interviewed?"

"No. Some of them escaped capture, and she's one of them. But we got a name. Our talker said it was Margaret Redstone."

His trickle of unease became a hot flare, and Daniels hit the accelerator and almost hit a passing car. "Redstone? Are you sure?"

"You think I'm a rookie, Daniels?" asked Lozano. "Yes, I'm sure. I'm assuming that's a relation to Mason Redstone? Has he mentioned her to you?"

"No."

"Well, she's still out there."

"Did you call Rem's house?" asked Daniels, shooting past a stop sign as a car blared its horn.

"I'm calling you," shouted Lozano. "I assumed you were there."

Daniels' mind raced. Margaret Redstone? Who the hell was she and what was her connection to Mason and Mikey? Was she a threat to Rem? Then another thought occurred to him which made him run the next light. Mikey was likely a nickname. Could her real name be Margaret?

"It may be nothing, but if it isn't…" said Lozano.

Another thought rang in Daniels' head. If Mikey and Margaret were not the same person, and they were siblings, could they be working together? Mikey had followed Victor in the past, but what if she'd never stopped? Had she been helping Allison?

Cursing, he swerved and passed a vehicle that honked. "Send a patrol over to Rem's, Cap. I'll there in two minutes." Lozano started to respond, but Daniels hung up and immediately dialed Mikey's number. It rang and rang, and then went to voicemail.

**

The light from the torches crackled, and the rope cut into his wrists. Rem struggled and fought to free himself but failed. Seeing Allison approach, he cried out, but was helpless to stop her. Gripping the knife, she climbed on top of him and held it to his throat. Laughing, she stroked his chest with her free hand, telling him that she wanted him and asking if he wanted her. He bucked his body to get her off, but she wrapped her legs around him and told him he was going to die. Arcing the knife, she punctured his jugular and began to slice him open. A scream stuck in his throat, and Rem opened his eyes, jolting awake.

The bright room briefly blinded him, and he was disoriented. Shaking and sweaty, he wondered where he was, and then recognized his living room. He was home, lying on his couch. Trying to push up, he went still when he heard voices and a distant phone ringing. He held his head. Where was Daniels? Who was talking? He trembled when a female voice yelled, and that familiar, gnawing fear returned. The voice was low, deep, and cold, and reminded him of a growl.

He gripped the blanket around him, wondering what to do. Had Allison found him? Was she searching for him? The phone stopped ringing, and he heard a shriek. Then there was movement, and shifting his position, he saw two females, one looming over the other, in his front entry. Trembling, he closed his eyes, not wanting them to know he was awake.

The second woman's voice was familiar. "What are you doing here?" it said.

Then the growl, and he cringed when he recognized it from when he'd been on the stone slab. "You're so stupid, Mikey. You should have known better. Now you're trying to pretend you're perfect? That you didn't do the things you did? You think that by helping him, it somehow absolves you from your crimes? I know you. I know your truth. You're just as small and pathetic as Mason and Max. I thought you had potential, but I was wrong."

Rem heard another shriek and quivered, his memories returning. Now he knew the familiar voice was Mikey, and a vague recollection bubbled up of her being with him earlier. Had she offered him water?

The cold voice returned. "Just because Victor and Allison failed, doesn't mean that I will."

"Stop it, Marge," yelled Mikey, and it sounded like she struggled. "You're crazy and always have been. I got out—I thought you did too—and were never coming back."

He heard a thunk and cracked an eye open. He saw the woman with the long dark hair, holding Mikey against the wall, and his insides curdled. For a second, he was back on the slab, terrified and desperate. Hearing that voice and remembering those icy blue eyes, he trembled and wanted to curl back into the couch and hide beneath the covers, but the woman had her fingers on Mikey's throat and a knife in her hand. "Stop it," yelled Mikey.

"Sorry, sis. I'll stop when I finish what I came here to do." She turned her head toward Rem, and he closed his eyes. "The light is destined to die today. Before the veil closes."

"Leave him alone," yelled Mikey. "Listen to yourself. You don't want to do this. You're not thinking. It's the damn drugs. They've messed with your head, just like Victor did." Mikey cried out, and Rem peeked an eye open. The woman had the knife against Mikey's throat.

"It's time you learned some respect. I tried to show you the way, and you rejected it. Decided to side with Mason and Max, and Mom died because of it."

"That wasn't our fault. That was Victor's fault." Mikey's voice shook, and he could hear the fear in it. Deciding to gather his courage and do something, he began to slide off the couch, praying Mikey would keep the woman talking.

His chest throbbing and his muscles trembling, he had to be careful to be quiet and not collapse, or this woman would easily kill them both. Getting to his knees on the ground, he dropped the covers back onto the couch, and spied a heavy book end on a shelf on the wall.

"It wasn't Victor's fault," said the woman. "All of you were to blame. Victor had to defend himself. You all turned on him."

"You're the one who turned, Margaret," said Mikey. "You left mom to die. If anyone is to blame, it's you. You knew what Victor was doing, but you did nothing to stop it."

Rem crawled over and used the wall to support himself as he rose up, his legs shaking like he was on unstable ground, but he held it together long enough to stand and grab the bookend, almost dropping it. He peered around the corner and saw the back of the growling woman and her long, dark hair as Mikey made eye contact with him.

"You stupid bitch," said the woman. "I'm going to slice your friendly detective's throat just as Allison planned, and you're going to watch."

She grabbed Mikey's shoulder, and Mikey pulled back and yelled. "No. Stop. Kill me," said Mikey, before the woman could turn toward Rem. "That's what you want, isn't it? This isn't about him, or Allison, or Victor. It's about me." Her voice rose. "Well, here I am. Do it. Cut my throat. Or are you all talk like I always thought?"

The woman cackled, and Rem almost faltered. He imagined her turning and finding him, aiming the knife, and coming at him. Allison's face flashed in his mind, and he almost lost his hold on the bookend.

"That's what you want, Mikey?" The woman's cold voice turned colder and deeper. "You want me to kill you the way Victor should have? The way I wanted him to kill you, by slicing you open like a fish?"

Rem heard a low gasp from Mikey.

"Then let's do it," said the woman with a hiss. "Say hi to mom for me."

Rem stepped out, seeing the glitter of the knife pressed against Mikey's throat. Raising the bookend with both hands, he moved quickly and before the woman could pull the blade across Mikey's skin, he slammed the bookend down hard on the back of the woman's head.

**

Daniels brought his car to a screeching stop in Rem's driveway and jumped out. He ran up to the entry, his gun drawn, and stopped when he saw the open door. Raising his weapon, he stepped inside, and found a woman with long dark hair, lying unconscious, blood dripping from her head onto the rug, and a knife in her hand. Mikey stood against the wall, pale and still, holding her neck, a trickle of blood running down it. Rem stood across from her, his chest heaving, still wearing his ripped t-shirt, his dirty hair hanging in his face, and his injured chest exposed. Holding a bloody bookend with shaky fingers, he stared at the woman on the floor, and then dropped it. The bookend hit the ground with a thud, and he backed up, fell against the wall, and began to slide down it.

Daniels holstered his weapon and debated who to check first. Stepping over the woman, he took the knife from her hand and put it out of reach. Rem made it to the ground and sat. Mikey straightened and stared at the bleeding woman.

"What the hell happened?" asked Daniels, checking the woman's pulse. It was strong and steady. He eyed Mikey. "Are you okay?"

Breathless, Mikey looked stunned. "I'm…I'm okay. Just a scratch. Check him first."

"Go sit," he said, "Before you fall over." He ran over to Rem, who looked pale and confused. "Hey," he said, squatting beside him. "How you doing?" He checked Rem's pulse, which was racing.

Rem was breathing hard, but he made eye contact and spoke softly. "I've been better."

Daniels hung his head and took a deep breath, grateful his partner was okay. He cocked his head at the unconscious woman. "Did you do that?"

Rem looked over, his eyes wide. "She was going to kill Mikey."

Daniels looked at Mikey. "Is this Margaret Redstone?"

Mikey nodded, still holding her throat. "She's my sister."

"How the hell many siblings do you have?" yelled Daniels. "Please tell me this is the last of them."

"It is," said Mikey. "I promise."

Hearing a siren approach, Daniels stood and cuffed Margaret, and decided he would let the arriving patrol call the ambulance. He returned to Rem. "Think you can stand?"

Rem laid his head back against the wall. His pupils had returned to normal, and he trembled, but not with the amount of fear he'd shown before. There were still deep creases beneath his eyes, his pallor was gray, and his cheeks were sunken, but he appeared more clear-headed. "I can try," he said. "But I'm gonna need some help."

"Hold on one second." Daniels stood and waved the officers in, telling them what happened and telling them to call an ambulance. He stopped beside Mikey. "Let me see your neck."

She lowered her hand, and he saw the crease, but it didn't look deep. "You'll live. We'll have the EMT's look at it. Stay there."

He returned to Rem, squatted, and took an arm. "C'mon, buddy. Let's get you back to the couch." He pulled and Rem tried to stand as

Daniels supported him. Rem's legs wobbled, but he managed to get balanced, and Daniels walked him back to the sofa, where he sat him down. Rem leaned over and put his head in his hands. Daniels grabbed the blanket and put it back over his shoulders. "You want to lie down?"

Rem didn't answer.

Daniels started to worry. "Hey, you okay?"

Rem let go of a long breath and whispered. "I thought I was going to die last night." He spoke so softly, Daniels almost didn't hear him. "I was so scared." He gripped his head.

"I know," said Daniels, measuring his words. "But it's over now. It'll take time, but it will get better."

"Will it?" asked Rem, he glanced over, his eyes weary. "I'm not so sure." His gaze fell on the woman on the ground. "And now I've got Victor's crazy followers looking for me." He closed his eyes and touched his injured chest. "I don't know if I can do this."

Daniels's heart fell. "I know it might feel that way now, but I promise, we'll get you through it." He squeezed his partner's shoulder and hated it when Rem flinched. "One day at a time."

Rem closed his weary eyes and sniffed.

Daniels tried to fill the silence. "How about once we deal with this, we get you showered, and then maybe you can get some food and a nap. That'll help. What do you say?"

Rem took a shuddered breath and nodded. Daniels paused, and seeing an officer wave him over, he stood. Keeping an eye on his partner, he couldn't help but wonder if Rem would ever be the same again.

CHAPTER THIRTY-ONE

Rem sat at his kitchen table, nursing a cup of coffee, and staring out the window. It had been a week since his near death at the warehouse, and it had been a long seven days. Once they'd gotten Margaret Redstone out of his house, he'd found the strength to clean up, get something light to eat, and had fallen asleep again, and that had been the reoccurring pattern ever since, except now he was able to sleep in his bedroom, as long as the lights remained on.

He'd finally convinced Daniels to sleep at home two nights ago, and he'd been on his own since, telling Daniels to spend some time with his family. Rem had done pretty well, despite the nightmares which plagued him each night. Sometimes he woke screaming or crying, and others in silent, muted terror.

His mind wandering, he thought about his upcoming afternoon. Lozano needed him to make a sworn statement about what had happened and couldn't wait any longer. Daniels would be picking him up later to take him to the station, and he dreaded reliving the hell he'd been through, plus leaving his house. He hadn't stepped outside of it since coming home a week ago.

He knew his partner worried about him, which is why Rem had sent him home. Daniels had enough to handle and was still dealing with his own demons, and he didn't need more. If Rem was going to fall apart, he'd do it on his own, and he wouldn't take Daniels down with him.

Stirring his coffee, which didn't need to be stirred and was now cold, he debated eating breakfast, although he had no appetite. He'd had little interest in food since Victor had taken him, and it still made him anxious to drink water. Sighing, he rested his head in his palm.

The doorbell rang, and he jumped, thinking immediately of Margaret, her long, dark hair, and her icy blue eyes. He wondered if she'd been the one to shoot the cashier at the liquor store robbery, although it could have just as easily been Allison. Telling himself to relax, he stood and warily approached the door, looked out the peephole, and saw Mikey.

Taking a relieved breath, he turned off the alarm and opened the door.

"Hey," she said. She stood in blue running shorts and a slim white t-shirt, and her reddish-brown hair with purple streaks was pulled back in a ponytail. The piercing in her nose remained. He couldn't help but stare at her shapely legs, which he'd never seen before.

"I know. It's not my usual look," she said. "But I don't always wear black." She stood for a moment while he nodded, unsure what to say. "Can I come in?"

"Oh, sorry." He stood back, and she entered. "Did I know you were coming?" He closed the door.

"Love the look," she said.

He looked down at his clothes. He was wearing his Superman sweatpants and a t-shirt with holes in it. "It's comfortable."

"Yeah, well, you need to change."

He frowned. "I do? Why?"

"Because we're going for a jog."

"We are?"

"We are. Your partner told me you like to run, and I hear you have a big day today, so you need to get out there and break a sweat."

Rem stared and shook his head. "That's why you're here? To make me run?"

Mikey waved at herself. "I didn't wear this just to watch. I'm running with you." She waved. "Let's go. Get dressed."

He chuckled. "You're funny."

She turned serious. "I'm not joking."

"Listen. Mikey. I appreciate your—"

"Shut up, Remalla."

He dropped his jaw.

"You can stand there and tell me whatever the hell you want, but I don't care. You need to get out of this house and do something for yourself, because if you don't, six months will pass, and you'll still be standing there in those same ridiculous clothes."

"Ridiculous?" He pulled on his pants. "I like Superman."

"Good for you. Do you like yourself? Maybe that's what you should be asking. Because if you have any shred of self-respect and want to find your way back to some semblance of normal, then you'll get your ass back in your room, and put on something more suitable for running, unless you want to wear that." She pointed. "And if you do, I'll be keeping my distance. My suggestion is that you change for both our sakes." She put a hand on her hip. "I'll wait here."

He stood in disbelief. This petite woman he'd barely known more than two weeks, was telling him what to do. Anger bubbled up, and he opened his mouth to argue.

"And don't tell me to get out. I've dealt with worse shit than you, so if you're coming at me, be prepared to get physical." Her eyes narrowed, and her gaze bore into him, and he got it then that she wouldn't be bullied. "Now go get dressed," she said again.

Rem warred with himself. The thought of going outside unnerved him, but at the same time, it might feel good to get out and move. Would he be able to even run? Would his body hold up? He sighed and figured maybe she was right. He had to try. "Give me five minutes."

"Good." She nodded and went to sit in the kitchen.

Twenty minutes later, they were slowly jogging down his street. The sun was out and the wind was light, and that sickening feeling Rem had felt when he'd stepped outside his door began to lift. The first five minutes had been hard, and he suspected he'd looked a little green, but Mikey hadn't said a word and just started to run, and he'd forced himself to follow.

Starting to sweat, he picked his speed and took a deep, full breath, and for the first time since being home, he didn't feel sick to his stomach. "There's a park up ahead. I usually take the trail."

Mikey jogged quietly beside him. "Sounds good. I'll follow you."

He headed down the path, seeing the few other people out, some walking their dogs, and others just walking. His mind stilled, and his body relaxed, and he settled into his pace. Entering the park, he took the trail that headed into the woods, and breathing harder, he ran a little faster. Images began to take shape in his mind, and he thought back, and couldn't stop himself from recalling Allison's assault and his captivity. Victor's face and then Allison's flashed in his head, and he remembered the feel of that dark room, and the sound of the mice. Picking up his pace, he recalled hearing the footsteps, then the hood on his head, and being dragged from that room, and then secured to that cold slab.

Breathing rapidly, he began to sprint, and sweat poured down his face and his back. In his mind, Allison straddled him, holding that knife and cutting him, and he broke into all-out run, moving as fast as he could, and let go of a moan, seeing Allison on top of him, her tasting his blood, and the knife to his throat.

Fury and rage erupted, and he darted off the trail and down to a small stream that ran along it. His side ached, and he was panting, and he kicked at a rock, and then another, and then found a big one, picked it up and threw it. He found another and another. Tears ran down his face as he threw and kicked the rocks, and then he bellowed in frustration, livid at what they'd done to him, and his helplessness. Spent and breathing hard, he fell to his knees by the stream, disgusted and enraged, and sobbed by the side of the water, knees soaked, palms in the dirt, and his body shaking, until he couldn't cry anymore.

Several minutes passed, his breathing slowed, and his fury subsided. Wiping his face and nose with his sleeve, he looked around but didn't see anyone, and figured if there had been a passerby, they would have assumed he was a drifter off his meds and would have steered clear. Pulling it together, he stepped away from the stream, back up to the path, and returned to the park. Mikey was sitting on a bench near the playground, and he walked up and sat beside her. He watched the kids play. "Sorry I took off on you."

"Not a problem. I figured you needed some time."

"I...uh...sorta had a mini meltdown by the stream." A toddler climbed the slide with his mother's help.

"Feel better?"

"Actually, yeah, I do."

She nodded. "Good, because there will be more. They tend to come out of nowhere, but I find them to be very therapeutic."

"Great. I can't wait." The child made it down the slide and landed on his butt. "How is it that you're hanging out with me? I assume you work somewhere. Is your boss that understanding?"

"He is, actually. It's Mason, so, yeah, he gets it. I do research for him, plus some financial and assistant stuff and any legwork he needs done. What he does can take its toll, so I try to ease the burden. Business has picked up recently, but there's a few weirdos out there, so I try and keep the crazies at arm's length."

"I guess I'm lucky you took my call and made the appointment."

"It was a toss-up, but you won me over with your insistence. I especially liked the part where you told me that there was an alien working in your building. I think that gave you the edge."

He chuckled and swiped some dirt off his shorts. "You know, you haven't said much about your experience with Victor."

Mikey studied her hands and sighed. "It wasn't as intense as yours, but it was longer. A lot longer."

"Care to share?"

Eyeing the playground, she sat back. "I was stupid and young. Back when we lived in Texas and Mason and Victor were friends, I had a little crush on Victor. Mason and I were close, and the three of us hung out a lot." She paused. "But then they moved out here, with Maxwell. I was in school in Texas, and Margaret..." She hesitated.

"I get the sense she was different."

She smiled. "You could say that. All us have some sort of ability and have managed it, but Marge was...I don't know...not quite right in the head. She was always in competition with us, and if one of us did well, she was plagued with jealousy. She could turn mean at the slightest provocation and lacked any empathy no matter how much misery she caused." A child began to cry, and Mikey looked over at him. "I'm very empathic, so I guess I got all of hers." Picking something off of her sleeve, she crossed her legs on the bench. "As the years passed, she became harder and harder to deal with, until eventually she left home, and not many of us had anything to do with her."

"How'd you end up out here?"

She swallowed. "Margaret contacted me. Asked me to come visit. I missed Mason and wanted to see him. Max is the oldest and was out of the house when I was still young, but Mason and I were always close. So, I came out. I stayed with Marge in the hope that maybe it would bring us closer together. She introduced me to her group of friends, which were actually Victor's group of friends." She bit her lip and took a second. "Victor started paying attention to me, and I was flattered. I liked it and started spending more time with him. Mason wasn't happy. At that point, he and Victor were on the outs, and Marge saw the rift and exploited it. She pushed me away from Mason, and before I knew it, I was caught up in Victor's world. He introduced me to drugs, and I was doing things I never would have thought possible, and I still struggle with it today. It was like I'd given all my control over to someone else, and he relished in abusing that power."

Rem recalled his night at Allison's. "I know the feeling."

Mikey stared off. "This went on for a while, Marge using me against Mason, while at the same time, feeding me to Victor like some sort of snack, and then we learned what Victor was doing to our mother, in an attempt to get back at Mason."

Rem sat forward. "What was that?"

Pensive, she rested her elbows on her knees. "You know that box in Mason's office? On the shelf?"

Rem nodded.

"Victor sent that to our mom. Nobody knew what it was until it was too late." Her composure slipped, and she bit her lip and took a second. "It was like that damn statue Victor mailed to your partner, only I think it was worse. My mother was already frail, but that box made her sick, and before Mason realized what was happening, it was too late. Mom didn't survive it."

Holding his stomach in disbelief, Rem remembered Daniels' mental torture and decline. Who could do that to somebody's mother? A memory flickered of Margaret Redstone standing beside him on that slab, and her reminding Allison about how she'd created the statues. He watched the kids on the swing but didn't say anything. Had Margaret played a part in killing her own mother?

"Mason went a little crazy after that. Turned the cops onto Victor, which is how Victor ended up in prison. Margaret disappeared after Victor went away, and Mason focused his sights on me. I was finally free from Victor's grasp, and he saw his opportunity. He'd lost mom, but he wasn't going to lose me. It's why he keeps that box on his shelf, to remind him of what's at stake, plus it's like the guilt trip he refuses to let himself off the hook for. No matter what I say, he won't take it down. It's also why he has to be safe and requires security. Some of Victor's followers didn't take too kindly to their leader being locked up and saw Mason's actions as a betrayal." She scratched her knee. "Anyway, it took a while for me to come around. I resisted Mason's help, but eventually, my old self surfaced, and I started to see the light, although it was a miserable experience. Mason stuck with me. I owe him my life." She looked at Rem. "Much like I owe you."

"Me? What did I do?"

Mikey's face furrowed. "My sister was about to cut my throat. You stopped her. I'd say that qualifies as saving my life."

"Oh, that."

Mikey rolled her eyes. "Yeah, that."

Rem sat back. "Seems we have some stuff in common."

"You could say that, which is why I plan to get in your face. You sit back and wallow in this, you'll never find your way back. I learned that the hard way. Thankfully, Mason didn't give up."

Rem crossed his arms, thinking of his outburst at the stream. "It's hard."

"It's the hardest thing you'll ever do, but it beats the alternative." She stood. "It can't be as scary as living in those Superman pants for the foreseeable future." She cocked her head. "You ready? We should head back before Daniels calls the authorities."

Rem studied her, admiring her tenacity, and stood, too. "I actually prefer my Batman pants."

Her mouth dropped open. "Please. Don't tell me you think Batman's cooler than Superman?" They started walking back.

"Are you kidding? It's not even close. Batman's got the car, the cave, and the casa. Not to mention a sidekick."

"Don't forget the mental angst," said Mikey. "The guy should be on meds. Superman comes from another *planet*, plus has superpowers. What's Batman got? A bunch of cool toys? No contest. Superman would kick Batman's ass in a street fight, no question."

"Whatever. All Batman needs is a kryptonite necklace, and it's curtains for Superman."

"The only way Batman's finding any kryptonite necklace is by using his bat rocket ship. Oh, wait," she said, pointing, "I forgot. He doesn't have one." She sneered at him.

"Not yet, he doesn't, but he's got everything else, so it's just a matter of time."

"Whatever," said Mikey. "I'm not holding my breath."

Walking back to his house, Rem couldn't help but smile.

CHAPTER THIRTY-TWO

Daniels sat at Rem's dining table, waiting. Mikey had told him her plan to get Rem out of the house, and he'd gone along with it, but he hadn't thought for a second that she'd succeed. Rem had hunkered down, and Daniels knew how difficult his partner could be. But when he'd arrived at Rem's, and found them gone, he half considered calling Rem just to be sure he was okay, and that Mikey hadn't tied him up and forced him out. Telling himself to calm down and that there wasn't a bogeyman around every corner, he made himself sit and wait. Rem and Mikey would be okay. It was just a jog. But then he thought of Margaret Redstone and the other crazy followers, and his worry percolated.

Bouncing his knee, he was about to pick up his cell when the front door opened, and Rem and Mikey walked in. Both were in running gear and tennis shoes and looked like they'd had a good workout. Rem's eyes were red, but his tension was gone, and he almost looked relaxed.

"Well, look at you two," said Daniels, standing. "How was your run?"

"It was great," said Rem. "I'll admit. I didn't want to go at first, but she wouldn't take no for an answer."

Mikey walked to the fridge and opened it. She pulled out two bottled waters. "He did fine," she said. "Better than me. That's for sure. But we're not done conquering demons yet." She held out a water to Rem. "There's another to face."

Rem saw the water bottle and stilled. Daniels tensed, too. Rem had been able to drink from a glass but had refused to drink out of a bottle. The mere sight of one made him ill.

"Mikey...," said Daniels.

Rem stared. "You weren't kidding about getting in my face."

"No, I wasn't." She held it out to him. "It's just a water bottle. It can't hurt you."

Daniels watched and waited, seeing the gamut of emotions play across his partner's features. His own gut churned, and he was about to take it from Mikey, when Rem reached out and took it first.

He held it, and Daniels saw him swallow. "You don't have to drink from it," said Daniels.

"Yes, he does," said Mikey. "It's just water. What are you going to do? Never drink from a bottle again?"

Daniels wanted to tell her to stop pushing; it had only been a week, but held still, letting Rem take the lead.

Rem stared, and Daniels caught the slight shake in his fingers, but then he twisted the cap. After a few seconds, he closed his eyes, as if trying to center himself, reopened them, and took a swig. Lowering the bottle, he paused, held it, and then put it on the table. "That's all I can do today."

Mikey smiled. "Good job. I'd say that deserves a glass." She picked one up from the drainer and filled it with the water from the bottle he'd put down. She held it out to him. "One step at a time."

Rem's pale face softened, and he took the glass. "Thanks." He eyed Daniels. "I'll go jump in the shower. Be right back." He stopped in the hall. "Oh, by the way. Mikey's coming over tomorrow night to watch a Spiderman marathon. She's inviting Mason, who apparently hates superheroes as much as you do. You and Marjorie and J.P. should come too, and you and Mason can discuss your favorite documentaries. We'll make the ton of pasta Mikey bought if you don't mind cooking it."

Daniels chuckled. "How could I possibly refuse that offer?"

Rem nodded. "Great. Be out in a sec."

"Okay." Daniels marveled at what Mikey had done. She'd gotten Rem to exercise, drink from a bottle of water, and invite people over for dinner.

Rem disappeared into his room as Mikey opened her own bottle of water. "How'd the run go?" he asked.

"Better than I thought. He had a moment off-trail, but he held it together."

Daniels shook his head. "I can't believe you got him to drink from that bottle. He's turned green every time he's seen one."

Mikey took a swig from her water. "No offense, but that's why I didn't want you here when I showed up. You two are like brothers. He's been through a lot, and you want to protect him. Your intentions are good, but he knows what to say to you to get you to back off. The longer he sits, though, the harder it will be to pull him out of the dark. I understand some of what he's facing, and it's daunting." She paused. "I love Mason to death, but he took it easier on me than he should have. I wish he would have gotten in my face a little more. I think I would have come around sooner if he had. But when you love someone, that's difficult to do."

Daniels couldn't deny she was right. "I thought I'd have to drag him kicking and screaming to the station. He was dreading it."

"It will still be an ordeal, but I think the exercise helped. I plan to be here at the same time tomorrow and we'll knock it out again. He'll need it after today."

"He'll love knowing you plan to come back."

"Every morning until he's back at work. It's good for both of us." She looked him over. "It wouldn't hurt you either. When's the last time you went to the gym?"

**

Not long after Mikey left, and after Daniels had promised to hit the weights at least three times a week from here on, Rem emerged from his room. Showered and clean, he wore a shirt and a pair of blue jeans that were loose on him. His face exuded more strain than before, and Daniels suspected he was anticipating his afternoon.

"You want to eat something?" asked Daniels. "Before we go?"

"I'm not hungry."

Daniels nodded, wondering how much to push. "I get it, but you might need your strength."

Rem gripped his neck and massaged it. "That may be true, but I also don't want to woof it all up during my statement."

Daniels thought that was smart. "Good point. Then how about we get something on the way home? I'll buy you a burger."

Rem nodded. "I may take you up on that."

Daniels sensed his hesitation. "You ready? Or you need a minute?" Rem sat at the table, and Daniels joined him. "What is it?"

Rem traced a crack in the table. "I've been thinking about this statement, and I remembered something." He paused. "I'm not going to mention it today, but I wanted to tell you."

Daniels prepared himself. He knew some of what had happened to Rem, but not all of it, and he'd been dreading the statement almost as much as Rem. "Okay."

Rem took a second and interlaced his fingers in a tight grip. "When I was on that slab, and she...Allison...was sitting on me with that damn knife," he cleared his throat, "she said something."

Daniels' heart thudded. "What did she say?"

Rem took a second. "I'd asked her what she was going to do to me, and in hindsight, that might have been a bad idea."

"Did she tell you?"

"Yeah, she did." Rem fidgeted and bounced his knee. "Just so you're prepared, she told me that she, and the others, were going to drink my blood after she slit my throat, so that they could stay young and pretty, I guess. I was supposed to be the light and Victor was the dark, and the veil was thin, or some such nonsense."

Daniels didn't let himself react, but took a long, slow breath. He had no idea how to respond. "Is that what you don't want to talk about?"

Rem shook his head. "No, not that. It was about the veil. She said she could sense others present and watching, from the other side, kind of like Redstone can, I guess." He hugged himself, and Daniels was reminded of the night they'd brought Rem home, and he'd huddled on the couch. "She said I had a contingent there for me."

"A contingent for you? From the other side?" Daniels frowned. "Like dead people?"

Rem sighed. "Yeah." He stared off. "She said there were two women protecting me, trying to stop her from hurting me." He hesitated. "I'm pretty sure one was Jennie."

"Allison said Jennie was there, watching over you?" asked Daniels. Did Allison know about Rem's past? He guessed if she'd dug deep enough, it wouldn't have been hard to find out. He shifted in his chair, angry about the mind games this woman had played with his partner.

"Yes." Rem spoke softly as the events replayed in his mind. "She didn't say who the second woman was, but they were both fighting for me." He closed his eyes. "I think they may have saved me. Those few seconds Allison took to tell me about them, may have been the few seconds that protected me, because you arrived just as she was about to kill me." He opened his eyes, and his face fell. "And it's messing with my head, along with everything else." He paused. "Was Jennie really there?"

"Why wouldn't she be?"

He leaned over and rested his elbows on the table. "I guess…" He held his head.

"You guess what?"

He let go of a deep breath. "For a brief second, I felt relief that maybe I was about to see her again, you know? I figured if there were a silver lining in that moment then that would be it. But…"

Staying quiet, Daniels let Rem take his time.

Rem moaned. "But then I thought of you, and I hated the thought of you finding me on that slab, my blood pooling on it, and knowing what those people had done."

Daniels tried to understand. "And are you regretting that decision now? That you didn't join her?"

"No…Yes…" He clutched his head. "Maybe. But I realized she was trying to save me. She didn't want me to die. She didn't…didn't want me to join her." He looked up, his eyes haunted, and his voice quiet. "And I can't help but wonder why."

"Because it wasn't your time. Believe me, if it had been, she'd have been first in line to meet you."

"Am I crazy?" He sucked in a ragged breath. "I think I'm going crazy."

"You're not going crazy. I promise. And personally, I'm thankful she's not ready for you. I think she was looking out for me too, you know? You're not the only guy she liked."

Rem's eyes rounded, and his shoulders came down. "You got a point. She was a little partial to you."

Daniels smiled softly. "I think she was looking out for both of us, partner."

Some of Rem's lost look and tension faded. "Maybe so. It's one of the few things in my life right now that makes sense." He looked away. "I guess I'll just plan to wait a little longer to see her."

"That's fine with me."

"I still wonder who the second lady was."

"Probably one of your crazy relatives. God knows you've got a few up there keeping an eye on you."

"Probably my late Aunt Geraldine. She was a little touched in the head. Always used to pinch my cheeks when I was little. I retaliated by sticking a Lego up her nose when she was asleep. She had to go to a doctor to get it out."

Daniels shook his head. "She sounds like the sort to keep you right where you were."

Rem loosened up and scratched his head. "It would be just her way of getting back at me."

"You about ready?" asked Daniels. "Anything else you want to mention?"

Rem released another slow breath. "Just that I'm glad you found me in time, and well...not dead, despite my ramblings about women beyond the veil."

"Me, too. I'll thank Jennie a million times over for not wanting you back yet."

Rem stood. "Maybe when this is over, and we're eating that burger, you can fill me in how you're doing? All we've done this week is talk about me, and it's getting old."

Daniels smiled and stood. "You got it. I'll fill you in on my beautiful wife and son, the dog my wife wants that I refuse to get, and my partner who thinks he's crazy, but he's not. He's just a little weird. You're gonna love it."

Rem chuckled. "I'm on Marjorie's side when it comes to the dog."

"I figured," said Daniels, and they headed out the door.

CHAPTER THIRTY-THREE

Daniels stirred the boiling pasta and felt a hand on his back.

"You bring the parmesan?" asked Marjorie, who came up beside him.

"It's in the fridge," he said.

Marjorie stirred the sauce in the pot next to the pasta. "Great." She looked down the hall. "Looks like he's doing okay today."

Daniels followed her gaze, seeing Rem and Mikey sitting on the couch in the living room, watching TV, and in a deep discussion. "Considering yesterday, and what he had to talk about, it's a one eighty. I half expected him to cancel this dinner."

Marjorie continued to watch. "I think it's her. She's got the magic touch."

Mason walked into the kitchen, glancing behind him, and holding a glass of wine. "They're both helping each other. Shared pain is easily released and does wonders for the soul." He grimaced. "However, they're watching a dreadful movie about a man who thinks he's a spider and arguing about who played him better. Are you telling me there's more than one of these movies?"

"Don't ask me," said Daniels.

"I think there's three," said Marjorie.

"Three?" asked Mason. "With three different actors?"

"I believe so," said Marjorie. "I personally liked Tom Holland as Spiderman the best. He's cute."

Daniels raised a brow. "Really?"

She rubbed his back. "But not as cute as you, honey."

"Yeah," he said. "Sure."

J.P. squealed from his high chair by the table. He was gnawing on a piece of cheese, and drool ran down his chin. Marjorie walked over and picked him up. "I'll change him since we're about to eat. Be right back."

"Okay. We've got a few minutes. No rush," said Daniels.

She nodded and left the kitchen with J.P, and Daniels stirred the sauce and the pasta.

"Looks like your family life has returned to normal," said Mason. "No aftereffects?" He eyed the amulet around Daniels' neck.

"None. I feel fine. No crazy dreams and sleeping like a baby."

"Good. You can probably take the amulet off then if you'd like."

Daniels touched the necklace, remembering what he'd been through. "I think I'll leave it on a little longer, just to be safe."

Mason nodded, then stretched his neck and stifled a yawn.

"What about you?" asked Daniels. "Are you sleeping, considering you've got those wacky statues sitting on your shelf?"

Mason shook his head. "The statues aren't the issue. My girlfriend kicked me out. I've been sleeping on the couch."

"Sorry to hear that."

"It's fine. I half expected it. Not many women quite understand what I do. I find it hard not to take it home with me, and sometimes the spirits like to get my attention, and they got hers, too. I think they were deliberate in scaring her off. I don't think they liked her." He set his wine down. "Mikey offered to let me stay at her place, but I prefer the couch."

"You can sleep on that thing?"

"It's not the couch that's the issue. It's more comfortable than you'd think. But I saw Margaret yesterday, and that's what kept me awake."

Daniels covered the sauce. "You saw your sister? What did she say?"

Mason's shoulders fell. "Let's just say whatever marbles she had are gone. She hates me, Mikey and Max. Blames us for everything. I can only hope her stay in that psychiatric ward is a long one."

"Yeah, well, don't tell Rem, but I went to Allison Albright's arraignment, hoping she'd be denied bail. Thank God she was, but when they took her away, she spotted me." Daniels paused, recalling the moment with anxiety. "Gave me a look I won't soon forget." He checked the pasta. "I'm praying they lock her up and throw away the key."

"It sounds like we've both been troubled with difficulties this week."

"Sounds like it. Considering your sister's mental state, I can't imagine they'd let her out anytime soon."

Mason nodded. "Let's hope. For our sake, as well as Remalla's. I wouldn't put it past her, or Allison, to come after him again if they had the opportunity."

Daniels chest tightened at the mere thought of it. "Let's just keep that between you and me, okay?"

"I agree," said Mason. "There's enough in this world to deal with without adding those two to the mix." He sighed and gestured. "Would you like me to set the table? I think our movie fans are still debating the acting chops of someone named Tobey?"

Daniels chuckled. "Sure. That would be great." He pointed out where the plates and silverware were to Mason, and Daniels started searching for a colander for the pasta.

Mason put the plates and silverware on the table, and straightened, eyeing Daniels, his face pensive. "Detective, there's something I need to say."

Daniels tasted the pasta and put the spoon down. Seeing the look on Mason's face, he turned down the heat on the sauce, and crossed his arms. "It sounds serious."

Mason shook his head. "It's not, but it's been plaguing me, and to be honest, is the other reason I didn't sleep well last night."

Daniels waited. "What is it?"

Mason came over and put a hand on the counter. "I don't normally read people unless requested to, but there's someone on the other side that insists I speak with you. She's quite assertive, and almost impossible to ignore."

Daniels held his breath. "Excuse me? You mean someone who's died? They want to talk to me?" He wasn't sure how to react.

"Not so much talk as send a message. Are you comfortable with that?" He paused. "I sense your skepticism."

Daniels wasn't sure what to say. "I'll be honest. This whole thing is strange. I'm not sure how I feel about it."

Redstone smiled softly. "This coming from the man who dreamed about his partner's almost fatal encounter, and whose memory of a painted bird likely saved his partner's life?" His brow arched. "Like it or not, I'd say you have a touch of ability yourself."

Daniels debated that but didn't deny it. "What's the message?"

"Thank you. I look forward to sleeping better tonight." He took a second. "It's a woman. I think a little older than you." He paused. "Did you have a sister cross over?"

Daniels' heart picked up its pace. "Yes."

"I think her name is Melinda. Or is it Belinda?"

Daniels couldn't believe it. He narrowed his eyes. "It's Melinda." He thought of his sister who had died when he was a teenager. Her death had changed the course of his life, but just as quickly he questioned Mason's integrity. It would not have been hard for him to do a little checking on Daniels' past.

Mason nodded. "She wants you to know that she's proud of you. She's with you often and loves Marjorie. She hangs out with J.P., too. Says he can see her."

Daniels tightened his jaw and couldn't help but feel the pain of her loss surface. He found it difficult to talk.

"She's funny. Always cracking jokes. Says she and Rem would have been fast friends. She keeps an eye on him, too." He stopped and held his chin. "She's saying something about her being the second? That she was the second woman? You have any idea what that means?"

Daniels froze and gripped the spoon in his hand. He recalled what Rem had told him about Jennie and the other woman coming to help him, and there was no way Mason could have known about that. Clearing his throat, his eyes welled. "Yeah. I know what that means."

"It seems so," said Mason. He gestured back toward Rem and Mikey. "She also wants to tell you not to worry about him." He hesitated. "I sense there's another woman who watches over Remalla." He stared off. "I can't quite get the name, but I think it starts with a 'J.'"

Daniels tried to breathe normally but failed.

"Your sister says to tell you that he's okay, and exactly where he needs to be."

Daniels eyed the two in the living room, seeing Rem laugh at something Mikey said, and nodded. "Tell her thank you," he said, his voice gruff.

"You can tell her that. She's listening all the time."

Daniels breathed deeply. "Anything else?"

"I think that's the gist of it." He picked up his wine and took a sip. "I'll finish with the table. Give you a second."

Daniels nodded and sniffed. He grabbed the dishcloth and dabbed his eyes, amazed at what Mason...and Melinda, had told him. He stood for a second and thought of his sister, and how close they'd been, and for a moment, felt the slightest draft on his skin, and sensed Melinda's presence.

Marjorie returned, holding J.P. "All nice and clean. Is the pasta ready?" She slid J.P. back into his seat.

Mason put some glasses on the table and grabbed the bottle of wine.

Daniels composed himself and shook off the memories. "I think so." He picked up the pot of pasta and dumped it into the colander in the sink. Once drained, he added the pasta and sauce to a large bowl on the counter and stirred it. Dabbing at his eyes once more, and thinking of how lucky he was, he yelled out to Rem and Mikey. "C'mon, spider people. Let's eat."

∞∞∞∞

Want more from J. T. Bishop? Go to jtbishopauthor.com and sign up for her newsletter to get short stories, missing scenes, excerpts, and a Daniels and Remalla prequel novella, *The Girl and the Gunshot*, plus future books for **free**. Follow J.T. on her Amazon Author page to be notified of new releases.

I hope you enjoyed *Of Breath and Blood*, but Victor D'Mato's reach runs deep. Get ready for Daniels' and Remalla's return in the next book in the series, *Of Body and Bone*. They'll chase a killer with unique abilities who's kidnapped a child, but his connections to an evil past, and Victor D'Mato, make him even more dangerous. Will Rem and Daniels pay the price? Enjoy an excerpt below.

And get ready for *Lost Souls,* the first book in *The Redstone Chronicles,* a crossover series with the Detectives Daniels and Remalla books. It features paranormal PI Mason Redstone and his sister Mikey, and it follows the events of *Of Breath and Blood*. Mason's ex-partner returns and asks for Mason's help to solve a murder. Can his old partner be trusted when Mason and Mikey risk their lives to help him? Enjoy an excerpt below for this one, too.

If you liked *Of Breath and Blood* and this is your first foray into the world of Daniels and Remalla and you'd like to read more, then check out the first book in the series, *Haunted River*. A ghost, a dead body, and a small town with secrets wreak havoc on Daniels' and Remalla's attempted vacation. Can they find a murderer before they become the next targets?

Or discover the *Family or Foe Saga*, where Detectives Daniels and Remalla first appear. When a serial killer with strange abilities, dark secrets, and an evil grudge strikes again, Daniels and Rem seek the help of a former detective whose psychic connection to the killer almost destroyed her. When the killer decides to make up for lost time and targets those he believes wronged him, can Daniels and Remalla stop him before he seeks his revenge? Enjoy *First Cut, Second Slice, Third Blow* and *Fourth Strike*.

Or, if you like light sci-fi with urban fantasy and a delicious romance thrown in, then check out Bishop's first series, *The Red-Line Trilogy*. One woman holds the key to unlocking a secret that will ensure the existence of a secret community. One man, assigned to protect her, will risk everything to keep her alive, but when he falls for her, will their destiny be enough to save them both?

And the Red-Line series continues with the sister series to the trilogy, *The Fletcher Family Saga*. A distant but deadly threat risks the lives of three unique siblings, but life can't stop because of who they are. They'll endure love, loss and a dangerous enemy determined to destroy them.

Either the trilogy or sister series can be read first. Take your pick. Boxed sets are available for both, too!

A NOTE FROM J.T.

I love to hear from my readers about their experiences with my books, and I'd love to know what you thought about *Of Breath and Blood*. This book was a little more intense than earlier ones, but I followed my muse and that's where it led. After the fun of writing *Haunted River*, I was ready for a fierce, edge-of-your-seat, fight for survival kind of story, and *Of Breath and Blood* fits the bill. Plus, it opens the door to some exciting future story lines as Rem fights to recover from his trauma, which won't be easy. Victor D'Mato's influence creates new enemies, and who knows what will happen with Allison? She might have a few cards up her sleeve, too. I also get the chance to dive into a new series featuring Mason Redstone and his sister Mikey. It will be a crossover, so the major characters from each series will be featured in all the books, with gives me some new creative opportunities. (Including a potential new romance for Rem. We'll see what happens between him and Mikey.)

Since the books from these series are intertwined, if you'd like to read in order, I've provided a chronological list of my books below.

Reviews are a huge plus and big help for an author, and potential readers. I would love it if you could please take a couple of minutes to leave a quick review for *Of Breath and Blood*. And if you'd like, please leave a few comments, too. I always like to know what my readers think.

As always, thank you for your time and readership. It is deeply valued and appreciated.

Now, on to the next book!

Books in Chronological Order

Although recommended but not required, in case you like to read in order…

Prelude to The Shift, a short story (free at jtbishopauthor.com)
Red-Line: The Shift
Red-Line: Mirrors
Red-Line: Trust Destiny
Curse Breaker
High Child
Spark
Forged Lines
**

The Girl and the Gunshot, a novella (free at jtbishopauthor.com)
A Hamburger Christmas, a novella
The Magic of Murder, a novella (featured in the anthology Talk Deadly To Me)
First Cut
Second Slice
Third Blow
Fourth Strike
Murder Unveiled
Haunted River
Of Breath and Blood
Lost Souls
Of Body and Bone
Lost Dreams
Of Mind and Madness
Lost Chances
Of Power and Pain

Lost Hope
Of Love and Loss
Lost Lives
Dominion
Lost Time
Illusions

ACKNOWLEDGEMENTS

Another book is complete, and again, I have many to thank. This doesn't happen alone, and I thank family and friends for their help, support and encouragement. It is truly appreciated.

I love writing about the bonds between loving family, deep friendships and the ties that hold them together. Plus, my fascination with the unknown thrown into the mix makes for a satisfying story and hopefully, adds a little more thrill for my readers.

I especially want to thank my fans. Hearing from you and knowing that you're enjoying my books makes all the hard work worthwhile. None of this would matter without your tremendous support. If I can help you escape from this crazy world for a short period each day, then I've done my job.

Here's to more stories, more fun, and more time for yourself. If you can have a little of that each day, you're on the right track.

"So much for taking a nap," said Mason.

"What the hell is he doing here?" asked Mikey.

"I think we're about to find out." Mason went to the door and opened it. Trick was standing in the small, wallpapered, outer office which contained only a desk and chair. Seeing Mason, he took off his hat. "Well, hell. Look at you." He ran his fingers over the brim. "How long's it been, Red?"

Mason crossed his arms and considered his response. They'd met and been assigned together during his tenure as a Texas Ranger. There had been a time when Mason would have called Trick his best friend, and they had been as close as Detectives Daniels and Remalla. Mason had envied that bond when he'd met the detectives, recalling his old partnership with Trick, but those days were long over.

"I figured it would be a lot longer," said Mason.

Trick shook his head. "Shit. You sure know how to hold a grudge. It's been years, Red."

Mikey poked her head out, and Trick grinned. "Is that you, Mikey?" His eyes trailed over her. "You've grown up."

Mason stiffened. "What the hell do you want, Trick?"

"Trick Monroe?" asked Mikey. "I remember you."

"I like to make an impression." Trick raised his hat, looking pleased with himself.

"I recall you being a lot more handsome," said Mikey.

Trick's face fell. "You haven't changed much."

"I like to make an impression, too," said Mikey.

Mason sized up his former partner. Trick looked much the same. His swagger and annoying charm remained despite their estrangement. It was a valued skill in a Ranger, or any cop. Trick could talk down a junkie threatening suicide and waving a gun better than any lawman Mason had ever witnessed. Everything in him wanted to throw Trick out, but he couldn't do it. A tingle moved through him, and Mason opened up, letting his senses guide him. A fuzzy image appeared behind Trick and Mason watched as Trick's grandmother came into view. Her eyes twinkled and her silver hair sparkled. She'd died a couple of years after Trick had joined the Rangers and been partnered with Mason. Trick had invited Mason for dinner at her place a few times, and she'd been a terrific cook. Smiling, she put a hand on Trick's shoulder and her voice echoed in Mason's head.

Trick shifted on his feet, and then scratched his shoulder. "You gonna talk to me, or leave me standing here like a fool?"

Mason relaxed, as the older woman faded from view. "You're lucky I liked your grandmother."

Trick squinted and Mikey shot him a confused look.

"She says 'Hi' by the way." Mason stepped back. "Come on in."

Trick gripped his hat. "God, are you talking to her? You still doing that dead people thing?" Trick walked into the inner office.

Mason closed the door. "It's my business. You know that's why I came out here. Some Ranger you are."

Trick put his hat on the coffee table. "I'm not a Ranger." He paused. "Not anymore."

"Sorry to hear it," said Mason. Despite their falling out, Trick had always been a first-rate investigator, smart as any high-ranking officer, and a solid partner. Thinking back on their days together, Mason missed being part of a team, and relying on and talking to someone who would back you up no matter what occurred.

Mikey raised her mug. "You want some coffee?"

"Love some," said Trick. "Thanks. Black is fine."

Mikey nodded and headed to the coffee machine.

Mason walked to his desk and sat. "What brings you here, and don't tell me you're just passing through."

Trick surveyed the room, his gaze briefly settling on the wooden box and plexiglass holder of the statues. "I barely saw you at your mom's funeral and you disappeared before we could talk, but I wanted to tell you it's a damn shame. She was a nice lady."

Mason interlaced his fingers and tried not to think about his mother. It would only upset him more. "Thanks." He waited as Trick stood anxiously, his face flat.

His mind wandering, Mason asked the question he should have avoided. "How's Cara?"

Trick groaned and shook his head. "You just can't let me off the hook, can you?"

Mikey finished with the coffee and brought Trick a mug. He took it and thanked her. Mikey stayed quiet, but leaned against the wall, watching.

"You don't seem to be saying much, so I figured I'd start the conversation." Mason leaned back and crossed his arms. "Did you think I wouldn't bring her up?"

"You know I haven't seen her in years," said Trick.

"How would I know that?" asked Mason.

"Don't you talk to her?"

"No. Why would I? My patience with her is about as non-existent as it is with you."

Trick sipped his coffee. "Last I heard, she married. Has two kids."

"Sorry to hear it didn't work out," said Mason.

Trick chuckled softly. "Sure you are." He gestured. "You mind if I sit?"

"Why not?" asked Mason. "You typically do what you want. Why stop now?"

Mikey pushed off the wall. "You know, I have a couple errands to run." She reached for her purse beneath the desk.

"What errands?" asked Mason.

"Oh, I don't know. I'll think of something." She tossed her purse strap over her shoulder. "You need anything while I'm out?"

Mason glared at Trick. "Maybe a shovel? I sense a lot of shit comin' my way."

Trick snorted and rolled his eyes. "While you're at it, pick up a violin. He can play it when you come back, and you can feel sorry for him."

Mason frowned, and Mikey winced and headed for the door. "I'll...uhm..." She looked between the two men. "...never mind. I'll just go." Not getting a response, she left.

Mason told himself to stay cool. Although he hadn't spoken to Trick in years, his old partner had not forgotten how to get under his skin, but Mason refused to be drawn into another inane discussion about his ex-wife. "How about we cut to the chase? Why did you come?"

Trick walked to couch and sat, holding his mug. Mason stood from his desk and approached Trick, waiting to hear the answer.

Trick sighed. "Chad is dead."

"Who?" Mason rested a hand on the back of the chair.

"Chad Howard. My stepbrother. Ruby's kid. You met him. Remember? Kid used to follow us around like we were superheroes."

Mason recalled a younger version of Trick with long legs and dirty hair pestering them with questions whenever they were around. "Chip?"

Trick ran a hand through his brown hair which was almost as long as Mason recalled Chip's used to be. "Yeah. I used to call him that. Kid could eat a bag of chips faster than a pile of racoons." He hung his head. "He grew up, though. Came out here last year for employment with his new wife. Her name's Cissy. Cissy found him dead on their sofa three weeks ago in their living room. She'd gone out for groceries." Trick paused. "He'd been shot in the head."

Recalling Chad, Mason's heart thumped, and he remembered how attached Chad and Trick had been. Even though they were stepbrothers,

Trick had considered Chad to be as close as Trick's two biological brothers. Taking a deep breath, he took a seat in the chair across from Trick. "I'm sorry. I know how you felt about him."

Trick put his mug down and picked up his hat. He fiddled with the brim. "After you left, we hung out a lot. He thought about becoming a Ranger, and made it into the Fort Worth P.D., but ultimately decided it wasn't for him. He became a security consultant and got a lucrative offer from a firm out here. He and Cissy found a place outside of San Diego, and I'd been planning to visit, but just hadn't made it out here yet." He studied his hat. "Maybe if I had…"

"You don't know if you could have prevented it," said Mason. "You likely would have come out and left, and he'd still be dead."

"He had something on his mind. Wanted to talk to me about it." He tossed his hat back on the table. "I should have paid more attention."

Mason nodded. He understood the pain of regret. "They know who did it?"

Trick rubbed his face. "They arrested Cissy."

Mason dropped his jaw. "His wife?"

Trick stood and paced. "It's absurd, but they insist she did it. They picked her up the day after the funeral. She's the spouse. Has no real alibi, other than she went to the store, came home and found him. They believe she shot him before she left, and then claimed that it happened while she was gone. Chad was killed with his own gun, but it wasn't a suicide. Whoever did it knew where the gun was, and where he lived. Chad must have let them in because there was no forced entry."

"How do you know she didn't kill him? How was their marriage?"

Trick flicked a pained glance at Mason. "Those two were closer than a couch and my butt during a Cowboy game. Chad met her his first year as a cop. He pulled her over for speeding, and they'd been together ever since. They were happy, and she is devastated by his loss."

Mason studied his hands. "You don't know for sure. They'd been out here for a year, and you hadn't seen them recently. Maybe that's what Chad wanted to talk to you about."

"Hell, no. I don't believe it. They were trying to get pregnant. Chad couldn't wait to be a dad, and Cissy couldn't wait to be a mom." He shook his head. "And even if they weren't happy, Cissy could have easily filed for divorce. She hated guns and doesn't even like scary movies. There's no way she would have shot him."

Mason considered what to say. In his experience, he knew how even the closest spouses could turn on each other. And as a medium, he'd seen and heard plenty of examples from those who'd passed on who'd expressed regret over their perceived neglect or unintended abuse of their significant other. And the ones left behind often struggled with how to deal with it.

Trick returned to the couch and sat. "Listen, I know what you're thinking. I'm too attached to this, and I need to let the law take it from here. But you and I know that sometimes the law gets a hold of something and refuses to see any other scenario." He pointed. "I think that's what's happening here. The police suspected Cissy from the start, and they're not even bothering to look for anyone else. And that's just not right." He hesitated. "Cissy deserves her chance to be proven innocent, and Chad's killer needs to be brought to justice."

"Doesn't she have an attorney?" asked Mason.

"She needs more than an attorney, Red." He stared pointedly.

Mason straightened in his seat. "Wait a minute. Is that why you're here? You want my help?"

"I know you do that SCOPE stuff. God knows I didn't understand your woo-woo issues back when we were partners, and I still don't get it, but I also know you were a damn good investigator, and you have a P.I. license out here. Plus, you're bound to have some connections. You have access to people and things that I don't."

"How do you know I have a P.I. license?"

Trick chuckled. "I'm not an idiot. I did a little research of my own before I came out."

Mason put his elbows on his knees. "Are you serious? You want me to help you investigate Chad's death?"

"Hell, yes."

"We haven't worked together in years, and the last time we spoke, you were very specific about where I should put my head."

"And you weren't to kind about what I could do with my mother." Trick sat back against the couch, looking worn and frazzled. "I know I did things I shouldn't have done, and if you ever want to talk about it, I'm all ears, but right now, I could use your help. The past is the past. There's nothing I can do about any of it. If I could take it back, I would. But I need to focus on the here and now, and you're my best bet if I want to find Chad's killer."

Mason moaned and held his head. "And if it turns out to be Cissy?"

"Then so be it. At least I'll know the truth."

Mason sighed, uncertain of what to do. "I don't know, Trick. Something tells me this is a bad idea. Maybe it's better we go our separate ways. I'm sure her attorney can find a good investigator."

Trick went quiet, and Mason waited for the outburst, but none came. Trick just tipped his head and spoke softly. "You owe me, Red."

Mason's heart fell. "Hell. You're gonna pull that card? I figured you screwing my wife made us even."

Trick grimaced. "Whatever. You two were separated at the time, and you'd already come out here, and she was lonely."

"Thank God you were around to make her feel better." He glowered. "I still had hopes that she would join me here."

"She didn't want to leave Texas and you know it, so stop blaming me for the loss of your marriage. I wasn't the cause, only the result."

"That's a convenient argument, coming from the man who lied to me."

"I promised her I wouldn't tell you. I honored that."

"What about your promise to me as a friend? What happened to that?"

"I never stopped being your friend. I tried to talk to you, but you wouldn't even give me a chance."

"I tend to do that when people show me their true colors."

"My colors haven't faded one bit. You're just too damn stubborn to see it, or even take a trickle of blame for the giant mess that was your marriage."

Mason's anger bubbled up, and he set his jaw. "This is why we shouldn't work together."

Trick leaned forward. "This is exactly why we should. We have some things to work out. And this is the time to do it. But if you think that your issues with Cara have somehow wiped out your debt to me, then you're wrong. I didn't break you two up, and you know it."

Mason grunted, and he stifled the urge to throw Trick out, and leave his past behind him, but the memory of his former partner's role in saving his life could not be forgotten, and in some part of his gut, he realized that he'd screwed up when it came to Cara. Taking a heavy breath, he made his decision. "Fine. I owe you." He raised a finger. "But once this plays out and we figure out what's going on, we're even. You got that?"

"I got it. Call me Even Steven."

Mason sighed and fell back in his chair. His days off were no longer off. "Then where do you want to start?"

The next morning, Daniels waved as Rem pulled up to the curb in front of Daniels' home and stopped. Daniels opened the door and slid in, admiring the sunny day and cool temperatures. "Morning."

"Morning," said Rem.

Daniels closed the door, and Rem pulled away. "Thanks for being on time," said Daniels. "That's two days in a row. I should have you pick me up more often."

"Yeah, well. You're lucky. I was up."

Daniels took a closer look and noted Rem's droopy eyes. "Didn't sleep?"

"Maybe a few hours." He stopped at an intersection.

"I thought it was getting better."

"Depends on the week...plus...other things." Rem hit the gas and continued down the street.

"What other things? Something I should know?" Daniels recalled Rem's comment from the previous night. "Is it about what you were going to mention last night before we got interrupted? What were you going to say?"

Rem didn't answer and turned onto another, busier street.

"Rem?"

"It's nothing. I shouldn't have said anything."

"Well, it's obviously something."

"You mind if we stop and get some coffee? I need gas, too."

"That's fine. There's a place right up here on the corner."

Rem nodded. "Perfect."

Daniels waited. "Well?"

Rem sighed. "Fine. I'll tell you, but you're going to get upset and before I deal with that, I need some caffeine in my veins. I can handle you better when I'm awake."

Daniels shifted in his seat. "What the hell is going on?"

"Just wait, okay? Don't freak out, at least not yet anyway. No one is in immediate danger and it's not life-threatening, and no, I'm not quitting." He flipped on his signal, turned into the parking lot, and pulled up next to a gas pump. "You go get the coffee, and I'll get the gas. We can talk about it after I have a few gulps." He reached for his wallet. "I'll get some cash."

"Keep it," said Daniels. "I'll get it. I'm going to need some coffee, too, to brace myself." He popped the door open. "Be right back."

"Okay." Rem turned off the ignition and popped the gas cap.

Daniels closed his door and jogged into the convenience store, wondering what Rem was going to say. His mind whirled but he told himself to relax; his imagination was probably far worse than the actual issue.

Entering the store, he saw the attendant up front. "Morning," he said.

The attendant nodded and waved, and Daniels headed toward the coffee section in the back. Rows of coffee dispensers filled with everything from breakfast blends to dark brews sat atop a counter along with various creams and sugars. Daniels grabbed two cups, one large and another small, and began to fill Rem's with a medium roast Columbian variety.

Out of the corner of his eye, beside the coffee aisle, and near a rear exit, Daniels noticed a young boy, probably a preteen, standing by himself. Looking over, Daniels noted the boy's unkempt appearance; his jeans were ripped, his shirt was dirty, and his brown hair was uncombed and unwashed. His freckled, pale face had a flat expression, as if he wasn't sure where he was or what to do.

Daniels' radar blipped on, and he watched the boy as he filled Rem's cup, and then filled his own. After a few seconds, he added cream and sugar to Rem's and then placed lids on each cup. The boy remained quiet and didn't move. Eyeing the store, Daniels saw a man in one of

the aisles, wearing a baseball cap. The man walked toward a refriger-
ated section, turned, and headed toward them. Nearing the boy, the man
came into full view, and Daniels saw him holding two bags of chips and
a six pack of soda. He was in his mid-forties, tall, thin, wearing his own
unkempt clothes, and Daniels could see close-cut brown hair beneath
the baseball cap.

He handed the chips to the boy. "Here, kid," he said. "Hold these."

The boy took the chips and turned his head. Cold crawled up Daniels' back when he saw that the child had a swollen cheek and eye.
Thinking of J.P., something shifted in Daniels and he recognized that
something was off. Watching the man and the boy, he realized the boy
was scared. Years of experience had taught him not to ignore those messages, and he couldn't start now.

Holding his coffees, he approached the man. "Hi, there," he said,
keeping his tone friendly.

The man stiffened and turned toward him, his face tense. The boy
looked up at Daniels.

"I know you?" asked the man. He lowered his arm and put his hand
on the boy's shoulder.

"No." Daniels saw a small tattoo on the man's wrist and debated his
next words. "I just happened to notice you two standing over here. Your
boy here looked a little lost. You two need anything?" He eyed the
child, whose gaze darted between Daniels and the man.

"We're good. Thanks," said the man. "Let's go, kid." He pushed on
the child's shoulder.

Daniels had no reason to stop them, but his unease grew and he
couldn't let them walk away. "You sure everything's okay? I just noticed his bruised face." He gestured toward the boy.

The man stopped. "He's fine." His posture straightened, and his eyes
narrowed. "Not that it's any of your business."

Daniels' narrowed his own eyes. "It might be, actually. I'm a detective. And I'd just like to make sure he's all right."

The man hesitated, but then sneered. "Detective, huh?" He chuckled. "Well, ring-a-ding-ding. What do you think of that, junior? A real-live detective."

Daniels glanced down at the child, who looked like he wanted to cry. He spoke to him. "You okay, son?"

The man took a step closer. "He ain't your son."

Daniels held his ground. "Maybe not, but if he's been abused, then that makes him my responsibility."

"Responsibility?" The man chuckled. "You hear that, kid? You're his responsibility now. I bet your momma would be happy to hear that." He squinted. "Boy's my nephew. He fell off his bike." He took another step toward Daniels. "You're relieved of duty, *Detective*."

That cold sliver became a spike, and Daniels gripped the coffee cups. "Is that true?" He looked down at the boy. "You fall off your bike?"

The boy didn't say a word, and Daniels wanted to grab his hand and pull him out of the store.

"Tell the detective." The man didn't take his gaze from Daniels.

The boy looked between them. "I...I...uhm..." He spoke so softly that Daniels barely heard him. "I don't know."

Daniels noticed the man's grip tighten on the boy's shoulder. "That doesn't sound like a boy who fell off his bike," said Daniels. "Maybe we should go to the station and talk about it."

"Station?" The man glowered. "I'm not going anywhere with you. We're leaving. And if you know what's good for you, you'll head in the opposite direction."

Daniels' skin tingled, and the hair on his arms raised. He wondered how far he should take this. He set his jaw. "Nobody's going anywhere until I know the boy's okay." The air electrified, and Daniels heard a buzz around him as if a swarm of bees was approaching.

The man took another step and encroached to within a foot of Daniels. Raising his hand off the boy's shoulder, he grinned. "Is that so?" He pointed a bony finger with a grimy nail. "We'll just see who's going where." The buzzing vibration grew louder as the man brought his finger closer and Daniels got a better look at the tattoo. He could read the word *Sam*. Anticipating the contact against his chest, he held still. If this guy touched him, he'd have grounds for an assault charge, and reason to bring him in. He waited, wondering what Rem would think when he walked out with this loser in handcuffs.

The boy suddenly spoke. "He...he's right. I...I fell off my bike. It's no big deal." He reached up, grabbed the man's arm, and pulled it down and away from Daniels. "I'm okay." His breathing came in quick gasps, and his face paled more. "He...he's my uncle. We just stopped to get some snacks."

The man's grin grew, and he dropped his hand back on the boy's shoulder and patted it. "See? He's just fine."

Daniels' mental war raged. The boy had backed up the man's story, but Daniels didn't believe him and he couldn't leave it alone. Something was up, and he sensed the boy was in danger.

"What's your uncle's name? He got one?" asked Daniels, holding the man's stare.

The boy didn't respond, and Daniels didn't blink. The man glared and opened his mouth to answer when Daniels heard a yell from the front of the store.

"Daniels. Where are you?" It was Rem's voice.

Daniels hesitated, and then glanced back. "Here."

Rem spotted him. "We got a call from Lozano. We got a ten fifty-four. We got to go."

Daniels cursed and eyed the drinks. He still needed to purchase them, and figure out what to do about the boy. "Be right there."

"You get the coffees?" yelled Rem.

"Yes...and no." He turned back.

"What are you doing back there?"

Daniels stopped cold. The exit door was open and the man and child were gone.

Made in United States
Orlando, FL
11 May 2024

46771668R00205